A. BERTRAM CHANDLER:

This is an If-Of-History Novel.

There have been many such. One popular "if" in recent years has been *if* Germany had won the Second World War. It could have happened, you know. *If* Hitler had launched a damn-the-expense invasion of England immediately after Dunkirk . . . *If* the German scientists had been first with the atom bomb . . . After all, Germany already had the means of delivery, the V2 rocket, and, on the drawing board, another rocket, capable of striking the eastern seaboard of the U.S.A. when fired from European launching pads.

Insofar as history is concerned I have tried to steer a middle course between Carlyle and Marx. Carlyle said, more or less in these words, "History is the biographies of great men." Marx regarded the great men of history as symptoms rather than causes. But great men *do* influence the course of events—and there have been men who were potentially great and who, had the cards fallen a little differently, would have achieved greatness or would have had greatness thrust upon them.

Such a man was Edward Kelly.

—*from the Foreword to the Original Edition*

KELLY COUNTRY

A. Bertram Chandler

DAW BOOKS, INC.
DONALD A. WOLLHEIM, PUBLISHER

1633 Broadway, New York, NY 10019

DAW Collectors' Book No. 639

DEDICATION

For Ned Kelly, a man who could have been king.

First DAW Printing, August 1985

1 2 3 4 5 6 7 8 9

PRINTED IN THE UNITED STATES OF AMERICA

AUTHOR'S NOTE

Sincere Thanks to

The Literature Board of the Australia Council, who awarded me a Senior Fellowship to enable me to work upon this project;

Mr. Goins, Curator of the Division of Military History, the Smithsonian Institution, Washington, D.C., who gave me much valuable information, including that regarding Francis Hannerman and his arms-dealing activities;

Mr. Philip D. Edwards, Technical Information Specialist, National Air and Space Museum, Washington, D.C., for unearthing for me the actual patent taken out by Dr. Solomon Andrews and for finding for me other information regarding that prolific inventor;

Miss Brenda Beasley, of National Archives, Washington, D.C., for helping me to find the full specifications for Professor Lowe's mobile hydrogen gas generator;

The late Professor Susan Wood of the University of British Columbia, Vancouver, who insisted that I somehow incorporate the Riel Rebellion into my fictional history and who found for me useful material on that quite nasty little civil war;

Mr. P. Maxwell, Secretary of the Union Shipping Group, Wellington, New Zealand and Mr. T. J. Lovell-Smith, Company Archivist, who supplied me with plans and specifications of the Union Steam Ship Company's *Rotomahana*, time-tables of the Company's trans-Tasman services in the mid-1880's and photographs of the master and officers of *Rotomahana* in what was then the Company's uniform;

Professor John Molony of the Australian National University, Canberra, with whom I had an interesting and informative talk regarding Ned Kelly;

Mr. & Mrs. McCay of the Kelly Country Motel, Glenrowan, who acted as my guides through the countryside;

Mrs. Susan Chandler, who has acted in an editorial capacity and who breathed a great sigh of relief when I returned to the Twentieth Century.

FOREWORD TO U.S. EDITION

Every nation has its folk heroes. Very often such heroes are picturesque rogues—and the passage of time has added a spurious glamour to the reputation of many a vicious criminal. The English have their mythical Robin Hood, who stole (it is said) from the rich to give to the poor. They have the real life highwayman Dick Turpin, who just robbed the rich to fill his own pockets. In the U.S.A. there is, among quite a few others, Jesse James. In Australia there is Ned Kelly. He is not the only bushranger in our criminal history but he is the one whose name is most familiar to every Australian. Perhaps it is his famous armor that makes him loom so large in the national imagination, as a sort of living prophecy of the panzer warfare of the twentieth century. Too, there was something of Robin Hood about him. When he robbed a bank he made a great show of tearing up the mortgages that he found in the strongroom. This endeared him to the poor farmers heavily in debt to the financial institutions.

And, unlike other glamorized and over-glamorized criminals of the period, he was a man who just might, had the cards fallen a little differently, have changed the course of Australian history and even, to a lesser degree, of world history. There were the stirrings of revolt, the poor farmers on their selections increasingly resentful of the banks and of the rich squatters, those landowners whose ancestors, like robber barons, had made their grabs during the early days of colonization. There was some sort of underground revolutionary movement, of which Ned Kelly was at least the figurehead. There was talk of a Republic of North East Victoria—and Kelly was known to many as the Captain of the North East.

Not only in Australia were the 1880s a time of ferment. Although the sun was still a long time from setting on the British Empire there were ominous storm clouds on the horizon. There was—as, indeed, there still is—trouble in Ireland. In Canada there was the Metis Revolt, also known as the Riel Rebellion. (It seems strange that the U.S.A. did not become somehow involved in this civil war. Perhaps if Riel had accepted the offer—which in actual history was made—of a regiment of New York Irish Fenians there would have been active involvement.)

It was in the late nineteenth century that the tide of the mechanization of warfare was beginning to flood. That well-known physician Dr. Gatling had invented and was manufacturing—and selling—his manually operated machine gun, although he was unable to interest the admirals and generals in a model with a much higher rate of fire operated by steam or electricity. A decade and a half before 1880 another physician, Dr. Solomon Andrews, had constructed and successfully flown a dirigible airship, a flying machine that, before the development of antiaircraft artillery, could have been used as an effective dive bomber.

And at the same time that Dr. Andrews was making his first flights over New York yet another physician-inventor, Dr. Bland, in Sydney, Australia, was attempting to raise money to finance the construction of his "atmoship"—a steam-powered dirigible. (He was unsuccessful.)

Steam-driven traction engines had already been used in warfare—for the towing of heavy artillery over muddy ground. One or two visionaries had toyed with the idea of arming and armoring such brutes.

The ideas were there, just waiting to be picked up and developed. But unfortunately (or perhaps fortunately) the admirals and generals of the time were lacking in imagination. Had Ned Kelly become a general—and why not? he was at least as well qualified for such rank as Gabriel Dumont, in Canada, who achieved fame as Riel's fighting general—he would have been able to make good use of such innovations as the airship, the steam-operated Gatling cannon and the armed and armored traction engine.

As is evidenced by his famous armor, he was not deficient in imagination.

But who was this Ned Kelly?

He was of Irish descent, as were many Australians of his time. His people originally came from Northern Ireland. His father, John Kelly, was the son of Thomas Kelly and Mary Cody. A famous bearer of the Cody surname was Buffalo Bill who, in actual fact, was distantly related to Ned Kelly. Kelly's mother, Ellen, was a Quinn. His father died in 1866, a year after his birth. His mother remarried in 1874, her second husband being George King, a Californian. It might be argued that King was an evil influence in the young Kelly's life. It is a matter of record that George King was a horse thief and that his stepson was a willing apprentice.

Perhaps I am being unjust to George King. It could be said that the Kelly clan exercised a bad influence upon him. By the time that he arrived on the scene those who were to become his in-laws were in constant trouble with the police—horse stealing, cattle stealing, brawling, assault. Whenever the usual suspects were rounded up there would be a Kelly or two, or more, among them. Together with—and an excuse for—this lawlessness was the hatred for the English Establishment and for those fellow Irishmen, the police, who wore the uniform of the English oppressors.

One policeman who became a special enemy of Ned Kelly was Constable Fitzpatrick, a notorious liar and womanizer. It seems that, when under the influence of liquor, he dropped into the Kelly cottage at Greta for afternoon tea, Mrs. Kelly just having baked a batch of scones. Also present was Kate, Ned's beloved sister. Fitzpatrick made unwelcome advances to Kate. Ellen Kelly intervened to protect her daughter's honor and struck Fitzpatrick on the wrist with a shovel, wounding him slightly. At this juncture Ned Kelly returned home and evicted the constable from the premises. Fitzpatrick reported to his superiors that his injuries were due to an unprovoked assault upon him by Ned Kelly who, he said, had drawn a revolver and fired at him. Allegations and counter-allegations confused the issue. Ellen Kelly was arrested as an accessory to the attempted murder of Fitzpatrick and given a jail sentence. Ned loved his mother deeply and this miscarriage of justice hardened his hostile attitude toward the police in particular and toward the Establishment in general.

Meanwhile a warrant was out for his arrest for his alleged complicity in the Fitzpatrick affair. He and four friends took refuge in the bush, in the wild, hilly country that he knew so well. He was tracked, eventually, by four well-armed policemen. These, early one afternoon, set up camp by Stringybark Creek. The next day two of the troopers, Kennedy and Scanlan, left the camp to continue the search for Kelly and his accomplices. Lonigan and McIntyre stayed behind. McIntyre shot some parrots to provide the wherewithal for a meal and the noise of the reports attracted the attention of Kelly and his followers. The police camp was attacked and Lonigan, an old enemy of Kelly's, was shot dead. McIntyre surrendered but when Kennedy and Scanlan returned attempted to warn them. Fire was exchanged. Kennedy and Scanlan were killed. In the confusion McIntyre escaped on Kennedy's horse.

And Ned Kelly had become an outlaw.

Without the support of the poor farmers and the laborers who, rightly or wrongly, regarded the Kelly Gang as their champions against the big landowners and the banks, Kelly's career as a bushranger and bank robber could not have lasted as long as it did. He could always be sure of finding food and shelter and, more important perhaps, information. He always knew just where the police would be looking for him and made sure that he would be somewhere else. He became a legend in his own time. Ballads were sung about his exploits, set to the music of traditional folk songs.

It was not only in the countryside that he had his supporters. He was regarded as a hero by many in Melbourne, the capital city of the State of Victoria. There was talk, even, of secession from the British Empire and the founding of an independent republic. It is not known to what extent an army of freedom fighters had been organized but there certainly seems to have been the nucleus of such a body.

And if there were a freedom army it had its traitors. One such was Aaron Sherritt, a Kelly family friend and also a paid police spy. This became known to Kelly and his lieutenants. At first Kelly wanted him left alone—hoping, perhaps, to use him as a double agent. But Joe Byrne and Ned's brother Dan were determined that Sherritt must be executed. They shot him down in the presence of his wife and mother-in-law—*and while this was happening four policemen, who were supposed to be protecting him, were hiding under a bed!*

And if there was a freedom army, it had the beginnings of an armored corps. Kelly knew that sooner or later there would be a real showdown with the police and that he and his men would have to face a murderous fire. He experimented with various materials. Sheet iron, readily available, proved ineffective. Steel was much better—but available only from a rather unusual source. So it was that the Kelly family's only plow lost its mold board, and so it was that several farmers whose smallholdings were in the vicinity of the Kelly homestead reported the mold boards of their plows stolen. A suit of armor fashioned from this material weighed ninety-five pounds. It would resist penetration by a rifle bullet fired at a range of ten yards. It traded mobility for protection.

After the execution of Aaron Sherritt it was hoped by Kelly that the police would be lured to the scene of the crime, near the town of Beechworth. He laid his plans accordingly. As he had thought would be the case a special train left Melbourne for Beechworth, via Wangaratta. Aboard this train were Superintendent Hare and other Victorian Police officers. There was an Inspector O'Connor, on loan from the Queensland Police, and his five black trackers, Aborigines employed for their skills in bushcraft. There were journalists. There were even two ladies—Mrs. O'Connor and her sister—just along for the ride. There was a pilot engine preceding the main train, it having occurred to Hare that an attempt might be made to tamper with the track.

Meanwhile the Kelly gang had prepared an ambush at Glenrowan, a village to the south of Wangarrata. Very conveniently there was a gang of platelayers there, engaged on maintenance work on the railway. These Kelly persuaded, at pistol point, to tear up the rails a short way north of the station. According to some, pro-Kelly historians his intention was not actually to derail the train, with inevitable casualties, but to trap it, blowing up the track south of Glenrowan after it had passed. Then Hare and his men would be captured and held as hostages until Kelly's demands for justice, land reform and for the release of his mother from Melbourne Jail were met.

It was a long wait; the special train was not running on time. Almost the entire population of the village, together with the railway workers, was confined by Kelly and his men to Mrs. Jones's hotel. Even the village policeman, Constable Bracken, was among the more or less willing guests at the party. Another guest, Thomas Curnow, the village schoolmaster, was allowed by Kelly to leave quite early so that he could look after—he said—his sick wife. There are those who say that Kelly's kindly nature was his undoing.

At last the train came, the noise of its approach carrying through the still, cold, night air. The time was about three in the morning. Curnow was ready for it. Using a candle and a red silk scarf belonging to his wife he was able to flag it down, then stammered out his story to Police Superintendent Hare. The police disembarked and almost immediately began to pour a murderous fire into the flimsy wood and hessian structure that was the hotel.

A very short while later somebody loosed two signal rockets. Were these supposed to call reinforcements to the beleaguered Kelly Gang or were they supposed to inform Kelly adherents in the vicinity that their leader's plans had gone awry? To this day nobody knows—but those rockets were fired. Meanwhile people were being killed and injured by the police fire, women and children among them. Even though a white flag was raised by young Dan Kelly, who tried to arrange a truce so that the villagers could escape from the by now almost demolished building, this was ignored by the police. Such was the hysteria of the gallant law enforcers that a message was telegraphed to Melbourne requesting that a piece of field artillery be sent to Glenrowan by rail. This cannon actually commenced its journey but before it had come very far some genius decided to set fire to what was left of the hotel.

For a while Ned himself was out of the picture. Early in the action he, in full armor, had left the hotel on some errand, possibly to fire the signal rockets. He had been shot at and wounded in the foot and arm, neither of which were protected. Apparently the pain from these injuries caused him to lose consciousness for a while. Eventually he recovered and tried to hobble back to the hotel. The police—whose fire, aimed at his body, had no apparent effect—fell back in terror. But Sergeant Steele kept his wits about him and aimed his shotgun at Ned's unprotected legs, bringing him down. (That same Sergeant Steele had to be restrained by his own men from killing Kelly there and then as he sprawled injured on the ground.)

When it was all over Ned was a badly wounded prisoner. Joe Byrne, Steve Hart and Dan Kelly were dead—as were the innocent old man Martin Cherry and the son of Mrs. Jones, the unfortunate owner of the hotel.

Ned was nursed back to health, stood trial for murder, was inevitably found guilty and was hanged, in Melbourne Jail, on November 11, 1880. After his execution public feeling was such that many of the reforms that he had been advocating were introduced. Certain sections of the press demanded that some members of the Victorian Police Force who had taken part in the siege be brought to trial on charges of manslaughter.

But in those times that would have been going altogether too far.

—A.B.C.

CHAPTER I

Every story must have its beginning and the beginning of this one was not quite two years ago. Or just over one hundred years ago. Some of it, perhaps, never happened. (But it must have happened; otherwise I should not be sitting here writing this.)

That morning I was doing what I am doing now. Writing. It could almost have been the same machine that I was using, a manually operated typewriter of German manufacture. I was working on yet another novel in the never-ending series in which I had become trapped, a further installment of the adventures—and misadventures—of a character who had been referred to by *Publishers Weekly* as "science fiction's answer to Hornblower." When I was interrupted by the telephone I'd gotten to an interesting part of the story; my hero was putting up a token resistance against the amorous advances of a beautiful, blonde, not too alien princess. I used a very appropriate word when my train of thought was disturbed by the insistent ringing. Nonetheless I did not answer the call until I had finished the sentence: ". . . made a major production of filling and lighting his pipe while trying to ignore her attentions."

The person from Porlock—I never finished that novel, any more than Coleridge finished "Kubla Khan"—was Duffin. Duffin was editor of *The Sydney Star*, one of our evening newspapers. He was less than a friend but rather more than a mere acquaintance. Now and again he would commission me to do scientific—or pseudo-scientific—articles for him. I assumed that he was about to do so again.

He wasted no time. "I'd like you," he said, "to do an article for us. The usual rates."

"Not UFOs *again*?" I demanded.

"No."

"Then what?"

"I'll tell you over lunch. You know that new Vietnamese place in the Cross? The one opposite the Wayside Chapel? I'll see you there."

He hung up and I got changed into something respectable. My hero would have to wait until late afternoon, or possibly the next day, for the consummation. (I wonder if he and that tow-haired trollop are still waiting, frozen in some kind of literary stasis . . .) I left the unfinished page, the half-written chapter, in the typewriter and went out to meet Duffin and to find out what was expected of me in return for the free lunch and the usual rates.

The restaurant was as good as Duffin had implied that it would be. The honey prawns were especially delicious. For a while we busily plied our chopsticks and sipped our cold beer.

And then . . .

"The Centennial's coming up," he said.

"Not for a long while," I told him. "In any case, it will be the Bicentenary."

He said, "I'm talking about the Siege of Glenrowan, not the First Fleet."

"History is not my field," I said.

"Even so, I want a piece from *you* about the Siege."

"From me? And all this time in advance?"

"It could take you some time to do it properly," he said.

"But it has already been done, and done, and done. People have written about it. There have been films."

"I want *you* to write about it."

"But I'm a fiction writer, a science fiction writer at that."

"You're a writer," he said patiently, "who is very interested in history, Australian history and one who has a definite connection with Glenrowan. You told me, a while ago, that an ancestor of yours was among that gang of platelayers whom Ned Kelly persuaded to tear up the track north of the station."

"He was. But if you're hoping that he left a diary, an eyewitness account of the events of that night, you'll be disappointed. He was there, as I told you, but he didn't approve of Kelly. In his later years he was a pillar of the Establishment, a respected and respectable shipmaster. He was notorious for only one thing. He would never, if he could possibly avoid it, have an Irishman in his crew."

"But he was there," insisted Duffin, "at Glenrowan."

"So were a lot of other people."

"True. But only one of them was your great-grandfather. Only one of them was the great-grandfather of a competent writer." He looked at his watch. "Finish your chili beef. We've an appointment."

"Who with?"

"Dr. Graumann. You must have heard of him."

"I have," I admitted. "The man who resurrected J. W. Dunne's theories about time. *Omni* published an interview with him a while ago. I didn't know that he was in Australia."

"Well, he is. Has been for some weeks now. We've been interested in his work. We've let him know that we shall pay handsomely for a *real* story. So far he has not come up with one. And then I thought of the Ned Kelly angle."

"Ned Kelly, and J.W. Dunne's theories . . ." I muttered. "It just doesn't make sense."

"It does," he assured me.

We got a taxi without any difficulty and drove out, over the Bridge, to one of those tall apartment blocks on the north shore of the Harbor. This Dr. Graumann, I thought, was doing himself well. But charlatans never seem to find it hard to persuade allegedly hard-headed businessmen to subsidize their activities. During the ride I had been recalling the *Omni* interview. I had gained the impression that Graumann was a refugee from the Bad Old Days of science fiction, the archetypical Mad Scientist. He had been trotting out as fact the tired old fables that were played around with and then discarded by science fiction writers years ago. And, obviously, had found somebody to sponsor his so-called research.

Graumann was on the top floor in a luxury suite, with a view. The wide window of his living room looked out over the Harbor and the Bridge. Graumann, himself, was something of a disappointment. He didn't look like a Mad Scientist. He didn't look like a charlatan, even. He was a very ordinary-looking middle-aged man, slightly pudgy, with close-cropped graying hair, dressed formally in a three-piece dark blue suit, white shirt and a blue, polka dot bow tie. He used his heavily black-rimmed spectacles more to gesticulate with than as an aid to vision. His gray eyes looked keen enough without them, keen and . . . fanatical? Perhaps—but it may have been that I was seeing what I thought I should see.

Introductions were made.

"Mr. Duffin has been telling me about you, Mr. Grimes," he said. His accent was that of a New Yorker, I thought. "Perhaps I shall have greater success with you than with the *real* Australians."

I told him, rather tartly, that I was real enough.

Duffin said, "Dr. Graumann means the Aborigines, Grimes."

Graumann motioned us to the chairs set around a low table. He took a seat himself, facing us.

He said, "Mr. Grimes, I have what some people would call an obsession. I believe, most sincerely, that Earth has been visited, more than once, in the distant Past, by beings from other planets. All over the world there are . . . relics. In this country there are your Aboriginal rock paintings, depicting humanoids wearing spacesuits. I had hoped, by the use of my techniques, to tap ancestral memories. . . ."

"So you're trying to find an Aboriginal Bridey Murphy," I said.

"*Not* Bridey Murphy!" he snapped. "My theories have nothing at all to do with reincarnation!" I feared that he would break the earpiece of his spectacles as he waved them at me. "My theories—which, to give credit where credit is due, are a development of Dunne's theories . . . You have heard of Dunne?"

His manner implied that he would be surprised if I said that I had.

"J.W. Dunne," I told him. "English mathematician and aircraft designer. Author of *An Experiment with Time* and *The Serial Universe.*"

He looked at me with some surprise and said, "So you have read his books?"

"A long time ago," I admitted. "A very long time ago."

"And what do you remember of them?"

"What started him off," I said, "were some very vivid premonitory dreams that he had. He . . . sort of worked things out. Most dreams, he reasoned, are based on memories of the Past—but a few are based on memories of the Future. Have I got it right?"

"Go on, Mr. Grimes."

"He used analogies. A photograph is a sort of two-dimensional presentation of your three-dimensional self. Your three-dimensional self, the one that's sitting across the table listening to me, is a sort of cross section of the four-dimensional *you*. The Fourth Dimension is Time."

"Crude, but adequate," he commented. "Go on."

"From birth to death you co-exist with yourself. Your spark of consciousness travels at a steady rate along your elongated four-dimensional being, your World Line, from conception to eventual demise. But when you are sleeping it is free to . . . wander, back into the Past, forward into the Future. And those glimpses of what is to come are the basis for premonitory dreams. And, I suppose, for such psychological phenomena as déjà vu."

He said, "Unfortunately I have not yet been able to send any of my subjects into the Future." He smiled bleakly. "Perhaps there is *no* Future. In any case, as Dunne made clear in *The Serial Universe*, there is an infinitude of possible Futures branching out from every instant of experienced Time. But the Past is immutable. And it is the Past that I am mainly interested in."

"As we are, too," put in Duffin.

"*Your* Past, sir?" Graumann's voice was scornful. "Something that happened less than one century ago. An event of no real importance, already well documented."

An angry flush spread over Duffin's normally pale, fat face.

He said stiffly, "We have given you more than a little assistance, Doctor Graumann, in your search for alien starmen." (*If there ever were such beings*, I could almost hear him thinking.) "I feel that you owe us something in return. And if what you consider to be only a minor experiment, of no interest to yourself, is successful we shall be happy to continue our sponsorship of your major research."

"Very well." Graumann returned his attention to me. "I am given to understand, Mr. Grimes, that a relative of yours, a paternal great-grandfather, was among those present at the so-called siege . . ."

"He was," I said.

"Now, this is important. Had he yet become a father? Had he yet initiated the chain of events culminating in yourself?"

"No. I can't recall the exact date but he married Harriet O'Connor, my great-grandmother, some years after the Glenrowan affair."

"There could have been children, by other ladies, before that marriage," said Graumann. "But it is of no consequence. You are in the direct line of descent. Before your grandfather was conceived your great grandfather had experienced the famous siege. That experience, therefore, is accessible. And now we return to Dunne's concept of the World Line. Yours is a continuation of that of his father, and his of that of *his* father, and so on and so on. You seem to have accepted the proposition that your spark of consciousness may travel back and forth during sleep, to revisit your Past, to preview your Future. What if that spark, that lens through which your mind inspects the Universe, could be induced to transfer, as it were, to your father's World Line, at the moment of your conception, to continue its Pastward journey? And then your grandfather's World Line . . . And your great-grandfather's. . . ."

"Why stop there?" I asked. "I've a pirate clambering around in the branches of my family tree."

"Pirates, especially minor pirates," sneered Duffin, "were two a penny. There was only one Ned Kelly."

"I am at a loss," said Graumann, "to understand this fascination with a criminal, a . . . a bushranger."

"But he was more than a bushranger," I told him. "Much more. He was a freedom fighter, the champion of the poor farmers on their selections and of the landless laborers."

"You obviously don't share your great-grandfather's opinion of him," said Duffin.

"Of course I don't. Why should I? I've never subscribed to the 'God bless the squire and his relations and keep us in our proper stations' philosophy. Ned Kelly may have been of humble birth—but, given his chance, he would have made something of himself."

"I agree," Duffin said. "That's why I want a late-twentieth-century man, you, to look at Ned, even though it will be through your ancestor's eyes. I want you to hear him speak, even though it will be through your great grandfather's ears. You, belonging to another era, will be an altogether unbiased witness. With you as an observer we shall, at last, meet the real Ned Kelly."

"I haven't yet agreed to be Dr. Graumann's guinea pig," I said.

"You'll be a mug if you don't, Grimes," said Duffin. "Even if the experiment doesn't work it will be material for you. You'll be able to use it in one of your far-fetched stories."

I turned to Graumann, who had been listening to us with slightly contemptuous amusement.

"Tell me, Doctor," I asked, "are your techniques dangerous?"

"So far, in this country," he said, "I have employed six subjects, all of whom were found for me by Mr. Duffin. Three women, three men, of Aboriginal descent. They experienced nothing worse than dreams, extremely vivid dreams, of the remote Past of their people."

"And no starmen," grumbled Duffin. "Not even a bunyip."

"But there were . . . hints," Graumann said. "Lights and noises in the sky."

"No more than hints," stated Duffin. "We shall be expecting more than hints from you, Grimes."

"What *are* your techinques, Doctor?" I persisted.

"A mind-liberating drug," he said. "Surely you have made your own experiments with such."

"Perhaps I have, but not by injection. I detest having needles shoved into me."

"The drug will be taken orally. And there are audio-visual devices to induce the proper mood in the subject. You will seem to sleep, that is all. You will awake, refreshed but with the memory of a remarkably vivid dream. I suggest that we make the first experiment now. The apparatus is set up."

"It won't kill you, Grimes," said Duffin cheerfully.

"Then why don't *you* try it?"

"I didn't have an ancestor at Glenrowan. Come to that, as far as I know none of my forebears was present at any really interesting historical event."

"All right," I said. "Let's get it over with. If I don't like it, there won't be a second time."

"There has to be a first time for everything," said Duffin fatuously.

CHAPTER 2

Graumann's laboratory, if you could call it that, had once been the master bedroom of the suite, complete with Harbor view. Now it was more like a museum with an odd mixture of art, history and technology all in the same confined space. On the walls were reproductions of Nolan's Ned Kelly paintings and also a large reproduction of the photograph that was taken of the bushranger shortly before his death. There was a suit of the famous armor that had been hammered out from plowshares. I looked at it curiously.

"It's the real thing," Duffin told me. "It cost us plenty to hire it. Go on, touch it. . . ."

I touched it. The metal was cold under my fingertips. And had my great-grandfather, I wondered, touched it all those many years ago when he, with the others, had been held by the outlaws in Mrs. Jones' pub, awaiting the arrival of the special train from Melbourne? It was possible. I felt that already I had established a link with the past.

Graumann was fussing around with the only piece of modern apparatus. The metal of which it had been constructed was bright, reflecting the light coming in through the wide window, contrasting shockingly with the age-dulled iron and steel of the armor and the ancient weapons—revolvers and shotguns and what I identified as a Colt revolving rifle.

I remarked on this latter.

"You seem to have slipped up there, Duffin. Those things were issued to the Union Army during the War Between The States. They weren't very popular. More than one chamber was liable to go off at once and a rifleman could lose the fingers of his left hand . . ."

"They were still around in 1880," Duffin said. "Fifteen years wasn't long in the life of a weapon in those days. And *this* is the one that Ned Kelly carried at Glenrowan. *He* didn't lose any fingers."

He lost more than just fingers at the end, I thought.

(But don't we all?)

Graumann stood back from the thing that he had been adjusting. It could have been a mobile. It was a band of metal, twisted through 180 degrees, a Mobius strip, resting on a disc of transparent glass or plastic which was mounted on an obvious electric motor housing. I'd played with Mobius strips made from paper, cutting them along their lengths and getting all kinds of odd results, but one made of metal . . . ? What was it supposed to *do*?

"If Mr. Grimes will sit in the chair . . ." suggested Graumann.

I sat in the chair, facing the Mobius strip affair. I could see, too, the Nolan paintings, the photograph of the heavily bearded Kelly and the suit of armor. I could see, too, through the window. A green hulled, red funnelled coaster, inbound to her Darling Harbor berth, was passing under the Bridge. It was a great pity, I thought, that Ned Kelly's last stand had not been made at sea. Ships have always fascinated me.

I was annoyed when Duffin drew the heavy curtains.

Now the only light in the room came from a ceiling fitting, the beam from which was directed onto the gleaming Mobius strip. This was moving now, the transparent turntable rotating. The humming of the motor was barely audible. Much louder was the music, a recording of a folksinger accompanied by a guitar. "The Wild Colonial Boy"? But hadn't that wild colonial boy been Jack Dolan, who had met his end some years before the Kelly gang became famous? Still, he had been, like Ned, a bush-ranger and, also like Ned, of Irish descent. Another song started "The Wearin' O' The Green," I thought. But it wasn't. It was "The Ballad of Ned Kelly," sung to the same tune.

I was dimly aware that Graumann was standing in front of me. He was holding a glass, half full of some dark liquid.

"Drink this, Mr. Grimes," he said. "Drink this, then watch the rotator."

I accepted the tumbler from his hand. I raised it to my lips, took a very cautious sip. The drug, as I supposed it to be, was almost flavorless but with a slightly acid tang. And weren't the Waters of Lethe supposed to be dark and bitter? But this draught was supposed to be memory enhancing . . .

I thought, but did not say, *down the hatch.*

I gulped, swallowed.

I settled back in the surprisingly comfortable chair and watched that gleaming, rotating, distorted circle, waiting with an odd feeling of anticipation for the twist in the metal band to come into view, again and again and again, as it turned. The rate of rotation seemed to be slowing—but was that impression, I wondered, subjective or objective?

And I asked myself, *is this all there is?*

Suddenly the humming of the motor was louder, much louder and, I realized the Mobius strip was now rotating in reverse, faster and faster, flickering in and out of focus. The light was dimming, was little more than an ominous ruddy glow, but that twisted metal band seemed to be gleaming brightly with a luminosity of its own. There was no longer any mood-setting music, just a roaring like that of a mighty wind.

The roar of the Time Wind blowing through the dark corridors of Eternity. . . .

I liked the sound of that. I must use it sometime, in something.

And there was another roaring noise, different, and coming from outside the room. That ship, I remembered. The one that I had seen passing under the bridge. She must be rounding Millers Point. For some reason she was very important to me. Union Steam Ship Company, with those hull and funnel colors. And it was in that employ that my great-grandfather had held command in his later years.

The roaring of the Time Wind sounded more like the wash of the sea along a ship's side. I could feel the deck rising and falling gently under my feet, the early afternoon sun warm on my back through the thin shirt. I could hear the creaking of cordage, the voices of the watch on deck as they went about their work, bringing up the mooring lines from the rope locker in readiness for arrival.

I opened my eyes.

CHAPTER 3

The memory was vivid.

No, it was not a memory. I was actually reliving the events of that long ago afternoon. I was reliving them, experiencing them, but could do nothing to interfere with the sequence. I was no more than an observer, an uninvited guest in my great-grandfather's mind.

The warm sun, the following westerly breeze and the old ship, with her flaking paintwork, her shabby, patched suit of sails, her spliced and respliced cordage, plowing steadily across the Bight, Medbourne bound . . . It was a pleasant afternoon watch—until Captain Flannery came up from his quarters. He was a drunkard, was Flannery—a drunkard and a bully. He was badly hung over. He staggered to the wheel and roughly pushed the helmsman aside so that he could peer into the compass bowl. Not surprisingly the ship fell off course. From overhead came a warning flap of threadbare canvas.

"Watch your damned steering!" he snarled at the seaman. Then, "You couldn't steer a scrubbing brush across a frigging washtub!"

The man made no reply but his face flushed angrily.

"Say something, you useless dolt! If you can't open your frigging mouth I'll have you in the Log Book for Dumb Insolence!"

I thought that it was time that I intervened. (Or my

great-grandfather thought that it was time that he intervened.) Morris was a good seaman, one of the very few
good seamen aboard the *Lady Lucan*. Left to himself he
did his work—any work at all aboard the ship—well but,
as I had learned, he hated being stood over.

I walked to the binnacle.

"Sir," I said to Flannery, "Morris has been steering well
all through his trick at the wheel, never so much as a
quarter point off course."

The captain glared at me with his little bloodshot eyes.
With that filthy ginger beard covering most of his face it
was impossible to read his expression; the overall impression was that of a rat peering out of a bale of oakum. He
straightened up, then almost fell against me. His breath,
as he exhaled gustily right into my face, was like a foul
emanation from a sewer.

"It's you . . ." he muttered. "So we do have an officer of
the blinking watch . . . I was beginning to think that we
didn't . . ."

I retreated before him, still facing him, drawing him
away from the wheel. If I was to be treated to one of his
outbursts—as I frequently was—I'd prefer it not to be
within earshot of one of the fo'c's'le hands.

"You . . ." he snarled again.

"Sir?" I asked politely.

"You and your blinking watch, mister! Never in all me
born days have I had to put up with such a shower of
mother-frigging bastards, all o' you about as much use as a
nun's privates . . ."

Even today that would be considered rough language.
In those days it was impossibly vile. What made it even
worse was that I got a faceful of Flannery's spittle.

I pushed him away from me.

He flailed out with both fists, one of them striking me
on the right shoulder.

"Useless, mother-frigging bastard!" he gibbered.

So I hit him.

He screamed and spat out broke, yellow teeth. He
clapped a hand to his bleeding mouth, scuttled to the
head of the companionway and vanished below. I rubbed

my sore knuckles with my left hand and looked at Morris. He looked at least as frightened as I was feeling.

He muttered, "I didn't hear nothin', Second. I didn't see nothin'."

"I wish I could say the same," I told him.

The Mate came up from his cabin. He was a good seaman, was Connery, a good officer. Without him the ship would have become more of a shambles than she already was. He was the nearest I had to a friend aboard *Lady Lucan*.

He drew me forward to the starboard rail, spoke in a low voice so that he would not be overheard.

"Paddy the Pig's been at me," he said. "What did you *do* to the old bastard, John? He was raving about mutiny on the high seas. He was wanting you hanged from the yardarm . . ."

I told him what had happened.

"You bloody fool," he said. "Why couldn't you keep your temper? Mind you, I've often had a helluva struggle keeping mine. Well, this is the way of it. He wanted you arrested and handed over to the police on arrival. I talked him out of it. It would mean promoting the bo's'n to acting second mate—and even the Old Man knows how useless *he* is. So you're to carry on with your normal duties—until we get to Melbourne. And then? He's a vicious bastard, as we both know. He'll have you up before the beak on a charge of mutiny on the high seas. There're at least a couple of men on your watch, cousins of his, who'll swear that they saw you strike him without provocation. . . ."

"Quinn and Halloran?"

"The same. If I were you I'd get packed—just valuables, your certificate and the like, some spare clothing. Then, after we're alongside and before Paddy can run screaming to the agents, the shipping master and the police, you just walk ashore and go on walking. Inland."

"But what shall I do to earn a living?"

"There's plenty of work in Australia for those who want it. You'll get by. You're a seaman. You've been in steam as well as sail. You should be able to turn your hand to most things."

"You said it, Peter. I'm a seaman. I don't especially want to be anything else."

"Just keep out of sight for a few months. Nobody bothers much about seamen who enter Australia illegally. Then make your way to Sydney and try to get a ship. You shouldn't have much trouble. You'll have your certificate with you."

"But no discharge book . . ."

"I'll try to get it out of the Old Man's safe while he's passed out. But even if I can't, any master wanting a second mate in a hurry won't be too fussy."

"I . . . I think I'll stay to face the music," I said. "I'm not afraid to tell my story in a court of law . . ."

But Australian courts, *I* tried to tell me, speaking from my knowledge of those times, are all for the Establishment, all against the little man. Captain Flannery, dissolute brute that he was, represented the Establishment. Too—the knowledge came to me in a flash—if the nineteenth-century John Grimes deviated from the script that already had been written even greater deviations would be possible. He might never meet and wed the lady who became my great grandmother, who made her own contribution to my genes. I liked me the way that I was. . . .

I listened to the voice inside my mind. I must have heard about Australian courts of law somewhere. And in any court, anywhere in the world, a ship's officer who had assaulted his captain, at sea, could require the sort of lawyer for his defense that he could never afford.

I looked at Morris, standing stolidly behind the wheel.

He would be of no use. He had made it plain that he did not want to get involved.

"Don't be a fool, John," said the Mate.

"All right," I said (to *me* as well as to him), "I'll take your advice."

"You're wise, if you should be cleared, if you stay on here, one of Paddy the Pig's pets might be dropping something on you from aloft, or tipping you over the poop rail on a dark and stormy night. . . ."

Neither I nor *I* had thought of that angle.

Jumping the ship would be the only safe course of action.

Suddenly I felt faint. The brightness of the day faded and all color seemed to be sagging down the spectrum. There was a roaring in my ears.

I heard, as though from a great distance (in Space or Time?) the Mate asking urgently, "What's wrong with you, John?"

There was blackness, utter blackness and then, at last, a single spark of light. Slowly, slowly it expanded until it became that glowing, twisted band of metal, still rotating but slowing to a stop.

Light flooded the room as Duffin drew aside the heavy curtains. It was not yet sunset. I watched a huge container ship, her decks piled high, sliding slowly under the Bridge, tugs fussing about her. A far cry, I thought, from that scruffy little tramp windjammer.

Graumann was making adjustments to the controls of what I was thinking of as his time-twisting machine. Duffin was standing over me.

"Well?" he asked eagerly. "Well?"

"Well *what*?" I countered.

"Were you at Glenrowan? Did you meet Ned?"

"No," I told him.

Duffin turned to Graumann. "Does this bloody contraption of yours ever work?" he demanded.

I said, "It does work." Both Duffin and Graumann were listening to me intently. "Either I had a very vivid dream or I experienced the events leading up to my great-grandfather's deserting his ship in Australia . . ."

Graumann looked a little happier.

"You relived the Past . . ." he half asked, half stated.

"That's what it felt like," I said. "It must have been some months prior to Glenrowan. It was summer. The ship had almost finished her crossing of the Bight . . ."

"Do you know anything about gunnery?" asked Graumann. "Gunnery the way that it used to be before the electronic devices made it more of a science than an art?" He went on, before either of us could reply, "I used to be in the Navy, you know. A Reserve commission. Gunnery fascinated me. . . ." Now he was lecturing us. "You fire your first salvo, your sights set for range and deflection. If you're very, very lucky, you hit the target. If you don't, you spot the fall of shot, left or right, under or over. Then you correct, and correct again if necessary. And again . . .

"You've spotted the fall of shot for me, Mr. Grimes. Could you tell me the exact date?"

"As a matter of fact I can. It was on my great-grandfather's birthday. January the 28th. And the year was 1880."

"Good. Good."

He rubbed his hands together gleefully. I could guess what he was thinking. During his past experiments, his futile quest for the mythical starmen, he had been shooting blind, as it were. Now he had a real target, even though it was not one of his own choice, had made a near miss and needed, to make a hit, only to bracket or ladder. But this analogy was a false one. *I*, or whatever part of me that was being fired from an artillery piece, was a guided missile.

"So . . . I must adjust . . . a fine adjustment . . . I don't suppose that you can remember the *exact* time of your experience . . . ?"

"It was shortly after four bells of the afternoon watch . . . Two o'clock in the afternoon."

"And the time zone?"

"In those days, Dr Graumann, ships did not adjust their clocks, as they do today, from zone to zone. They kept apparent time. Or tried to. The idea was that the sun should be at the meridian on the stroke of eight bells."

"No matter, Mr. Grimes. You will home to that crucial point at Glenrowan just as you homed to that crucial point at sea. . . ."

"How do you know about it?"

"Mr. Duffin has already told me something of your family history."

"All right. That was a crucial point. If great-grandfather hadn't socked Captain Flannery on his own poop *I*, almost certainly, should not be here now. But Glenrowan?"

"Also crucial," said Duffin. "When the police were pouring their fire into Mrs. Jones' hotel a stray bullet could easily have found your ancestor. There were civilian casualties, you know. It's amazing that there weren't more." He produced a pocket cassette recorder. "And now, while the good doctor is setting his sights for the next salvo, will you tell me just what you experienced?"

I said, "I'd like a transcript. After all, it's *my* experience."

"You shall have one," he said generously.

CHAPTER 4

Oddly enough—or not so oddly—there was no discussion as to whether or not a second attempt to reach Glenrowan was to be made that day. Even the guinea pig, myself, had no misgivings. While I talked into the cassette recorder I was conscious of Graumann's tinkerings with his apparatus, was wishing that he didn't have to take so long about it. Dimly I was aware that, outside, the light was fading fast. But it would not be a dark night; a full moon was rising as the sun fell below the horizon.

"And that's that," I said at last. "End of story. Oh, I do know what happened afterwards. Great grandfather did jump ship in Melbourne. He was able—thanks to the Mate—to take his papers with him. He was at Glenrowan, as you know. After the siege he got away from there as fast as he could. He was afraid that the police might be looking for a Pommy deserter and mutineer as well as Australian bushrangers. But nobody worried him, or worried about him. In Sydney he got a job with the Union Steam Ship Company, as second mate. And after that, as the saying goes, he never looked back."

"And are *you* ready to look back again, Mr. Grimes?" asked Graumann, who seemed to have finished doing whatever it was that he had been doing.

"Yes," I said. Then, "But what if it's a bracket? What if

your next shot is under? You'll probably treat me to another taste of nineteenth-century seafaring."

"The next shot will be on target," Graumann said confidently.

So I made myself comfortable in that deep chair again and gulped another glass of that drug, whatever it was (I hoped that it was not habit-forming) and listened to the folk songs and watched the rotating Mobius strip. It was like staring at a powerful magnet with your rods and cones made of soft iron. Then, as before, there was what I had thought of as the roaring of the Time Wind . . .

. . . which was beginning to sound, I realized, like too many people talking all at once.

CHAPTER 5

I looked out through my great-grandfather's eyes, listened through his ears. But I knew what was going to happen; he did not. He was wondering, *What have I gotten myself into?* He knew that the special train was expected from the south and that the track had been torn up north of the station—he had been among those persuaded, at revolver point, to take part in this work. And yet he knew something that I—until then—did not, that it was not Ned Kelly's intention to derail the train but to trap it at Glenrowan by blowing up the lines, south of the station, after it had passed. That scheme, the taking of hostages to be followed by a demand for the release of the outlaw's mother from Melbourne jail—and by a demand for land reforms—might have worked. On the other hand it might not. But I, from my twentieth-century vantage point, knew that the hostage technique sometimes works.

In my own Time I was somewhat pro-Kelly but I had found it hard to excuse the murders at Stringy Bark Creek and the proposed massacre of a trainload of people, civilians as well as police, with two women among them, at Glenrowan. But now I knew that there was no massacre intended. And insofar as Stringy Bark Creek was concerned, how much mercy would the policemen, Lonigan especially, have shown the outlaw if he had not fired first?

But I was here to observe, not to philosophize.

That old man, playing a violin when he was not sipping from a mug . . . Would he be Martin Cherry? And that lad who was singing, in a high, clear voice, "The Minstrel Boy" . . . Mrs. Jones' son? Like old Cherry, a victim of the inexcusably reckless police fire . . . What would happen if I were to tell them, "Get out of here or you'll be dead within hours!"

As before, on the poop of *Lady Lucan*, there was a sort of mental osmosis. My ancestral host was perturbed by the thoughts that were coming unbidden, into his mind. How did he *know*, as know he did, that old Cherry and young Jones had not much longer to live? How did he know that those three young men (*I* was surprised by their youth), Dan Kelly, Steve Hart and Joe Byrne, were also doomed and that their leader had less than five months to live?

I looked at Ma Jones—a woman not old but stout and motherly—with pity. And what of her? Her son killed—*no*, murdered—and her means of livelihood destroyed. I dipped into my great-grandfather's memories. She had been kind to him during his stay in Glenrowan with the other members of the railroad maintenance gang. She had treated him to drinks, to a meal or two. "It's a nice change," she had told him, "to meet somebody around here who's not a bloody Irishman!"

And there was the little club-footed Curnow. He, the village schoolmaster, in his respectable black suit, with high white collar and black cravat, obviously considered himself several cuts above his rough fellow "guests" in the Glenrowan Hotel. He sat by the blazing fire, sipping his drink sullenly, talking only when he was talked to. During my stay in the village I had met him more than once and had been looking forward to a conversation with an educated man. But, as far as he was concerned, I was just another laborer with brains to match. He had no time to waste on such as I. And now he was being forced to waste hours in the company of his intellectual and social inferiors.

But he'll get his revenge, I thought.

How do I know that? I—the other I, my great-grandfather—wondered.

I was here, I told myself, to observe, not to go putting thoughts into people's heads. Where was Kelly? He must have gone out shortly prior to my arrival at Glenrowan. I could guess why. Soon I should have to do the same but was reluctant to leave this overheated room—the blazing fire, the oil lamps, the people—for the bitterly cold night outside. I'd go when I had to go, but not before. Ned Kelly, I hoped, would prevent any of his unwilling—although most of them seemed to be enjoying themselves—guests from answering the call of nature.

Kelly came back in, followed by a blast of freezing air.

And he was young, too, I realized. Not even the full black beard could disguise the fact. He was young and he was a giant and he moved with arrogance. His eyes were pale blue flames in his ruddy (what could be seen of it) face. Yet when he spoke his voice had a soft, Irish lilt to it. Should he be so minded he could charm the birds out of the trees.

"I've been listenin' " he announced, "an' still there's not a sound o' the train a-comin'. But come it must, an' when it does . . ." He addressed himself to his brother, to Hart and to Byrne. "There'll be no bloodshed. I want them alive—Hare an' all his puppies an' O'Connor an' his black devils. Ye can't drive a hard bargain when ye've only dead men to exchange for what ye're wantin'. An' it's justice we're wantin'—justice for my mother an' for all the selectors of the northeast . . ."

He went on. It was a rambling speech but, obviously, it came from the heart. The man had the makings of an orator, a rabble rouser. To me, the twentieth century me, he was preaching to the at-least-half-converted. In my own time descent from convicts was no longer something to be concealed but, instead, to be boasted about. Governor Bligh was at last being looked upon as the tragic hero of the Rum Rebellion and the officers of the New South Wales Corps as the villains. And Ned Kelly, of course, was beginning to be regarded as more of a freedom fighter than a mere bushranger.

And as for my great-grandfather—he wasn't sure. Although he had tried to adapt to his new surroundings he was still very much a fish out of water. As a ship's officer (would he ever be one again? I knew that he would be; he did not) he believed in duly constituted authority, even though he himself was technically guilty of the crime of mutiny. This Kelly, spellbinder though he might be, was both a criminal and a rebel. He had robbed and murdered.

And yet . . .

And yet, he thought, a real murderer would have given that special train no chance at all. He would not have caused the rails to be lifted, making a gap that was sure to be spotted in time by an alert engine driver. He would have planted a charge, detonating it when it was bound to do the most damage.

Meanwhile I was watching Curnow.

Soon, I thought, very soon he will be making his move. He will appeal to Kelly, taking advantage of the big man's generosity and decency, telling him that his sick wife will be worried about him and asking to be allowed to leave to go home. I thought, *the little rat!* I made my way through the crowded room to where he was sitting. Somehow, I realized, I was more and more in control of my great grandfather's mind. Perhaps it was because he had been drinking quite heavily, alternating thick, treacly rum with warm bitter beer. It was as though his body were being handled by a pilot and a co-pilot, with the co-pilot (myself) usurping more and more of the control.

"Can I get you a drink, Mr. Curnow?" I (he, or both of us) asked.

"Thank you, Grimes," he replied coldly. (The lack of an honorific annoyed me.) "I'd like a small rum."

To give him Dutch courage, I thought, *or to keep out the cold when he walks along the tracks with his candle and his box of matches and his red scarf . . .*

I shouldered my way through the crowd, being cursed by one of my Irish workmates as I jostled him, causing him to spill his beer. Mrs. Jones was busy behind the bar.

"Can I have a rum, please?" I asked.

"Surely, Johnnie. Here you are."

She poured a generous measure.

I fumbled for money. (How much did a glass of rum cost in these days?)

"It's on the house, Johnnie. Thanks to Ned I'm doing a roaring trade tonight. I can afford to shout you a drink."

"It's not for me," I said. "It's for Mr. Curnow."

"Then I will take yer money. That stuck-up little bastard isn't getting a free drink off me."

I paid, letting the nineteenth century me take over. I was wondering what had come over me, to be buying a drink for Curnow. I thought, *I must be drunk*. And then as I stood there, watching the ungrateful schoolmaster lift the glass to his bearded lips, I had a vision of what would be happening very shortly. The bullets tearing through the flimsy wooden walls, the shouting and the screaming, old Cherry and Mrs. Jones' son fatally hit, others injured. . . . And Byrne and Hart and Dan Kelly dead. (But they were criminals.) And Ned Kelly brought down, to stand trial and eventually to be hanged. . . .

He deserved a chance. All his ravings about a Republic of North East Victoria were just that—but if he were to live, only a little longer, some much needed reforms could be made. (They were made eventually, of course, but why not a little sooner?)

I was more than a little drunk. So was I. Nobody knows what the mind is—but the brain is no more (and no less) than an organic computer. This computer, snugly encased inside my ancestor's skull, was malfunctioning owing to the presence of too much alcohol in the blood. I was sharing his brain, the computer, with him. He was affected by its defective workings. So was I. He had experienced a flash of prevision—based on my memories of what I had read—and knew, in his muddled way, that he could do something to save his friend, Mrs. Jones, from the tragedy that shortly was to come upon her.

And I?

I was an interfering bastard, I suppose. I had decided to give Kelly his chance. After all, what difference would it really make? The Siege of Glenrowan was only a minor eddy in the main stream of human history.

And anyhow this was all only a dream, wasn't it? Wasn't it?

I realized that Curnow had finished his rum and had gotten to his feet. With his lurching gait he was making his way to the leader of the outlaws.

"Mr. Kelly . . ." he was saying, with oily politeness.

"Yes, Mr. Curnow?"

Don't listen to him, Ned! I thought but did not say.

"It's my wife. She is not well, as you know. She will be worrying about me. I am not usually out so late."

Kelly looked down at the little schoolmaster.

"Off ye go, then. Never let it be said that I caused any member of the fair sex needless worry. . . ."

I tried to push through the crowd to where the two men were standing but everybody seemed determined to get in my way. And then Curnow, displaying quite considerable agility, wormed his way through the gathering to the door. Steve Hart stopped him. Curnow started to expostulate then Kelly called, "It's all right, Steve. He has to go home to look after his good lady."

Not without reluctance the young outlaw let the schoolmaster out into the night. He slammed the door after him and truculently barred my way.

"Where d'ye think ye're off to, Limey?"

I said, not untruthfully, "I'm busting for a Jimmy Riddle."

"Let him through, Steve!" roared Kelly. "He can't hold his liquor!"

There was an outburst of laughter, directed at me.

Hart unlocked the door again. I brushed past him with unfeigned urgency. The cold air was like an electric shock to the exposed skin of my hands and face and, in seconds, permeated my clothing. Shivering, I walked hastily to the nearest tree, unbuttoned and fumbled, managed to get cleared for action before I wetted my trousers. It seemed as though that steaming stream would never stop.

At last I finished.

I looked along the road that Curnow would be taking to his house. The moon, just past its full, was high. I had no trouble in seeing him, although he now had a fair start on me. There was no mistaking that little, black figure hobbling along the rough track.

I started to walk after him.

He must have heard me. He quickened his pace.

I walked faster.

He started to run.

I ran.

It wasn't much of a race. At the finish he panicked and scuttled into the brush at the side of the road, attempting to hide. He tripped and fell heavily, squealing like a trapped rabbit.

I stood over him, panting.

At last he rolled over on to his back and stared up at me. Relief showed on his face.

"Grimes . . . It's you . . . I thought that it was one of them . . ."

"Yes. It's me."

"What . . . What do you want?"

"To stop you from stopping the train."

"What are you talking about?" he demanded, all injured innocence.

"You know."

"Help me up, Grimes," he appealed. "My wife will be worried about me."

And then we both heard the noise coming from the south, faint at first then becoming louder and louder. The distant rattling, the chuffing . . . It could be only the long-awaited special train, the train itself and, running ahead, the pilot engine. . . .

"Help me up, Grimes!" Curnow was beginning to sound desperate. "Help me up!"

One of his legs was twisted at an unnatural angle. It must have been at least badly sprained.

"Grimes! You must help! Make a fire on the tracks! You must stop the train!"

"Why?"

"Damn you, man! You know what the blackguard Kelly intends to do! If he gets away with it there will be anarchy all through the north east of Victoria!"

And you won't get your reward, I thought. How much had it been? Five hundred and fifty pounds?

He said, "Stop the train—and we'll share the reward . . ."

I crouched over him. The train was getting close now. I had to stop him from shouting as it passed. It was unlikely that the driver of either the pilot engine or of the following locomotive would hear him—but it was possible. I clamped my hand over his mouth. He tried to bite me. He gasped and abandoned the effort when I slammed my other hand, hard, into his belly. I was able to watch the train as it passed, was deafened by the mechanical clangor.

The pilot engine was first. Its headlamp, I noticed, was very dim, almost out. The other engine was having no such trouble. I could see through the windows into the lighted carriages—men in uniform and in civilian clothes. And two women—O'Connor's wife and sister-in-law.

But the leading engine seemed to be slowing. There was the shriek of escaping steam. So much, I thought, for my attempt to change, even if in only a very minor way, the course of history.

The pilot engine most certainly was slowing. The driver's intention must be to stop at Glenrowan station.

But the special train itself did not slow down. Its driver whistled impatiently. (He must have plenty of steam to waste, I thought.) I released Curnow, left the road for the railway track to try to see what was happening. The pilot engine was picking up speed again, although by this time the two locomotives were almost in contact.

The train vanished around the bend beyond the station.

And then I heard the crash.

CHAPTER 6

I left Curnow sprawled there, moaning, and began to hurry back to the station. I could hear the loud hiss of escaping steam, the shouting and the screaming. There was a burst of gunfire. Then, with shocking suddenness, from somewhere ahead and to the right of me, a signal rocket climbed into the moonlit sky. The green stars of its bursting—the dull thud of the explosion seeming to come long seconds after the pyrotechnics—were bright even against the moon. There was more shouting, distant, that I thought came from the neighborhood of Greta. And a blazing beacon fire flared into life on the black, brooding bulk of Morgan's Lookout.

As I ran past Mrs. Jones' hotel I saw people standing outside the lighted doorway—women and children but only a very few men. The others must all be at the scene of the train wreck. I turned away from them to make my way down to the station, jumped from the platform to the tracks. Now to run was far from easy; the sleepers were so spaced as to make rapid progress impossible. Too, this part of the line was in the cutting and partly in shadow. There was light coming from ahead but it was unsteady and blinded rather than helped me. It came from a fire. Wooden railway coaches, I thought, and overturned oil lamps. . . . The van with the police horses must be one of

43

those blazing; the screams of the trapped, tortured animals were drowning out those of the human victims.

But somebody was fighting. I heard a ragged volley, then another.

The wreck was just beyond the cutting where the line curved on to the embankment. It was a horrible tangle of shattered wood and twisted metal in the ravine, self-illumined by the licking flames. But there were people still alive in the wreckage and others who had crawled or been thrown clear and who were taking what cover they could. Moonlight and firelight were reflected from rifle barrels and from the metal buttons and badges of uniforms—and from the sweat-shiny, black faces of the five native trackers from Queensland. They, from the not very effective cover of trees and bushes, were fighting back with grim and vicious determination, firing, reloading, firing again.

Somebody grabbed my arm.

A female voice demanded, "Is that you, Flanagan? Where are the others? Didn't they see the rocket?" Then, in tones of great disgust, "Oh, it's *you*, Limey . . ."

I asked, "What's happening?"

"Can't ye see for yerself, ye English eejit?"

I looked at the pale face under the wild, dark hair, saw that it was Kate Kelly.

"Can't ye see for yerself?" she repeated. "Ned never intended this. The fools should have stopped in time. We ran to help them, to save the horses if we could, an' the people. Then the black bastards fired on us. Dan is dead. He wasn't wearin' his helmet. Others were hurt . . ." She paused briefly. "The murtherin' police bastards! They can fry in hell now, all of 'em!"

We stood there together, united in some strange companionship, watching the giant figure walking slowly along the track to where he could bring his revolvers to bear upon the surviving police. The cylindrical helmet added to his already considerable height, the body armor to his bulk. Smoke and the steam from the ruptured boilers eddied about him. He was like some figure out of mythology—or like some huge, implacable robot from the science fiction of my own proper time. Now and again he staggered as he walked; perhaps he was stumbling over irregularities in the ground, perhaps not all the bullets fired at him were missing. But if they hit him they were doing no worse than to inflict bruises.

And where was Sergeant Steele, I wondered with the twentieth century part of my shared mind, to shoot with his shotgun at Kelly's unprotected legs to bring him down?

Byrne and Hart, both in full armor, joined Kelly. They were followed by others, armed but not armored. The three outlaws were the storm troopers, premature panzers. They must have been a terrifying sight but most of the surviving police stood their ground. Their fire was ineffectual; that of Kelly and his two companions was not. They aimed and fired their weapons with slow deliberation, making every shot count. At the finish two men panicked, broke cover and tried to run. They were trapped in the undergrowth and died with their backs to the enemy.

Kelly turned away from the scene of carnage, faced his supporters. He thrust his pistols into the deep pockets of the overcoat that he was wearing over his armor. His hands went up to his helmet, lifted it slowly from his head. He let it fall to the ground, where it clanged hollowly.

He said, his voice slow and grave, "Bear witness, all of ye, that this killin' was none of my intention. The fool in the pilot engine should have seen that the tracks were up. . . ."

And perhaps he would have done, I thought, *if he'd been allowed to stop at the station to fix his headlight. . . .*

"And the other fool should not have been treadin' so hard on his heels that he could not stop in time.

"But we came runnin', did we not, to save whom we might from the wreck. An' they fired on us as we came. My brother Dan they killed, and Mrs. Jones' son, an' even poor old Cherry, that ancient, harmless man. . . . *They* killed, an' so we were forced to kill." He sighed gustily. "Ah, well. It had to come to this."

I was aware that the crowd, now, was much bigger.

"Ned!" many voices were shouting. "Ned! The Captain of the North East! We're with ye, Ned! We're with ye!"

And then something—I hoped that it was something,

one of the horses, not somebody—started to scream loudly again in the burning wreckage. I remembered those two women who had been in the special train. I could smell not only smoke but scorching meat.

The acrid, sickly-sweet fumes eddied about me, thicker and thicker, choking me, blotting out the moonlight and the flames from the burning coaches.

There was a roaring in my ears.

Was I going to faint?

And what would Kate Kelly, to whom I was a member of a despised and hated race, think of me if I did?

I clung desperately to consciousness.

But loudly in my ears roared the Time Wind, bearing me back to where (and when) I really belonged. No longer could I hear the voices of the crowd, the crackling of the flames. No longer could I see the flaring fire. (But the stench of burning flesh lingered in my nostrils.)

There was a light, no more than an incredibly distant spark. It expanded slowly. It became. . . .

No, not the slowly rotating Mobius strip that I was expecting.

It became a complexity of spidery, spinning wheels, set at odd angles each to each, spinning, precessing, seeming ever to be at the point of fading into invisibility but never quite doing so. . . . Precessing, and dragging my mind with them through the warped Continuum. . . . Precessing but spinning ever more slowly. . . .

Coming to rest.

The overhead light that had been focused upon the device went out. Somebody drew the curtains apart, exposing the big window. I looked out to a view of the harbor and of the floodlit Bridge, with a large container ship inbound under its span.

The bridge?

It was in silhouette against the moonlit eastern sky—the pylons to the north and the south, the graceful catenary of the cables slung between them. A suspension bridge. . . .

But this was Sydney, wasn't it? Not New York. Or San Francisco.

Hadn't the bridge *always* looked like this?

Where did I get the idea from that it had been affectionately nicknamed "The Coathanger"?

The lights came on.

I looked at Graumann and at the big, bearded man who was standing beside him. Had I been out for long? Long enough for the scientist to get changed into a different suit. (I resented this. Surely he should have been watching over the controls of his weird machine.) He was now wearing a tweed outfit and gold-rimmed spectacles instead of horn-rimmed ones. His companion, too, was in tweed, Irish tweed, an expensive looking Donegal. At first I could not place him. I was certain of only one thing. He was not Duffin.

Yet his face, what I could see of it, was hauntingly familiar.

He towered over me as I sat in that deep chair.

He said, "So ye're back. So ye saw it all, the start of it, as it really happened?"

I said, "Yes. I was at Glenrowan."

"So now ye'll be able to make a start on the book. *The* book. The history, written by an eyewitness . . ."

"I still think," put in Graumann, "that you, too, sir, should go back yourself to experience the events. After all, your ancestor played a major part. *The* major part. . . ."

"Later, perhaps, Doctor. I've too much on me plate now, both at home an' overseas, to be able to afford the time." He turned to me. "An' anyhow, you're a scribbler, which I'm not. You're best able to get the History finished in time for the Centenary. An' you'll do it."

It was an order rather than a request but it seemed to need an answer.

"I'll do it, Ned," I said to the Hereditary President.

There was a moment of panic until I remembered that "Ned" was more of a title than a Christian name.

CHAPTER 7

I suppose that a psychiatrist would diagnose my state of mind as schizophrenia—but my personality is not split. I am no Dr. Jekyll and Mr. Hyde. I and me are both writers, stylistically almost indistinguishable. One of me writes (wrote?) science fiction but is a student of history. The other writes historical romances but reads science fiction for relaxation. Until I was persuaded to be Dr. Graumann's guinea pig neither of us was aware of the existence of the other. Yet there is the parallelism. We share a common ancestry, including a French Canadian great-grandfather on my mother's side, a German grandmother. My admixture of chromosomes and genes is such that I have to be the essential *me*. Nonetheless environment has played a part in my shaping.

For example—when I was a boy in this here and now, in the Republic of Australia, science fiction, in those days mainly of American origin, was as impossible to come by as hard pornography. (The Church honestly thought that it was pornography, and what customs officer was not a faithful son of the Church?) So historical romances were my staple diet during my formative years. When I started to write it was no more than natural that I wrote the sort of stuff that I enjoyed reading. By the time that the relaxation of censorship came, and with it my belated discovery of a field of literature dealing with other worlds and future times, I had established myself in a comfortable and fairly lucrative rut and saw no reason why I should try to clamber out of it.

In my other life I cut my teeth on Verne and Wells and all the American science fiction magazines that I could lay my hands on. When I made my first short story sale it was to one of these.

There are other differences. One of me loves Asiatic food—Chinese, Vietnamese, Korean, Japanese—the other has only my memories of what such meals look like and taste like. From the foundation of the Republic onwards there was a very strict White Australia policy. But, as I have said, I can remember the dishes that I used to enjoy (am still enjoying on the other time track?) and consider the most exotic restaurants that *we* have, Italian ones, a poor substitute for the many and various Oriental eating places.

But this will change, already is changing. For many years, despite our participation in foreign wars, we successfully maintained our cultural isolation. We can do so no longer. The dams have burst and the alien floods are surging over our country. Many fear that we shall lose our national identity. And that is too big a price to pay for the opportunity to sample again such delicacies as honey prawns!

Meanwhile I walk the city streets, just waiting, like so many others, for whatever will happen next. Sometimes there seems to be very little that is familiar and much that is strange. The Town Hall is an oasis of familiarity in an utterly alien desert. But then, suddenly, everything is normal and as it should be, well-remembered—the Cathedral on the hill with its twin Gothic towers reaching to high heaven, still the tallest building in the southern hemisphere, and the Harbor Bridge, built to the same design as but more graceful than its sisters in New York and San Francisco, and the Opera House, a secular version of St. Peter's in Rome . . .

So far we have escaped serious damage although we have had our share of street fighting. Fortunately only small calibre weapons were, for most of the time, employed although the buildings along the Circular Quay were shelled by a rebel destroyer. There have, so far, been no air raids.

Most services are now functioning more or less normally.

There is little live entertainment on our TV screens, however.

Of late prime time has been taken up by the trials in Melbourne.

CHAPTER 8

When I wrote the last chapter I was getting ahead of myself.

But, after all, the world hasn't come to an end. Life must go on. And, as far as I'm concerned, I'll carry on with what I was doing before the . . . interruptions. My original sponsor will not be able to pay the balance of the agreed upon fee for the definitive history, the eye witness account—but there must be some publisher who will be interested. Fortunately I still have all my notes; my flat was not among those looted during the riots. They are filed in the correct order. Now I must work from them, fleshing out the bare bones, the brief, unvarnished accounts of events, with interpretations and opinions and a narrative that is more than a mere catalogue of facts and dates.

I was present, as I have already set down, in the mind of my great-grandfather at the Glenrowan Massacre—as it is still called in English histories. This first slaughter—of police and pressmen and those two foolish, unlucky women (who had no business there)—was the consequence of accident and misunderstanding. (It was also the result of my meddling. Had I been able to foresee recent events I think that I would have allowed Thomas Curnow to play with his red scarf and candle.) I was also present at the more recent Glenrowan Massacre—as it is referred to in the Australian history books. This second one was deliberate, cold-blooded murder. My great-grandfather was among the few survivors.

After that first experiment the Kelly ran me back to my Potts Point flat in the presidential Cadillac. (In both my lives some place names are the same, others differ. In this here and now Governor Darling is no longer commemorated either in suburb or harbor; much is made in the history books of his brutality however.) I was grateful for the lift. I was still confused, disoriented, very much a gawking stranger in my own city. I do not think that I should have been able to cope with public transport or even to find my own address unaided.

Kelly did not drive himself, of course. He and I sat in the back of the huge car, secure behind armor plate and bullet-proof glass, while a green-uniformed sergeant of his bodyguard acted as chauffeur, a lieutenant sitting beside him.

The hereditary president was in an expansive mode, expansive and philosophical.

"So we're together again, Johnnie boy," he said. "Ye're helpin' Kelly, just as your great-grandfather helped Kelly. Who knows what would have happened if he hadn't stopped Curnow?" He laughed. "Probably 't'would have all come right in the end. A man born to be king was the first Ned. I've often thought that 't'was a great pity that he was bitten by the republican bug. . . ." He laughed. "But I'm royal, amn't I, in all except the crown. Just as the Kennedys are in our fellow republic. Not that I've had much time for them of late. After Jackie took the bullet meant for John at Dallas he started goin' to the bad. You never met her, did you? While she was livin' she was behind him in his—our—struggle with the Godless commies in the Nam. An' you know what happened after he took up with that English bitch. . . . Lady Caroline Winster, claimin' relationship with every royal house in Europe an' as red as old Charlie Marx himself . . . Did he *have* to marry her? An' then . . ." He mimicked a female voice talking in a very English accent. "John, dear, you really must not continue being unkind to our brown brothers in Vietnam.

And what about our Australian allies, you ask? What about them, John? They have no more right to be interfering in the affairs of other nations than we have. If President Kelly has any sense and decency he will withdraw his forces when you withdraw yours." Kelly laughed. "Well, *I* didn't withdraw. But, God, how I hate that Marxist Lady Muck!"

(I remembered the other Marxist Lady Muck. Kelly should have remembered her too. After all she—the Countess Catherine von Stolzberg, nicknamed Red Kitty—had played a major part in the Australian Revolution.)

I asked, "What about Red Kitty?"

"What about her?"

"She was a Marxist and a Lady."

"Things were different in those days, Johnnie."

"Why don't *you* go back, Ned, to see how things really were?"

"I've already told ye. I've too much on me plate. Things going not too well in the Nam. The students an' the unions wantin' a pull out. The Yanks an' the Poms tryin' to bring pressure to bear on me. Besides—you're a writer. I'm not. An' I'm payin' you for the job, aren't I?"

And you're afraid to have your mind tampered with, I thought. I wished that I'd been so afraid. I looked out through the thick glass of the window on my side at the unfamiliar supporting cables of the Bridge, which we were now crossing. A train, bound for the northern suburbs on the monorail, whined past. Memories flashed into my mind of Brennan's early attempts at giving Sydney an ultra-modern public transport system, his fantastic, tight-rope-walking carriages balanced by gyroscopes. . . . After that first, disastrous crash he had done some rethinking and come up with something very like the monorail train I had ridden recently in Tokyo. (In which life?)

The waterfront at Wooloomooloo didn't strike any false notes and the ships in their berths were just ships, although deck cranes were more in evidence than derricks. There were some unfamiliar—but, in this world, familiar— funnels; three vessels displayed proudly floodlit green shamrocks on a golden ground. Australian National Line, of course.

Macleay Street was very much the same as it always had been—but there was no El Alamein Fountain. Instead there was the heroic figure of a soldier, in bronze, holding threateningly a bazooka-type weapon. A name came into my mind—the Tobruk Memorial. (I preferred the fountain to this piece of statuary, even though it commemorated General O'Connell's defense of Tobruk and the breaking of the thrust of Rommel's panzers.)

We came to Tusculum Street, which I knew slightly in one life and very well in this other. There was nothing at all strange about it.

"Ye'll be picked up in the mornin', Johnnie," said Kelly. "Goodnight to ye. Sleep well. Don't dream too much."

The lieutenant got out of the car and opened the door for me. He stood there at attention, very smart in his green tunic with the silver braid and breastplate, the saffron kilt. His hand came up to his bonnet (he was not wearing the full dress helmet) in crisp salute. I bowed in reply (I had no hat to raise), stood on the sidewalk and watched him resume his seat. Kelly raised his hand in an almost regal gesture as the vehicle sped off.

I fumbled for my keys, let myself into Tara Tower. I found it hard to remember which floor my flat was on, finally stabbed blindly at the control panel in the lift and hit the right button without thinking. I had no trouble, then, in recalling the flat number.

My working-cum-sitting room was as untidy as its counterpart in the other life. My typewriter was on the desk and in it a sheet of quarto with carbons. What had I been writing when the telephone call had disturbed me?

He looked down, with mingled pity and contempt, at the grossly obese body of the dead eunuch. The man should have fled rather than to attempt to fight a master swordsman such as himself, should have run, screaming, to raise the alarm, to summon the other harem guards. He wiped his blade on a richly embroidered wall hanging, returned it to its sheath. While he was so doing the Princess came slowly out of the bedroom. Between her short, brocaded jacket and her diaphanous harem trousers her naked skin was palely luminous. Her long, golden hair was unbound. She gazed at him with invitation in her blue eyes, her full, red lips slightly parted to display her flawless white teeth.

"My Lord Francis Delamere," she murmured. "I was sure that you would come for me. . . ."

And then she was in his arms, sagging against him, her body warm and soft against his own . . .

"Take your place in the queue, darling," I muttered sardonically. "This is a bad time for blonde princesses."

I poured myself a stiff whisky, added a token ice cube. I intended to get books, historical works, from my reference shelves so as to get myself established mentally in this Time and Place. But I would have a drink first. And then, suddenly, I was very tired. I stumbled into the bedroom, undressed and fell into bed.

I expected that I would dream, but I did not.

I hoped rather than expected to wake up, in the morning, when and where I really belonged.

But when the clock-radio-alarm woke me with the news it was to tell me of more Communist victories in Vietnam and the continued withdrawal of Australian forces toward Saigon.

CHAPTER 9

A car was sent for me at ten o'clock that morning.

It was a government vehicle but not the presidential Cadillac. It was an AWM Delaney, comfortable rather than luxurious, its paintwork the drab green of the Australian Army. The driver was a uniformed corporal, a sandy-haired, nuggety-faced little fellow who was far from being a model of military elegance. His tunic, with its display of canteen medals, fitted where it touched. His saffron kilt looked as though it had been used to polish his boots—but if this were the case it was not the footgear that he was wearing now.

He got out of the car to open a rear door for me. I told him that I would sooner ride in front. This was a mistake as he was a non-stop talker.

"Have ye been seein' the mornin' papers, sir?" he asked. "Things are bad in the Nam an' it's gettin' worse they are. Maybe I shouldn't be sayin' this to ye—but I'm after thinkin' that we should ha' pulled out when the Yanks did. I did me spell in the Nam an' I know what it's like. The people there hate our guts—an' why shouldn't they? Why shouldn't they be let to have their revolution in peace—like the Yanks had theirs an' we had ours? What's the world a-comin' to if ye can't settle yer family squabbles without all sorts of strangers a-buttin' in?"

Like the French during the American War of Indepen-

dence, I thought and would have said if given a chance. *Like the Americans in Australia*. If it had not been for The Battle of the Chesapeake Capes, between the French and British fleets, quite probably there would never have been an American Republic. And then—what of the Australian Revolution? Would there have been aid from France or, more probably, Germany?

Would Australia have then become no more than part of the German Empire?

We were driving along Deirdre Street, part of the light, mid-morning traffic, when I heard the growing uproar that was coming from the direction of St. Martin's Place.

"What's that?" I asked.

"The bloody students an' the like," said the corporal, "an', like as not, the man Cairns a-stirrin' 'em up. Och, he's a real shit-stirrer, that one!"

"Nam . . . Out!" I could hear. "Nam . . . Out! Nam . . . Out!"

"Aren't those your sentiments?" I asked sarcastically.

He snarled wordlessly.

"Didn't you say . . ."

"An' amn't I entitled to be sayin' it? I've done me time in the Nam. I've an arse full o' shrapnel to prove it. But puppies who've never worn uniform or been under fire. . . ." He turned to glare at me suspiciously. "An' have ye been under fire? Sir?"

"Yes," I told him—but not that it had been during the first Glenrowan Massacre.

"And were ye in the Nam?"

"No. And I'm not sorry."

He grunted and returned his attention to his driving. He slowed as we approached the top end of St. Martin's Place. Police were on duty to prevent sightseers from clogging the highway but ours, being an Army vehicle, was allowed to loiter. We looked down to the crowd around the Glenrowan Column and on the steps of the GPO, could hear the voice of the orator on the plinth of the monument, amplified by a bullhorn.

"The President must be made to see reason . . ."

"Nam . . . Out!" roared and screamed the crowd, waving their placards. "Nam . . . Out!"

"It is the right of every people to rebel, as our fathers rebelled. . . ."

"Nam. . . . Out!" Nam. . . . Out!"

And was that mounted police trotting into the Place from James Street? No. It was cavalry, the sunlight reflected from their helmets and breastplates, from their drawn sabres.

". . . teach the young bastards a lesson . . ." I heard my driver mutter.

There were soft explosions as the first petrol bombs were thrown from the Post Office steps—dull reports and burgeoning upbursts of flame and smoke. Horses were screaming. People were shouting and screaming. And somebody, somewhere, was using an automatic weapon. Horses were down and their riders beaten with placards, kicked and trampled. There was more, and heavier, automatic fire from the Post Office. There was a great, triumphant yell as the cavalry withdrew, leaving behind half a dozen horses, down and struggling in the petrol flames, screaming. . . . Half a dozen horses and four men, motionless. . . . The other two men were trying to run for safety but they were pulled down. . . . It looked, from where we were, as though they were being torn to pieces. . . .

"Jaysus . . ." the corporal was whispering. "Holy Jaysus . . ."

From somewhere to our right a voice was bellowing, "You! Corporal! Clear the way! Get the hell out of here!"

We turned to look into the twin muzzles of the heavy machine guns of the leader of a squadron of Leprecaun armored cars.

"Let's do as the man says," muttered the corporal. He accelerated madly.

Behind us we could hear the gunfire, the shouting and the screaming. There was a heavy explosion. The armored cars weren't having things all their own way.

CHAPTER 10

Graumann was waiting for me, opening his door immediately upon my ringing the bell.

"So you made it all right," he said. "The riot. . . . We wondered if you'd gotten caught up in it."

"My corporal driver," I told him, "has a great concern for his own skin. As soon as the shooting started he got the hell out. Fast." I looked around. "Where's Ned?"

"Mr. Kelly," he told me, "*was* here. Then he received a call from the officer commanding this military district and left hurriedly. But he said that I'm to . . . That we're to carry on with the research. He suggested the Glenrowan Massacre."

"But I've already been through that."

"There were two massacres, were there not, in your history? Both of them were important."

Yes. Both of them had been. Without the first one there would not have been the second.

"Your great-grandfather had a knack for surviving. . . ." Graumann went on, the suspicion of a sneer in his voice.

I tried to remember what he had told his family, his children and grandchildren, of the second massacre. He had been there, I know. I had gained the impression, from what my father had told me, that he had not been at all proud of the part that he had (had not) played.

"Shall we go in to the laboratory?" asked Graumann.

I looked at my watch.

I said, "It's almost my lunch time."

He said, "The mind-liberating drug works better on an empty stomach."

"The first experiment," I told him, "was successful enough, and I'd just had a good meal. That first time. I was *there*, and *then*. I was on the poop of the *Lady Lucan* in my great grandfather's mind when he beat up Captain Flannery. . . ."

He looked at me oddly, then demanded, "What are you talking about? There has been only one experiment so far. The one during which you relived the first Glenrowan Massacre."

"And interfered," I said.

"Interfered? What do you mean, Mr. Grimes? Oh, it's a matter of historical record that your great-grandfather stopped Thomas Curnow from flagging down the special train. That was Curnow's story and you've confirmed it, almost a century later. But *interfering*? Rubbish, Mr. Grimes. The Past is immutable. What happened, happened. *You* were just there as an observer, nothing more."

"Then," I said, "why not send me back to the first massacre again? So that I can refrain from interfering with Curnow . . . It will be interesting to see what happens then."

"The Past is immutable!" he almost shouted. "And if you *could* interfere you'd be wiping yourself out. Your ancestor probably would never have married the woman he did. His children would have married differently. And theirs. You wouldn't be *you*. Or—" the thought seemed to be especially distasteful "—I *me*."

"But the various marriages and begettings could still have been the same," I insisted. "Unlikely, perhaps—but unlikely things do happen."

"Impossible," he snapped. "Utterly impossible. We have wasted more than enough time in this futile discussion. Please come into the laboratory."

Things were as before.

There was the view of the Harbor and the Bridge until Graumann drew the curtains across the wide window.

There were the antique weapons and that suit of plow-share armor and the old photographs. There was the taped music—"The Ballad of Ned Kelly." There was the weird machine that I was thinking of as the Time Twister, the gleaming complexity of spidery wheels set at all sorts of odd angles each to each and the control panel, part of which could have been a color TV screen, but now dead and gray. There was the deep, comfortable chair. And there was the glass of dark, bitter fluid, the mind-liberating drug, that Graumann handed to me.

He said, "The controls are set. Glenrowan. Tuesday, June 30, 1880."

I said, "I'm not sure that I like this."

He said, "You agreed to take part in the experiment. I understand that you are being paid well, whether or not you write your book. Your history."

That was true enough—but at the first Glenrowan Massacre I had discovered that I am not the stuff of which war correspondents are made. It's one thing to read about people being killed, or to watch it on the screen, but when you are *there*, your nostrils assailed by the stinks of blood and of burning flesh, when bullets are whipping past your own ears, it's different. I had expected, that first time, to be no more than an observer. I had found that I was to be a participant.

At the touch of a switch the machine came to life.

The wheels began to turn, faster and faster, shimmering in the illumination of the overhead light. The screen came alive, the colors of the spectrum washing across it. There was the illusion of depth. The spinning wheels were pre-cessing, at right angles to the applied force (what force, and how applied?) and, somehow, at right angles to all the normal dimensions of Space. They were precessing, tumbling, fading and yet never becoming completely invisible, dragging me with them back along my World Line—and along the World Lines of my father, and his father, and his father . . .

Loud and louder in my ears was the roaring of the Time Wind while my vision blurred and dimmed.

And I was cold, the thin drizzle soaking through my clothing.

I was cold and I was tired.

With the other laborers I had been clearing wreckage from the track, preparatory to making good the section of the line that we, under Kelly's orders, had torn up.

The smell of charred wood and burned flesh, acrid and sweet, still lingered although the bodies had been removed.

CHAPTER II

"There's a train a' comin'," said Reardon.

We all of us stopped working, straightened up and stood, listening.

"If he's bound for Wangaratta," said Murphy, "he'll just have to cool his heels until we're finished here. An' Jaysus knows when that'll be."

Louder and louder came the noise of the approaching train, carried by the light, chill breeze from the south. Its whistle sounded mournfully.

"It's stoppin'," Reardon said unnecessarily. "At the station."

"An' where else would it be stoppin'?" demanded Murphy.

"A train stopped *here*, didn't it?" countered the other. He laughed. "All change here for Heaven. Or the other place."

"Yes, it's stopped all right," said one of the others.

We pulled out pipes and pouches. This was as good an excuse for a smoke-oh as any. We lit up.

"Do ye think it's the troopers?" somebody asked.

"Could be," Reardon said. "There'll be inquiries about this bad business. Now, boys, remember this. If they come askin' us questions—we know nuthin'. Oh, we tore up the track, we can't deny that, but there were a dozen of 'em, big bastards all, Kelly an' all his gang, a-standin'

over us with guns an' revolvers, threatenin' to blow the
head off anybody who wouldn't work."

"There was only four of 'em," objected Murphy. "Countin'
Ned himself."

"If we says that there was a dozen, there was a dozen,"
snapped Reardon. "We was here. They wasn't."

From the south, from around the bend, came the sound
of an explosion. There was a series of regularly spaced
heavy reports, which the twentieth century me identified
as the noise of a slow firing machine gun of some kind.
(Nordenfeldt or Gatling? I wondered.) There was another
explosion. An artillery piece of some kind, I decided. (At
the time of the Siege of Glenrowan, on that other time
track, I recalled there had been talk of bringing a field gun
from Melbourne.) The machine guns were opening up
again, firing with slow, deadly deliberation.

There was shouting. There were screams—but they didn't
last long.

We stared at each other out of white faces.

"Jaysus!" muttered Reardon at last. "Holy Jaysus!"

Murphy hefted his pickaxe.

"Come on, ye lily-livered cowards! Are ye goin' to stand
here, while people are bein' slaughtered by the bastard
English, doin' nothin'?"

"We are, Mick," said Reardon sadly. "What can we do?
By the sound o' things they've at least two of those new-
fangled coffee grinders—an' somethin' heavier. Loaded with
canister, no doubt. . . ."

Murphy spat.

"If that's the way ye're feelin', Paddy. . . ."

"That's the way I'm feelin'—but I'm not likin' it. If we
had guns 't'would be another story."

"Then let's be gettin' out o'here, Paddy, afore they
come an' do for us."

"No. We're never bushmen—an' at least some o' the
troopers are. They may have more black trackers with
'em, too. They'll just hunt us down if we run. Back to
work, all o' ye. Pretend ye've heard nothing. Pretend
ye're little, innocent, woolly lambs. After all, 't is none of
our quarrel, which is selectors 'gainst the squatters."

"An' Irish 'gainst the haythen English!" shouted the belligerent little Murphy, his sprayed spittle white against his black whiskers.

"Later, perhaps. Later. But not now. I've seen it too often in the Ouldh Country, clubs an' pitchforks 'gainst muskets an' bayonets. Let somebody put guns in our hands—*then* we fight. But not till then. Back to work, all o' ye!"

We heard the horsemen riding along the track but feigned deafness.

A very English voice brayed, "You men! Who is in charge here?"

We straightened up slowly and turned to face the riders.

The man who had spoken was in well-cut, obviously expensive civilian riding clothes over which the belt, with its holstered revolver, looked incongruous. Behind him was a large, heavily bearded, senior police officer in uniform and, a little to the rear, a naval officer, a lieutenant looking more than a little absurd and uncomfortable on horseback. Six mounted police, their carbines at the ready, brought up the rear.

"You men! Who is in charge here?"

"May it please Yer Honor," said Reardon, "I am. As ye can see, 't is repairin' the track we are. Ye can be on yer way to Wangaratta soon as we're finished . . ."

"I know that, you fool." He turned to the police officer. "Superintendent Nicholson, what was the name of that man Curnow told us about? The man who stopped him from flagging down the train?"

"Grimes, Captain Standish."

"Grimes? That's not an Irish name." He returned his attention to Reardon "You! Is one of these men of yours called Grimes?"

I tensed, ready to make a bolt for it.

I heard Reardon say slowly, "Grimes? As Yer Honor says, 't is not an Irish name at all, at all. . . ."

"I know that, you fool. Where is Grimes now?"

(And where was Curnow, I wondered. When would he make his appearance to identify me?)

"Well, now, that I can't be tellin' yer, Yer Honor. He went a-ridin' off, ye see, with Ned Kelly an' his cutthroats. . . ."

"Riding off? Don't lie to me, man. I'm told that this Grimes is a sailor, a deserter from his ship. What would he know of riding?"

"We've a sailor on horseback with us, Captain Standish," said Nicholson.

The naval lieutenant grinned sheepishly.

"Pah!" barked Standish contemptuously. "But it doesn't much matter. I still think that the story Curnow gave us in Melbourne was a pack of lies, told to make him look important and to qualify him for a share of the reward when the Kelly gang is run to earth . . ."

"But if this man Grimes rode off with the Kelly mob," pointed out Nicholson, "it's proof of the truth of Curnow's tale."

"Not necessarily, Superintendent. The man's a criminal, isn't he? A deserter from his ship. He's doing no more than consorting with his own kind. But we'll be getting his own story when we take him, with the others. If we take him alive, that is. . . ." He glared down at Reardon. "You! Get your men fallen in! Follow the Superintendent back to the station. The rest of us will be behind you." He drew his revolver. "I shall give the order to fire if necessary."

"Captain Standish," began Nicholson.

"Yes, Superintendent?"

"I think that we should all of us keep behind the laborers."

"You will lead them, sir. Let us have no further delays."

So we shambled along the track, behind the slowly riding Nicholson, acutely conscious of the loaded weapons leveled at our backs. It was some small consolation that the police officer must be similarly conscious.

Apart from the station and the police barracks Glenrowan was in ruins. Canister from the field gun, manned by men of the Victorian Navy, had devasted both hotels, McDonnell's as well as Mrs. Jones' establishment. The more humble dwellings had not been spared. Fires were still burning. There was a small group of prisoners, Mrs. Jones among them, huddled in the heavy drizzle. I wanted to go to her to offer some small (and useless) word of comfort but I was a coward. She would recognize me and might cry out my name.

"The next time," Standish shouted to us, "that an outlaw persuades you to tamper with the railway tracks—remember this! If you didn't have work to do I'd put you all under arrest with these others. But the next time—if there is a next time . . ."

"Yer Honor . . ." Reardon pointed to where our tent encampment had been. A hail of canister shot had shredded the shelters. "Where are we goin' to sleep?" He swept his hand around to first one ruined hotel and then the other. "An' where do we eat?"

"You will have to manage somehow," Standish said coldly.

"I will arrange for a train to bring you more tents and supplies," said Nicholson.

"*Your* job, Superintendent," Standish told him, "is to scour the countryside. Greta has yet to be dealt with, for a start. And you can get these wretches . . ." he gestured toward the prisoners ". . . out of my sight. There's a coach for them, isn't there?"

"And the bodies . . . ?"

(So there had been killings.)

"These men should be capable of digging graves."

I never knew whom it was that we buried. The naval ratings manning the Nordenfeldts had fired high, smashing the faces of the victims. All I knew was that there were five men and one woman.

Reardon cursed almost continuously while he plied his shovel.

"The dirty English bastards, they'll pay for this day's work. . . ." The policeman standing guard over us pretended not to hear. After all, he was an Irishman who, obeying orders of foreign conquerors, had taken up arms against his own people. "The dirty, mother-fucking English . . ."

I felt an acute sense of shame for my own race.

I looked down into the last grave, still to be filled.

I stared at the dark, wet earth, into the murky puddle that had already formed on its bottom. I thought that I was going to faint.

There was a roaring in my ears—the roaring of the Time Wind.

CHAPTER 12

Once again I found myself sitting in that comfortable chair, staring at the complexity of precessing gyroscopes that, having dragged my mind back to the Present, was slowing to a stop. I turned my regard away from the machine to look at Graumann. There was somebody with him, a man in uniform, his face somehow familiar. *Duffin* . . . I thought. *Duffin?* But what was Duffin doing in this rig of smart, gold-braided green tunic and saffron kilt? I stared at him. He was taller than the Duffin I had known in the other life, leaner, fitter looking.

"You're back," said Graumann unnecessarily. "Did you see the Glenrowan Massacre?"

"Yes," I told him.

"Good. We shall get your impressions of it down on tape while they are still fresh in your mind. But, first of all, Major Duffin would like a few words with you . . ."

So this *was* Duffin—but a Duffin whose ancestry was not quite the same as that of the editor on the other Time Track. And it was obvious, from the way that he was looking at me, that this was the first time that we had met.

"Mr. Grimes," he said, "I have come from the President. Ned is concerned for your safety. . . ."

He arranges for me to have a ringside seat at both Glenrowan massacres, I thought, *and now he's concerned.*

"There has been rioting in the Kings Cross area," he

68

said. "There have been casualties. The indications are that there will be more trouble."

"And so?" I asked.

"You are an important man, sir. The President thinks that you will be safer if you stay in this building until you have completed your research for the project."

"But I have to go back to my flat," I told him. "My books . . . My typewriter . . . My work in progress . . ."

"Your work in progress is here," he said. "If you need a typewriter we can provide one. Also clothing to your requirements and toilet necessities." He stood by the window and pointed. "Surely you do not want to go back there at this time?"

I got out of my chair and stood by him. I looked. Beyond the Bridge, from somewhere in the Kings Cross area, there was smoke, and plenty of it. Fires. What was burning? How had the fires started? Were there casualties, and how many?

I said, "I had no idea that things were so serious."

He said, "You saw something of the riot this morning, didn't you? And there's trouble in the other cities, and any place at all where there's more than two men and a dog the demonstrators are out, some of them violent. But you wouldn't know, would you? You writers live in your ivory towers. You haven't a clue as to what's happening in the real world."

"Not all of us," I told him. "What about . . .?" I searched for names in my mind. "What about Burchett? and Hardy?"

If I'd been intending to make the major lose his temper I could not have been more successful.

"Don't name those traitorous swine in my hearing!" he shouted. "If they ever set foot back in this country they'll be strung up—and I hope that it's me that's pulling on the rope!" He glared at me suspiciously. "And are you one of those smuggling their seditious writings into Australia?"

I said, truthfully, that I was not. I wasn't fool enough to say that among the books in my flat was a copy of Burchett's *Vietnam Tragedy* and one of Hardy's *The Dream Turned Sour*. I hoped that the major would not send somebody there to pick up my possessions for me.

He turned to Graumann.

"Doctor," he said, "the apartment next to yours has been . . . vacated. Mr. Grimes will be moving in for now. The President considers your work to be of vital importance—so you and Mr. Grimes will be under military protection. Neither of you will leave this building without the permission of the officer in charge—me—or without an escort. Is that understood?"

"Yes," said Graumann doubtfully. "But. . . ."

"There aren't any buts, Doctor."

"But I would remind you that I am a citizen of the United States of America."

"Here by the invitation of the Republic of Australia—and under the protection of the Republic."

"Protective custody?" Graumann found the courage to sneer.

"You could call it that. Once you've done the work for which you're being paid—handsomely, I understand—you will be free to leave."

"We'll see what the American Consul has to say about that!" blustered Graumann.

"If you were thinking of telephoning," Duffin said, "then forget about it. All calls from this building are now routed through the Army exchange. And now, Mr. Grimes, shall we inspect your new premises? And while we are doing so you can tell my supply sergeant what your requirements are. We want you to be comfortable and happy in your work."

CHAPTER 13

We fed, that evening, in the sitting room of my new apartment—Duffin, Graumann and I. We used the crockery, cutlery and glassware that had belonged to the previous occupants. The quality of the china, stainless steel and crystal in sharp contrast to that of the meal itself, takeaway Irish stew brought to us by a private soldier from the nearby Monaghan's restaurant. I asked the Major what had happened to the previous occupants of the flat. He told me that the man of the family was in government service and had obeyed orders which, in his case, had been a transfer to Glenrowan at short notice.

"Very short notice," I remarked.

"No, Mr. Grimes. Not very. We had this eventuality in mind. And don't you be worrying about Mr. and Mrs. Maloney. There have been very well compensated. I wish that I could come by promotions as easily."

Graumann said morosely, "I'm worrying about me."

"You're being paid, aren't you, Doctor? And paid well. And now, both of you, listen to me. Ned's been on my back. . . ."

"Do you mean the President, Major Duffin?" asked Graumann coldly.

"I mean the Kelly, Doctor Graumann. Like the first Kelly, he's Ned to all who know him. Anyhow, while he's away at the capital he's put me in charge of this operation.

And he wants the work stepped up. The way things are, at home and abroad, he wants that book written and published by last Thursday at the very latest. No matter how things turn out it will be a sort of enduring monument to the Kelly family."

"Erected by myself," Graumann said sourly. He added hastily, as he saw the way that I was looking at him, "And by Mr. Grimes. But I don't mind telling you, Major, that I wish I were back in the U.S.A. right now. If President Kennedy and his advisers had allowed me to carry on with my *real* research I'd never had been tempted by *your* President's offer. . . ."

"But I thought that you came here, to Australia," I said, "to use your techniques to try to find out something about visits by alien starmen in prehistoric times . . ."

He stared at me.

"Alien starmen?" he demanded at last. "Whatever gave you that crazy idea? Although, as a matter of fact, the researches that I wished to carry out at home were connected with prehistory. I wanted to prove that, long before Columbus, the Phoenicians made the Atlantic crossing and actually established colonies on the East Coast. You may know that at one time, during the last century, many people believed that the Amerindians were of Semitic origin. . . ."

"And then, of course," I said, "there were the ancient Chinese navigators making their landings on the West Coast. . . ."

"Ye'll be dragging in St. Brendan next," said Duffin with an approach to joviality. "But tell me, Dr. Graumann, why should President Kennedy not have approved of your project?"

"He did not disapprove of the project, Major Duffin. He disapproved of the source of my funds. You have heard of the Beauregard Corporation?"

"Yes, of course. We used Beauregard grenade launchers in the Australian Army and, until recently, the Beauregard automatic rifle was standard issue."

"An ancestral Beauregard was an officer in the Confederate Army during the War Between The States. The Beauregards still maintain that the South should have won

KELLY COUNTRY / 73

that war. John Beauregard, the Corporation President, heard somehow of my theories and my project, offered to fund me and give other assistance . . . Without the computer time placed at my disposal it would have been years before I could make a start. But there was a condition. A crazy one, quite crazy."

"Which was?"

"Essentially it was that he'd help me if I helped him."

"Help *him*?" asked Duffin. "How? Oh, I begin to see. Send his mind back in Time into that of his ancestor so that he could relive the battles of the War Between The States in person."

"But why should President Kennedy have taken a dim view of that?" I put in.

"Because Beauregard's idea was, as I have said, quite crazy—yet it was a logical sort of craziness. He thought that he would be able to exercise some influence over the mind of the ancestral Beauregard. Just imagine it—a senior officer in the rebel army getting mental nudges from a late twentieth-century armaments manufacturer . . . And, furthermore, an armaments manufacturer who knew how close some of those battles actually were and how the tide could have been made to turn the other way by the slightest of pushes, properly applied . . ."

Just as I applied a slight push, I thought, remembering, *when I pushed Curnow off his feet . . .*

"Beauregard talked too much about it," went on Graumann, "to people whom he thought that he could trust. Washington's a bad place to do that sort of talking. I was in his office when the polite young men in gray suits came calling. They allowed me to stay while they had their conversation with him. There were no overt threats, little more than a strong hint that a very lucrative small arms contract might be going elsewhere. And then one of them noticed me and mentioned that it could be worth my while to pay a visit to the Australian Ambassador. I remember his words. 'Unlike Corporation President Beauregard,' he said, laughing, 'President Kelly is not interested in changing history. He only wants somebody to write an eyewitness account of what actually happened.' "

"But how did Ned know about you?" I asked.

"Just knew, I guess."

"The Kelly and Kennedy families are still on corresponding terms," said Duffin, "in spite of the disagreement over the Nam. But this man Beauregard . . . Changing history! What a mad idea!"

"Quite mad," agreed Graumann. "I kept telling him that the Past is immutable but he wouldn't listen to me." He laughed. "Grimes, here, is a good enough writer and that's all. He just could not affect the course of events at any of the scrimmages at which his ancestors were present."

"Ancestors?" asked Duffin. "I thought that there was only one involved. His great-grandfather."

"The President," Graumann said, "wants as complete a history as possible from Glenrowan to the present day."

Duffin found some excellent port wine—the Maloneys had done themselves well—and we sat and sipped and watched the News on TV. It was far from cheerful. As well as coverage of what seemed to be a general collapse in Vietnam, there were shots of a disaster at Port Kennedy, on the Moon, where an inbound rocket had crashed on to the Administration Dome and pictures of the wreckage of *Minnehaha*, the latest and most luxurious dirigible of the Trans-World Airways fleet, broken apart in midair, over the Grand Canyon of Arizona, by a PLO saboteur's bomb.

It made a change, I found myself thinking, *from jumbo jet crashes . . .*

CHAPTER 14

"So His Highness The Hereditary President wants a hurry-up job," grumbled Graumann the following morning. "Hereditary President . . . Why the hell can't he just call himself king and be done with it?"

"You've the makings of a dynasty in your own country," I told him. "The Kennedy clan."

We had just finished a light breakfast in my sitting room. Major Duffin had eaten with us and then left us to our own devices. Graumann was now speaking with far greater freedom that he had allowed himself when the officer was present.

"I don't like working under pressure," he went on. "It puts me off when the military are breathing down my neck."

"But you used to be military yourself, you told me. U.S. Navy."

"Whatever gave you that idea, Mr. Grimes? I was never in the armed forces." He poured himself some more coffee and sipped morosely. Then he brightened. "But I admit that a hurry-up job suits me too. I want out of this country before the balloon goes up. . . ."

"Have you used your . . . your time-twister to get a preview of the future?"

"I have tried, Mr. Grimes, I don't mind admitting. But for some reason it doesn't work that way. As I've said before, the past is immutable but there's an infinitude of alternate futures branching out from every moment of experienced time. But you've read and watched and listened to the news as much as I have. There's the increasing unrest as the unpopular war drags on. Why you people couldn't have pulled out of Vietnam when *we* did I just don't know."

"President Kelly," I said, "pledged support to his coreligionist, President Ky, just as he did to President Ky's predecessors."

"And what good has it done either of them? While you people have been squandering millions of dollars on this useless war, we've been able to afford the space exploration program. We're established on the Moon. It will be Mars next."

"Unless the Russians beat you to it."

"One thing is certain," he said, "*you* never will unless you come to your senses and stop pouring money down the Vietnam drain." He drained his cup, put it down in the saucer with a clatter. "Now Mr. Grimes, I've been giving this matter some thought. The hurry-up job. We've established that you're capable of what a sensational writer would call Time Travel. So far your travels have been . . . episodic. Back to the past for a hasty look, then back to the present to get your impressions down on tape while they're fresh in your memory . . . But if you spent longer periods in your great-grandfather's mind—weeks, or even months—your research for the book would be completed sooner. But I'll be frank. There's a risk."

"Too right there is," I agreed. "My mind's away for, say, a fortnight and my body's sitting in that chair of yours, quietly starving to death."

He said, "It would not be like that at all. You must have noticed that the time you spent in the past, each time at Glenrowan, was much longer than the time elapsed in the present. If I were to make a really fine adjustment to my controls I could have a year experienced in the nineteenth century equivalent to only five minutes here and now."

"Or bring me back before I left?"

"Don't be stupid."

"So what is the risk, then?"

"That you will be, as it were, trapped in the mind of your ancestor. One of my subjects in the U.S.A., an American, suffered that fate. *I think*. All that I know is that he never recovered consciousness. He is still in hospital, a human vegetable."

"And how long did you send him back for?"

"On that occasion for a full month. On previous occasions for day trips only. But other subjects spent as long as six weeks in ancestral minds and suffered no ill effects."

"Have you any idea why this man—I suppose that it was a man—was unlucky?"

"As a matter of fact I have. He was a no-account person. Weak, a drifter. An alcoholic. His ancestor was a powerful Chief. It could be that he just did not want to come back. Or it could be that his ancestor's powerful mind just . . . just absorbed his weak one."

And my mind, I thought, *had been able to take control of that of my great-grandfather*.

He said, persuasively, "You're a successful man in your own field, Mr. Grimes. You have too much to lose in the present if you allow yourself to be trapped. . . ."

But, I thought, remembering family history, *I might like being an Admiral*. On the other hand, I liked being a twentieth-century writer.

"Suppose," he went on, "I send you back for a week, just to see how things work out. To Glenrowan again, just after the second massacre. . . ."

I said, "All right. I'll give it a go."

CHAPTER 15

I looked down into the last grave, still to be filled.

I stared at the dark, wet earth, at the murky puddle that had already formed on its bottom. I stood aside to make way for those who were carrying the last body, who lowered it into the hole with a rough reverence, who arranged it with some pitiful semblance of dignity, the legs straightened and the arms crossed over the chest. An almost clean (but not for long) handkerchief was spread over the shattered face. The man who had performed these last rites clambered out of the grave.

"You men! Get on with it!" ordered Standish.

"Shouldn't there be some sort of service?" asked the naval officer.

"We've no time for that now. If any priest cares to come out later and mumble the right words we shan't try to stop him." Then, to us, "Get on with it, I said!"

So we got on with it, throwing shovelful after shovelful of muddy earth into the gaping hole, concealing the last evidence of Standish's crime. The last evidence? No. There were the gutted buildings, still steaming under the drizzle. There were the survivors, now herded into the waiting railway coach. There were those other witnesses, the railway laborers.

I still wonder why Standish did not have us rounded up with the others and shipped to Melbourne Jail. After all, we had torn up the track, albeit under duress. We were accessories to the derailment of Hare's train and the subsequent massacre. It is possible that we were left at large so that we could talk, so that we could spread the news about the countryside of what happened to those unwise and disloyal enough to harbor and abet the Kelly Gang. My twentieth-century persona is far better read in history than my nineteenth-century one. (He just helped to make history.) I know that savage reprisals are effective—as a short-term policy. They cease to be effective when oppressed peoples are the recipients of aid from rich and powerful overseas friends.

Standish and his masters never dreamed that Kelly and his supporters had such friends. Oh, there was Ireland, of course, but she was neither rich nor powerful. She would never be more than a nuisance.

We stood there, miserable in the freezing drizzle, watching the train pull out of the station. It had been switched onto the southbound track so that it could by-pass the torn-up rails and continue on to Wangaratta. There, presumably, the locomotive could be end-for-ended ready for the run back to Melbourne. On this journey, we hoped, the train would bring the food and shelter promised us by Nicholson. Of course, we could sleep in the station but we were hungry and we wanted something better to drink than rainwater.

Legally what we did was looting—but so many illegalities had already been committed in and around Glenrowan that ours was a very minor crime. We rummaged through the ruins of the two hotels and of the cottages, finding articles that had survived both gunfire and hand-initiated incendiarism. In the station waiting hall our pile of booty grew—two bottles of rum, one of brandy, four of various wines. . . . A half dozen loaves of bread, neither rain-sodden nor too badly charred. . . . A few tins of sardines. . . . Other tins with their labels burned or washed off but apparently intact. . . . A canister of tea . . . One of sugar . . . A small sack of damp flour . . . Cooking utensils . . .

It became obvious that not all the liquor discovered was being turned in. A few of the men were reeling drunkenly, speaking wildly and incoherently. One of them was shouting that we should tear up all the tracks and burn the station to the ground. "That'll teach the English bastards," he yelled, "that they can't be triflin' with the Irish!"

"Shut yer trap!" Reardon told him.

"An' who are you to be throwin' orders around? There's only one man I'll be takin' orders from—and that's Ned!"

"Shut yer trap!"

"I'll shut *yours* for ye!"

The wild blow never connected. Reardon's counterpunch did, catching the other man full in the mouth. He crashed to the floor and sprawled there, dribbling scarlet blood and white fragments of broken teeth over his beard.

Reardon licked his bleeding knuckles, wrapped them in a none too clean handkerchief.

"Any more for any more?" he asked. There was no reply. "All right, then. Just watch it. An' you, Mike, try an' find some kind o' locker to get the booze stowed in. After there's been some soberin' up we must have a talk. All of us. . . ."

He looked at me, made a beckoning gesture with his head. He went out onto the platform. I followed him. We stood there, sheltered by the overhang of the roof from the rain.

He said, at last, "What d'ye make of it, Johnny?"

Until now it had always been a half-contemptuous "Limey."

I said, "What should I make of it?"

He said, "Ye're an educated man an' ye're not one to take everything the bosses say as gospel. I could have turned ye in, ye know. . . ."

"I know. And thank you."

"I'd sooner have your thanks, Johnny, than those of the police. But, tell me, do ye think that Ned's risin' will ever come to anything? They call him the Captain of the North East—but what are rifles an' revolvers against the kind o' weapons that *they* brought up today?"

And what use, I thought, will late-nineteenth-century field artillery be against airships? (I was remembering things that were not yet in my great-grandfather's memory—although they would be.) I could have told Reardon that the Australian Republic was coming into being, that we had witnessed the first birth throes. But I did not. If I had done so he would have thought me quite mad.

I said, "There may be Kelly sympathizers in the army, such as it is, and in the navy. . . ."

He spat. "Ye know how it is. Ye've seen it today. Once an Irishman puts on uniform he'll turn his gun against his own people for pay. An' what about the English navy? There're their battleships in every Australian port, with their men and their guns. . . . But, damn it all, Johnny, as long as Ned has men flockin' to his banner he stands some kind of a chance. . . ."

I liked Reardon. I did not want to influence him either way. Perhaps if I encouraged him to join the rebels he, in consequence, would have only a short time to live. I just didn't know. All that I knew was that he played only a very short and relatively minor part in the history that I was reliving.

He said, "There's somebody a-comin'. . . ."

There was somebody coming, a solitary rider on a tired horse. There was somebody coming, riding side-saddle. She rode slowly up to the station, mounted the ramp on to the platform. Her long skirt and her blouse were rain-soaked and mud-spattered. There was more mud on her pale face, framed by the wild, dark, unbound hair.

She stared down at us with icy contempt while the snort of her horse, relieved at being at last allowed to rest, sounded like one of derision.

"Call yerselves men," she whispered at last. "Near to a dozen o' ye—an' what did ye do when the English came, a-murderin' an' a-burnin'. . . ?" She glared at me. "I'd expect nothin' better from you, Limey, but as for you, Reardon, an' all the big, strong Irishmen. . . ."

"They had a cannon, Miss Kate, an' some of those new-fangled quick-firin' guns. We'd nary a weapon. . . ."

"Ye'd yer picks an' shovels an' crowbars. . . . Help me down, Reardon. I want off this saddle. I've been chased dear knows how many miles. They did to Greta what they've done here, but I got away. . . ."

Reardon held out his arms to her and she fell into them

rather than dismounting. For a few seconds she sagged against him, then straightened up and pushed herself away.

"Have ye a fire in there, Reardon?" she demanded. "I must get the chill out of me bones. An' hold me horse, will ye?"

She snatched up the dangling reins, thrust them into the Irishman's hands. The animal, which had been about to wander off, back down the ramp, snorted reproachfully.

As she strode into the booking hall Reardon said to me, "She's a wild one, is Kate Kelly. Wilder than Ned himself. But 't is pleased I am that they never caught her. Prison'd be the death of such as Kate. . . ."

From inside the booking hall there came a burst of drunken laughter and slurred speech.

"Look who's here, boyos! 'Tis the Queen o' Greta herself!"

"How about a kiss, Kate? I'll gi'e ye a sup o' brandy for a kiss. . . ."

"I'll gi'e ye the bottle for more'n a kiss! Hold her boys while I get the skirts off her!"

"There're some bad bastards in there," Reardon said to me. "An' 'tis a long time since they had a woman!"

He dropped the reins, ran into the booking hall. I followed him. I heard the crash of breaking glass and a woman's scream. Then there was a sharp explosion.

The acridity of burned powder assailed my nostrils, mixed with the sharp sweetness of spilled brandy. Backed against the ticket office window was Kate Kelly. Her blouse was torn from her left shoulder. There was a pistol in her right hand, a shiny Derringer, with over-and-under barrels. Sprawled on the floor was Murphy, the blood pumping from the wound in his chest mingling with the spilled liquor and the broken glass. His limbs were still twitching. The other laborers were grouped around him, growling menacingly but held at bay by the weapon that slowly fanned from side to side, aiming at each man in turn.

"Out o' the way, ye eejits!" roared Reardon.

He shouldered his way through the angry crowd, confronted the girl.

"Ye'd better be gettin' out o' here, Miss Kate, afore ye do any more damage—an' before these boys o' mine tear ye to pieces. An' give that toy o' yours to me!"

"Ye think I'm a fool, Reardon?"

"That I do, Miss Kate—but ye're not the only fool around here. Not by a long sight. Give!"

I thought that she was going to pull the trigger and then, suddenly, she reversed the weapon and handed it, butt first, to Reardon. He used it to cover her retreat as she walked slowly to the door, keeping at distance the men who would have attacked her. Only he and I followed her outside.

"Ye'd better go to Ned," he told her, "wherever he's hidin' out. Tell him that his mother'll soon be havin' company in Melbourne Jail—Ma Jones an' the others. Tell him that Dan has company in the cold ground . . ."

"An' I'll be tellin' him, too," she said bitterly, "that ye turned me away, in the cold an' the rain, afore I had a chance to warm me back at your fire."

" 'Tis more than yer back that would ha' been warmed, Miss Kate. But that was no excuse for murther . . ."

"Murther, ye say? 'Tis no murther when a woman defends her honour 'gainst drunken scum."

"When that woman's name is Kelly, Miss Kate, 't'will be murther, in any court in Australia. Off with ye, afore Murphy's chums pluck up their courage."

"So that's the way of it. Let's have me pistol back, Reardon."

He said, "I'll be keepin' it. I may be needin' it meself."

"So ye're scared o' your own men," she said contemptuously.

She looked for her horse. It had wandered back down the ramp, had found a thick clump of grass and was dejectedly eating.

"Maeve!" she called. "Maeve!"

The animal pricked up its ears but made no further move.

"Then I suppose I must go to her," she sighed.

I accompanied her to ground level while Reardon watched the booking hall door. She picked up the dangling reins and then looked at me expectantly. What was I supposed to do? The experiences of my great-grandfather, whose mind I was sharing, were all of ships and the sea. Horses did not come into them.

"What are ye waitin' for, Limey?" she demanded.

Memories came unbidden to my mind, recollections of Western films that my twentieth-century self had seen. I stooped, cupping my hands. She put one, small, muddy boot into them. I straightened up, lifting her. There was a non-revealing flurry of long skirts and she was back in the saddle, reins in hand. And then she was gone, without so much as a gesture of farewell, riding through the light rain toward Morgan's Lookout.

I rejoined Reardon on the platform. He was playing with the Derringer tossing it from one big hand to the other.

I said, "I wish you'd let her take that thing."

He said, "It has to stay here, Johnnie. As evidence."

"So you're going to tell the police that Kate shot Murphy? That she was here?"

He laughed. "O' course not. We found this pretty little toy in the ruins of Ma Jones' hotel; 'tis somethin' that she must ha' kept for her own protection. Not that t'would ha' been much use against artillery! Murphy had taken drink an' was playin' with it, wavin' it about. I tried to take it away from him an' it went off . . ."

"Will the others back up your story?"

"They'd better," he murmured. "They'd better. The arm of Sinn Fein's a long one, even out here."

He turned, started to go back into the booking hall.

His way was blocked by O'Hara.

Behind him stood the other men. They were holding iron bars and other weapons. I saw two long carving knives displayed threateningly.

CHAPTER 16

"Get out o' here, Reardon," growled O'Hara. "You an' the Limey. Both o' ye."

"What the hell is this?" bellowed Reardon.

"What d'ye think? I'm a-givin' ye a chance, that's all. Some are for holdin' ye, both o' ye, until the police do be comin' back. Ye're. . . ." He searched his mind for the word. "Ye're accessories. Accessories after the fact. Ye helped the Kelly bitch to escape after she murthered poor Paddy."

"There'll be more murtherin'," threatened Reardon, gesturing with the little pistol.

O'Hara laughed scornfully. "Ye'd get only one o' us, at the most. D'ye think I don't know how many bullets them things hold?"

Just one shot, I thought, and then the mob would be all over us. Only a small mob, to be sure, but vicious. By the looks of them we should be lucky to survive until the train returned with Nicholson and the promised supplies.

"Can't ye see?" pleaded O'Hara. "We're givin' ye a chance. Get out, afore minds are changed."

Reardon shrugged, then thrust the Derringer into one of his pockets.

"Come away, then, Johnny," he said to me. "We'll leave these bastards to stew in their own juice." Then, to

O'Hara, "Be sure to present my compliments to Mr. Nicholson when he comes callin' on ye."

He turned, walked slowly along the platform to the ramp. I followed him. I did not like turning my back on the hostile crowd but nothing worse came after us but shouted abuse. Clear of the station we stood there in the rain, cold and miserable.

"Where do we go?" I asked at last.

"The way that Kate went. She seemed to know where she was goin'."

"You think that there's some sort of camp on Morgan's Lookout?"

"I'm hopin' so. If we can't find shelter o' some kind we'll not see the night out."

We set our feet on the upward track.

That walk is not among my pleasanter memories.

We trudged upward, the cold rain soaking through our clothing, adding its moisture to the perspiration induced by the unaccustomed—as far as I was concerned—exercise. Our bodies were hot in the muffling layers of damp cloth but every time we stopped for a breather the chill penetrated coats and flannel shirts and underwear. During one such rest period, when we had tried in vain to light our pipes with sodden matches, we heard the noise of a train. We looked back and down to see it pulling into Glenrowan Station.

And were the horse-carrying trucks still part of it? Would the horses be discharged and then, with armed troopers on their backs, be coming after us? If they did we should have to break away from the track and hide in the bush. It was not a pleasant prospect in this weather.

"Nicholson's no fool," said Reardon at last. "Night's almost on us an' he'll not be riskin' his men in the bush, in the dark." He laughed. "In any case, the boyos'll not be tellin' him which way we went."

"Why not? They threw us out, didn't they?"

"But that was *them*, ye see. 'Twas their idea o' justice. But it comes natural to them to be lyin' to the police. Nicholson'll be lookin' for us in Benalla."

I said, "I hope you're right."

We continued our upward journey.

We heard the train leaving but did not look back again. Eventually we were climbing rather than walking, clutching at undergrowth for support. Dislodged rainwater fell on us in heavy showers. It was becoming darker and darker. How long would it be before the moon was up? I didn't know, although during my days at sea I could have known. All that I knew was that it was past its full and that it would be well into the evening before we derived any benefit from its light.

"Melbourne Jail'd be better than this . . ." gasped Reardon.

I was, by this time, inclined to agree but I asked, "What do they do to accessories to murder?"

"I. . . . I don't know. . . . Is it a hangin' crime?"

I said that I was a seaman, not a lawyer.

At last it was too dark to go on. I thought ruefully that if this were an English forest the trees would give us good shelter from the rain. (But I could not imagine circumstances in which I should be fleeing from the police in England.) These blasted gum trees, giving neither shade nor shelter . . . We found a rock that overhung the path. Under it the ground was almost dry. We sat down gratefully. We tried again to light our pipes, without success. We listened to the sounds of the bush—the small scurryings, the bird and animal calls, some raucous, some almost sweet. And always there was the steady *drip, drip, drip* of the rain.

Reardon, unable to smoke, chewed tobacco. It was a habit that I had never acquired, although it was common enough at sea. To keep Reardon company I pulled a stem of grass, chewed that.

He spat, with a noisy splatter.

He said, " 'Tis gettin' on, we must be, or we freeze. . . ."

I said, "I'm freezing now."

"Then let's get a-goin'. We can take it careful."

"Where to?"

"Kate came this way, didn't she? An' I've heard that there's some sort of a camp up this mountain. . . ."

I remembered the beacon fire that I had seen flare into life halfway up the Lookout on the night of the derailment, the first Glenrowan Massacre. There had been somebody here then. Was there still somebody here?

It was lighter now, despite the overcast. The moon was up. We got to our feet, our joints creaking. Fortunately our eyes had become accustomed to the darkness and we were able to continue our upward way without overmuch difficulty. The stiffness of our joints wore off and soon we were sweating again.

"Hold!"

The man who stepped out from the bushes was no more than a dark shadow but I could see clearly enough that he was holding a weapon of some kind—a rifle? a shotgun? —and that it was pointing at us.

"Hold!"

We stopped, maintaining our balance with difficulty.

"Who the hell are ye?"

"Well, 'tis a long story. . . ."

"Then cut it short. Me trigger finger's liable to twitch."

"Kate . . ." began Reardon. He seemed to sense disapproval. "Miss Kelly, that is. . . . She shot a man, one o' the men in the gang. We helped her get away. The gang didn't like it. Told us to get out or they'd be handin' us over to the police . . ."

"So you're Reardon and Grimes. Miss Kelly's been this way. She's not here now. She's off to find Ned. . . ."

"An' where is he?"

"Ye think I'd be tellin' ye without his say-so? Anyhow, she told me what's been happenin' at Glenrowan an' places around. I heard the gunfire up here meself an' saw the fires. . . ."

"Talkin' o' fires . . ." said Reardon hopefully.

Obviously he could smell, as I could, the faint odor of wood smoke, mixed with the mouth-watering aroma of cooking meat.

The sentry, as he must be, laughed.

"So ye think I'd be welcomin' ye with open arms? Miss Kate didn't speak at all highly about all o' ye down at Glenrowan. Doin' nothin', ye were, while people were bein' slaughtered by the big guns. An then ye were lootin'. An' then, when she came on ye, tired an' cold an' saddle sore, tryin' to treat her like some loose woman from the stews o' Melbourne town."

"She shot and killed a man," I said. "We helped her to escape. And then the gang turned on us."

"Is that the case?"

"I swear by the Blessed Mary that it is," said Reardon.

I was surprised, despite Reardon's obvious sincerity, despite the sacred oath, when the gun was lowered.

"All right. I believe ye. I thought, at the time, that Miss Kate wasn't tellin' all o' the story. A Kelly she may be, a Kelly she is, but no lone woman'd be a match for a dozen Irishmen.

"Come."

We followed him off the track, into the bushes, ducking to avoid low branches with their water-laden foliage. We came to a clearing. In it was a rude construction that was neither hut nor tent but something of both, an affair of canvas and brushwood. Just inside its entrance a sullen fire was burning and on it was a pan. Beyond it loomed a tall man, illumined dimly by the feeble firelight, pointing a rifle at us as we approached.

"All right, Joe!" called our guide. "Here're two more refugees from Glenrowan to stay at our palatial hotel. If their stories are true, if they're who they say they are, Ned'll have use for 'em."

CHAPTER 17

The hut (or the tent) was a miserable, makeshift affair but it kept most of the rain out—and most of the smoke from the dispirited fire in. Still, there was at least the illusion of warmth. There was the hot stew, which was tasty enough, and then there was tea, sweetened with condensed milk and fortified with rum. We slept then, Reardon and I, huddled under the filthy, borrowed blankets. I doubt that the twentieth-century me would have been able to sleep in such conditions—but this was not the first time that my great-grandfather had snatched a brief spell of rest without first removing his wet clothing, sprawled on a hard bed. For some—although not all—physical tiredness is the world's most effective sleeping draught.

So I slept. I suppose that our hosts maintained some sort of sentry routine; after all there was the possibility that one of our late workmates at Glenrowan had told the truth to the police, including the information as to the direction in which Reardon and I had last been seen heading. But the police would not be at all likely to come trampling through the bush during the hours of darkness.

I awoke when somebody shook me roughly. I opened my gummed-together eyes, saw that it was not only broad daylight but that the weather had improved and that outside the crude hut the sun was shining brightly. I looked up into the bearded face of Kelly.

He said jovially enough, "Ye can certainly stow it away, Limey. The way ye were snorn' they must ha' been hearin' it in Melbourne."

So I had been snoring. I didn't need anybody else to tell me that; my mouth and tongue were dry, felt as though the skin was cracking. And my back ached and all my joints were stiff.

I threw off the sour-smelling blanket, came to a sitting posture with almost an audible creak and croaked, "Ned. . . ."

"In person, Limey, singin' an' dancin'."

I saw on the earth floor beside me a tin mug. It had contained somebody's tea. There was a quarter inch or so of dark brown fluid still remaining. I picked it up, drained it, swilled it around my mouth, spat out the sediment of tea leaves.

"So ye miss havin' a steward to bring ye yer mornin' tay," gibed Kelly.

"I wasn't a captain," I said.

"But ye were an officer, they tell me. An educated man. I can use such. What d'ye know about guns, Limey?"

I told him, "You'll know more about guns than I do, Ned."

"I don't mean rifles and pistols," he said. "I mean the big stuff, Cannon. An' those new-fangled quick-firers."

As a matter of fact I—or, to be more exact, my great-grandfather—did know something about artillery, although not much. As an apprentice he had served in a ship trading in Far Eastern waters where piracy was still one of the hazards of seafaring. This vessel had been armed with four carronades. Although he (I) had never seen a shot fired in anger—or defense—he had served in the guns' crews during practice shoots. The Old Man—who liked, now and again, to kid himself that he was captain of a battleship rather than master of a tramp windjammer—held these with some regularity, paying out of his own pocket (he said) for the ammunition so consumed.

I said, "I have fired a carronade."

"An' what's that when it's up an' dressed?"

"A sort of short cannon, but heavy enough. For close quarters only."

"Still, a cannon, But these other things. . . . These Gatlings and Nordefeldts . . . What d'ye know about them?"

"Not much. But I'm sure that they're quite easy to use. Any fool can turn a handle."

"Any fool—an' any murtherer. Kate's been tellin' me of what was done at Glenrowan. An' tellin' me, too, of the reception she got from the bold railway men. She wants her Derringer back."

I said, "I haven't got it."

"I have it," said Reardon, who had been awakened by our voices.

"Then let's be havin' it," Kelly told him, holding out his big hand.

He accepted the little weapon, broke it to check the loading of it, snapped it shut and thrust it into his pocket.

"All right. The pair o' ye did help Kate, so far as ye were able. Which wasn't much. Ye're on the run now. It could be that I could find a use for ye. A railwayman an' a seaman. I know that ye can tear up tracks, Mr. Reardon, an' lay down tracks. An' you, Mr. Grimes, know somethin' about the big guns. Ye know all about ships too—an' that could just be useful to me. . . ."

"You with a navy, Ned!" exploded Reardon. "I know that they call you the Captain of the North East—but ye'll niver be an admiral!"

"A president," he said, "employs admirals."

"Ye as president, Ned!"

"An' why not, Mr. Reardon?" Kelly was deadly serious. "An' why not? I've made no secret of my wantin' an independent republic of North East Victoria. I have my followers, as well you know. What Sinn Fein has failed to achieve in the old country I shall achieve here."

"Why stop at North East Victoria?" asked Reardon. If there was a faint note of derision in his voice Kelly either did not detect it or chose to ignore it.

"Why, indeed? Australia is ripe, I'm tellin' ye, for the overthrow of the English—the London bankers an' politicians an' all o' Mrs. Brown's puppies. An' the squatters—these robber barons whose fathers came out with the New South Wales Corps an' helped themselves to mile after square mile o' precious land. North East Victoria is just the beginning. . . ."

"But ye'll still be needin' Sinn Fein, Ned," said Reardon.

"I'll be needin' anybody at all, at all who'll be willing to take up arms, to help with guns an' money, with money an' guns. I tell ye, both of ye, that I'll accept help from the Devil himself."

And he would, I thought (remembered). He would. Surely American Big Business and the American military establishment were as much representative of His Satanic Majesty as their British counterparts.

"But to hell with the Devil!" he went on. It's men I'm wanting', *good* men. You, Reardon, an' you, Limey. Ye've skills, both o' ye, that I can be usin'."

I knew, with my memories of history (the wrong history? the history in which I had become trapped), what the outcome would be. Reardon did not. But it was not Reardon who hesitated; it was I. I had seen what the outcome would be, a century later, and I wasn't at all sure that I liked it. (But was the world that I had lost because of my interference at Glenrowan so very much better?)

"I'm with ye, Ned!" said Reardon.

"Count me in," I said.

(Yes. *I* said. My co-pilot, my great grandfather, whose mind I was sharing, was unable to wrest the controls from me.)

CHAPTER 18

The nineteenth century me had ridden a horse now and again while staying between ships, on an uncle's farm in East Anglia. The twentieth century me had never had anything to do with the brutes. And now I was going to have to ride from the lookout post to Kelly's main encampment. I was not looking forward to it.

Kelly had come to his Mount Morgan observation station with three men and five horses. The spare horses had been laden with supplies for the observers. They would carry Reardon and myself on the return journey. It would be better than walking, I supposed—but only just.

It was some little consolation to me that Reardon was no more at home aboard a horse than I was. Had we not been placed in the middle of the little troop, with Ned Kelly in the lead and his two men bringing up the rear, we should never have been able to control our beasts. But they were, fortunately, docile animals, brought up to follow the leader. The reins that Reardon and I held in hands that, in his case, were more accustomed to pick and shovel and, in mine, to wheel, tiller and halyard were little more than ornaments.

We rode on through the late morning, along trails that wound through bush and rocky outcroppings. We paused for a late lunch in a clearing. I was grateful for the opportunity to stretch my legs—and to rub my aching buttocks.

The bread that we devoured was stale and the cheese hard and dry, but it was welcome enough. The water, from a canvas bag, had an organic flavor which was only partly hidden by the added rum. After the meal we sat and smoked, talking little. Then Kelly pulled a big gold watch out of a waistcoat pocket, looked at it and gave the order to remount. He and his men watched amusedly as Reardon and I struggled to resume our saddles. We managed at last. (Our horses, as I have already said, were docile animals.)

We rode on through the afternoon, the wintry sun warm enough but a threatening chill in the light breeze. It seemed to me that we were steadily gaining altitude, although every now and again we descended into small valleys through which ran streams that were little more than trickles. We rode on, and as we rode the bushrangers began to sing. Their favorite seemed to be "The Wild Colonial Boy"—but it was the new version, the one that I had heard sung in Ma Jones' hotel.

There was a wild colonial boy, Ned Kelly was his name,
He robbed the rich to feed the poor, and so he gained
his fame. . . .

We rode on and, when the sun was just about to dip below the hills, came to the main encampment. This was on top of a hillock and the ground all around it had been cleared of trees and bushes, affording an unbroken field of fire. There were two sizeable slab huts and half a dozen tents. There was a flagpole, even. The banner flying from its peak was, more or less, the one made famous, decades ago, at the Eureka Stockade—a white cross with a star at the end of each arm and at the center. But the cruciform design was not on a dark blue field but on one of emerald green, and in the upper canton was something that at last I recognized as a harp.

There had been a stockade at Eureka—and there was a stockade here. There were men behind it and their rifles were leveled at us as we approached. Then I heard a shout, " 'Tis all right! 'Tis Ned an' the others!"

Logs were lifted to clear an opening and we rode through.

We dismounted. As far as I was concerned I fell off the horse. At least the ground, which was damp enough to be almost soft, made a change from that infernally hard saddle. I looked up to see Kate Kelly staring down at me, laughing scornfully.

"So ye've joined us, Limey! Our sailor on horseback!"

"It's as a sailor we might be needin' him, Kate," said Kelly. "I've cavalrymen enough to mount another Charge o' the Light Brigade!"

"But all ye have now," she pointed out, "are rifles that must ha' seen service in the Crimea an' shotguns that came out wi' the First Fleet. An' a few pistols. Talkin' o' pistols—did ye get my Derringer back?"

"Here 'tis." He handed her the weapon, butt first. "But I'll be obliged if ye'll not be shootin' any more Irishmen with it."

She laughed and said, "Ye're a fine one to be talkin' of shootin' Irishmen."

"But in English uniforms, Kate. Don't be forgettin' that."

Men had taken the horses and were leading them away. I got to my feet and followed Kelly into what seemed to be a mess tent. There was a rough wooden table with benches. There was a huge, steaming kettle of tea. There were bottles of rum and brandy. There was a leg of mutton, charred on the outside and almost raw inside. It was tough but tasty.

Reardon and I stayed at one end of the long table, eating and drinking.

Ned Kelly, with Kate and with Joe Byrne and Steve Hart, sat at the other. They ignored us as we ate and drank, made no attempt to keep their voices down.

"Glenrowan must be avenged," said Kate.

"I must gather me forces," said Ned.

"Gather yer forces. Gather yer forces. Men'll not come flockin' to yer banner, Ned, till ye've somethin' more to show 'em than a couple of ambushes. Stringy Bark Creek . . . What sort o' battle was that, I ask ye? The wrecked train at Glenrowan? Oh, 't'was a little better, perhaps—but too many people have suffered because of it. Too many people have found out that givin' aid to the Kelly Gang can bring the Law hard down upon them. Oh, ye'll have to show the world that Kelly can avenge—ay, an' protect—his own."

"I was thinkin'," said Kelly, "of goin' into Beechworth for more supplies . . ."

"An' just how do ye propose to lug tons o' foodstuffs an' the like from Beechworth to here?"

"Money an' gold are easy enough carried on horseback."

"An' here we have a shop just around the corner to spend the money in."

"Money an' gold are always good to have," he said. "There're plenty o' both in the Beechworth banks."

"And there're plenty o' police there," she said. "Some o' them must ha' been involved in the massacre. . . ."

"Murtherin' bastards," he said.

"To be executed for their crimes," she told him.

"Why not?" he whispered. "Why not?"

CHAPTER 19

I didn't take part in the raid on Beechworth—the Battle of Beechworth as it is called in the history books. Neither did Reardon. Kelly told us, not unkindly, "Ye're neither o' ye horsemen. Ye sit the saddle like sacks o' murphies, both o' ye." Kate, to her intense annoyance, was also excluded from the raiding party. Ned put her in charge of the encampment, our little fort in the wilderness. She was commander of the garrison, such as it was—Reardon, myself and two elderly men, small farmers whose selections had been repossessed. McLeod and Brown were their names. They could have been twins—little, gray-headed, wizened men whose heavy, grizzled beards could not hide the bitterness of their expressions. Our armory consisted of a couple of muzzle-loading shotguns, three Martini-Henry rifles, a Colt revolver and Kate's Derringer. There were, too, horses on which we could (hopefully) make a getaway should this be necessary. Of these only Kate's mare, Maeve, looked capable of outrunning a fast-walking man.

So there we were, the five of us, with Kate in a foul temper and McLeod and Brown resenting being put under a woman's command—a woman, moreover, who considered herself exempt from the camp's domestic chores. They took orders from her, but grudgingly. They were cunning enough to get lost whenever they suspected that orders were about to be given.

But they stood with us, with Kate and Reardon and myself, to watch the fifteen men and the twenty horses—five of them with equipment of various kinds, ammunition and four suits of the famous armor—ride away down from the stockade, then up the slope of the next hill, vanishing over the crest. They had a flag, even—a smaller version of the one flying from the fort's flagpole.

Then—"How about gettin' this . . . midden cleaned up?" said Kate. "There's garbage to be buried; even though its midwinter there're still flies. There're the pots to be scoured. An'. . . ."

"Is it orders you are giving, Miss Kate?" asked McLeod dourly.

"It is, Mr. McLeod. Me brother made it plain that I'm to be in charge until he's returnin'."

He muttered something under his breath. I caught the word "woman."

"So I'm a woman, am I? Yes—an' proud of it. An' you're a big, strong man. Tell me, Mr. McLeod—have ye iver killed a man?"

He mumbled, "No. . . ."

"Well, I have." She might not have been the fastest gun in the North East but the little Derringer, from some recess in her clothing, appeared in her right hand as though by magic. "I have, Mr. McLeod. If ye're not believin' me, just be askin' Mr. Reardon or Mr. Grimes."

"I wish that you'd put that thing away, Miss Kate," said Reardon. "You've done enough damage with it already."

"I made me point, didn't I? That a woman's honor is not somethin' to be taken from her by drunken louts."

"Did she kill a man, Mr. Reardon?" asked McLeod.

"She did that."

"Come on, Frank," said McLeod to Brown, "let's be getting the bones and spud peelings out of the way."

They drifted off.

"How to win friends and influence people," I said.

Both Reardon and Kate Kelly laughed at this.

"Ye've a fine way with words for a Limey," gasped Kate.

"I must remember that an' use it meself some time. But there's work to be done, the pair o' ye. I want this camp to be a place fit to live in by the time that Ned an' the others come back."

"*If* they come back," muttered Reardon.

But I, with my memories of histories read in the late twentieth century, knew that there was nothing to worry about—from the viewpoint of a Kelly supporter that is.

They came back, just before sunset, at the end of the third day. By this time Kate was becoming impossible to live with. During the daylight hours she spent most of the time on the crude lookout platform that we had constructed for her from spare timber, scanning the circumscribed horizon with a battered old brass telescope. (I had had to show her how to use it). She insisted on watches being kept throughout each night, losing sleep herself to make sure that the sentries (us) were not dozing off. All of us—Reardon and myself as well as McLeod and Brown—were on the verge of open mutiny.

But Kelly came back, riding over the brow of the hill at the head of his men with, by his side, Steve Hart carrying the green and gold banner. I was with Kate on the lookout platform. Suddenly she removed the telescope from her eye, thrust it at me.

"Here, Limey. You're more used to this thing than I am. 'Tis himself, isn't it?"

I steadied the instrument against the stanchion that I had put there for that purpose, adjusted the focus. Yes, the man in the lead was Ned all right and the standard bearer was Steve Hart. But there were considerably more horses than had set out. And more men. I tried to make a count. The original fifteen had been increased by one. There was a stranger riding immediately behind Kelly. A young man, it looked like, who was unusually (for these days) clean shaven. He was bareheaded and his hair was almost shoulder length. He did not seem to be a prisoner.

I said, "Looks like Ned's picked up a volunteer. . . ."

"Who is it?"

"Nobody I know," I said.

"Mr. Reardon," she shouted down from the platform, "get the stockade opened up, will you? Ned's back!"

I clambered down the rough ladder to ground level, joined Reardon and the other two in pulling the heavy logs to one side. (If we were to stay here, I thought, a proper gate would have to be made.) As we were standing there, regaining our breath, the leaders of the cavalcade came riding through the opening—Kelly, and Hart, and. . . .

I knew now who it was, despite the male apparel. In the photographs I had seen (would see) in the history books she was older and more conventionally attired, with much longer hair piled and coiled about her head in the fashion of the time. But now she was looking around the camp with interest—and at Kate, who had come down from the lookout and was standing there, staring at her.

"Who's this?" Kate Kelly demanded sharply.

"Kate, my dear," said Ned, "allow me to introduce another Kate—though 'tis Kitty she prefers to be called. . . ."

"Kitty?"

"Well, if 't'is formal ye'll have me be, the Countess Catherine von Stolzberg. Stolzberg's somewhere in Germany. . . ."

"An' do I address ye as Yer Highness?" asked Kate tartly.

"Kitty will do, Miss Kelly." The voice was a musical contralto, the English sounding good with no more than a trace of accent.

"I bid ye welcome," said Kate in a voice that made it plain that she was doing nothing of the kind. "This is Liberty Hall. Ye can spit on the mat an' call the cat a bastard."

CHAPTER 20

Ned Kelly's tent wasn't large enough to be dignified by the name of Liberty Hall—but there were two cats there. Kate and Red Kitty were almost at the claws out, spitting and snarling stage. It was a case of intense dislike at first sight.

There were five of us in Ned's cramped quarters—Ned himself, Kate, Kitty, Reardon and I. It had been almost impossible to talk over the evening meal—a hastily prepared stew of tinned meat and onions, washed down with rum-fortified tea. The men were bragging about their exploits in loud voices and every now and again bursting into song. The Kelly version of "The Wild Colonial Boy" was the favorite. Nobody noticed when the subject of the revised version of the bush ballad got up from his seat at the head of the rough table, making a beckoning gesture with his head to Kate, Reardon and myself. There was no need for him to do the same to the German countess; she rose when Ned did and walked with him out into the night.

He was first to enter his tent. A match flared and then, after a short interval, there was the soft, yellow light of the hurricane lamp hanging from the ridge pole. His huge form was in black silhouette against this illumination as he held the flap aside so that Kitty could enter. Against his bulk she was slim, frail almost—but I knew already that there was no frailty in her makeup. Courteously Ned held the flap clear until all of us were in the tent.

Kitty, I saw, had already made herself at home, was sitting on the rough bed, had lit for herself a long, slim cigar. In her male clothing she was surprisingly elegant, her auburn hair glinting in the lamplight, her almost violet eyes surveying us appraisingly as we came in. She was like a queen holding audience with her faithful subjects.

Ned took his seat beside her. Kate glared at her brother and the other woman, then found for herself a folding stool. Reardon and I looked around for seats but there weren't any. We sat on the ground.

Ned pulled out his pipe, filled it from his tobacco tin. Red Kitty produced matches, lit it for him. I was wryly amused. It is a sure sign of infatuation when a man lets a woman light his pipe.

"Well," he said, "I'm sure that ye'll all be wantin' to know what happened in Beechworth. . . ."

"First of all," said Kate, "perhaps ye'll be tellin' us what *she's* doin' here. . . ."

"And why should I not be here, Miss Kelly?" asked Kitty sweetly. "After all, I am a revolutionary, like yourselves. I came to this country as a fact finder, to discover, on behalf of my comrades in Europe, what conditions are." Her wide, scarlet slash of a mouth opened in a smile that displayed almost dazzlingly white teeth. "I did not expect to stumble upon the beginnings of a revolution."

"*You* a rebel?" sneered Kate. "You? An aristocrat. . . ." She made it sound like a dirty word.

"Yes. I am not only one of Karl Marx's disciples. I count him as a personal friend."

"Karl Marx? An' who might he be when he's up and dressed?"

"You do not know? You really do not know? I find this hard to believe. Karl Marx, Miss Kelly, has written books that will shake the world, that will change the world. They will become the bibles of the toiling masses."

"Don't blaspheme, woman!" flared Kate. "There is only one Bible!"

"And religion," said Red Kitty, "is the opium of the people."

"If only the Father were here . . ." began Kate furiously.

"Enough! Enough!" roared Kelly, holding up his big hand. "Enough! Religion we must have, we always will have. An' I'll ask you to remember, Kate, that Kitty, here, is our guest. . . ."

"*Your* guest," she sneered.

"Quiet, damn ye! Well, ye'll have been askin' yourselves how things went at Beechworth. They went well, even though the town was crawlin' wi' police, far more than usual. There was even Nicholson himself, stayin' at the hotel. They must ha' been expectin' us to be comin' after the gold in the bank." He laughed. "Expectin' us they might ha' been—but that dawn I could ha' ridden in wi' drums an' fifes an' taken the Town Hall while they were still rubbin' the sleep out o' their cowardly eyes . . .

"Mind ye, we did not advertise our presence. We stopped outside so I could get me battledress on, an' Steve an' Joe put on theirs an' Dan's suit was a good fit enough for Paddy Malone. We came ridin' in quiet like, an' after a bit of a drizzle the streets were muddy enough to muffle the thumpin' of our horses' hooves. We saw the first peeler outside the Town Hall. He must ha' been half asleep. He didn't see us till we were on top o' him. I dropped him wi' just the one shot before he had his rifle as much as halfway up.

"But when ye fire somethin' even so small as a revolver in the middle of a quiet country town in the hush o' just before sunrise—well, 'tis a cannon ye might as well be firin'." He laughed. "In two shakes of a lamb's tail windows were a-flyin' open an' heads wi' the nightcaps still on 'em were peerin' out to see what was happenin'. Most of 'em ducked back inside when they saw me an' the boys. . . ."

"I did not duck back inside," said the Countess. "I saw men in armor, on horseback, and it was like something out of our old legends. . . ."

"An' I saw ye there in the window," said Kelly, "with your red hair just kissin' your white shoulders . . . Like a queen ye were, out of our old legends."

The pair of them looked at each other through the smoke cloud of their own generating, the acrid fumes from his pipe, the only slightly more aromatic ones from her cigar.

"Get *on* with it!" snapped Kate.

Ned glared at his sister and demanded, "Am I to tell the story my own way? After all, 'tis my story. Well, as I was sayin' before ye interrupted me, I dropped the policeman before he could do the same for me. Then somebody started shootin' at us from an upstairs window. He was a good shot, I'll say that for him. I've a dent in me breast-plate to prove it. Almost knocked me out o' the saddle, it did. But young Steve was a good shot, too. The fool was showin' himself. An' then there were the other fools—they'd taken the time to put their uniforms on—who came pourin' out into the street. Oh, such a reputation for cowardice they had that now, when any sensible man would ha' been firin' from cover, they had to show the world that they were heroes.

"I told me men who hadn't armor to take cover in doorways an' the like while Steve an' Joe an' Paddy an' myself rode to the attack. Oh, the weight o' fire they were pourin' at us would ha' knocked us off our horses for sure if they'd been shootin' straight. But they weren't. Oh, if I were a glazier in Beechworth I'd be makin' me fortune now repairin' all the broken windows!

"We galloped down on 'em, the four of us, our revolvers blazin'. Not that it was much of a gallop, our horses weren't all that nimble, what with the weight of our armor as well as ourselves. Kitty tells me that the knights of the olden days were ridin' animals more like plowhorses than what we ride today . . . But no matter.

"The police had plenty o' time to break to let us through—but they were too busy scrambling clear to take aim an' fire as we were among them. If they'd used their heads they could have brought our horses down for sure. But we were takin' aim an' got seven o' the bastards. When we turned, to come back at 'em, they were runnin' for the hotel. The boys, shootin' from their cover, brought down three more o' them. Oh, 't'was a real battle, I'm tellin' ye. Bullets flyin' everywhere, an' as we were chasin' the last o' the peelers into the hotel it was our own side that nearly got us.

"We couldn't ride our horses in after 'em so we had to dismount—an' gettin off a nag with all their weight of ironmongery on ye isn't all that easy . . ."

"In olden times," said Red Kitty, "the knights used to be hoisted up on to their horses by a sort of crane. . . . Perhaps, Ned, you could get somebody to make something of the kind for you. . . ." She looked at him fondly. "But those knights were *little* men . . . Once, not so long ago, I tried to put on one of the suits of armor we have in the Schloss . . ."

"An' what the hell's a Schloss?" demanded Kate.

"The Schloss von Stolzberg. Our family castle, Miss Kelly. As I was saying, I tried to put on one of the suits of armor. It was too small for me. The olden knights were little men—not big, strong giants like Ned, here."

Kelly was almost purring but said, "Let me get on with the story, Kitty. An' you, Kate, pipe down. As I was tellin' ye, we got off our horses an' followed the police into the hotel. They were in the bar, five of 'em. We shot it out. Oh, the criminal waste—the smashed bottles an' the golden liquor minglin' wi' the blood on the floor. . . . The reek o' gunpowder an' the smell o' whisky an' brandy an' rum enough to make ye drunk. . . . An' over the crash o' the gunfire the sound o' women screamin' somewhere—in the kitchen, maybe, or the upstairs rooms. . . .

"Then it was over.

"Joe said, his voice echoin' up from inside his helmet, 'We've earned ourselves a drink—if there's a bottle left unbroken. . . .' He put up his hands an' lifted the helmet from off his shoulders, let it drop to the floor with a crash an' a clatter. The other two did the same, then went behind the bar to find what was left on the shelves. I didn't interfere. Killin' people—an' runnin' the risk o' bein' killed yerself—does give ye a powerful thirst. But first I had to go outside to tell the boys what was happenin'—an' to make sure that our horses hadn't taken off for Wangaratta or Glenrowan or even Melbourne. 'Twas lucky that I didn't take me own helmet off.

"I was makin' for the door when I heard a shot behind me. It missed, but only by a whisker. I turned around—an' there, comin' down the stairs, was Nicholson. He was all dolled up in his full uniform, all gleamin' braid an' buttons, an' looked like a general, no less. He had a revolver in each hand. I had, too, come to that—but I hadn't reloaded them. I was wearin' me belt with the ammunition pouches an', still facin' him, I fumbled for bullets after I'd stuck the pistols in me belt an', at the same time, kept on walkin' backwards. The hallway carpet had been rucked up with all the scufflin' an' me right heel caught in somethin' just as one o' Nicholson's shots hit me on the right shoulder.

"I went over with what sounded, to me, a crash like a bull in a china shop. (Afterwards Joe an' Steve an' Paddy, told me that they'd heard nothin'—neither the shootin' nor me goin' over with a wallop to shake the very foundations. It could be that all the firin' in the bar had deafened 'em—but they must already ha' been into the hard stuff an' deaf to the world in consequence.)

"Anyhow, there I was, flat on me back an' more than half stunned. I tried to move but could do no more than sort o' feebly flap me arms. An' I knew that me arms weren't protected by the armor, an' neither were me legs. Just four shots from Nicholson an' I'd be crippled for life—what was left of it. I could *hear* him comin'. *I* wasn't deaf—or it could be that the helmet sort o' magnified sounds. *Thud, thud, thud* . . . An' how long before the first bullet smashed an elbow or kneecap?

"Then the little, narrow strip o' light, the slit in me helmet through which I was lookin', was blotted out, just as the sound from Nicholson's big boots stopped. But I could still see. I could see the muzzle of a revolver—big as a cannon, it looked.

"An—'Say your prayers, Kelly,' I heard. 'Ye've come to the end o' yer dirty road, ye cold blooded murtherer!'

"I heard a shot but I felt nothin'. An' it wasn't anything like as loud as I'd been expectin'. An' the light was streamin' in through me helmet slot again as Nicholson fell away from me, takin' that ugly, great revolver with him.

"But was I dead after all? Was it the big, violet eyes of some holy angel that was starin' down into mine?"

" 'T'wasn't an angel's eyes, that's obvious!" sneered Kate.

"I make no claim to be an angel," said Red Kitty. "I saw

that the Superintendent was about to murder Ned, so I
. . . intervened. Luckily I had thought to bring my pistol
with me when I came down from my room to see the
fighting. I had already heard about your brother, of course,
and about his valiant fight against the capitalist oppressors.
I had heard the police boasting about what they had done
at Glenrowan. There was only one side that I could possibly be on."

"And so you have cast your lot among outlaws," I could
not help saying.

"I am a servant of the revolution," she told me. "I had
never expected it in this country so far removed from
Europe and the Americas. But you Australians have set
the example that all must follow. I am proud to be among
you."

I looked at her, sitting on the bed beside Kelly.

Insofar as Australia was concerned she had been in the
right place at the right time.

CHAPTER 21

Nobody was surprised—although many were disapproving—when Red Kitty moved in with Ned.

"What they do is their business," I said to Kate, one morning while we were making an assessment of the gold, bags of dust and small nuggets, plundered from the bank in Beechworth.

"Ye wouldn't understand, Limey," she sneered. "Ye're as bad as all yer Godless breed. We Irish are a moral people, not like you. We obey the dictates of the Church. An' what burns me up is the thought o' Ned wallowin' in sin wi' that scarlet woman while his poor mother—*our* poor mother—is languishin' in Melbourne Jail. . . ."

I said, "The Countess is a very attractive woman. And clever. And influential."

"And a whore." (She made two syllables of the offensive word.)

I said, "She's not hawking her body around the camp."

"Once she's tired o' Ned she will be."

I said, "I doubt it."

"Whether or not she does—we'll not be gettin' the support we should so long as Ned is flauntin' her in the eyes of the world."

I said, "We are getting support. Volunteers are coming in. There's been trouble in Benalla and Wangaratta, with police killed. The McIlwraith Station was raided and looted. . . ."

"An' that wild man Mike McGinty has frozen on to the carronade that old man McIlwraith had to protect his property an' has set himself up as a little king in his own fort—all because he now has a cannon an' thinks that he can thumb his nose at everybody. Includin' us."

I remembered my reading of history—on which Time Track?—and recalled how Parnell, a leader of the Irish Home Rule movement, had lost popular support because of an adulterous affair.

I said, "Ned will have to marry."

"What? *Her?*"

"Why not?"

"She's no better than a whore. He's already slept with her."

I said, "Come off it, Kate. You know as well as I do how many couples in this country—good Irish couples—have shacked up together and not gotten married until a priest has happened around—very often to officiate at a few christenings as well as at the wedding."

She said, " 'T'wouldn't be right."

I said, "Why the hell not?"

"If ye must know—'tis because she's not one of us."

"You could say the same about me," I said.

"I could—an' with truth." She stared at me. "No. One of us ye most certainly are not. Ye're even more . . . foreign than most Limeys. An' do ye have the gift o' second sight? 'Tis seemed to me, more than once, that ye've ever known too much about what's goin' to happen. . . ."

"Intelligent guesswork," I said.

"An' these queer turns o' phrase o' yours. . . ."

I said, "I suppose I have a way with words."

"Ye have that. Well, now, with yer second sight do ye see Ned marryin'?"

"I do," I told her.

"To bring a priest out here'll cost money."

I made a not very successful attempt to juggle with two little bags of gold dust and a small nugget.

I said, "We've more than enough here, in dust and nuggets and coins and notes, to bring out the Pope himself."

She pretended to be shocked but laughed nonetheless.

"Father Flynn in Wangaratta would not be so expensive. An' he can be trusted. . . . I might, I just might, go there meself to persuade him. I know the old b —gentleman, I mean, quite well. But do ye swear to me that it's in the stars that Ned must marry that woman?"

"I do," I said.

"Then so be it." She sighed. "Ellen Kelly, our mither, is a strong woman—but she hasn't the education, the knowledge of the world. I'm strong meself—but a sister can't push a man the same as a wife can. An' Ned, for all his strength an' brains, needs pushin'. He's like some proud stallion, runnin' nowhere at all, at all, 'less there's a gentle yet firm hand holdin' the reins. Or, as I suppose ye'd say, a tall, proud ship under full sail but never makin' port unless there're cunnin hands on the wheel. . . .

"Even so . . ." She spat. "This Kitty bitch!"

"It's not only who she is," I said. "It's who she knows."

"I suppose that's the way of it . . ." she sighed.

But *I* was not one of the witnesses at the wedding of Ned Kelly and the Countess Catherine von Stolzberg. My great-grandfather was. He must have been bewildered when he was left, once again, in full control of his brain, must have wondered what had made him say and do all the things that he had been saying and doing.

And I was making my report to the Kelly in twentieth century Sydney.

CHAPTER 22

I finished dictating into the recorder, then sipped gratefully from the tall glass of cold beer that Graumann handed to me.

Kelly—he was back from the capital, from Glenrowan—stood scowling down at me.

He said, "I was hopin' that ye'd have been among those present at the Battle o' Beechworth."

I said, "But I wasn't. Or my great grandfather wasn't. He was no horseman."

"But couldn't *you*. . . ?"

"No," I said. "I'm no horseman either. In any case—what would have happened if I'd interfered with the script?"

"It's already been written," Graumann said. "It can't be altered."

Can't it? I thought

"I suppose that we have to be content with what we've got," grumbled the President. "But tell me, Johnny, what was he *really* like? The first Ned, I mean . . ."

"Very like you," I said. "Tall, with a heavy beard . . . A commanding presence . . . But bulkier . . ." I stared at him. "But was he? Or have you been putting on weight? I haven't been away all that long. . . ."

He laughed.

"Armor is coming back into fashion in the Kelly family," he said. He smote himself on the chest and the sound was duller than it would have been had he been wearing normal clothing. "A present from Cousin Jack in Washington. Supposed to keep out bullets better than a string vest keeps in warmth. There've already been two attempts on me life." He started to shout. "I wish to Jesus God that I could string up every one o' the bastards that want me out of the Nam! An' that goes for Cousin Jack's brother Ted, sent here from the States as a special envoy to try to persuade me. He'd be better employed savin' his girlfriends out o' cars sunk in the river. . . ."

He quieted down. "So I'm like the first Ned, ye say? Game as Ned Kelly . . . That goes for me, I hope, as well as for him. I gave me word that I'd save the Nam from the commies—an' when did a Kelly ever break his word? And now tell me—what was she like?"

"Kate?" I asked.

"No, not Kate. Red Kitty. My great-grandmother."

"Tall," I said, "for a woman. Any slimmer and she'd have been skinny. Rather too much nose and a wide mouth. Hair that was red rather than auburn. Eyes violet rather than blue. A dead shot with a pistol—anything from a Derringer to a Colt revolver. At home on horseback—although she preferred astride to side saddle. She was wearing male clothing all the time that I was in the camp. From a distance she'd have passed for a good-looking lad. But only from a distance."

"She sounds quite a girl," said Ned.

"She was. But you wouldn't have liked her."

"An' why not? After all, she's me great-grandmother."

"And also a communist," I said. "A faithful disciple of old Karl himself. And do you think that *she'd* have liked what you're doing now, in Asia?"

He growled, "Enough o' that. Your job is to research the Past, not to advise me on foreign policy. Bear it in mind, will ye?"

He strode out of the room.

"You've upset him," said Graumann worriedly.

"I know."

"Don't do it again, please. He might throw you into one of his prisons for punishment and that will hold up the project. And *I* want the project finished so I can get back to God's Own Country before the balloon goes up."

"Have you been trying to look into the Future?" I asked him.

"Yes. I didn't get much. Only hints—but they were bad enough."

And that was all that he would tell me.

CHAPTER **23**

A Dr. Shaughnessy examined me and pronounced me sound in wind and limb after my long trance but insisted that I should be given at least two days to get my strength back before taking part in further experiments. He was frankly puzzled by the whole business.

"Just what is going on here, Dr. Graumann?" he asked, his fat, florid face worried. "Ye're not a medical doctor, are ye? Ye aren't qualified to be puttin' a subject under for a long period, or even a short one. Ye're lucky that he's not starvin' an' dehydrated. . . ."

"We saw to it that he took fluid nourishment, Doctor," said Major Duffin.

"Ye could ha' killed him. I don't like this business at all, at all."

"If you have any complaints, Doctor," said Graumann stiffly, "I suggest that you take them to the President."

That shut Shaughnessy up. In sulky silence he repacked his bag and left the bedroom. I took a much needed shower—arrangements may have been made for feeding me, after a fashion, but none for excretion. There had been . . . leakage. I got dressed in clean clothing. I joined Graumann and Duffin at the dinner table. I was hungry, although not ravenously so. The sight and the smell of the steaks that an orderly set on the table made my mouth water.

During dinner we watched TV. It was not suitable entertainment to accompany a meal. Yet another military disaster in the Nam, with shots of exploding rockets, burning houses and fleeing civilians, with full sound and color. All that was missing was the smell of the roasting flesh of those trapped inside the buildings. (I did not finish my steak, which was rather too well done, anyhow.) Then there was an anti-war demonstration in Brisbane, brutally suppressed by the State Governor's police, Bjelke's Bullies as they were so aptly nicknamed. Even Duffin could not hide his disapproval of the use of heavy machine guns against a peaceful march. There was very brief coverage of an interview with the American President's envoy, Senator Edward Kennedy. He was barely given time to say that his brother did not approve of Australia's continued participation in the Vietnam war before there was a switch to a coverage of the latest welfare riots in Washington D.C.

Then, "You'd better get some sleep, Mr. Grimes," said Graumann. "I want you fit to make another historical excursion tomorrow."

I said, "Dr. Shaughnessey said that I should have at least a two-day break."

He said, "I am running this experiment, not Dr. Shaughnessy. And President Kelly has told me that he wants the eye-witness history written as soon as possible." He smiled bleakly. "As I do myself." He pulled a small pillbox out of a side pocket. "I persuaded the good physician to leave me these. Take two, with water, before retiring." He smiled again and wished me happy dreams.

CHAPTER 24

I did dream that night—if it was a dream. Yet there was no time-twisting apparatus to send my spark of consciousness swirling back along the world lines.

(The next morning I told Graumann about it. He said that he had been expecting something of the kind and that it must have been a side effect of the most recent experiment, when I had spent a much longer time in the Past than on prior occasions. My hold on the here-and-now had been weakened, he said. Given the right stimuli I could regress—to anywhere and anywhen. After all, I had more than one great-grandparent. Or, come to that, grandparent.)

I left Graumann and Duffin at the dinner table, slurping their coffee. (It smelled good; I would have liked some myself but Graumann told me that I had to sleep.) I went into the bedroom, closed the door after me. I got undressed. I did not feel at all tired. So I took two of the pills, washing them down with cold water from the vacuum flask on the bedside table.

Whatever was in the things was most effective. I went out like a light before I'd gotten properly into bed.

My name was Pierre de Gruchy. I was standing, with others, on the bushy bank of a river. All of us were armed, most of us with a motley collection of rifles that, even at this historical period, were almost museum pieces. As I looked around I saw a small group of tall, dark-complexioned men who carried, as their weapons, bows and arrows.

Pierre de Gruchy knew what it was all about. *I* didn't. Delicately I probed his mind. The year was 1885. It was early in May. The pine trees—that seemed so wrong to anybody, like myself, used to eucalyptus—belonged in this landscape. But I had to be careful, far more careful than when I was sharing the mind of the ancestral John Grimes. That great-grandfather had been a man of some education and of wide experience of the world. Insofar as religion was concerned he regarded himself as an agnostic. Bewildered he must have been more than once when I had taken control—but he had not rushed to the nearest priest to have himself exorcised. Pierre de Gruchy would be all too liable to do just that.

So—I was very cautious. Great-grandfather Pierre must have felt something scratching in his mind. He was becoming increasingly uneasy—but so was everybody else waiting at this riverside ambush. Gabriel Dumont was no exception, was prowling back and forth, in the limited space allowed by the clearing, like some large, hungry cat. I watched him and, inevitably, made comparisons. He did not have Kelly's essential . . . nobility? Yes. Nobility. Or Kelly's handsomeness. At first glance he could be dismissed as a scruffy little half-caste—his stocky build made him look shorter than he actually was—with a dirty beard, wearing stained, buckskin clothing. There was more stubborn French peasant in his face than noble Red Indian.

And yet—he had it. Charisma. Not to the same degree as Ned Kelly, but strong enough.

The sun was high in the southern sky and warm. There were insects, some harmlessly irritating, some biting. We were sweating in our rough clothing. I looked at the Amerindians. I thought they they would have been far happier dressed for battle as their ancestors had been, in warpaint and breechclouts. Pierre de Gruchy tried to dismiss the indecent notion from his mind. To him even partial nudity was both obscene and indicative of heathen savagery.

Dumont stopped his pacing to speak to one of his lieutenants.

"They are late," he complained.

"The *Northcote* is slow," said the man. "And perhaps she is having trouble at the shallows. It is there that we should have laid the ambush."

"It is there," said the Metis leader, "that they would have expected to be ambushed. It is the American, Howard, who is late."

"Can he be trusted, Gabriel?" asked the other man. "After all, he is an officer of the Army of the United States. He might think that his proper place is with the General Middleton."

"He is a soldier, Jean, and will follow his orders. The Irish, who influence his government, want America to support the good Catholics both in Canada and Australia. So Louis Riel has told me."

"Louis Riel!" Jean spat untidily and sputum glistened in has black beard. "I care nothing for him. *You* are our leader, Gabriel."

"Louis," said Dumont patiently, "is an educated man. I am not. He can read books and he can write. He can talk to important people as an equal."

He is only a schoolmaster," persisted Jean stubbornly. "You, Gabriel, are our general."

Up the slope somebody was shouting, "They are coming! They are coming!"

Dumont turned and bellowed, his voice resonant and powerful, "Do you see the steamer? The *Northcote*?"

"No! It is the Americans, with their guns!"

It was the Americans with their guns.

There were two of the things, each on its own carriage and with its own limber, each drawn by four horses. They negotiated the rough track down from the brow with some difficulty, the horses slipping and scrabbling for hoofhold. The air was loud with American curses. At last the guns were down to the small clearing, which was hidden from view riverward by bushes. The horses were unharnessed, led back to the top of the bank.

The leader of the newcomers was, like his men, dressed in breeches and brown flannel shirt, high boots and a wide brimmed hat. He was clean-shaven—or would have been so if he hadn't missed at least three morning shaves. There were no insignia on his clothing, yet he conveyed the impression of being in uniform.

He demanded, "Who's in charge here?"

He looked around at us all and did not quite sneer.

"I am, Captain," said Dumont.

"You are Dumont? General Dumont?"

Where is your uniform? said his expression.

"You may call me that, Captain."

"My rank is lieutenant, sir. Lieutenant Arthur L. Howard, Second. Connecticut National Guard. At your service, General."

"In my service, M'sieur, you are a captain. I so appoint you."

"I'll not argue, General. Now, what do you want me to do?"

"There will shortly be a steamer passing this point, the Hudson Bay Company's *Northcote*. It has stores and reinforcements for General Middleton's army. I want it stopped."

"And these are the babies that'll stop her for you, sir! Old Doc Gatling's bouncing babes!"

So these were not, as I had thought at first, misled by their carriages and limbers, field guns of large calibre. The bronze casing around the revolving assembly of ten 0.5″ barrels had contributed to the erroneous impression. I (we) watched curiously, as did everybody else, while the Americans prepared their machine-gun battery for action. The weapons were very much of a frightening mystery to Pierre de Gruchy but *I* recognized such features as the oscillating gear and elevating screw. And it was Broadwell drums being taken out from the limbers, each loaded with four hundred rounds—less than thirty minutes' sustained firing.

(Some of this information leaked into my great-grandfather's mind. He was beginning to wonder how he knew so much.)

"Steamer comin' roun' the bend!" came the hail from up the bank.

Yes, here she came. The twentieth century me had been expecting something on the lines of a Mississippi river queen—but this vessel was no more than a shabby, scruffy, even, riparian workhorse. I saw the walking booms—with the aid of which she could crawl over sandbanks—projecting forward. Her decks were protected with what I thought were sandbags, piled high, with loopholes through which the barrels of rifles projected. There was no makeshift armor around the pilot house, however. I could see the scarlet coats of many officers and somebody in dark blue, presumably the *Northcote*'s captain, and the white-shirted helmsman. Smoke poured from the pair of tall, thin funnels, set athawartships forward of the wheelhouse, and sparks, clearly visible even in the bright daylight. The *thump*, *thump*, *thump* of the engines carried across the still water, through the calm air, as did the threshing of the sternwheel.

She came on steadily into the narrows.

And on, and on. . . .

A single rifle shot rang out. One of Dumont's men, unable to contain his impatience, had fired.

"Stop shooting!" Dumont roared. "Stop shooting, you fools!"

But he was too late. That first, premature shot sparked off a ragged volley from his undisciplined forces.

There was a screaming roar of escaping steam as *Northcote*'s engines were stopped as the preliminary to going astern. Her whistle sounded shrilly in a series of short blasts. Howard, cursing loudly, was shouting at his men to swing the guns around so that they could be brought to bear upon the steamer, himself lifting the trail of one of the carriages. But, with the sternwheel not yet turning in reverse, the ship was still making headway through the water, was still coming on. The troops on the port side of the deck, secure (they thought) behind their protection, had opened fire. Fortunately for us they still could not see any targets.

Northcote was going astern at last—just as Howard, who had been fussing with the elevating screw of one of the Gatlings, ordered, "Fire!"

The gunners bent to their handles. Twenty rounds rapid, a quick flick with the left hand to turn the Broadwell drum so that the next twenty rounds came over the hopper, twenty rounds rapid . . .

The pilot house . . . disintegrated, was blown into shreds of wood and splinters of glass by the concentrated fire of the gun of which Howard had assumed personal command. Only one man, one of the army officers, staggered out of the wreckage—and was swept overside by a hail of bullets. A funnel, literally sawn through at its base, tottered and fell like a tree.

The return fire was heavy at first but uncoordinated. Then the barricade of sandbags collapsed suddenly. But it was not bags of sand but sacks of grain which had been commandeered from some warehouse along the river; once the sacking was ripped the golden wheat poured out and overside in an unstoppable torrent and the redcoats, suddenly exposed, were mown down before they had a chance to fall to the deck or to seek cover. In a matter of seconds there was nothing but the occasional single shot, fired by a wounded or dying man, barely heard above the steady, deafening hammering of the Gatlings.

The sternwheel was still threshing but the ship was utterly out of control and was listing heavily to starboard as the grain sacks, that had been protecting the deck to port, emptied. She swung so that her bows were toward us, bringing the soldiers on the starboard side of the steamer under Howard's murderous fire. She backed away from us, wallowing like a stricken whale. She grounded, stern first, on the far bank. Her superstructure was being shredded away. Her scuppers were running with blood.

(How often, as a small boy reading sea stories, had I come across that expression? Now I was seeing the real thing. I did not like it. Neither did great-grandfather Pierre.)

"Captain!" Dumont was bellowing to Howard, "Stop firing! For the love of the good God, stop firing!"

But the American either could not or would not hear. Empty drums were lifted from the guns and full ones dropped in their place and the sweating gunners were spinning their handles and Howard, deaf to everything but the infernal rattle of his killing machines, was staring through his binoculars at the stricken ship. He must have thought that it was the Gatlings that brought about the ultimate disaster. Perhaps it was. A stray shot could have somehow jammed the safety valve—and then, with the sternwheel embedded in mud or straining against immovable rock, the steam pressure in the boilers, already dangerously high, had built up, and up—.

The dreadful roar of the exploding boilers shocked me into wakefulness, asprawl in the sweat-dampened, tangled bedsheets.

CHAPTER 25

The following morning, after breakfast, I taped the account of the dream (if dream it was) while it was still fresh in my memory. Graumann and Major Duffin listened while I spoke into the microphone.

When I was finished Duffin said, "Ned'll not be liking this."

"Why not?" I asked.

" 'Tis a waste o' time, that's why. Correct me if I'm wrong," he went on sarcastically, "but weren't you hired to write an account of the *Australian* revolution? You aren't bein' paid to go traipsin' off to Canada."

I said, "It all ties in."

He demanded, "Who the hell cares about this man Dumont?"

"Lots of people did, at the time," I told him. "He was, in his way, a brilliant military leader. Most historians are of the opinion that Louis Riel supplied the brains involved in the Metis Revolt, and Gabriel Dumont the brawn. But Dumont wasn't short in the brain department, even though he had never received any sort of education. He was very quick to see the advantages of automatic weapons after Howard's demonstration of the Gatlings. Riel was the rabble-rouser, the letter writer, the fund-raiser. It was Riel who made the deal with Francis Bannerman in New York—

and it was Bannerman who had political clout, in that city and, even, in Washington.

"But don't forget that it was Dumont who was the fighting general."

"And where did it get him in the end? Swept under the mat after Canada was incorporated in the U.S.A., to die in obscurity. As far as *we* are concerned he was nobody."

"Don't they teach you history at the Glenrowan Military Academy?" I asked. "Didn't you learn, there, that the Australian and Canadian revolutions were . . . complementary? That Sinn Fein had its agents among their co-religionists, the Metis in Canada, as well as in Australia and in the U.S.A.? And, too, *our* President's great-grandmother, the famous Red Kitty, had friends, good friends, in Washington. . . . Oh, it was a tangled web, all right, and the biggest, fattest spider was the U.S.A. If we'd had a common border with them we'd have gone the same way as Canada."

"I was taught," he said stiffly, "that American involvement in the Metis Revolt was to take the heat off us. Off Australia. If the English navy had not been lured away from our ports to show the flag off Vancouver. . . ."

"It wouldn't have been much use if it had stayed here," I said. "After all, we had the Andrews dirigible."

He said, "It would not have been long before effective anti-aircraft artillery was developed. . . ."

"The English," I told him, "still hadn't developed effective anti-aircraft guns at the time of the Boer War. If Kruger hadn't fallen out with the reigning Kelly—over religion, of all things! —our Air Force would have won the war for him. As it was—as you should know—once the Australian forces were withdrawn the Boers collapsed."

He said stiffly, "I have studied the Boer War campaigns, General Morant's book was required reading."

Graumann was becoming impatient with both of us.

"Gentlemen," he said with a touch of anger, "may I remind you that if it had not been for *my* country, the United States of America, the pair of you would not be sitting here, as citizens of the Australian Republic, arguing about history."

"It's just a matter of luck—and logistics—that we aren't having this argument as American citizens," I said.

"Logistics?" he asked.

"The art of getting there fustest with the mostest, as one of your generals—I think—once said. In those days, the days of the first Ned, we were one helluva long way from both England and the States. That was our salvation. Canada wasn't so lucky. Neither was Ireland, with only the Irish Sea as a moat between it and England, and with England already strongly entrenched in the north. The Irish rising was foredoomed from the start."

"Ireland rose," said Duffin heatedly, "to divert the English attentions from Australia."

"Ireland rose," I said, "because the Irish thought that we were diverting attention from them."

He said, "Of course, your name is not Irish."

I said, "It's not. But where was *your* great-grandfather, Major Duffin, when the flag of the Harp and Southern Cross was raised?"

"For your information, Mr. Grimes, both my great-grandfathers were soldiers in the Army of the Irish Republic and were among the defenders of Dublin, during the siege."

"But they were not here," put in Graumann. "They were not among the first Kelly's trusted officers. Mr. Grimes' great-grandfather was. That is why he, and not you, is the subject of my experiments. Perhaps, if there is time, you will be allowed to do some research into the Irish history of the period." He paused and said somberly, "If there is time."

"What do you mean?" demanded Duffin.

"I mean that I want to get out of this bloody country!" snapped the scientist.

"Scared of the Yellow Peril?" the major sneered.

CHAPTER 27

My next excursion into the Past was a controlled one, to a predetermined time and place. Once again I sat in the chair in the darkened room, hypnotized by the spinning, precessing wheels, the glimmering, tumbling rotors. I was drawn away from the here and now, back to the there and then. *There* was the camp, the fortress in the bush. *Then* was a morning in the early February of 1881.

The camp was larger than when I had last seen it, had acquired an air of permanency. There were more of the bark-roofed slab huts and there had been a proliferation of tents, not crude affairs of sagging canvas but neat, military-looking shelters. There was a carronade emplaced to cover the path up to the main gate of the stockade; it could be effective should attackers make their approach by this route. This weapon was my toy; Kelly had appointed me Master Gunner. Unfortunately there was not enough ammunition for a practice shoot; Mike McGinty had parted with the gun willingly enough—it was far too clumsy a thing to drag around on his guerrilla raids—but had maintained that he had no powder to spare. And there were no cannonballs. In a situation such as ours, I was thinking, canister would be the most effective—but there was no canister. I was looking at the cannon, wondering if it would be possible to load the thing with sacks of stones. And why not? I was asking myself. At short range such fire would be deadly enough. After all, the China Coast pirates fired almost anything at all from their guns—including, it was said, horseshoes for luck . . . But I wasn't at all happy about the carriage with its four little wheels, suitable enough for trundling over a ship's deck but not for shifting the carronade to another firing position over rough ground. Perhaps Reardon, I was thinking, could made a proper field gun carriage for me. . . .

Kate interrupted my thoughts.

"Johnny," she said.

I turned to look at her. Very smart she was looking this morning—as she did most days now—with her lustrous, dark hair piled high on her head, with her spotless, ruffled white blouse, her long black skirt from under the hem of which peeped the toes of her highly polished black boots. Very feminine she was these days, in deliberate contrast to the assumed masculinity of her brother's wife. (But Red Kitty, despite her male attire, always looked very much a woman.)

"Yes, Kate?" I asked.

"His Highness is wantin' ye," she said sourly.

I said, "It's nice to be wanted."

She laughed without much warmth. "It makes a change, so it does. Since he took up with Her Ladyship 'tis little enough time he's had for any of us, even me, who's his own family. An', talkin' o' family, when's he goin' to do somethin' about gettin' mither out o' Melbourne Jail?"

"Don't ask me," I said. "I only work here."

"Work, ye call it? Playin' around wi' that stupid, great gun, drivin' the boyos till they're sweatin' their guts out, goin' through the motions wi' make-believe gunpowder an' make-believe cannon balls, luggin' the thing all around the stockade but niver so much as firin' a single shot. . . ."

"Somebody might hear it if we did," I told her. "Sound carries, you know, and cannon fire, out in the bush, would be a dead give-away. In any case, we've no powder to spare for practice. We have to keep what we have, which isn't much, for the real thing."

"An' it can't come soon enough for me," she said viciously. "I'd like to be in some fightin'. *She* goes out on raids wi' *him*, but *I* don't. My job is to have a hot meal ready for 'em when they come ridin' back. If 'twas aboard one o' yer ships 'tis the chief steward ye'd be callin' me." She shrugged. "Oh, well, I suppose 'tis better'n bein' the crock washer an' spud peeler.. . . ."

"You said that Ned wanted me," I reminded her.

"He does that."

"What for?"

"He wants yer ter meet the stranger who rode in wi' Joe an' the others this mornin'. The one wi' the sack over his head. The Yank."

"So he's an American?"

"I just told ye that, didn't I?"

I patted the carronade and then walked with her toward the large hut, the headquarters hut, outside which was the flagpole with the banner of the Harp and the Southern Cross at its peak, stirring lazily in the light, warm breeze.

Ned was sitting at the head of the rough table. At his right was Red Kitty, very smart in scarlet silk shirt, open at the throat, and narrow black trousers tucked into high, gleaming, black boots. She was smoking one of her long, thin cigars. Below her sat Joe Byrne and Steve Hart. My attention, however, was mainly for the stranger, sitting to Kelly's left. He was a tall man, beardless but with a heavy moustache. He was wearing a blue flannel shirt and tan riding breeches, brown lace-up boots. There was a revolver holster at each hip but both were empty. He must have surrendered his weapons before being brought to the camp. He turned in his chair to look at me as I came in.

"Major Donnelly," said Kelly, "this is Mr. Johnny Grimes, my master gunner. Johnny, this is Major Donnelly, who's come all the way from New York to talk to us."

There was handshaking.

Donnelly said, "And so you, sir, are in charge of that antique I saw by the gate . . ." He added, before I could take offense, "Don't get me wrong, sir. The carronade was a good weapon in its day, and still is. But there are better ones."

I said, "A poor thing, but mine own."

"*Mine* own, Johnny!" laughed Kelly. "Don't ye be forgettin' it. 'Twas good gold I paid Mike McGinty for it.

An' if the major, here, has his way 'tis more good money I'll be payin' out. He must think I'm made o' money."

"But I'm telling you, Mr. Kelly," said Donnelly as he resumed his seat, "that you have backers in the United States. I represent them, as well as Francis Bannerman, Dr. Richard Gatling and . . . others. There is the Harp In The South Committee in New York, with a distant cousin of yours at its head. . . ."

"A distant cousin of mine, Major Donnelly?"

"Yes. Colonel William Cody, better known, perhaps, as Buffalo Bill. He is interested in what you are attempting to do in this country of yours. He is a romantic. . . ." He looked around the table. "As are we all."

"Speak for yourself, Major," I muttered.

"What did you say, Mr. Grimes?"

"You heard me."

Donnelly laughed. "But then, with that name, you aren't one of us, are you?"

"Neither am I," remarked the Countess quietly.

It was Kelly's turn to laugh. "But ye're one o' us by marriage, Kitty me girl. For all yer fancy German title ye're Mrs. Kelly. We'll have to find a colleen for Grimes to marry so that he's one o' the family. . . ."

I looked at Kate, sitting across the table from me. She looked back. She smiled a little scornfully and shook her head.

There was an interruption. A Mrs. Haggerty, one of the wives of whom there were now several in the camp, came in with a big tray upon which there was a huge, steaming teapot, sugar bowl, milk jug and mugs. She was followed by Mary O'Dea, a pretty, red-haired, unmarried girl, with fresh-baked scones, butter and a tin of jam. The refreshments were set down with a clatter and the women, obviously in awe of the visitor, departed. I heard one of them whisper to the other, "A Yankee gineral come to see our Ned. . . . Things is lookin' up. . . ."

So rumors start.

Donnelly looked at the tea things.

"Would there by anything stronger?" he asked.

Kelly looked at Kate, Kate sighed audibly, pushed back her chair and stalked out of the hut. When she returned she was followed by Mary O'Dea, who carried a tray on which were brandy and rum bottles, a water jug and an assortment of unmatched glasses.

The serious talking did not start until mugs and tumblers had been filled and pipes and cigars ignited and drawing well. I took brandy and water myself. (The sun was as nearly over the yardarm as made no difference.) I was pleased that Mary had had the sense to fill the water jug from one of the big canvas water coolers. It was far from being ice water and there was a definitely organic flavor but it was, nonetheless, considerably less than lukewarm. I helped myself to a scone, split it and applied butter and jam. I wished, not for the first time, that Ned, on one of his "shopping trips," would lay in something else than plum-and-apple. . .

"If ye can listen with yer mouth full, Johnny," said Ned, "I'll fill ye in. Major Donnelly, here, represents the government of the United States."

"Not officially, Mr. Kelly," said Donnelly. "Not officially."

"You're here for the U.S. Army, Major?" I asked.

"I hold my commission," he told me, "in the New York State National Guard. Not the Army. But I have contacts. If you must know, I am on the payroll of Francis Bannerman of Broadway, New York." He took a hearty swig of neat rum. "You must have heard of Frankie, even here at the bottom of the world."

"The second-hand arms dealer," I said.

"That is how he started," Donnelly admitted. "But you, sir, are hardly in a position to sneer at second-hand arms. How many previous owners has that precious carronade of yours had? By whom has it been fired, at whom has it been fired? Oh, it is still a good gun. I could buy it from you at a price that you would consider generous and still resell it at a good profit . . ."

"I'm not sellin' my artillery," growled Kelly. "An will ye come to the point?"

Donnelly refilled his glass. "Very well, Mr. Kelly. As Mr. Grimes has said, Francis Bannerman is famous as a dealer in second-hand arms. But I have been trying to persuade him that there could be more money in new— and when I say new I mean *new*—weaponry . . ."

"But rebels," I said, "can't afford such until they become the government and start printing their own money."

"I've already told you," he said, "that the Irish in the U.S. of A. are behind you and are raising money. And there is talk of volunteers. . . . D'ye know, I might even be among such some day."

His speech was beginning to become slurred. He would have been wiser, I thought, to have stuck with tea.

"But I'm too valuable to Frankie. His ideas merchant, he calls me. 'Frankie,' I said to him, 'Frankie, you're making *pennies* selling arms to raggedy-arsed South American revolutionaries so as they can fight today's battles with yesterday's weapons. What you should do is make millions of dollars selling arms to governments so as they can fight today's battles with tomorrow's weapons.' Get me?"

"But we are not yet a government, Major," said Kelly.

"Neither was Georgie Washington when he started fighting his little War of Independence. But the French trusted him, didn't they? And he made good."

"But these *new* weapons you're talking about," I persisted. "They're bound to be hellishly expensive, at first, anyhow. Surely your Mr. Bannerman, and the people he's representing, like Gatling, would have taken them first to the established governments. They're the ones who have the money."

He glared at me. "D'ye think we haven't tried that? That *I* haven't tried that? But they're stick-in-the-muds, all of them. And even with the . . . the conventional stuff, you English colonies are all the same. Your armies an' navies, such as they are, can use arms only if they've been approved by *and* supplied through Mother England. And as for your politicians—they're even worse than ours, an' that's slobbering a bibful! I know. I was out here last year. An' what was I told by some stuffy colonel commanding one of the volunteer regiments?" He put on a not very good parody of an English upper class voice. " 'Warfare, my good man, is a matter for soldiers, not for engineers!' "

"Tell Mr. Grimes about the weapons you're trying to peddle, Major," said Kelly. "I'd like to be hearin' his opinion of 'em."

"Very well, sir. A Gatling gun operated not by a man turning a handle but by its own little steam engine. Bigger calibre. Faster rate of fire. An' a steam engine doesn't get tired. . . ."

"An' where're ye gettin' all the steam from?" asked Joe Byrne. He then made a coarse suggestion and wilted under Kate Kelly's glare.

I said thoughtfully, "Such guns could be fitted aboard ships. Steamships—or even sailing vessels, as long as they had a good donkey boiler. . . . But we don't have any ships.

Yet, I thought.

"What about trains?" asked Kelly. "*Armored* trains. . . ." (He had a fixation on armor.) "Yes, a train. An armored train, with an extra locomotive along for the steam for the guns . . . I'll have to have a word wi' Reardon about it . . . An' armored trucks for the horses, with a ramp, so the cavalry could come chargin' out for the moppin' up. . . ."

"But why horses?" asked Donnelly. "There's a lot of work being done in the States on steam traction engines that can get across almost any sort of country. And fast."

"Armored traction engines!" scoffed Kelly. "Now ye're talkin' nonsense!"

"Talking nonsense, ye say? I'm not. An' I'm tellin' you, now, that we've more than steam guns an' traction engines to offer. At a price, of course, at a price. . . ."

"Then what have ye got?" demanded Joe Byrne in a *put up or shut up* sort of voice.

"What have ye got?" echoed Hart.

Donnelly spoke slowly and carefully, endeavoring to give the impression of sobriety.

He said, "We, Francis Bannerman that is, have the honor to represent Mr. Solomon Andrews, son of the famous inventor Dr. Solomon Andrews. Dr. Andrews willed to his son his patent on the Aereon. . . ."

"The Aereon?" asked Kelly.

"Yes, sir. The Aereon. A flying ship. It flew, Mr. Kelly. It flew. But old Dr. Andrews could gain no support either from the military or from commercial interests. Perhaps if Mr. Lincoln had lived . . . *He* was interested in the Aereon, but the assassin's bullet removed him from this world before he could issue the orders for the construction and launching of the world's first flying fleet. . . ."

I thought that Donnelly was about to cry into his rum.

"A flying ship!" Ned Kelly was laughing so hard that he sloshed his own drink all over the table "Now ye are havin' us on, Major Donnelly!"

"He is not, Ned," said Red Kitty quietly. "When I was a small girl, seven years old or so, my parents visited New York, taking me with them. One day there was excitement. I remember it very well. People were running out into the streets, looking up into the sky and pointing. And there *it* was. No, it was not a balloon. It was like two fat cigars, side by side, with a long car hanging below them. I could see people in the car. And the ship was soaring and swooping, flying in circles . . ."

"Just blowin' wi' the wind, Kitty," said Ned. "Like balloons always do. I've seen a balloon, ye know."

"It was not just blowing with the wind, Ned. It was flying against the wind, across the wind. There was a long flag, a streamer, flying from the back of the car. It was standing straight out, not hanging limply."

"Ye actually saw this, Kitty?" demanded Kelly.

"I did."

"And so did I, lady," said Donnelly, looking at her almost with affection. "And so did I. It must have been on the same day."

"It's a small world, isn't it?" I remarked.

"Niver mind yer cheap philosophy, Johnny," growled Kelly. "Jist tell us what ye make o' this . . . thing. Ye're the expert on ships, sailin' ships. I know that ye can tack, as ye call it, beat to windward. Could a flyin' ship do the same?"

My great grandfather did not know the answer—but I, in his mind, did. He thought, *I don't think that it could be done, tacking a balloon like a ship. . . .*

I thought, *You're right, up to a point. . .*

I felt his emotions, something between mere uneasiness and stark terror.

You again! *Who are you? Where are you from?* Then, *My God, am I going mad?*

I thought, *Don't worry. It will all come right in the end.
You have my word for that. Believe me, I know.*

Kate Kelly inquired sweetly, "Cat got your tongue,
Johnny?"

I said, "I'm trying to reason this out . . ." (Actually I
was trying to remember what I had read about the early
Andrews airships, the ones relying upon the juggling of
buoyancy and ballast rather than the compression and
decompression of the gas cells.) I turned to Donnelly.
"I'm just kicking ideas around, Major, to see if they yelp
. . . Let's try this on for size . . . The Aereon, as Dr.
Andrews called it, sort of glides through the air. . . .
There are seabirds, you know, that cover enormous dis-
tances just by gliding. . . . Anyhow, at the start of a flight
the airship has positive buoyancy, with all the weight,
crew and disposable ballast, at the after end of the car . . .
It will be, as we would say at sea, down by the stern . . .
When the moorings are slipped it won't go straight up like
an ordinary balloon . . . It will glide up, at an angle, steep
or shallow according to the trim . . ."

"Go on, Mr. Grimes," said Donnelly.

"When it—how shall I put it?—when it reaches its
ceiling gas is valved and the trimming weight shifted
forward. The ship then has negative buoyancy and glides
downward. The steeper the angle, the higher the speed.
And so on, and so on, as long as there's ballast to jettison
and gas to valve. And at all times you'll have steerage way.
You'll be making way through the air as a surface ship
makes way through the water . . ."

"You sure know your onions, Mr. Grimes," said the
major. Then, with sudden suspicion, "But how do you
know all that? It's . . . s'posed to be secret . . ."

"The principles of shiphandling," I said, with not quite
sober pomposity, "are essentially the same in any medium."

"Listen to who's swallowed the dictionary," gibed Kate.

Her brother looked at me. "Between the three o' ye,"
he said, "you, Kitty an' the Major, ye've almost convinced
me that the Andrews contraption would fly. But you'd
never get *me* up in one of those things."

CHAPTER 28

We had dinner in the headquarters hut—a huge roast of beef with boiled potatoes, a plum pudding for afters, all of it washed down with hot, sweet, milky tea. (Donnelly despised this latter, and said so, and stuck to rum.) It was not, by today's standards, at all a suitable meal to be eaten just after noon on a hot summer day but we all, with the possible exception of Red Kitty, enjoyed it. She was still not used to having to fight the flies for her food. She said irritably, "Don't you think, Ned, that you could have some muslin, or something similar, put up at the doors and windows?"

"See to it, Kate," said Kelly to his sister.

"Anything at all to oblige Her Ladyship," replied Kate. If her look had been lethal the other woman would have died on the spot and Ned would have been *hors de combat* for at least a month.

Kelly filled and lit his pipe, sat back in his chair. "Get this mess cleared away, Kate, will ye?" he said.

Kate said nothing—her silence was more eloquent than words—but got up from the table and stalked out of the hut. She returned with Mrs. Haggerty and Mary O'Dea. She resumed her seat while the two women removed the debris of the meal. She condescended to accept a slim cigar—a peace ofering?—from the countess and sat sulkily smoking.

Donnelly, speaking around his own cigar, a fat one, said, "Thank you for an excellent meal, Mr. Kelly."

" 'Tis Kate ye should be thankin', Major. She's in charge o' such matters. She's my—" he fumbled for words "my commissariat officer. Would that be right?"

"It would, Mr. Kelly." Donnelly hiccupped loudly. "It would. Quite an organization you have here. A commissariat officer . . ." He took the cigar from his mouth and pointed it at me. "And a gunnery officer. *And*, as I discovered when I made my first contacts in Melbourne, a very, very efficient intelligence service . . ."

"The people, my own people, are behind me," said Kelly proudly.

"But they're . . . *little* people," Donnelly said. He added hastily, "Don't be getting me wrong, Mr. Kelly. They're the salt of the earth. They're my people as well as yours. Is mine an English name? It isn't, any more than yours is. But it's the *big* boys we're needing on our side." He lowered his voice, speaking confidentially. "Mr. Garfield is interested in what is happening here, down under. Don't let it go any farther, Mr. Kelly, but before I came out here I was called to the White House. We had a talk, Mr. Kelly, the President and I. Quite a talk. . . ."

"So ye're hintin' that I can expect help from your country?"

Donnelly looked at Kelly owlishly. I think that he had suddenly realized that a surfeit of rum had loosened his tongue.

He said, speaking slowly and carefully, "I made no hints, Mr. Kelly."

"But you did, Major Donnelly," said Red Kitty. She smiled dazzlingly at him. "But it is nothing to be ashamed of. We are all friends here. I, as you know, am neither Australian nor of Irish descent—and yet I have espoused the just cause of Ned and his people."

"You have, lady, you have," Donnelly almost whispered. "You have, and I respect you for it."

"And is your Mr. Garfield to give *us* cause for respect?" she asked.

He said, "I am not an accredited envoy."

"But you have talked with the President and his advisers.

Tell us, should we receive help from the United States, even though it is no more than the turning of a blind eye to arms shipments and even the raising of an army of volunteers, what is the *quid pro quo*?"

"The *what*, lady?"

"What is in it for you? For America, I mean, rather than for you, personally, and your employer, Mr. Bannerman?"

The major sat lumpishly, still staring at the countess, his cigar smouldering, forgotten, on the table before him.

Then he said, "All right. I'll spill the beans. The U.S. of A. is a Pacific Rim nation. So is Canada. So is Australia. And we're all of us white men's nations. We have a common enemy. The Asiatic hordes."

"The Yellow Peril," put in Byrne. "The Chinese."

"No, Mr. Byrne. Not the Chinese. The Japanese. They are clever—and treacherous. Mark my words, all of you! In years to come they will burst out of their little islands to attempt to conquer the world. And who will have to stop them? The *white* Pacific Rim nations, that's who. Canada. Australia. The United States."

"So you want Australia to become part of the American Empire, Major?" asked Red Kitty interestedly.

"We are not imperialists, lady," said Donnelly stiffly.

"I wish that I could believe you, sir. Our struggle is against British imperialism. Are we to win this fight only at the cost of being swallowed up by a greater and even more ruthless empire?"

He looked at her reproachfully and said, "We do not want dominions, lady. Only strong and loyal allies."

"So you say. But, tell me, how are the arms that you have almost promised us to be paid for? Oh, I know that your Colonel Cody and his people have been raising money—enough, no doubt, to pay for second-hand rifles and Gatling guns. But what about the new, improved Gatlings? What about the Andrews flying ships? They will be *very* expensive, will they not?"

He said, incautiously, "Australia is a rich country, your ladyship. Or a potentially rich country."

"And so," put in Kate, "we've to mortgage ourselves up to the hilt to pay for these new-fangled toys".

Kelly growled. He knew all about mortgages. He had

torn them up, on more than one occasion, when he had found them among other documents in the strongrooms of the banks that he had robbed.

He said heavily, "I think, Major, that ye should be payin' *us* for tryin' out yer new toys for ye . . ."

I said, "Why not? After all, it's quite obvious. The conservative admirals and generals won't touch the new weapons with a bargepole—but there are younger, less hide-bound officers who'd like to see them tried out of somebody else's country in somebody else's war. Why shouldn't we get free samples?"

Everybody stared at me.

Then Donnelly laughed. "Why not?" he asked. "Why not? Frankie Bannerman has never given out free samples yet—but there's a first time for everything. I'll tell you what. Once you people get your paws on to a steamship or a locomotive you'll get a free trial of the steam-operated Gatlings. And, meanwhile, the first shipment of second-hand arms, already paid for by the Harp In The South Committee, will soon be on its way to you."

"But we do not yet hold a seaport," said Kelly. "And, as Johnny is always after remindin' me, the ships of the English Navy control our seas."

"I'm sure that your Mr. Grimes," Donnelly told him, "has heard of crates marked AGRICULTURAL MACHINERY that have contained another kind of ironmongery."

"I have," I admitted. "And I've carried such crates. Once from New York to some Godforsaken river port in South America. One slipped from its sling as it was being discharged and broke open when it hit the wharf. There was all hell let loose. We were lucky that we, the ship's crew, didn't all finish up in jail."

"We'll all of us be lucky", said Kate somberly, "if we all don't finish up in jail—or worse. Oh, 'twas a nice little risin' we had while we had it all to ourselves—but now, wi' all these outsiders buttin' in, it's gettin' out o' hand. Your mob, Major Donnelly. I din't like it at all, at all. Haven't ye heard the old sayin'? He who sups wi' the Devil needs a long spoon."

"You're not calling Uncle Sam the Devil!" snarled Donnelly.

"Many have called him that," said Red Kitty sweetly. "I have little doubt that many more will do so in the future. But there are times when one welcomes help from the Devil himself."

"As I do!" almost shouted Ned. "D'ye think I *like* bein' an outlaw when I was born for better things? D'ye think I like havin' no better home to offer me wife than this slab hut? If Old Nick offers to get me a palace for ye, Kitty girl, that's an offer I'll be takin'—an' to hell wi' the price!"

"An' what if he offers to have ye crowned King, Ned?" asked Joe Byrne sardonically. "Will ye make the deal? An' then will ye be makin' all o' us Dukes an' Duchesses, same as Napoleon did for all his friends an' relations after he'd crowned himself Emperor?" He stared rudely at Red Kitty. "A Duchess is higher than a Countess isn't she, Your Ladyship?"

"She is," Kitty replied icily. "But I have no wish to become a Duchess. And Ned has no desire to become King—although I have no doubt at all that he will become President."

"From Log Cabin to White House," I murmured.

Donnelly glared at me and said, "That was not funny, Mr. Grimes."

"It was not meant to be, Major. But Mr. Kelly will be no more improbable a President than some who have held that high office in your country."

Joe Byrne sloshed brandy and water into his glass. He got unsteadily to his feet.

"Ladies an' gentlemen an' . . . an' our distinguished guest. I give ye a toast. To Ned Kelly, President of the United States of Australia!"

We drank the toast.

I knew, of course, that the toast would come true.

And Red Kitty knew too, in her own way. In another era she would have aimed for the presidency herself. But in the nineteenth century, she would have to be content to be First Lady.

The power behind the throne.

CHAPTER 29

Ned and Red Kitty had gone into their bedroom and
Donnelly was sleeping it off in one of the tents and Steve
Hart and Joe Byrne were continuing the party in the main
mess hut with others of the men and a few of the women.
I could have joined them but did not. I still was not one of
them; now and again I had overheard myself referred to as
"Ned's pet limey." Only Kelly and Reardon seemed fully
to have accepted me.

So I was standing by the carronade, enjoying the breeze
that had sprung up with the setting of the sun, smoking
my pipe and hoping that the fumes of burning tobacco
would act as a deterrent to the mosquitoes and other
flying pests.

I was joined by Kate. It was still light enough for me to
see that she was in a bad temper about something. She
gestured toward the mess hut from which came the sound
of drunken singing, the Kelly version of the "Wild Colonial Boy."

She said, "There'll be a fine old mess in there come
mornin'—dirty plates an' glasses, broken bottles, an' worse.
An' who'll be havin' to clear it up? Not Her Ladyship,
that's for sure. Me, that's who."

"You've women for that sort of work, Kate."

"But who has to drive the lazy, slatternly sluts? No. If
't'wasn't for me this camp'd be more of a pig sty than 'tis

already." She produced a pipe of her own, filled and lit it. She leaned back against the barrel of the gun. "An' it sure has some odd pigs in it these days. . . . A German countess. A Yankee officer who's also a hard talkin' salesman. An', in case ye think ye're bein' left out, *you*. . . ."

I said, "I suppose it is a bit odd finding an English seaman in this outfit."

"There's nothin' odd in yer bein' a seaman or a limey. It's *you* that's odd. These queer expressions ye come out with every now an' again. Not all the time, but . . . Her Ladyship's noticed it too." She laughed. "We do talk a bit when Ned's not around. . . ."

"All girls together," I said.

"Like I was sayin'. These queer expressions o' yours, this . . . this *new* way with words. An' ye seem to know so much about other things. Like when ye were tellin' us how the Andrews flying ship works."

"I must have read about it somewhere," I told her.

"In the cards? In a crystal ball?"

"In a book." (That was truthful enough insofar as my twentieth century personality was concerned).

"An' did this book o' yours tell ye how all this is goin' to come out?"

I said, "There's no such book."

She pushed herself away from the carronade, drew herself to her full height and stood facing me. Her face was no more than a pale blur in the dusk but her wide mouth was darkly vivid. Her eyes seemed to gleam like those of a cat.

"But there will be a book, won't there? Somebody'll be writin' the history o' these troublous times. I wish I could catch just a glimpse o' the pages."

And what would she read?

The few years of not overly successful show business, I thought, after Ned's execution. . . . Then marriage and parenthood, settling down. . . . And then, after the stupid exposure of her wild past by a traveling showman, the lonely death by drowning. . . .

But that was on another Time Track and, besides, the wench was dead.

Not yet she wasn't.

She said, "Ye know, ye English bastard, but ye're not tellin'."

I asked, "How could I know?"

"But ye do. An' what's yer price for tellin'?" She smiled dazzlingly, even in this dim light. "Ye must have a price. All men have a price—all men that are men, that is . . . D'ye think I didn't notice ye makin' sheep's eyes 'cross the table at me while we were havin' dinner?"

She was very close to me now, our bodies almost in contact. I could smell her, the scent of young, healthy womanhood, the not unpleasant tang of female perspiration. Almost without conscious volition I put an arm about her. She did not resist. I put the other arm about her and—foolishly, perhaps, began to have doubts. After all, she was Ned Kelly's sister—and Ned, in the past, had dealt harshly with Kate's suitors. But there was nobody to see us; those who were not at the party in the mess hut must be sleeping, possibly even the lookout at the top of the wooden watchtower. Even if he were awake and alert he would need night glasses to see us—and it would be many decades before such things were invented.

As I have said, I put my arms about her. I was pleasantly surprised. I was expecting to feel the resistance of female armor-plating, a whalebone-stiffened corset, but there was only resilient softness. I brought my mouth down to hers. We kissed warmly—and then, abruptly, she pulled away from me.

She said, "Ye stink, Johnny . . ."

I thought that she was using the words in the metaphorical sense and asked, in an offended voice, "How so?"

"When did ye last wash yer shirt?"

"I've been busy lately."

"When did ye last wash yourself?"

I tried to remember, rummaging through my great-grandfather's memories. I came to the conclusion that he had conformed altogether too readily to the mores of those among whom his lot had been cast. To seamen, cooped up together aboard a ship, personal cleanliness is important. To landsmen, especially landsmen of a certain class, it is not.

"Come on!" she said.

I followed her.

She did not lead me, as I had been expecting that she would do, to the small hut that was her living quarters but toward the stockade. Just to one side of the main entrance, now, of course, closed there was a gap between two logs, barely wide enough for anybody of slim build to squeeze through. More than once I had pointed this out to Ned, saying that it was a weak spot in our defenses. He had laughed, saying that it would be fun to pick off the hated coppers as they squirmed through, one by one.

It was to this gap that Kate took me.

She was the first to wriggle through. I followed her. Sure footedly she was making her way down the rough path toward the stream. The moon was coming up and there was light enough for us to see our way, to avoid major obstacles. We reached the bank, at the point where the rivulet widened into what was almost a small but shallow lake. I stopped to stare at Kate. She stood there, unembarrassed, slipping out of her white blouse and then loosening the fastenings of her long, black skirt, letting this garment fall about her feet. Her bodice was next to be removed and then, rather awkwardly hopping from one foot to the other, she stepped out of her long, frilly knickers. She was naked then, save for her gartered black stockings and high, lace-up boots. To the twentieth century me the spectacle was as incongruous as erotic—a Playboy Femlin in this day and age!

She whispered, "What are ye gawkin' at? Have ye never seen a woman before as God made her?"

(The last time, in great-grandfather's memory, had been in a waterfront brothel in Santiago).

She sat down on her spread-out skirt.

"Help me to get me boots off," she ordered.

I squatted down at her feet, busied myself with laces. As a seaman I was used to dealing with cordage in poor light or no light at all. It was as well, as I was not watching what my fingers were doing. I was looking at her as she sat there, her body palely luminous against the black material of her skirt, against the dark bushes in the background. In this light her nipples seemed as black as the luxuriant growth at the jointure of her thighs.

I pulled the boot from her right foot, and then did the same for the left one. Then I put out my hands to a stocking top and she waved them away.

"Ye're not touchin' me," she said, "till ye're clean."

Herself she rolled the stockings down her strong, fine, white legs and then she sprang to her feet, running down to the little beach that was more mud than sand. She fell forward into the water and then began striking out for the opposite bank. I could see the pale glimmer of her limbs and body under the surface as she swam.

She turned over to swim on her back, lazily, only just keeping herself afloat.

"Come on," she called. "Come on! Are ye afraid o' the water, an' ye a sailor?"

As a matter of fact I was. In those days very few seamen could swim. If one fell overboard from a sailing ship the chances of being picked up were extremely slim and swimming ability would only prolong the agony of one's passing.

But who was in charge here—myself or great-grandfather?

I tore off my shirt—a button went, but perhaps I could persuade Kate to sew on another—then unbuckled my belt and let my trousers fall. I could not, of course, pull them past my heavy boots so there was more delay. Finally I was stripped and wading out after Kate. The water was almost warm, just cool enough to be refreshing. I let myself fall forward and, although part of my mind experienced very real terror, my arms and legs struck out in the motions remembered from another century, from a hundred years in the future.

I was a faster swimmer than Kate—she had yet to learn anything better than the breast stroke—and soon overtook her. But she evaded my clutching hand easily enough, turned and started back to where we had come from. I kept pace beside her.

We found our footing, began to wade out to the bank. I couldn't keep my eyes off her.

Then, "Stop," she ordered. "Where ye are. Sit yerself down."

"Why, Kate?"

"Just do as I say."

So I sat down, the bottom soft but slightly gritty under

my bare buttocks. She squatted beside me, scooped up a double handful of the sandy mud, began to scrub my back with it. The texture was as greasy as it was gritty. Undeniably I was enjoying this. Both of me were enjoying it. Then, when she was done with me, I attended to her, my hands lingering on her firm breasts with their erect nipples, straying between her open thighs. Her own hands were bold in their caresses. At last we went back, briefly, into the deeper water to rinse off. Hand in hand, we made our way up the bank to where we had left our clothing. She stretched herself out on her spread out skirt, opened herself to me, knees lifted. I lowered myself on to her. My mouth found hers and while we were kissing her hands found me, guided me in.

And then the mosquitoes found us.

Oh, we managed, despite the pests, spreading my clothing on the rough grass and using her skirt and underwear to cover us. It was not as good as it should have been, perhaps, but it was good.

And then she whispered, "I've paid you, Johnny, haven't I? Tell me, what is in the book? About me?"

"There is no book'" I insisted.

"But there is . . . Perhaps not somethin' made o' paper an' bound in leather, but. . . . There are men an' women who can read the futures an' I think ye're one o' them."

"Kate," I told her, "when Ned goes to Melbourne to raid the jail, to rescue Ellen, don't go with him."

"But I must, Johnny. I must. She's me mother as much as she's Ned's. But what's this about a raid on Melbourne Jail?"

I said carefully, "I think that there will be one."

I *had* read about it, of course, in one of the histories of the War of Independence. The author of this work had not considered Kate Kelly to be of any great importance, had just mentioned in an offhand sort of way that she had died during the raid. He didn't even bother to say how.

"And about time. An' Ellen? What about her?"

"She'll be all right."

(But she wouldn't be. She would mourn the death of Kate and hate Ned's foreign wife with her foreign, atheistical ideas.)

"An' me?"

"You might get killed."

"An' so might we all, mightn't we? Isn't this a war we're fightin'—not that there's been much fightin' of late."

Suddenly she seemed to believe no longer in my alleged ability to foresee the future. Her mouth was busy again, and her hands, and it was quite some time before we resumed our clothing and walked slowly back to the stockade. We re-entered the camp unobserved, despite the now bright moonlight.

Poor Kate, I wish that she had taken my advice—but what would have been the effects? It is probable that what had started that night would have gone on, and gone on, and even though there were contraceptive techniques in those days they weren't all that reliable.

But suppose I had been trapped, as the saying goes, into marriage. . . .

Suppose Kate Kelly had become my great-grand-mother. . . .

Then I shouldn't be me.

Quite possibly I wouldn't have happened at all.

And then would the train of history have been shunted on to a different track at Glenrowan?

CHAPTER 30

The next morning Ned called a conference of his officers. Red Kitty was there, of course. So was Kate. And Donnelly, looking very much the worse for wear, was present as an observer.

Ned sat at the head of the table.

"Ladies and gentlemen," he said with grave formality, "I have called ye here to discuss a matter of great importance. I'm thinkin' that the major, here, needs proof that we're more than a band of outlaws. He should have a story that he can take back to New York, to Colonel Cody and the Harp in the South Committee, to Francis Bannerman, and others. We must show that we have the strength to strike at will . . ."

"Who's Will?" asked Joe Byrne.

Nobody laughed and Kelly froze the would-be jester with an icy glare.

"We must show that we have the ability to strike at will," he went on. "That we have the ability to deliver a blow at the very fortress of the rulers of this State. And that we have supporters in the capital who will assist us, who will fight by our side. I needn't be tellin' ye that my good friends—*our* good friends—in Melbourne are keepin' me informed as to the feelin' in the city. People are thinkin'—as we're thinkin'—that there're men and women in Melbourne Jail who should never be there. I have kept my plans secret until now. But, this very morning, I get word from Fergus O'Connor that all is in readiness. . . ." He produced a crumpled letter from his shirt pocket and spread it out on the table. "There will be the riot in and around Russell Street and, if all goes well, the blowin' in o' the prison doors wi' blastin' powder. An' that's when *we* come ridin' in, to snatch me mother, an' others, to bring them back here. . . ."

"We'll not be doin' much gallopin'," said Byrne, "after we've ridden our nags all the way from here to Melbourne."

"We shall be takin' the train into the city from Wangaratta," said Kelly. "Fergus'll have horses waitin' for us at Spencer Street Station. As for gettin' back here we shall have to take our time, campin' in the bush, avoidin' towns an' villages where there'll be police an' rats wantin' to make a few guineas informin' on us."

"People know us in Wangaratta," objected Byrne. "D'ye think that when we walk into the railway station to buy our tickets that a hue an' cry won't be raised?"

"Have ye never heard o' disguises, Joe?" asked Kelly. "Take off that beard o' yours—an' who'll be recognizin' you?"

"An' are ye takin' *your* beard off, Ned?"

"I'm havin' it trimmed. One o' those neat, pointy jobs."

"T'is like a German count ye'll be lookin'," growled Byrne sourly. "An' will ye be wearin' a monocle?"

Kelly considered this seriously. The idea seemed to appeal to him.

"No," he said at last. "T'would be interferin' wi' me aim."

"You think you can pull this off, Mr. Kelly?" asked Major Donnelly.

"Why not, major? Get a good riot goin' an' in the general confusion a few strong, determined men can do what they set out to be doin'. Fergus'll be runnin' the riot; I'll be runnin' the rescues."

"I'd like to come with you," said the American. "If you'll have me, that is."

"Why not?" Kelly said.

"Is that wise, Ned?" asked Red Kitty. "Is that wise, Major Donnelly? There will be shooting. There could be casualties. And if an American citizen is among those injured, or killed, there could be international repercussions."

Donnelly laughed. "There were plenty of outsiders involved in *our* War of Independence, lady. The German mercenaries on the British side. French volunteers, like Lafayette, on ours. But I shall just be along as an observer."

"Bearing arms?"

He said, "I always carry samples of my employer's wares. Which reminds me, Mr. Kelly, when can I have my Navy Colts back? I feel kinda naked without them."

"You shall have 'em back, Major, when we leave this camp for Wangaratta."

"Is that wise, Ned?" asked Byrne. "Shootin' in the back is rather a favorite pastime in the U.S.A."

"Ye've got to trust somebody some time," Kelly told him. "And now, Joe, I want ye to select six volunteers, good men, to come with you, the major an' myself to Melbourne. Fergus has promised to have a dozen horses waitin' for us at Spencer Street. One for each o' us an' three spares. . . ."

"Can Ellen ride a horse?" I asked.

"Better'n ye can, Johnny. Ye'll niver make a horseman, Johnny. That's why I'm leavin' ye here, in charge o' the camp. Apart from anythin' else ye're the only one who knows how to fire the gun."

"So if Johnny's in charge here," said Kate, "there'll be no need for me to hang around like a bad smell. Make that five volunteers, Joe, not six. I'll be ridin' wi' Ned."

"Make it *four* volunteers, Mr. Byrne," said Red Kitty. "Did you think that I would be left out?"

"Kate . . ." I began, looking at her.

"Kitty . . ." began Ned, looking at the countess.

"Kate," I said, "I wish you wouldn't. . . ."

"Don't be interferin', Johnny," said Ned. "This is a family matter. Kate's a Kelly, isn't she? 'T is a proud name an' she's a credit to it. I'd sooner have her behind me than many a man." He frowned suddenly. "An' what's it to you whether Kate rides with me or not?"

"He has these English ideas 'bout a woman's proper

place," sneered Kate before I could answer, before, with my reply, I could incriminate myself. And her.

"But as ye've said, brother, I'm a Kelly. An' proud of it. If our mither's to be rescued I want a part of it."

"And I am a Kelly too," said Red Kitty. "By marriage. I am coming with you. After all, I have ridden with you on other raids."

"Not like this one'll be, Kitty girl. Wi' mobs in the streets an' guns firin'. Melbourne'll be like a hornets' nest. . . ."

"With ourselves as the most vicious hornets of all, Ned. I am coming with you."

And that, most obviously, was that.

"I wonder," asked Major Donnelly plaintively, breaking the silence, "if I might have a hair of the dog that bit me last night?"

CHAPTER 31

That night, when the camp was quiet, Kate and I went down again to the billabong. Again we swam. Again we made love, despite the attentions of the hungry mosquitoes.

And then she said, "Ye were right, Johnny, about the raid on Melbourne Jail. But I must go. 'Tis as though me doom's upon me. 'Tis as though I was a . . ." she searched for a metaphor ". . . a railway engine, wi' no option but to keep to the rails laid down for me. . . ."

"But you don't *have* to go!" I almost shouted.

"But I do, Johnny, I do. But I'll be careful, darlin', I promise ye."

"You—careful, Kate? Don't make me laugh."

"I'm wishin' that I could make ye laugh. All day 'tis been as though ye were goin' to a funeral. . . ." She got slowly to her feet and stood there in the moonlight, tall, proud and naked. She rather spoiled the effect by swatting at a mosquito that had alighted on her left breast. "Shall I let ye into a secret, Johnny? Shall I tell ye why I *must* go with Ned to Melbourne now? 'Tis because *she's* goin'. She's only a Kelly woman by marriage—an' I'm one by birth. 'Tis a matter o' pride, Johnny. Family pride. Ye don't have much o' that in England, do ye, 'less ye're one o' the aristocracy. In Ireland we're all aristocrats, wi' royal blood in our veins . . . We all of us have the . . . the obligation to do what we must do."

"There's nobody says that you must go to Melbourne."

"And nobody," she flared, "that says that I mustn't. Not even you."

I remained sprawled on the ground and kept my silence. How much was selfishness, the urge for self-preservation, ego-preservation? I had discovered, that first time in Glenrowan, how tampering with the Past could result in a rewritten Future. Fantastically the essential *I* had not been changed, the chain of begettings had not been broken. But others, such as Duffin, had been affected.

"Cat got your tongue?" she demanded sharply.

"No, Kate."

"Then what d'ye have to say to me?"

I said, "If you want to go, you'll go."

"An' after all yer fancy talkin' aren't you goin' to beg me not to?"

Again I was silent.

I thought, *I'll promise you this, Kate. When I write the history, you'll be getting more than just a footnote.*

She said abruptly, "I must be gettin' some sleep. 'T'will be a heavy day tomorrow. Shift your carcass off me clothes, will ye?"

I got to my feet and watched her dress. By the time that I had resumed my own clothing she was halfway back to the stockade.

And that was it.

CHAPTER 32

That next morning—fine and clear, with the promise of heat to come—I watched them ride out from the camp.

Ned, in his fine black broadcloth and snowy linen, with his jacket open to display the gold watch chain looped across his waistcoat, could have been some prosperous farmer, even a member of the squatocracy. Oddly enough the trimming of his luxuriant beard had made him look older rather than younger. Byrne and Hart were now clean-shaven and they *did* look young. Hart, in his rather cheap finery, a loudly checked not very well fitting suit, was a corner boy on horseback, a mounted larrikin. Donnelly was clad in black but an air of flashiness was imparted by his white Stetson. (*So he thinks that he's one of the good guys* . . . I thought sourly.) He looked like what he was—a Yankee traveling salesman. The other men had the appearance of what they had been before enlistment under the Kelly banner—small, struggling farmers. Small, struggling farmers now attired in their poor best for a day in town.

Red Kitty I hardly recognized. I had become so used to seeing her in mannish attire that the sight of her—long-skirted, veiled, with a smart little hat almost hiding her glossy auburn hair, riding side-saddle—seemed altogether startling. She raised her riding crop to me in salute as she passed me, standing by the carronade. And then there was

Kate, bringing up the rear. She was as smartly attired as was her brother's wife, looked just as much the great lady.

"Look after yourself, Kate!" I called.

She reined in and sat there, looking down at me gravely. Her eyes, behind the short veil, were very bright.

"And you look after *your* self, Johnny, Don't go blowin' yerself up wi' that dirty great gun while I'm gone. . . ."

Ned turned and came riding back to us. I think that he was suspecting that there was something between Kate and myself and that he was actuated by brotherly jealousy.

"Come on, Kate," he said gruffly. "We've a train to catch. An' you, Johnny, try to keep things in order while I'm gone. I've told the boys they're to take orders from you. Don't let 'em go strayin' off into the bush or goin' out on raids o' their own." He laughed. "An' don't go firin' that cannon 'less ye absolutely have to. I know that ye're just itchin' to let the thing off!"

"I'll fire a twenty-one gun salute when you come back," I said.

"Ye'd better not. Where's the powder to come from?"

He turned and rode away, followed by the others.

"Good luck, Ned!" I called after him.

"Good luck!" came the shout from the other men and women left behind in the camp. There was a ragged cheer.

I leaned against the carronade and filled and lit my pipe. I was joined by Reardon.

"What would yer orders be, admiral?" he asked.

I snapped, "Don't call me that."

He laughed, "All the others are callin' ye that, Johnny boy, even if 't is only behind yer back."

"As long as they obey orders while Ned's away they can promote me all they like, I suppose."

"It's if Ned doesn't come back ye'll have to watch yerself. They hate ye, some o' them. Ye're English. Ye've been an officer. An' . . . An' . . ." A deep blush suffused his already ruddy face. "An' this business between you an' Miss Kate. . . ."

"What business?"

"D'ye think people don't know? This camp's like a small village but more so, if ye get my meanin'. Ye can't let off a fart in the middle o' the night without wakin' everybody up. There's them as would ha' been runnin' to Ned about your carryin's on but I've managed to keep 'em quiet. But ye'll have to watch yer step, both o' ye, once Ellen's here. She'll not stand for any tamperin' wi' her precious daughter."

I said, "Things will be . . . different."

He said, "They'd better be, Johnny."

I changed the subject. "Have you thought any more about making a proper carriage for this thing?"

He stood back so that he could look at the carronade.

"Yes, I've given the matter some thought, Johnny. But I have to get a pair o' wheels, somethin' like the wheels of a trap but heavier. They'll have to be strong. Ye've the weight o' the gun itself, an' then there'll be the recoil when ye fire it. If ye ever do fire it. I'm lookin' forward, meself, to gettin' some o' those fancy quick-firin' cannon that Donnelly promised us. The ones worked by little steam engines. . . ."

"And meanwhile," I said, "we have to make do with what we've got."

And then, accompanied by Reardon, I strolled away from the main gate of the stockade to make my morning rounds of the camp.

Things seemed to be more or less in order. The lookout was in his post on top of the crudely constructed wooden tower. The women were reasonably busy in the kitchen hut, preparing the midday meal. The mutton stew smelled savory enough but I wished that I could have had a luncheon of cold meats and salads to look forward to. Mrs. Haggerty noticed my expression and asked sharply, "Isn't yer lordship satisfied, then?"

"Everything's just fine, Mrs. Haggerty," I lied.

"An' why shouldn't it be, when I'm doin' the cookin'?"

To pacify her I sampled a ladleful of the stew straight from the pot and nodded my approval.

In other parts of the camp men were cleaning weapons and overhauling other equipment. I recalled what Donnelly had said about fighting today's battles with yesterday's arms. But that, in this day and age, wasn't such a grave disadvantage. It was only in the latter days of the twentieth century that military technology advanced at a gallop rather than a crawl.

Most of the men ignored me; only a few acknowledged my presence with a surly nod.

I said to Reardon, "I feel as popular as a pork chop in a synagogue."

He stared at me and then laughed loudly. "Ye do have a foine way wi' words, Johnny boy. I must remember that one."

We went into the hut in which our ammunition was stored, what there was of it. There were the cartridges for the fairly modern rifles and revolvers, a barrel of black powder for the muzzle loaders. I decided that it would do no harm to have the carronade loaded and ready for instant action and told Reardon of my intention.

"An' why not?" he asked. "It takes time to load one o' them things, doesn't it? Even wi' trained gunners—the like o' which we don't be havin' here."

I agreed. I looked around the store and found a small sack. As far as I could remember it was about the same size as the powder bags that we had used for loading our carronades while sailing off the China Coast. I filled it, using the wooden scoop that was handy by the powder barrel, secured its open end with a short length of ropeyarn. Accompanied by Reardon I carried it back to the gun. It went easily enough into the muzzle. I picked up the rammer, pushed the charge back as far as it would go. Shouldn't there be wadding? That could wait for later. An old shirt would do.

"An' what about a cannonball?" Reardon asked. "I didn't see any o' such in the shed."

"I didn't see any canister either," I told him, "but we'll make do."

Back in the arsenal—if so it could be called—I found another little sack. I took it to the hut that had been converted into a smithy. Our blacksmith, a sullen giant named O'Meary, ignored Reardon and myself while he shaped a red-glowing horseshoe on his anvil. Finally he was finished, picked up the artifact with his tongs, dipped it, hissing, into a bucket of water. He lifted it out, dropped it with a clatter on to the workbench.

He turned to look at us, at me.

"An' what are you wantin', admiral? Can't ye see I'm busy?"

"Do you have any metal scrap?" I asked. "Or old nails?"

"Old nails I have, admiral, but I'm usin' 'em. There's no hardware store just down the lane out here, ye know. Or hadn't ye noticed?"

"What about . . . this?" I stirred a little heap of rusty scrap in one corner of the shed with my boot. "Surely this is no use?"

"I could be usin' it some time."

"Mr. O'Meary," said Reardon, "Mr. Grimes could be usin' it very shortly. An' I'm remindin' you that Mr. Kelly left Mr. Grimes in charge while he's away in Melbourne."

"Mr. Grimes is not in charge o' this smithy. *I* am."

"Mr. Grimes is in charge of *everything*, until Mr. Kelly returns."

He took the bag from my hand, stooped down to fill it with the smaller pieces of scrap iron while O'Meary watched, glowering.

He asked, "An' will this do, Mr. Grimes?"

"It should be just the shot, Mr. Reardon. Of course, we should include a horseshoe, just for luck."

"Ye've got all ye're gettin'!" growled the blacksmith. "An' what ye want it for the blessed Lord alone knows . . ."

We loaded the carronade—an old shirt for wadding to hold the bag of powder in place, then the improvised canister shot. And then, with the assistance of a couple of loafers pressed into unwilling service, we camouflaged the weapon with bushes hacked off close to the roots. As we worked I wondered if this was the way that things actually had happened or if, once again, I was interfering with history, altering its course. (But my great-grandfather had known far more about carronades than I did and, I thought, it was his part of the shared mind that was now taking charge.)

And now all that I had to do was to await the return of Ned and his raiding party.

CHAPTER **33**

I was not expecting them back the following day; nonetheless I made sure that a good watch was kept and that the lookout tower was doubly manned. In spite of protests I insisted that this double manning be maintained throughout the night and all through the day again. I saw to it that rifles and shotguns and revolvers were kept loaded, ready for instant use at all times. Oh, they hated me, these undisciplined rebels, these anarchists—although, good sons of Mother Church that they were, they would have hotly protested against the attachment to them of that label. They hated me, not only because of my attempts to run a taut ship but because I was the foreigner, the outsider, a renegade representative of that race whom all good Irishmen have hated since Cromwell—and before. It was fortunate that one of their own, Reardon, had befriended me, was acting during this period as my lieutenant.

It was in the early afternoon of the fourth day that Kelly came back. The duty lookouts were efficient, despite the oppressive heat. One of them clanged the bell—looted from what chapel?—that had been hung from one of the stanchions of the watchtower canopy. The noise of the thing—it was more of a clatter than a chiming—brought us all out running, abandoning our half-finished meal to the flies.

I scampered up the ladder to the lookout platform.

There was no need for the men already there to point; I could see the two parties of horsemen approaching. I snatched the battered old telescope from one of the lookouts, steadied it against a stanchion, focused it. Yes, there, in the lead, was Ned—but he was not alone on his horse. In front of him was a woman, leaning to him, her arms about him. (It says much for his horsemanship that he was able to control his steed so hampered.) Kate? Red Kitty? No. This woman's uncovered, untidy hair was white. . . .

And the others. . . .

Red Kitty, although somehow, somewhere she had found time to change back into male attire . . . Joe Byrne . . . Steve Hart . . . Major Donnelly . . . Costello . . . Gilligan . . .

But no Kate. . . .

I turned the glass on to the pursuers.

There were police, blue-coated, white-trousered . . . There were troopers from one of the volunteer cavalry regiments in their scarlet and gold, their sabers drawn and brandished, flashing in the light of the sun that, at this moment, broke through the clouds.

I handed the telescope back to the lookout, fell rather than clambered down the ladder to the ground. Reardon had already got the main gate open so that Ned and his party could ride into the camp. It was unlikely that his men would be able to get it shut again before the police and the soldiers reached it. Riflemen were manning the stockade but could not yet risk opening fire, would not be able to do so until Kelly and his people were out of the way.

The police were not so hampered. They were shooting, the reports of their revolvers sounding no more dangerous than firecrackers. I did not think that they, firing from horseback, would be able to do much damage.

The spike was ready by the carronade, and the slowmatch and a little tin of black powder. I thrust the spike down the touch-hole to pierce the powder bag. I poured the priming powder into the hole. I lit the sputtering slowmatch and waited, to one side of the breech of the cannon, my view partially obstructed by my crude camouflage of bushes.

I could hear the thudding of the hooves, coming closer

and closer. They were laboring hard, both fugitives and pursuers. There was shouting. Some cavalry officer was shouting, in a very English voice, "Forward, boys, forward! Tallyhoo! Tallyhoo!"

Kelly was through, thundering past me and then reining to an abrupt halt. He roughly disengaged his mother, dropped her into Reardon's waiting arms, then dismounted himself. The others were through. Men were struggling with the heavy logs, trying to lift them back into place before the police and the soldiers reached the stockade.

"Leave it!" Kelly was roaring at them. "Leave it, ye ijits! Let the dog see the rabbit!"

(And I was the dog . . .)

Through the screen of leaves and twigs I could see the blue coats and the scarlet coats, the reflection of sunlight from brass and steel.

"Tallyhoo! Tallyhoo!" that English fool was still shouting.

And what would the spread of my home-made canister shot be?

It was a bullet from a police revolver that decided me. As far as I was concerned it was a near miss. It struck the little tin of priming powder. There was a sharp explosion just behind me and something—fragments of metal, I discovered later—stung my calves painfully. My hand, holding the slowmatch, came down. The powder in the touch-hole flared and, almost immediately, there was the roar of the main charge detonating. The screening foliage was swept away by the fiery gale and I saw the center of the line of charging horsemen disintegrate. I was deafened by the blast so I did not hear the screams—but Reardon told me later that it was the most dreadful sound that he had ever heard.

I heard nothing but I saw too much.

There was the riderless horse trying to run and then falling, its hooves entangled in its own trailing intestines. There was the young, blond moustached officer—the one who had been shouting "Tallyhoo! Tallyhoo!"—staggering forward on the stumps of his legs, still brandishing his sword, until a shot from one of the riflemen manning the stockade brought him down. There was the headless policeman still astride his miraculously uninjured but terrified steed, galloping away from the scene of the carnage.

There were the survivors.

Some came on and were mown down by the enfillading fire of the riflemen. Some turned to run—and of these at least half the number were swept from their saddles by rebel bullets.

There was the chase, when the vengeful Kelly and his men, on fresh mounts, came charging out from the camp.

But, even so, there were a few, police and cavalrymen, who made good their escape.

CHAPTER 34

And that was what the historians have called The Battle In The Bush.

It was a very small scale affair, little more than a skirmish. It was noteworthy in one respect: it was the first use by the rebel forces of artillery. That ancient carronade, a veteran of sea warfare, dragged across the country by bullockwagon, its first Australian owner a wealthy squatter who never had a chance to use it, its second Australian owner a very minor guerrilla chief who didn't know what to do with it, its third Australian owner the Kelly himself, fired the shot heard round the world.

When the shooting was over it was Joe Byrne who was in charge of the tidying up—the gathering of weapons and equipment from the bodies of police and cavalrymen, the putting out of their misery of badly wounded horses. Kelly, with his wife and his rescued mother, retired to his hut and did not emerge for the rest of that day. Major Donnelly joined me by the cannon, condescended to help me with the sponging out of the barrel and the preparation of the weapon for further use. (The men whom I had been trying to train as gunners had been requisitioned by Byrne for the scavenging and burial parties.)

"What happened to Kate?" I demanded.

He said, "She . . . she got drowned. . . ."

"*Again?*" I asked stupidly.

"What do you mean, Mr. Grimes?" he demanded.

"I . . . I had a dream about her . . ." I lied. "A very vivid dream. . . ."

"And it's come true, has it? Dreams often do, you know. . . ." He lit one of his vile cigars and spoke around it. "She came through the fighting, all right, and that was something of a miracle. It was she that lit the fuse to the blasting powder that blew in the jail doors after the man that should have done it got shot. It was a short fuse, too. By rights she should ha' been spattered all over Russell Street . . .

"Oh, she was in the forefront, Miss Kate, from the time that we got off the train at Spencer Street an' found the horses an' the men waiting for us there. I was not expecting the reception we got. It was like a president—no! it was like a king coming home after a long exile. I thought that it would just be Mr. Kelly and the few of us riding up to the jail but it was like a procession—it *was* a procession, a light procession! —marching up that wide, dusty street toward the prison. They were singing. They were singing that song of yours about the wearing of the green. There were green and gold flags and men were wearing green hats and sashes.

"At first there was nary a policeman to be seen and then they started showing up in side streets, some on foot and some on horseback. I think that they were surprised by this turnout. More'n surprised. Scared shitless, like as not. Waiting for orders before they dared *do* anything.

"So we rode and marched and sang on our way to the jail, the crowd growing all the time, the torches flaring and the light reflected from a collection of weapons that even I had never seen the like of before—and me a Francis Bannerman salesman! There were pitchforks, I swear. There were muskets that'd have been considered old-fashioned at the time when we threw the British out of *our* country. Some of the mob must have been Kelly supporters—but more of 'em were just out to enjoy the riot and to get involved in the looting. Behind us I could hear the crash of shop windows breaking and screaming and shouting.

"We turned into Russell Street, I think it was. Or we

tried to make the turn. There were police there, trying to set up some sort of barricade, and there were red uniforms among the blue ones. Redcoats. Soldiers. There was an officer with a plumed hat astride a big white horse, waving a sword.

" 'Halt!' he was shouting. 'Halt, in the name of the Queen!'

"And Mr. Kelly sang out, 'The only queen I recognize is my mother, and it's her we've come to save!'

"The soldiers were forming up, leveling their rifles. So were the police. That British colonel shouted, 'Halt! Halt, or I open fire!' And Mr. Kelly went riding up to him, not fast, casual almost, with his wife and his sister following close behind him.

" 'Let us through, sir,' he said, polite as you please, 'or it will be the worse for you.'

"And that red-coated fool tried to use his sword on Mr. Kelly, made as though to strike him on the head with the flat of the blade. He was not looking at the ladies, both of whom had pistols out. I don't know which of them it was who fired first; the shots sounded as one. The colonel reeled in his saddle and dropped that silly sword with a clatter and then his horse was bolting, with him slumped and bleeding, already dead for all I know, back through the police lines.

"Mr. Kelly yelled, 'Follow me, boys!' and was galloping after him, he and the ladies, and myself and Mr. Byrne and Mr. Hart and all the rest of us who had horses under us. There was screaming and shouting and shooting and we were through, those of us on horseback, while the mob, those on foot, tore into the police and the soldiers.

"Like a fortress, that Melbourne Jail is. There were men firing at us from the windows but they weren't very good shots and when we got close under the walls they couldn't bring their rifles to bear. One of the men who'd met us at the station had a canister of blasting powder with him and he put it down at the bottom of those huge, iron-bound doors. I got down off my horse to lend him a hand—after all, I am something of an expert in these matters. I said to him, 'That fuse is too short . . .' He said, 'What the hell do you know about it, you Yankee know-all?'

"And then we were under fire again. Some of the police had broken away from the main struggle and had seen what we were about to do. Bullets were flying all round us. The man with the blasting powder was hit, killed. Mr. Kelly and the Countess were still mounted and were leading a charge against the police. I scrambled back aboard my own nag—luckily it hadn't run off—and followed them, blazing away with my revolver. Out of the corner of my eye I saw Miss Kate running, on foot, toward the big doors.

"The blast almost knocked me off my horse. I turned back, pulled up just in time to avoid trampling Miss Kate. She must have been trying to run clear after she lit that short fuse. But she was tough, that one. She got to her feet, her clothes in rags about her, smouldering in places, and screamed, 'Come on! Come on, all o' ye! The doors are down!'

"And down they were, what was left of them. Mr. Kelly and the others came thundering back—they had made short work of those few police and soldiers—and together we rode and ran, a raging crowd of us, into the jail. The warders were cowards—or wise men. Anyway it was that explosion must have shaken them. They threw down their rifles and ran. We caught one of them, a sniveling little runt who was actually pissing himself with fear. When he found out that we weren't going to kill him he led us, willingly enough, to the woman's quarters, to the cell in which Mrs. Kelly was confined. He didn't have the keys, of course, but Mr. Kelly blew the lock in with his revolver. Some of the others were dealing with other doors the same way but *he* was concerned only with his mother.

"He knelt beside her—she was still sitting on her bed—and the old lady threw her arms about him. They were both of them sobbing. She was saying, over and over, 'I knew ye'd come for me, Ned, but 'twas a cruel long time . . .'

"And then Her Ladyship threw in her two bits' worth. She said, 'Isn't it time that we were getting out of here, Edward? We've stirred up a hornets' nest in this town.'

"Mrs. Kelly stared at her and asked in a very cold voice, 'Who is this woman, Ned?'

"It's me wife, mother,' he told her, 'Catherine . . .'

"It was obvious to me that there was no love lost between the two women. It was obvious, too, that the Countess's reference to a hornets' nest wasn't far short of the mark. In spite of those thick, stone walls I could hear the noise of gunfire coming from outside. It didn't seem to be close yet but it sounded, to me, as though somebody were clearing the streets and making a drive toward the jail. There was the occasional boom of a cannon. There was a nasty rattling that could have come from either Nordenfeldts or Gatlings. I knew that the Victorian Navy had such weapons.

" 'Mr. Kelly', I said, 'the Countess is right. It sounds to me as though there are reinforcements for the police coming up. With heavy guns.'

"He said, 'Then we stand and fight.'

"The Countess said, 'Don't be a fool, Edward. That's only a mob out there supporting you, more interested in looting and murdering and burning than real fighting. They'll run like rabbits at the first discharge of canister, at the first volley from the machine guns. They'll be no match for disciplined forces.'

" 'They already have been,' he said stubbornly.

" 'Only a handful of policemen and soldiers,' she said, 'armed only with rifles and revolvers. The mob will never stand against artillery.'

"I was surprised when Mrs. Kelly supported her daughter-in-law. 'Ned,' she whispered, 'she is right. If ye stay here you will be taken and killed. You must get away, back to your own people, away from this gutless city rabble. You must escape so that you can fight again, when the odds are more even.'

"And then Miss Kate came in. She said, 'The horses are waiting outside. We must get out of here, out of this cursed city. The word is that men from the Navy are on the way with heavy guns. And I've seen what such guns can do. At Glenrowan . . .'

"So we got the hell out of there. I felt a heel, leaving our friends in Melbourne to face the wrath of the authorities. But they knew the city; we did not. They would be able to melt away into the back alleys. I felt a heel. We all felt like heels.

"And Mr. Kelly, back on his horse, tall in the saddle, shouted on those still around to hear him 'I shall return!' "

CHAPTER **35**

"But what happened to Kate?" I demanded.

"I'm coming to that," said Donnelly. "But let me tell the story in my own way, will you? I was there and you were not." He lit a fresh cigar. "Yes, I was there . . ." he repeated.

A peacetime soldier, I thought, and not even a real professional, still reveling in his one taste of military adventure, still reliving battle and chase, still both surprised and elated by the discovery that when hot lead was flying he had acquitted himself not too badly.

"So you were there," I admitted, "and I was here. But if I had not been here, with the carronade loaded and ready, it would have been just too bad for you and the others."

He said, "You'd have done better with one of our Gatlings, loaded with canister."

I said, "I did the best I could with what I had. And it was bad enough. *But what happened to Kate?*"

"I've already told you. She was drowned. It was one of those stupid accidents. It happened that very night—or, to be more correct, in the small hours of the following morning. We slipped out of Melbourne, all of us, with old Mrs. Kelly on her horse in the middle of us. She can ride, you know. Riding seems to run in that family. Anyhow, there we were, with Mr. Kelly in the lead and Miss Kate bringing up the rear. Behind us the sounds of gunfire got fainter and fainter. We looked back now and again and could see the glare of the fires that had started, reflected from the rising smoke.

"Mr. Kelly knows the country like the back of his hand. He led us away from the highway, on to bush tracks. There was a river—don't ask me the name of it—that we forded. The water came up to the bellies of our horses. There must have been rocks on the riverbed. My own nag stumbled more than once; so did those that the others were riding. But we got across all right—we thought—and rode on through the dark forest.

"And then I heard Mr. Byrne shout, 'Kate! Where's Kate?'

"Mr. Kelly called a halt. We counted noses. Miss Kate wasn't among us. So we turned back. We came again to the river. 'Kate!' Mr. Kelly shouted. 'Kate!' There was no reply, of course, although some damn' bird squawked as though laughing at us.

"We dismounted then and spread out along the bank. Downstream from the ford we found bushes broken as though something big, some big animal, had forced its way through them. Miss Kate's horse? It must have been. And then, further downstream, we saw something white tangled in the branches of a fallen tree that was lying out on top of the water. Mr. Kelly went wading out and cried for help. I joined him, and Mr. Byrne and Mr. Hart. It was Miss Kate all right who was in the clutches of that dead tree. What little light there was was reflected from her white skin. Her clothes had almost been torn off her by the explosion at the jail and the current had stripped her still further. . . ."

I remembered the luminous body of her as we had swum in the billabong—and now this cheap, Yankee huckster was telling me how he had defiled it with his eyes.

I said, "Please spare me the lubricious details."

"What was that? Why can't you talk plain English? And if you keep on interrupting me you'll never get the story. We lifted her away from the tree, up the bank. We put her down on the ground, very gently. She looked as though she was sleeping. But she wasn't. She was dead. Somebody struck a match and we could see a dark bruise on her left temple. Her horse must have stumbled—even more badly than the other horses had done. She had been riding sidesaddle and was easily thrown. She had hit her head on something, knocking herself out. She had drowned without knowing it.

"Only twice in my life have I seen and heard a grown man bawling like a child. This was the second time. Mr. Kelly sat there by his dead sister with the tears streaming down his face, into his beard, making a dreadful sort of loud moaning noise. It was his mother who comforted him, and . . . and rocked him, whispering, 'Hush, Ned. Hush. All yer cryin' 'll not bring her back. . . .'

"And then the other Mrs. Kelly, Her Ladyship, said, 'Shouldn't we be getting on before the police pick up our trail?'

"Mr. Kelly looked up at her and said, 'But we must give poor Kate a decent burial . . .'

"She said, 'We have no spades.'

" 'Then let her have a funeral pyre!' Mr. Kelly told her.

" 'Are you quite mad?' she asked. 'A fire will attract attention—and that we do not want.'

"He got to his feet and I thought that he was about to strike her. She stood her ground, glaring back at him.

"Then—'She's right, Ned,' said Mr. Byrne. And, 'She's right,' said Mr. Hart.

" 'You must do what you think best, Ned,' his mother told him.

"So we carried poor Miss Kate into the bush and heaped branches over her. And Her Ladyship, who somehow had kept a bag with her all through the action, went off behind some trees and came back dressed in shirt and trousers, saying that riding sidesaddle in the bush was asking for trouble. Again I thought that Mr. Kelly was going to strike her but his mother stopped him. She said to him, 'The woman has sense, Ned. I almost wish that I had something more sensible to change into. . . .'

"So we rode on. Come daylight, we made ourselves a sort of camp in the bush and two of the men, whose faces had not been plastered all over posters like those of Mr. Kelly, Mr. Byrne and Mr. Hart, rode into a village that was not far distant and came back with bread and cheese and some bottles of ale. They told us that the news—good or bad, depending upon which side you were on—was traveling fast and everybody knew about what was already being called the Battle of Melbourne. The Victorian volunteer regiments had been mobilized and special police were being recruited. Much of it must have been no more than rumor—after all, mobilizations and recruiting campaigns don't swing into action overnight. . . .

"But mobilization of some kind there must have been. And spies, informers, there most certainly were. Mr. Kelly's intention was to make the last leg of the journey back to the fort by night, entering it just after sunrise. But there were horsemen out, police and cavalry, and although we shook them off time after time they picked up the trail again. There were shots fired at us, although from a distance. There was that village through which we passed where the people stared at us sullenly and one man shouted, 'Get out of here, you bloody outlaws! We don't want to be another Glenrowan!'

"Mr. Hart pulled out his revolver and shot him dead. Everybody ran into their houses then, except for some woman who knelt by the body and screamed curses after us.

"At the finish we were being chased. Mounted police and soldiers were galloping after us, shooting from the saddle. A lucky shot got old Mrs. Kelly's horse. It went down in a heap, sending her sprawling. Mr. Kelly turned back and grabbed hold of her just as she got to her feet, scooped her up to hold her in front of him. And then, as we were pounding up to the fort, the main gates open for us and nothing, as far as we could see, but a pile of brushwood in the opening. I was doing you an injustice. I was thinking, *Where in hell is that man Grimes and his museum piece now that we need 'em?*"

He relit his soggy cigar.

He said, "But I still think that you'd have done better with a Gatling!"

We turned to look at Red Kitty, who was approaching us from the headquarters hut.

"Mr. Grimes," she said. "Major Donnelly. We are to abandon this camp and make our way into New South Wales."

CHAPTER 36

Later I learned that Ned, having won this victory against superior forces, had been determined to stay in his fort, there to fight off any further attacks. It had been the two women, his mother and his wife, who had at last persuaded him to abandon the camp. Red Kitty argued that it would not be long before more troops were sent and that these men, having been told of what had happened to the first attack, would bring with them light artillery and machine guns. Kelly's own carronade had been effective only because of the element of surprise.

Ellen Kelly knew little of military matters but what she had to tell her son saddened him. When she began her prison sentence she had been regarded as something of a heroine, even by a few of her jailers. But feeling had, over the months, hardened against her. By many, even those of her own race, she had come to be regarded not as the mother of a valiant freedom fighter but as a woman who had brought into the world a vicious, cold-blooded murderer. There had been the killing of the police party at Stringy Bark Creek, followed by the First Glenrowan Massacre. Women had died when the train had been derailed —the wife of Inspector O'Connor and her sister. Women and children had died at the Second Glenrowan Massacre— killed, it is true, not by the rebels but by the police and

military, but killed nonetheless. Had it not been for the
first massacre they would still be living.

And there had been more deaths and destruction of
property, although these crimes were attributable not to
Kelly but to other self-styled freedom fighters who were
little more than bandits taking advantage of the growing
unrest in Victoria. But Kelly was the Captain of the Northeast, wasn't he? Kelly was the leader of the revolution.
Anything done for gain or for sheer love of brutality by
men not under his command he was being blamed for.

Kelly was stubborn but the two women wore him down.
(It must have been the only time that each took the same
side as the other in an argument.) Finally they made up
his mind for him—and once his mind was made up he
acted, and saw to it that everybody else sprang into action.
It was a measure of the man's force of character, his
charisma. He was not a colonel or a sea captain issuing
harsh orders to disciplined soldiers or seamen who, despite the apparent unreasonableness of the commands,
would obey them, albeit sullenly. He was a civilian (still),
enforcing his will upon an untidy organization of other
civilians, women as well as men. (Luckily there were not
any children to complicate matters.)

There were horses enough for everybody, with spare
animals to carry bags bulging with supplies. There were a
few carts—but these we should not be taking with us. I
found this out when, at last, I was able to catch Ned's
attention to ask him for some men to load the carronade
onto one of them. He told me, "Ye'll have to leave your
toy behind, Johnny."

"But," I said, "it's the only artillery we have."

"We'll be gettin' more. An' better."

"We don't have it yet. And the gun can go on one of the
carts."

"We're not takin' the carts. 'Tis bush trails we'll be
following', not roads. We'll be travelin' light. An' fast." He
turned away from me to shout orders to his lieutenants.
"Pack what ye can, Joe—an' anything ye can't make sure
that the bloody coppers can't use it! An' don't be forgettin'
that ammunition's more important than food. Tucker we
can always get. . . ."

I walked back to the carronade. Reardon joined me by the weapon.

He said regretfully, "I just about had one o' the carts made over into a gun carriage. But ye'll not be needin' it now."

"I shan't," I said. Then, "I wonder if the blacksmith has stowed all his gear into the saddlebags yet. . . ."

"What d'ye need, Johnny?" Reardon asked. "I'll go to see him; he doesn't like you much."

"It's mutual. Oh, just a hammer. And a cold chisel. And a file, perhaps . . ."

Reardon returned in a short time with the tools I had asked for. I always had with me the spike, which had been used to pierce the cartridge casing. I pushed it down into the touch-hole as far as it would go and then hammered it home. Reardon took over then; he saw what I wanted and was more used to working with metal than I was. It did not take him long to cut off the blunt end of the spike so that there was no protrusion, nothing that could be gripped in an attempt to withdraw the stoppage. A few strokes with the coarse file finished the job off neatly.

The carronade would never fire again.

We mounted our horses, joined the long cavalcade. I was not the only one, I noted, sitting a horse like a sack of spuds. Mine would not be the only backside rubbed raw when, eventually, a halt was called.

CHAPTER 37

It is possible to sleep in the saddle.

It is possible to sleep in the saddle even when your legs are painfully cramped and your buttocks blistered. I tried to stay awake but the day had been too much for me and now, even long after sunset, the air was still warm, and humid, and the only breeze was that created by our own passage. The muffled sound of the horses' hooves as they plodded over the soft grass of the bush trail had a soporific effect and the calls of nocturnal birds and animals sounded fainter and fainter in my ears, more and more distant.

Somebody was snoring.

No, it was not me. It was Reardon, who was riding just ahead of me. I could just see, in the dim starlight, that he was hunched down, slumped in the saddle. Somehow he was not falling off. It was the sight of him, I think that encouraged me to relinquish my own precarious hold on consciousness. It was not only that I was tired. There was so much that I wanted to forget, if only temporarily. The news of Kate's death. The dreadful slaughter for which I had been responsible when I applied the slowmatch to the touch-hole of the carronade. The hunting down of the survivors. . . .

Somebody was snoring.

It was me.

*　　*　　*

I awoke with a start, made a frantic grab for the reins with hands that, somehow, had become empty. The light blinded me.

And I found that I was looking at the gleaming complexity of gyroscopes, still spinning, still precessing, but slowly, slowly, ever more slowly, until the timetwister, as I was thinking of it, was motionless.

"So ye're back," said Ned Kelly.

I stared at him. He looked all wrong in his smart, late-twentieth-century attire. And who were the two strangers with him—one in civilian clothing, the other in what seemed to be a military uniform of utterly unfamiliar style.

"He's back, Mr. President," said Dr. Graumann.

"He looks dazed," contributed Major Duffin.

I recognized the two strangers, was coming to a slow realization of where and when I was.

"And what did you see this time, Mr. Grimes?" asked Kelly. "Ye've been away long. Where ye at The Battle In The Bush?"

"Yes . . ." I muttered. Then, "Where's my carronade?"

Kelly stared at me, then laughed.

"Ye know where it is. 'Tis where it's always been, mounted outside me palace in Glenrowan with a handsome brass plate to commemorate the part played by your distinguished ancestor. . . . I've often thought that 't was a great pity that me own ancestor didn't start his own peerage. Then the first Johnny Grimes would have been made an Earl or the like, an' you'd be an Earl yerself . . ." He was in an expansive mood. "That limey sailorman surely earned a title. That idea of his to make the move from Victoria to New South Wales so that the rebels had a port to bring in arms and volunteers from the States . . ."

I said, "It wasn't like that at all, Ned."

He said, "So ye're sayin' that the history books are wrong? That the move into New South Wales and establishing a stronghold in Twofold Bay wasn't old Johnny's idea. It must have been. He was the seaman. He knew all about ships an' all the problems goin' with them . . ."

"He just went along for the ride," I said. "It was the Kelly's wife and mother who talked him into abandoning the camp—and for reasons nothing at all to do with a deep-water port. Oh, it all came right in the end, as things have a habit of doing."

He frowned heavily. "Not always, Johnny. Not always. While ye've been away things've been getting worse. In the Nam, an' here in the Republic. Our American cousins are bringin' more an' more pressure upon us to get out o' Indochina. An' Kennedy's been wined an' dined at Peking, wi' the Cong top brass as fellow guests. Dear knows what the world's a-comin' to. . . .

"An' at home Cairns is still loose, still shit-stirrin'. 'T'wouldn't be so bad if 'twas only the students an' the like who were with him—but the crew o' the assault carrier *Clontarf* mutinied when they got orders to proceed to Saigon. There's been trouble, too, in the Army and the Air Force . . ."

It seemed that the light was dimming and that Kelly's voice was coming from farther and farther away.

I heard Graumann say, "Sir, sir, he's slipping back. . . ."

And then there was the rim of a glass against my teeth and the scientist was saying, "Drink this, Mr. Grimes."

I sipped the bitter drug, whatever it was. It took effect almost immediately. My vision cleared, my hearing returned to normal.

Graumann said, "May I suggest that you tape your story now, while you're still lucid? And then you can sleep."

"I must go to the bathroom first," I told him.

Major Duffin helped me to my feet. I walked to the bathroom unaided, did what I had to do. When I was finished I found that I was both hungry and thirsty. When I returned to the laboratory I said as much, refused to speak into the recording apparatus until Duffin had organized a pot of coffee and a plate of thick ham sandwiches. Kelly was furious but Graumann took my part. "He's been *working*, Mr. President, even though he's just been sitting in the chair. He's been burning energy. He must replenish it."

So I gulped my coffee and munched sandwiches. The ham was disappointing. It was almost flavorless. I remembered the ham that I (or my great-grandfather) had eaten now and again, home-smoked, unruined by preservative chemicals. Even so, it stilled the grumblings of my belly.

The recorder was produced. I spoke into it, pausing now and again to sip more coffee, to smoke. Once or twice Kelly interrupted me with questions.

"This man Donnelly . . . Did he come with ye into New South Wales?"

"No. He made his way back to Wangaratta. The understanding was that he would report back to his principals in the U.S.A. as soon as possible. As we all know now, he did. . . ."

"And how were things, really, between Ellen and Red Kitty?"

"I can report only on what I saw and heard in the camp and during the march into New South Wales. They were strong women, both of them. One was a devout Catholic, the other an atheist. One was old—although by today's standards she wouldn't have been. One was young. But they both loved Ned. They both knew that he was a man born to be king. Each, in her own way, pushed him. But when you saw them together—as I did, once or twice— the hostility was obvious."

"But without them, both of them, Ned would never have become what he did," said the President. He laughed. "An' I'm havin' to manage on me own, without some woman behind me, pushin'. I'm not doin' so bad. I'm doin' better than cousin Jack, with his Pommy wife dictatin' American foreign policy!"

Are you doing so well? I wondered, but did not say aloud.

I went on with the dictation of my story.

CHAPTER 38

As before, I was very tired. After I had finished the recording sesson I went to bed. Ned Kelly wasn't too happy about this; he had wanted to question me further about his distinguished ancestors. But, autocratic as he was, he still knew that I had to be humored, pampered almost. Without me the authentic history of the Australian Revolution would never be written.

So I undressed, took a hot shower that revived me only temporarily, then slid between the cool sheets. I barely had time to make myself comfortable before I went out like a snuffed candle.

I was sitting at the breakfast table. Before me was the plate of ham and eggs that Mary, our maid, had just set before me. Sitting across from me was my father, the admiral. He was ignoring his own meal and his face was hidden from me by the *Sydney Morning Herald*, which newspaper he was holding in hands which, I noticed, were shaking.

He lowered the paper. The normally ruddy skin of his face was as white as the hairs of his beard.

He growled, "This means war . . ." Suddenly he smiled grimly. "They'll have to call me back from the retired list. I'm the only senior officer who knows both air and surface craft."

"What do you mean, sir?" I asked bewildered. "Surely what's happening in Europe is no concern of ours. We've no reason to love the English or the French. . . ."

"Neither have the Americans, Johnny. But the sinking of the *Lusitania* was one of the factors involved in their taking sides—and she wasn't even an American ship. *City of Bathurst is—was—*an Australian ship. With an Australian crew and passengers, carrying an Australian cargo."

"*City of Bathurst?*" I repeated.

I remembered her launching at Newcastle, my father and I having been among the guests. I remembered watching as the First Lady, tall and proud despite her age, had swung the bottle of champagne to shatter on the high stem. And there had been the cheering as the ship slid down the ways, and the President, an imposing, bearded figure in his black frock coat with the green sash, had gravely raised his top hat in salute . . .

"*City of Bathurst,*" said my father. "Read all about it."

He passed me the paper. A corner of it drooped into the marmalade dish but neither of us worried about such trivialties.

CITY OF BATHURST SUNK BY GERMANS screamed the headlines. ATROCITY IN BAY OF BISCAY.

There was a picture, captioned, OUR ARTIST'S IMPRESSION OF THE CRIME.

That pen and ink sketch was scarcely a work of art but it was shocking in its impact. There was the Zeppelin, with the black Maltese Cross and the Imperial German Eagle unmistakable on its bows. There was the big, three-funnelled ship going down by the head. There was the swarm of tiny biplanes which, launched from the aerial giant, had dealt the death blows to the stricken liner with their accurately delivered bombs. There were, in the foreground, crowded lifeboats and others floating bottoms up.

The dateline of the accompaying story was London.

The British cruiser HMS Sheffield *today landed survivors from the Australian Republican Line's* SS City of Bathurst *at the French Port of Brest. The ship was bombed and sunk by aeroplanes launched from a German Zeppelin, believed to be LZ15. The missiles destroyed the liner's wireless apparatus before any call for help could be trans-*

mitted. The dastardly attack was made despite the fact that the City of Bathurst was not only flying the Australian flag but also had the Australian flag painted on her sides.

Captain Mulligan, who leaves a wife and four children in Sydney, went down with his ship. Mr. Costello, of Melbourne, the liner's Chief Officer, is among the survivors.

He told our correspondent in Brest, "It was piracy. Nothing else but black-hearted piracy. We were steaming along, minding our own business, when we sighted the airship. We all turned out to look at her. People were taking photographs. We watched her lowering the aeroplanes out of her belly on sort of trapeze affairs. We thought that her skipper was just putting on a show to impress us. Even when those aeroplanes came flying over we weren't at all worried. People, children especially, were waving to the German pilots. And then I heard the screams. I looked down from the bridge. People were falling. I heard the rat-tat-tat of the machine guns that those b------s in the aeroplanes were firing. And then the bombs came. One of them hit the bridge, and the wireless room. It was all confused after that. The Old Man was wounded. His face was all blood but he was still in charge. He ordered me down to get the boats away. It was like a nightmare. There were dead bodies all over the boatdeck. There were fires breaking out. You couldn't hear yourself think for the noise of escaping steam. The ship was listing, more and more heavily. But the boys did well. They did as well as any crew could have done in the circumstances. The one thing that scared me was the thought that those b------s in the aeroplanes would come back to finish their dirty work. . . ."

I read on. I learned that 314 people, passengers and crew, were missing, believed killed. I learned that City of Bathurst's cargo—frozen meat and butter, wool, tallow and dried fruits—had been consigned to the British Ministry of Supply.

From outside, in the hall, I heard the ringing of the telephone. It stopped.

Mary came in and addressed my father. Normally she

was a pudding-faced wench but now excitement was making her almost pretty.

"Admiral Grimes, sir. It's for you."

"Who is it, Mary?" he asked unnecessarily.

" 'Tis the Admiralty, sir," she told him.

"They want me back, Johnny," said my father to me.

And that was the dream, if it was a dream.

I had slipped back in Time, into my grandfather's mind. Through his eyes I saw his father, my great-grandfather, the man whose life I had shared. With him I had experienced quite a lot—that undignified brawl on the poop of the tramp windjammer *Lady Lucan,* the Glenrowan affair, the Battle In the Bush. From my reading of history I knew what his fate would be, going down in flames in his flagship, the Brennan metalclad *Deirdre,* at the height of the fifty dirigible raid of Kiel.

But that experience I should never share with him.

CHAPTER 40

Another breakfast, but this one in real life (but was it?) and not part of a dream . . . Another breakfast, but with an army mess corporal serving the meal and not a pretty (sometimes) maidservant. Another breakfast, but sitting opposite me a major, more or less in my age group, and not an elderly, retired admiral.

As Admiral Grimes had been in the dream, Major Duffin was reading the *Sydney Morning Herald*. This morning, however, there was no report of a disaster in the Bay of Biscay. Splashed over the front page were reports of more disasters in Viet Nam.

Duffin laid aside the paper, picked up his coffee cup and gulped noisily.

"Wars . . ." he muttered. "Wars. Nothing but wars. Oh, I'm a soldier but I can't help feeling, now and again, that Australia should have kept out of all these foreign involvements from the very start. The Boer War. The First World War . . ."

"And the Second World War," I said.

"That was different, Grimes. The Japanese attacked us, plastering our naval base at Darwin just as they plastered the Yanks at Pearl Harbor."

"And the Germans," I said, "attacked *City of Bathurst*, a neutral ship, in the Bay of Biscay."

"Oh, yes. That dream of yours that you were mention-

185

ing just as we started breakfast. It would have been better if you'd actually been there, aboard the ship, instead of reading about it in the paper."

"Better?" I asked. "How so? That was the sort of party that I prefer not to be invited to. Being bombed and machine gunned in an unarmed ship isn't my idea of fun."

"And your great-grandfather, the man whose career you're supposed to be reliving instead of wandering off to Canada and the Bay of Biscay and the good Lord knows where else. . . . He led the raid on Kiel, didn't he? It's a pity that you weren't there."

"I couldn't have been," I told him. "You know how this Time Travel business works, going back along the World Line. Once great-grandfather had a son he—how shall I put it?—became out of bounds. And I was in the mind of that son, my grandfather, only until *he* became a father . . ."

"And your grandfather wasn't in the Navy, so he wasn't at Kiel."

"Just as well," I said. "Did you ever make a study of that battle?"

"Not in any great detail," he said. "The Army historians tend to ignore fighting that took place in the air or at sea. I could tell you all about the Battle of Berlin. An uncle of mine was a panzer colonel. But Kiel? No."

"Kiel," I told him, "was the main base both for the German Navy's submarines and its Zeppelins. Insofar as the submarines were concerned access to the North Sea was either via the Kattegat or the Kiel Canal. It would have been suicidal for Allied surface craft to attempt to run the Kattegat and, of course, the Kiel Canal was out of the question. . . ."

"I don't suppose that the Allied captains had any German money to pay their canal dues," said Duffin.

"Very funny. Anyhow, Kiel was bristling with anti-aircraft batteries. Nonetheless it was decided to carry out a large-scale bombing attack. The most suitable ships were the Australian dirigibles, the Brennan metalclads. They had a high ceiling for those days, 20,000 feet. They were armed with electrically operated one-inch Gatlings, with a fantastic rate of fire. Even should German fighter planes succeed in climbing to engage them the Gatlings would make mincement of the enemy. And the metal skins of the dirigibles, although not armor, would stop the average German machine gun bullet. Too, the gas cells were self-sealing. Brennan—he was a very versatile scientist and engineer—as well as being the designer of the ships themselves had also developed the bombs that they would use. The 'borrowing bombs.' One of these, falling as much as two hundred feet away from one of the canal locks, would cave it in."

"You seem to have done your homework," said Duffin.

"It's family history," I told him. "And, as you know, I am something of a historian. For a while I've been toying with the idea of writing a novel set during World War I. I've done plenty of reading up—including Luft Admiral Strasser's memoirs.

"Strasser was as devoted an airshipman as my great-grandfather. It was Strasser who pressed the development of the recoilless 88 mm cannon. At the time when the allies mounted the raid on Kiel four Zeppelins were so armed—LZ70, LZ71, LZ72 and LZ73. Like the Brennan metalclads these dirigibles had a high ceiling. The other ships, older and smaller, could clamber as high as 15,000 feet. These had only a few machine guns for their own protection but each carried at least a dozen fighter aeroplanes.

"The night of the raid was brightly moonlit, with a clear sky. The wind over the North Sea was easterly, at about ten knots. The allied air fleet lifted from the Royal Navy's Airship Base at Pulham, in East Anglia. There were twenty Australian metalclads, led by the flagship, *Deirdre*, in the van. There were ten French semi-rigids. My understanding is that these ships were among those present despite my great-grandfather's lack of confidence in them. There were ten Royal Naval airships of essentially Zeppelin design. Finally, there were ten of the Royal Navy's airship aircraft carriers to provide fighter support should it be required.

"The fleet flew an almost direct course for Kiel. It has been argued that Admiral Grimes should have made a devious approach. It has been argued that he should have waited for an overcast night. But the French semi-rigids could carry fuel sufficient only for the round trip, with no deviations. And, in those pre-radar days, the admiral had to *see* his targets—the Kiel Canal, the U-Boat pens, the Zeppelin sheds. The surface ships of the Royal Navy were supposed to have cleared the North Sea of all German vessels. But there were two German submarines at large—U27 and U33. Both of these vessels had resurfaced to recharge their batteries. Both of them sighted the eastbound air armada. Both of them broke radio silence to report what they had seen. Admiral Strasser got his warning.

"Oh, I can envisage it. The hasty mustering of the flight crews and the ground crews, many of them called from their warm beds. There were married quarters at Kiel—and there must have been quite a few unmarried ladies who were giving comfort to the brave boys of the Luft-Marine. I can just see those airshipmen clambering aboard their Zeppelins, still buttoning up their trousers. I can see the big ships being walked out from their sheds, silvery in the moonlight. Damn it, I can *hear* the splashing of the water ballast as they lifted. And there were the colored signal lamps and the flickering of the searchlights as Morse messages were flashed from ship to shore, from ship to ship, from shore to ship . . . And the throbbing of the engines and the shouts and, in the distance, the thudding of the anti-aircraft guns, at Heligoland, opening up. . . ."

"Anybody would think," commented Duffin, "that you were there."

"I wasn't. Or wasn't I? It all seemed so vivid. There is German blood in the family, of course. A maternal grandmother. She could have been at Kiel. Anyhow, Strasser got his ships into the air. He launched his Taube fighters as soon as the Allied fleet was sighted, just crossing the coastline. They made for the leading ships—*Deirdre, Kathleen, Fiona* and *Maeve*. They got close, too close. After all, a big airship, even without lights, is easy enough to see in bright moonlight. A smaller fighter plane is not. But once they opened fire, once they'd betrayed themselves, they'd had it. The Gatlings blew them to shreds. Not that the Pommy Camels, launched from the Royal Navy's carriers, did much better against the Zeppelins. LZ40 was hit but not badly. She lost gas but there was no fire. And LZ43 had somehow bungled the launch of her Taubes and so the fighters were airborne just in time to fight off the Royal Navy's planes. They had not been expecting such opposition.

"*Deirdre* stood on, with her bomb-aiming officer peering into his sights, waiting for the first indications of canal locks, of U-Boat pens, of Zeppelin hangars. He must have been dazzled by the upward-stabbing searchlights, by the anti-aircraft shell bursts, although these were well short of their target. And I can just imagine that frosty-faced old bastard of an admiral, my great-grandfather, in his control cab, getting the situation reports from his officers and growling, 'Tell those bloody Frogs to close up! They aren't much use but we can use their firepower.' (As a matter of fact the French Hotchkiss was a very effective air-to-air weapon. But, like the Australian Gatling, it didn't have the range.) And, 'Why can't the Poms send their aeroplanes where they're needed? It's the 70s they should be going after, not the old crocks . . .'

"Strasser kept out of range of the Australian Gatlings. His four 70s had climbed to the same altitude as my great grandfather's metalclads and then he had turned, running away (as it seemed) from the raiders. Soon Kiel would be spread out below the Allied raiders, a helpless victim. At the same time the German air fleet was being slowly overtaken. The aeroplanes from both sides, the Camels and the Taubes, were still dogfighting but nobody, as far as I can gather from my reading of the various accounts of the battle, was worrying much about them. They were just nuisances, capable of drawing blood, just as a mosquito is, but no more than nuisances. This was an affair of big ships. It was the only airship battle in history—but, of course, nobody at the time knew that. *Deirdre* and *Kathleen* opened fire on LZ40—crippled and lagging—with their belly Gatlings. This time there was a fire. She went down in a great flare of blazing hydrogen. And LZ38, too, had fallen astern of the main German fleet. She was just within Gatling range. There was another, slowly falling, funeral pyre.

"Meanwhile—according to Strasser's own account of the action—his gunnery officers had their eyes glued to their rangefinders. The Gatling gun flashes enabled them to keep the pursuing ships in their sights. Too, there was the bright moonlight. Even so, it was not easy gunnery. Laying and training the big guns meant that the ships themselves had to be laid and trained. It was more like firing a torpedo from a submarine than an artillery piece from a surface vessel. But, at last, *Deirdre* was within range of the 88s. The four super-Zeppelins, the Z70s, made the necessary alterations to course and attitude so that all four stern guns could be brought to bear. They fired almost as one.

"According to the captain of the British R49, one of the few ships that returned from the raid, 'One moment the Aussie flagship was there. And then she wasn't. There was just a shower of burning wreckage. Then one of the other Aussies bought it. We flew through where she had been but came through with nothing worse than a few holes burned in the envelope. We were too busy hooking on our planes, pulling them in for refueling and rearming, to worry much about it at the time. . . .'"

Duffin asked, "Are you sure that you weren't there, Mr. Grimes?"

"I've told you, I wasn't. But I've read all the accounts of the action—Australian, English, French and German. The Battle of Kiel was *the* airship action, with big ships slugging it out of relatively short range. The aeroplanes didn't play much part after the first flurry; the hooking on and launching procedures weren't all that easy to carry out in the heat of battle. Things were different after the Americans put their flying drainpipes into the air, making the recovery and launching of fighter-bombers much easier, far less time-consuming. But at Kiel the flying drainpipes were still no more than an aeronautical engineer's dream . . ."

"You know your airships," Duffin said.

"I should. Great-grandfather, the admiral, was one of the world pioneers of lighter-than-air military aviation in Australia. I wonder what he could have said if, while he was second mate of that tramp windjammer which brought him here, somebody had told him what his end would be. . . ."

Even as I spoke I was losing my hold on the here-and-now. I was no longer *me*, either of the late twentieth century *me's*. I was in a woman's body and mind. It was a strange experience, a frightening one. The odd clothing, the nothingness where familiar organs should have been, the top-heaviness about the chest . . . And was the mind that of my German grandmother? It must have been. I was cold and terrified, standing with others out in a street, deafened by the futile thunder of the anti-aircraft guns, by the explosions of the falling, earth-shaking bombs. I was looking up at the fire in the sky where the big ships were wallowing in their orgy of mutual destruction.

There was a burgeoning flower of flame far greater than any of the others had been. I knew, somehow, what it was. It must have been when R38, on fire but still under control, succeeded in putting herself alongside Dietrich's LZ72.

"Wake up!" Duffin was saying irritably. "Wake up, Grimes!"

The spell was broken. I took the last piece of toast from the rack and helped myself to a liberal application of butter and marmalade.

"When you've quite finished," said the major, "you'd better get ready for another session with the Good Doctor's time-twister. Ned's leaning on him and leaning on me. He wants that history written by last Thursday at the very latest."

CHAPTER 41

It was good, I was thinking, to be out of that blasted bush and back where I belonged, by the sea if not actually on it. But I couldn't help wondering, as I strolled down from Ned's headquarters to the pier, how long it would be before we were on the run again. Quite fantastically the New South Wales authorities had been virtually ignoring us. It was a sort of armed truce. As long as we kept our noses clean in New South Wales what we had done in Victoria was of no interest. We had heard that the Victorian Government had considered sending the turret warship *Cerberus* to clean out the "nest of outlaws" in Twofold Bay—and we had heard, too, that the government of New South Wales had intimated that it would consider an armed incursion into its territorial waters an act of war.

Red Kitty, I thought could claim at least some of the credit for our immunity. Although she was the black sheep (the black ewe?) of her aristocratic family she knew people who knew people who knew people, all over the world. And what about the Americans? As far as we could gather, huddled in our little corner at the bottom of the world, the Harp in the South Committee seemed to have faded into obscurity. Yet money must still be coming in. Somebody had chartered that little, rusty steamship alongside the Eden jetty. Somebody had paid for her cargo of agricultural machinery, consigned to the company that recently had acquired an office in Eden, Stolzberg Brothers. (Were there any Stolzberg Brothers? I had asked Red Kitty. All men are brothers, she had replied with sweet, revolutionary simplicity.) Somebody had greased the right palms to ensure that nobody got too curious about the contents of those crates and packing cases.

It was a cold day, but fine. The wind was from the south but there was good shelter in Twofold Bay from such weather conditions. It was too rough outside, however, for the fishermen to be out. At least a dozen boats, their masts bare, their gear stowed, were alongside at the northwest berth. Their crews would be among the watersiders discharging the American steamer's cargo on the southeast side.

I walked out on the rough, heavy planking of the jetty, stood watching the work in progress. Briefly I was enveloped in a cloud of raw-smelling, wet steam from the leaking cylinders of the rattling steam winch aboard the ship. A crate was being lifted from the main hatch, was hoisted clear of the coaming. Guy ropes tautened and slackened as the single, swinging derrick swayed its dangling load outboard to plumb the waiting dray.

Then the sling slipped and the crate fell heavily, striking between the wagon and the wharf stringer. It burst open.

And here was trouble. Daniels, the chief and only Customs Officer, was among the onlookers on the wharf. Surely even he, in front of witnesses, no matter how heavily he had been bribed, could not pretend to ignore a consignment of Henry repeating rifles or even something heavier, such as a disassembled Gatling.

I went to stand beside him, prepared to whisper, "It's worth another couple of hundred if you ignore this . . ." He watched as a wharf laborer and the American chief mate cleared away the splintered wood to reveal gleaming, well-greased metal.

"Doesn't seem to be damaged, Mr. Grimes," said the mate cheerfully.

"And what would it be for?" asked Daniels.

I said, "I wouldn't know, Mr. Daniels. I'm not a farmer."

"I've never seen such a tiny steam engine," Daniels persisted. "It's almost a toy. It must be for something . . ."

The mate, Muldoon, grinned at us. He said, "You're just not up to date in this part of the world. In the States we use these little engines to drive all sorts of farm machinery. Like chaffcutters."

"You're an ingenious people," said Daniels.

"We are that," agreed Muldoon, winking at me.

"Get it on to the dray," I said to two wharfies who were standing nearby. "Mr. Reardon's waiting for this."

"That bloody platelayer," muttered one of the men, spitting a gob of tobacco juice in the general direction of a narrow gap in the wharf planking. "Puttin' on the airs an' graces of a real engineer. You should see the way that he carries on in that dirty great shed o' his. Makin' us unload the ironmongery from this dray as though 't'was crates o' eggs. . . ." He scowled directly at me. "He an' the rest o' you should ha' stayed on yer own side o' the border."

"But they're bringing money inter the town, Bill," his companion told him. "An' wi' the fishing as bad as it has been, we need it."

"But where does the money come from, mister?" demanded Bill, addressing me again. He was a big, heavily bearded, surly brute, the sort of man that I'd hated having to have on my watch when I was at sea. "I'm not like some people I could mention. *I* don't like gettin' my hands dirty when I take my pay. Where does the money come from? Don't think that we don't know who your boss cocky is, even though he's callin' himself Kennedy . . ."

"What's in a name, Bill?" said the other wharfie. "An' why shouldn't he be settin' himself up as a gentleman farmer? Where, now, is the harm in that?"

"He's killed men," persisted Bill.

"What of it? What's been happenin' in Victoria's no concern of ours. No doubt any killin' done was in self-defense. They're a bad lot, those Victorian police. Even worse than ours. An' now, like a wise man—*if* Mr. Kennedy's who you're hintin' he is—he's left the Victorians to squabble among themselves an' makin' a fresh start here. With a wife like he's got—a looker an' rollin' in money—

why should he want to carry on bushrangin'? He's no fool."

"And not a bushranger either," I said.

"An' I'm not a poverty stricken fisherman whose boat is three-quarters owned by the Bank o' New South Wales," muttered Bill. "An' what are *you*, or what aren't you, Mr. Grimes? What's a Pommy deep water sailorman doin' mixed up wi' the *Kennedy* gang?"

Daniels' ears were flapping almost audibly and I thought that it was time that an end was put to this conversation.

"I'm the wharf superintendent," I said shortly. "And, as such, I'd like to see this dray and its load on the way up the hill."

"Proper little Cap'n Bligh, ain't he?" sneered Bill. "All right, Admiral. We'll get this load o' ironmongery delivered to your Lord High Engineer."

The driver of the dray cracked his long whip. The six great, surly bullocks bestirred themselves into reluctant motion. The wheels of the clumsy wagon began to turn, creaking and squealing about their axles. The two wharf laborers pulled themselves up on to the open back of the vehicle, sat with their legs dangling, facing aft. Bill spat again, this time just missing my right boot.

"With all the *machinery* you've got now," said Muldoon, "I'm surprised that you and your Mr. Reardon haven't set up a tramway system of some sort."

"We've more important things to be doing," I said.

"I've no doubt that you have," agreed the mate with a smirk. "No doubt at all. But one o' those traction engines we discharged earlier'd be better'n a bullock wagon."

"The first one's still being assembled," I said.

That was not quite a lie.

The first one was already almost completely assembled, behind high fences, covered with tarpaulins when not being worked upon. As a traction engine, as a traction engine only, it was ready to take to the road.

Shortly after my conversation with Muldoon and the others on the jetty I, together with Ned, Red Kitty and Reardon, was walking around the hulking, ungainly brute, admiring it. It was more, much more, than just another traction engine. Oh, there was the cylindrical boiler, with the fire box aft and a tall funnel forward. But the rear wheels, two pairs of them, were unusual. They were sprocketed and around them ran a heavy iron chain with iron plates bolted to the links. And the cab was more like an armored turret than the driver's control position on an ordinary locomotive, and was a sort of two-story construction.

"Tis an interestin' lookin' contraption," said Kelly.

"It is that," agreed Reardon. "That man Dr. Gatling's an engineer I'd like to be meetin' sometime."

"Dr. Gatling," said Red Kitty, in a school mistressy voice, "did not design this vehicle himself. One of his work managers did. They way I hear it, the good doctor wanted an engine capable of carrying his guns over any sort of country, a steam-driven, armored car. Steam to turn the wheels *and* to operate the machine cannon."

"An' what speed will this thing be after doin'?" asked Kelly.

"Five miles an hour over any sort o' road. A bit less over fields. A lot less over rough country. I'm just tellin' ye what it says in the book."

"It'll be a hog on coal," I said.

"Or wood, Johnnie—but there's always plenty o' that around. On the side o' the tender there're racks for axes an' saws for wood-cuttin'. The Yanks think o' everything."

"This thing'll never replace the horse," said Kelly.

"Show me a horse, Ned, that'll carry a steam-operated Gatling," said Reardon, "an' I'll believe ye."

"Have ye any o' the Gatlings assembled yet?" Kelly asked.

"D'ye take me for a miracle worker? One thing at a time's all I can be doin' wi' the sort o' help I've got. 'Tis a great pity the railway doesn't run to Eden. I could knock ye up an armored train, bristlin' wi' Gatling cannon, in no time at all, at all."

"You shall have your trains," said Red Kitty, "after we have taken Wangaratta. And with the trains we shall take Victoria. And then—all Australia."

"Aren't ye gettin' ahead o' yourself, girl?" asked Ned.

She said firmly, "I am not. There's a discontent enough

among the toiling masses, as well you know. Once the workers see that you are winning they'll flock to your banner, all over this island continent."

Ned looked at her, looked long and hard at the tall, slim woman in her mannish attire, her copper hair gleaming in the sunlight. In spite of his beard (now neatly trimmed as befitted his new image) I thought that I could read his expression. Was there doubt? Uncertainty? Fear, even? (No. Never fear.) But there was a sort of what-have-I-got-myself-into-now? look. He had found a snug haven across the border in the aptly named Eden and, I really believe, would have been content to settle down there, a prosperous farmer, backed by his wife's wealth and protected by her political influence. His bushranging days would be something to look back upon, a source of stories with which to amuse his children and grandchildren. He had never, I think, really taken it seriously when his Victorian supporters had referred to him as the Captain of the North East.

But now the ships were coming in from the U.S.A. —the scruffy little *Baltimore Belle*, now alongside discharging, was not the first—with their cargoes of "agricultural machinery." There was the growing stockpile of Henry rifles and Colt revolvers. There were already a few Gatling guns—both the relatively small calibre hand-operated models and the bigger, deadlier steam-operated ones.

And in Victoria the revolution was simmering, with at least three guerrilla leaders in the field who were little more, were no more, than bandit chiefs. Unless there were real leadership—and soon—the people, Red Kitty's toiling masses, would support the government in its efforts to restore law and order. Too, not for much longer would the premiers of the other Australian states be able to ignore the Victorian troubles.

There had to be a real leader.

And both Ellen Kelly and Red Kitty knew who that leader would have to be.

CHAPTER 42

I was sitting in the chair watching those shimmering, glimmering gyroscopes spinning ever more slowly, coming at last to rest. I looked up at Major Duffin and Dr. Graumann.

I asked, "What did you bring me back for? I was in the Past for little more than five minutes . . ."

"Longer than that, Mr. Grimes," said Graumann stuffily.

"Not much longer," I said.

"It's himself that's wantin' ye," Duffin told me. "He's gettin' impatient. The truth of it is that he wants tales about his valiant ancestor to sustain him through these troublous times. . . ."

"Ye could put it that way, Major," said Kelly coldly. None of us had heard him enter the room.

"Ye know how 't is, Ned," Duffin said placatingly. "We all of us need a bit o' buckin' up the way things are goin' in the Nam. An' at home."

"Dr. Graumann," Kelly said coldly, "is Mr. Grimes fit for interrogation?"

"I'm not a medical doctor, sir."

"But ye call yerself a doctor. An' you're in charge o' this experiment." The big, bearded man turned to. "How d'ye feel, Johnny? Do ye feel up to a good yarn, just the two of us, over a pot or two?"

I said, "I could do with a drink."

"Good. Then come wi' me. I've rooms set aside for me personal use in this warren. There's no need for either o' ye to come with us, Doctor and Major. Johnny an' I are capable o' waggin' our tongues without outside assistance."

I got up from the chair, followed the burly, tweed-clad figure out of the room, along the corridor to a doorway where two smartly uniformed soldiers, their highly polished breastplates and cylindrical helmets ablaze with reflected light, were standing guard.

I raised my glass to Ned and he raised his to me.

I sipped the aged, very smooth, Irish whisky appreciatively.

Kelly said, "I'm needin' to be cheered up, Johnny boy. I want to be reminded of how it was with the first Ned, besieged in the town of Eden, surrounded by enemies ashore an' afloat, until, with his faithful few followers, he broke out and carried the war back into Victoria. . . ."

I said, "It wasn't like that at all."

He glared at me. He demanded, "Are ye sayin' that the history books are tellin' lies?"

"Not lying, exactly," I said. "Just not sticking too closely to the truth."

"But ye were in Eden, weren't ye? Ye took part in the march on Wangaratta."

"When I was snatched back into this Time," I said, "the march was being planned. The armored tractors had not yet been fully assembled. Orders had not yet been passed to the guerrilla bands operating in Victoria."

"But the siege, man. The siege of Eden. The hardships, the danger, the privation—an' only the courage an' heroic presence o' the first Kelly holdin' things together . . ."

I said, "It wasn't like that at all. There wasn't any siege. The New South Wales authorities just ignored us. I didn't know what strings had been pulled, were being pulled, or by whom—but we just went about our business, our ostensible businesses, farming and importing, and paid our bills and taxes and that was that. We were rich, you see. There was Red Kitty's money. There was the money coming in from the U.S.A.—not only from Irish sympathizers but from people such as the railroad kings who wanted to get a toehold in Australia. Nobody talked about the multi-nationals in those days—but they were already in existence."

"If what ye're sayin' is true, if ye've been dreamin' the truth an' not a pack of lies, Ned, the first Ned, must ha' been like a caged lion before the break-out for Wangaratta. . . ."

I had to say it.

I said it.

"He was sitting pretty, and he knew it. He had become a landowner, thanks to his wife's money, and he didn't want to rock the boat. But all the time those Americans were sending in shiploads of arms when he'd sooner have had *real* agricultural machinery. And all the time he was being nagged by both his wife and his mother—his mother still crying about the death of Dan be avenged and his wife waving the red flag and spouting Karl Marx. And there were Joe Byrne and Steve Hart pining for action, and the emissaries from across the border begging the Captain of the North East to return from exile and take charge. And there was Reardon—it's fantastic how the official histories hardly mention him at all—assembling the American toys, the war-tractors and the machine cannon, and sulking because he wasn't being given the chance to play with them."

Kelly growled, "Ye're robbin' Ned of his glory."

"I'm not. I remember, with my great-grandfather's memory, what he was like at Glenrowan and at the Battle in the Bush, what he was like during the retreat into New South Wales. He was a leader, a born leader. . . .

"But he was not the first leader who had had to be pushed."

The Kelly finished his drink in one gulp, waited impatiently until I had finished mine. He replenished both glasses.

He said, "Then Ned, the first Ned, was lucky. He had a strong wife and a strong mother, both pushing. I've nobody. Just meself—an' I'm in a jam that the sainted Ned would never, could never have dreamed of. But I'm a Kelly, just as he was. I'll not desert me friends, any more than he did. Ye may say what ye like—but he did go back into Victoria. An' if life in Eden was as pleasant as ye're tryin' to tell me, that makes his action all the more noble.

"But life was simpler in those days. There weren't all the intellectuals out snipin' at anybody, like meself, wi' guts enough to fight a just war. Then everything was black and white . . ."

"And red," I said. "Don't forget that your ancestress, Red Kitty, was an early Marxist. And green. Without the help of the Irish in the U.S.A., and the abortive rebellion in Ireland itself which distracted the attention of the English, our Australian War of Independence would never have gotten off the ground. And yellow, the color of gold. What a complicated mess it was. The old, well-established imperialism of England and the nascent American imperialism . . . American big business just starting to flex its muscles . . . And the first missionaries of the new religion preaching the Gospel according to St. Marx . . . And the German Empire sending its tentacles out into the Pacific . . ."

He told me, "Enough, Johnny boy. What ye've been sayin' could get ye shot for treason in these times. But shall we forget that this talk ever took place? I want that history, the true history, written an', the way 'tis, ye're the only man that can be writin' it.

"Time's a-gettin' short. Ye've no idea o' the pressures bein' brought to bear on me, both at home an' from abroad. The Kennedy clan are a disgrace to their name an' I'm not a man to dance to a Yankee piper's tune even though he may claim that the blood o' Irish kings runs in his veins.

"Finish yer drink an' get back to the man Graumann an' his time-twister. An' I hope that when next we talk ye'll be able to tell me about the real Ned, the King, the warrior."

CHAPTER 43

I took my place in the chair again, facing the as-yet motionless assembly of gleaming rotors.

"That president of yours!" complained Graumann. "Storming in here and demanding that *the* definitive history of your war of Independence be written and ready for press by last Thursday at the very latest. I think that he regards that book, if it ever does get written, as his enduring monument. I suppose that he gave you a pep talk. . . ."

"Sort of," I said.

"And so you're to scurry through the years, as it were, just witnessing the high points. After all, you'll have your great grandfather's memories of what happened in between."

"But what's the rush?" I asked.

"You should know. You're the Australian, I'm not. But I do know that when overseas wars go badly, and there's discontent and rioting at home, some sort of balloon is liable to go up at any minute. After all, you've already had one revolution in this country."

"You've had two in yours," I said.

"And so you're overdue for your second one. Relax, now. Drink this. If I've the settings right you'll find yourself in Wangaratta, for the battle."

The rotors began to spin, to spin and precess, to tumble, dragging my soul, or my mind, or *something* of me back across the decades.

I was riding with Reardon in the cab of one of the huge, armored traction engines. With us was the fireman who, at a word from the engineer, flung open the furnace door, hastily raked out hot ashes and then flung in another four billets of wood.

"We shall soon be needing all the steam we can get, Johnnie," Reardon said.

Yes, we should be, and not only for driving the tracked vehicle over the fields.

"Keep her going," I ordered unnecessarily. "When you come to the main road carry on into the town."

I clambered up the vertical ladder into the gun turret. As in the driver's cab there were only narrow slits in the armor for vision, although there was a wider aperture through which protruded the multiple barrels of the one inch Gatling, allowing the gun a limited traverse to left and to right. The afternoon was cold, with a thin drizzle, but it was hot in the compartment. The air smelt of sweat—from the gunner and the loader and, I suppose, from myself. It was the little steam engine at the side of the machine gun, with the steam pipe running to it from the boiler, that had raised the temperature.

I looked ahead.

There was the grassy, sparsely wooded hill that we should have to surmount before plunging down to the main road. And there, too, was the tall, thin, smoke-and-spark-belching funnel of the traction engine. It was a fault in the design of the vehicle that, somehow, had escaped everybody's notice. The gunner would have to be careful, very careful, not to shoot it away. I looked to the left. One of the other two tractors was there, not quite abeam, a little astern of us. I noted how its tracks were tearing muddy gouges in the grass-covered soil. I looked to the right. The third member of our mechanized attack force was having trouble, was stopped. I could see its crew gathered around its left hand track. Something—a rock or a dead tree limb—must have gotten between the treaded chain and the rear sprocket wheel. There was a sudden, hissing roar as the safety valve released excess steam pressure.

But we could not afford to wait until the blockage was cleared. For all we knew our presence might desperately be required in the town. I pulled out my watch. The time was five minutes after one in the afternoon. We were late already. The attack by Kelly's bush cavalry, spearheaded by an armored elite, must already be under way.

We crested the brow of the hill. The gray-yellow of the road was ahead and below. There was no traffic on it to concern us, not so much as a pedestrian. The Cobb and Co.'s coach, I knew, would not be due in for some time. (And what would its driver and his passengers think when they found the town in rebel hands?)

We clanked and rattled down the slope. Reardon, I was pleased to see, was steering to avoid obstacles such as rocky outcroppings and trees and large bushes. (The driver of the third traction engine must mistakenly have thought that he could go through and over anything.) To the left the town came into view. There was smoke, thick black smoke, mingling with the drifting veils of drizzle. I thought that I could hear the sound of small arms fire, but the noise of our progress was such that I could not be sure. The boom of something heavier—a large field gun?—was unmistakable.

There was a ditch by the roadside. It did not stop us, any more than the low hedge did. And then, as we turned to the left, toward the town, we were running more smoothly, picking up speed. Reardon gave a toot on his whistle. The traction engine following us replied.

My gunner did not need me to tell him to stand by his weapon. He knew the drill. He opened the drain cock to allow any accumulated condensation to drip from the cylinder of the little engine. There was a brief spatter of falling hot water, then the sharp hiss of escaping steam.

He said, "I hope she works, Mr. Grimes."

I said, "She worked fine at the practice shoot, Peter."

"Yair. But that wasn't the real thing."

"We were using real ammo."

Now we were rattling past the occasional roadside cottage. I saw curtains drawn furtively aside and pale faces peering out through the small windows. This would be a day when people would stay indoors, behind the illusory security of their walls, listening to the sounds of warfare and hoping that the tide of battle would not flow their way.

From a long way astern I heard a shrill tooting. I looked out through a rear vision slit. The number two traction engine blocked most of the view but, beyind it, I could just make out number three, dense smoke pouring from its funnel, trying to catch up.

I shouted down through the hatch to Reardon, "Sound three long blasts and slow down!"

Our whistle screamed as I had ordered. I hoped that the driver of number two would remember the sound signals that I had worked out and that the number three man would not think that the order to reduce speed referred to him.

But before long number three was back in station and I gave the order to resume full speed. It was a pity that the road was not wide enough to allow line abreast formation. I became conscious, very conscious of the fact that number two's Gatling was pointed directly at us. Of course, he would have to blow his own funnel away before his shells hit our cab but the thin metal of the smokestack would barely be capable of stopping a well-flung stone. I hoped that number two's gunner was not too trigger happy. Who was it? I remembered. It was a man called Flynn. A wide man, violent in his cups. And he would have been quite capable of including a flask of rum in the contents of his tucker bag.

The town was getting close now. I could see that buildings were burning. The noise of gunfire was becoming louder. There was the hammering of machine guns—Gatlings or Nordenfeldts—and I knew that Ned's cavalry had no such weapons with them. The authorities must have learned of the impending attack on Wangaratta and stationed troops there and, to judge from the machine gun fire, a detachment from the Royal Victorian Navy.

We came to a scene of recent fighting. On either side of the street the windows of shops and houses were smashed, walls pocked with bullet holes. And there were bodies, of men and horses. Some of the men were uniformed, in blue and white, in blue and scarlet. Some wore only the identifying green sash over rough civilian clothing. At first Reardon tried to steer our clumsy war wagon around the bodies but soon realized the futility of this. We stood on, hardly noticing when our wheels and tracks crushed a human body into the mud, feeling the lurch when a horse was the ineffective obstacle.

Then we were coming under fire—so far only from rifles. There were troops or police or sailors in the houses on either side of the street. The fire was almost ineffectual but we were unable to reply to it. The Gatling could traverse only over an arc of 40°, 20° each side from straight ahead. To bring the machine cannon to bear we should have to turn off course and—I thought with the twentieth century part of my mind—this clumsy traction engine was no Tiger tank. The wall of a house would stop it dead and make a stationary target of us. I saw that our funnel was spurting smoke from a dozen holes along its length. As long as it remained in place, however, the natural draught into and through the furnace should not be effected.

We turned a corner and were heading almost directly for a large building that, I discovered later, was the Town Hall. There was fighting going on around it; it seemed to be under siege. I saw the blue and white of police uniforms, the blue and scarlet of one of the Victorian volunteer regiments. I saw the field gun with its crew of white-capped sailors. And they were working hard and fast to get their piece swung around, to bring it to bear upon the approaching traction engines. If they scored a direct hit on us, armor or no armor, that would be it.

"Peter," I said to my gunner, "as soon as you can get a clear shot, without blowing away our smokestack, let the bastards have it!"

"All ready," he said.

I yelled down the hatch to Reardon to slew a little to the right. There was a street lamp standard in the way but it was not sturdy enough to stop us. Neither was the light, ornamental fence enclosing somebody's front garden. The field gun was deployed now and I saw the charge being rammed home, the shell being carried by a big man who was about to drop it into the muzzle.

"Fire!" I shouted.

The little steam engine chuffed and then, as the multiple one-inch barrels began to turn about their central, longitudinal axis, that harmless sound was drowned out by the hammering of cartridges exploding in rapid succession. The loading of the drum magazine was canister shot. Its effect was . . . horrible. The field gun, its crew no more than bloody tatters of flesh and clothing, fired harmlessly as a dying hand jerked the lanyard.

Somewhere a Nordenfeldt was rattling away, its rate of fire slower than that of our Gatlings, its reports sounding almost shrill in comparison to the noise made by our larger calibre weapons. It was firing at us. Nothing came through the armor of our turret but the clangor of the striking shots was deafening. And I saw the odd, conical protuberances appearing. I wondered what they were, then realized that they were dents seen from the other side.

"Tell Reardon ter bring 'er round, Guv, so's I can get that bastard!" growled Peter.

As he spoke our smokestack, looking like a stick of chewed celery, collapsed. We were blinded by the gritty smoke that poured out from the hole on top of the boiler casing, that came eddying through the vision slits. The steady *chuff chuff chuff* of our engine did not falter—but soon it must start to do so. We had lost our natural draught and our furnace, before long, would be no more than a useless smoulder. Once we lost steam pressure we should be robbed of both mobility and the power to operate our gun. Too, until the smoke cleared we were running blind.

"Stop her!" I yelled down the hatch to Reardon.

We lurched to a halt. The safety valve blew deafeningly. (Oh, the waste of steam that soon we should be needing desperately!) But I knew that there was pressure still, pressure enough to operate the heavy Gatling for more than just a few rounds as long as we found a target before the boiler cooled.

The Nordenfeldt seemed to have stopped firing. I looked

out through the left-hand vision slit; the smoke was clearing now and I could see what was happening. Number two traction engine was pumping shell after shell into a two-story house, the ground floor of which seemed to have been a draper's shop. There was blood and there was broken glass and there was a bedragglement of tattered fabrics, once gaily colored, now only filthy, tattered rags. And was that a dead woman among the wreckage? I was relieved to make out that it was only a broken wax dummy.

There were men still living, the crew of the Nordenfeldt gun. They came staggering out from the ruins of their strongpoint, led by a naval lieutenant in a tattered uniform, capless, with blood running down his face. He was surrendering, was waving a piece of white—or once-white—fabric.

Flynn, the gunner in the number two tractor, deliberately depressed his Gatling to its limit and blew the officer and the naval ratings to shreds with one long burst. It was murder, cold-blooded murder, and I had done nothing to stop it.

(What could I have done? I could, I suppose, have ordered Cease Fire but I had not anticipated that anybody under my command would ignore the flag of truce.)

"Cavalry approachin', Guv," said Peter urgently.

I looked out through the forward slit. There was now only a trickle of smoke from the hole where the funnel had been. I could see that the horsemen were a mixed bunch—police troopers and soldiers and about half a dozen men in civilian clothes. Some were waving swords, others were firing their carbines from the saddle. The fools were coming at us from right ahead.

"There's still steam, Guv," said Peter.

"Then use it!" I told him.

I could see the faces of the leading cavalrymen clearly when Peter opened fire. There was the fat colonel—as I think he was—in his gold-braided, scarlet and blue finery, brandishing his sword. There was the more soberly clad sergeant of police, firing his carbine as he galloped. There were the other faces—plump and thin, clean-shaven, bearded, moustached—and the mouths opened wide as men shouted. I couldn't hear the shouting for long; the

noise inside our turret was deafening as soon as the multiple barrels started to turn, as soon as the heavy cartridges
began to discharge.

And there weren't any faces any more—and when Peter
brought the gun to maximum depression there weren't
any more horses. There was just a tangled mess, a tangled
mess of bloody flesh and splintered bone on the ground,
the muddy, bloody ground, that jerked and twitched as
the canister hail drove into it, through it, mashing it into
the sodden earth.

That was just the leaders of the charge.

Those bringing up the rear were able to rein in, to try
to turn, fighting, literally, among themselves for a clear
run to safety. We would have got them nonetheless. We
would have got them, had not the little steam engine
affixed to the side of the Gatling mount emitted a last,
feeble *chuff* and stopped, its piston in mid-stroke.

The other two traction engines could now bring their
guns to bear. Flynn, in number two, opened up too soon;
a hail of canister shot clanged and rattled on the armor of
our turret. A few balls actually penetrated but their force
was spent. Number three made better shooting. A scythe
of projectiles cut down the last half dozen of the troopers
as they bolted into a side street.

And now here was more cavalry, riding out from behind
the Town Hall. The visibility had worsened, smoke from
the Gatling fire mingling with the misty drizzle. Number-
two tractor opened fire again, once more before the gun
could be brought properly to bear. There was confusion
among the horsemen; they shied away from the eruptions
of mud and steam as the bullets struck the ground. But
Flynn's driver was turning, bringing the vehicle around to
the gunner's requirements.

But who were these horsemen?

Was it green that they were wearing, broad, green
sashes over civilian clothing?

"Sound the cease fire!" I yelled down the hatch to
Reardon.

"What am I going to use for steam?" was his reply.

So much for my whistle signals.

I fell rather than clambered down from the gun turret,

brushed past Reardon and his fireman, knocked up the dog securing the side door. I dropped down to the ground. I ran—slipping at times, stumbling over . . . things—to a position midway between Kelly's troop and the clumsily turning traction engine. I was waving my arms and bawling, "Stop! Stop! Hold it, you fool!" I suddenly realized that I was looking right into the muzzles of the multiple one-inch barrels. A touch on the trigger that opened the steam valve and I should be swept, a bloody mess, into the mess that the canister would make of Kelly and his men. (Even his famous armor would be little or no protection against such devastating fire.)

Arms still held aloft, I walked slowly toward the traction engine. Surely Flynn would recognize me. (And if he did, might he not be tempted to get loose with his Gatling? He did not like me and, more than once, had made it plain that he resented my authority.) I walked on, trying to look braver than I was feeling, and as I did so I saw the muzzles of the gun being depressed to cover me. I had to fight down my urge to scurry out of the field of fire.

I heard the sound of plodding hooves. I turned to see that Kelly had ridden up beside me. He was a towering figure on his horse, his armor gleaming wetly. The green sash worn diagonally over his upper body was torn and the metal of his breastplate was dented in many places. Even that crazy Flynn would have no excuse for not recognizing him.

Kelly said, "Ye were late on the scene . . ." His voice from within the cylinderical helmet had a strange, booming quality. "Ye were late on the scene—an' then ye tried to blow us all into Kingdom Come."

"That bloody Flynn!" I swore. "He's trigger happy."

"He's *your* man, Johnny. Ye're the commodore o' this squadron o' dry land battleships. Surely ye know that the senior officer has to take the blame for everything." He laughed. "An' that's something that I'm beginning to find out for meself!"

We were out of the field of fire of the Gatling now, walking along the length of the traction engine towards the driver's cab. I saw that the caterpillar tracks were clogged with bloody shreds of flesh and clothing. I forced myself to ignore the sight but, even so, had trouble in keeping my last meal down. I swung myself on to the stop up to the cab—and was almost knocked off it when the iron door was flung open from the inside. I climbed up again—to confront Flynn, who had come down from his gun turret.

Like a little, sandy-haired pig, he was, glaring at me out of mad, blue eyes.

"How was I ter know. . . ?" he began, and then his regard shifted to Kelly, looming large and ominously on his horse. "T'was all your fault, Mr. Grimes," he said virtuously. "Ye should ha' sounded the Cease Fire."

"An' you, Mr. Flynn," boomed Kelly, "should ha' seen that we were not wearin' English uniforms an' that all of us were displayin' the blessed green o' Mother Ireland. 'Tis lucky we are that our fight for freedom did not come to an inglorious finish, at your hands, just five minutes agone."

"I still say that Mr. Grimes should ha' given the order to cease fire," muttered Flynn sullenly. "The way that he made us learn all his silly signals, an' then forgettin' ter use 'em hisself."

"Why didn't ye sound the Cease Fire, Johnny?" asked Kelly.

"Because I couldn't, Ned," I told him. "We'd used the last of our steam for a final burst of fire from the Gatling."

"An' why was there no more steam? Ye're the man that knows all about such matters; I'm only a rough bushranger." Despite the muffling effects of the helmet his voice was hard and sharp. "Why was there no more steam?"

"Because," I said, "my bloody funnel had been shot off. Because, with no natural draught to speak of, my bloody fire wouldn't burn. Because . . ."

There was a sudden burst of shooting from a side street. There were wild yells as the Kelly cavalry swung into action, went charging toward this last upsurge of hostile activity. Red Kitty, I saw, was in the lead. She was clad in a lighter version of her husband's armor, probably more picturesque than effective. Her head was uncovered and her hair was gleaming, even in this diffuse light. She had found herself, somewhere, a cavalryman's sabre and was waving it above her head. Fleeting thoughts passed through my mind of Joan of Arc. (But the only voices that Red Kitty was hearing were those of Karl Marx and his more vocal disciples.)

"I'll be seein' yer later, Johnny," said Ned. "I'd better be seein' that me boys don't go gettin' into trouble. Just ye an' yer hunks o' animated ironmongery guard the Town Hall while we do the last moppin' up."

He went galloping after his men.

CHAPTER 44

So we took and held Wangaratta and, the very next day, Beechworth was ours after only a token resistance by the town's few police defenders. This time I rode in the number-two traction engine—Reardon was still fabricating a new smokestack for number one—and, with number three, spearheaded the assault. Flynn was left behind and Kelly, himself, acted as my gunner. He was, of course, in command of the assault although Red Kitty rode at the head of the cavalry. Despite his remark to the effect that armored vehicles would never replace the horse he was quick to recognize the value of the land ironclads. He liked the look of them. With their towering gun turrets, seen end on, they were something like himself when, in full armor, he made his ponderous, seemingly invulnerable advance on an enemy. He . . . identified.

We rumbled up to the police station, the horsemen behind us. We put a burst of canister into the walls, blew in the door and the windows. When the dust cleared an ashen-faced inspector cautiously emerged, waving a large, white handkerchief. The same gentleman took up to the mayor, a portly, bewhiskered individual, who assured Ned that he had always been sympathetic toward the small farmer and the working man and said that he hoped that the new regime would bring a return of peace and prosperity to the State of Victoria.

There wasn't any new regime yet—but we did not tell the mayor that. We held Wangaratta and Beechworth and, by this time, the authorities in Melbourne would know about it and be planning a counter attack in force. But the guerrilla chiefs would also know and throughout the state, those bands, some small and one or two large ones, would be taking advantage of the unrest and embarking on fresh campaigns of looting and terrorism.

"I don't like what I've been hearin'," said Kelly as we discussed matters around the big table in the Wangaratta Council Chambers. "All this robbery an' murder. That man Gilligan—General Gilligan, he calls hisself. They say that at Seymour he robbed the banks. . . ."

"You've robbed banks, Ned," Joe Byrne pointed out. "Ye can't tell me otherwise. I was there too."

" 'Tis true, Joe. But we didn't line up all the staff first and shoot 'em dead. We didn't . . . molest the bank manager's wife an' his teenage daughter. We didn't . . ."

Red Kitty was lighting one of her slim cigars. When she had it going she said through the smoke, "We can turn this sort of thing to our advantage. Victoria is falling into anarchy. The government is weak in this sort of situation and the armed forces are badly led. The people want a strong man on a white horse to take charge . . ."

"I haven't got a white horse," said Kelly.

"But you've a horse. And you have the panzer-wagens. . . ."

"The *what*?"

"The armored wagons, of course. And you are a superb cavalry leader. With your armor and your cavalry you will be able to mount a blitzkrieg."

"And what's *that*, woman?"

"A lightning war."

"I wish that ye'd speak English."

"I thought," she said, "that you do not like the English."

"No more I do." He looked at me and added grudgingly, "O' course, there are exceptions."

"Thank you," I said.

"Talkin' o' panzerwagens an' blitzkriegs," said Reardon, "I'd like to be able to work on the train we captured here. What'd ye be callin' an armored train, Miss Kitty? But no matter. The armor's no problem—sandbags'll have to do till I can get me paws on to some decent iron. But the guns . . ."

"Kevin Doyle, in Eden, will be havin' the word very soon how things are here," said Kelly. "An' then he'll be sendin' the wagons with the guns an' the ammunition."

"Over more'n two hundred an' fifty miles o' bad roads an' hilly country."

"But the traction engines we left to do the job'll be faster than bullock teams," said Kelly. "About four days, would ye say? With a bit o' night drivin'."

"Assumin'," said Joe Byrne, "that there are no ambushes. I think, Ned, that ye should send a party to escort the supply train in from the border."

"An' split me force?"

"Just ten men, say," went on Byrne. "Under young Steven here. . . ."

"I'll be happy enough," said Hart. To one of his age the prospect of an independent command was attractive.

"An' one o' the—" he grinned—"panzerwagens, wi' Johnny in charge. He can play at bein' back on a ship."

"Suits me," I said.

"But who'll be the . . . the general, like?" asked Steve Hart jealously.

"You, o' course, Steve," said Kelly. "I've nothin' against Johnny, here, but, after all, ye've been with me from the beginnin' an' Johnny's a Johnny come lately."

I didn't think that the remark was very funny but all the others did, even Red Kitty.

"Meanwhile," said Reardon, "we can tear up the tracks somewhere between here an' Glenrowan just in case they send more forces against us by train. 'Twill be easy enough to fix the rails again when _we_ want to use 'em."

"Ye're the expert on such matters," Ned told him.

He filled and lit his pipe and then slowly turned his head as he looked at us, one by one.

"Who'd ha' thought it," he said, "only three or so years ago? I was on the run then, an outlaw, an' me mother, Ellen, was in Melbourne Jail. An' now Ellen's livin' in comfort, in luxury even—as, indeed, she should be doin'—an' I . . . An' I . . ." He paused, staring around the table. "An' I am a bushranger again, just as I'd got to like bein' a gentleman farmer."

There was a silence. We all looked at him, wondering whether or not to take him seriously. Then Red Kitty laughed, with an odd mingling of scorn and affection.

"Of course, Edward," she said, "you are a bushranger. But ask yourself how did the kings and the dukes and barons get their start? Just as you are getting yours. By robbery. Violent robbery. But there is one great difference between them and you. They were robbing for the wherewithal to buy power for themselves and their families, for their descendants. *You* are robbing the rich for the wherewithal to buy the power so that it may be handed back to its rightful owners, the toiling masses. You are robbing the English plutocrats and their lackeys of a rich colony that they had misused and oppressed, to hand it to the workers who will make full and proper use of this land. . . ."

Her speech seemed to ignite a fire in Ned.

"Aye," he declaimed. "There has been much injustice in Victoria—as well my mother an' myself know. As you're sayin', Kitty girl, it's up to me to be puttin' things to rights."

"Victoria?" she scoffed. "You will be putting things to rights in all of Australia."

"Easy now, easy now," he said. "I've no quarrel with New South Wales an' the other states. Don't be forgettin' that New South Wales harbored us, even though there must be warrants out for our arrest after the Jerilderie affair . . ." He scowled. "I'll not be bitin' the hand that's been feedin' me."

"Do not deceive yourself," she told him. "There are wheels within wheels. As far as the government of New South Wales is concerned, you are only a very small cog." She frowned. "I am sorry, I did not put that well. As far as the government of New South Wales is concerned you are a pebble in the machinery of the governance of Victoria. It is not likely that in this country there would be a War Between the States, as there was in the U.S.A., but the possibility is present. For example, New South Wales wants free trade between the Australian colonies. Victoria does not. And, no matter what the history books may tell you, the causes of wars are economic."

He said, "You're losin' me."

"Then listen properly.

"You have nuisance value, Edward. There are men, powerful men, in Sydney who deplore the withdrawal of British warships from Australian ports and waters so that they may make their presence felt off the Pacific coast of Canada, a counter to the American Navy. London regards the Riel Rebellion as a threat to the Empire, especially since Washington has sanctioned the supply of American arms to the Canadian rebels and has done nothing to discourage the raising of volunteer regiments to fight for Riel. Dumont has his military advisers from the United States Army. They are being used, of course, Riel and Dumont, although they do not yet realize it. Ever since it came into being the U.S.A. has thought that Canada should be part of its territories."

"And are *we* being used?" demanded Kelly. "Am I being used? Am I just a pawn in the game bein' played by President Arthur against Mrs. Brown "

Red Kitty laughed. "Of course you are—although I doubt if the good Mr. Arthur knows what the stakes are. The railway kings and the mine owners know. As for Mrs. Brown—I have it on good authority that she regards you as merely a minor nuisance too far from England to worry about. And the faithful John Brown, whose brothers spent some time in this country, has been telling her about the sins of the squatters and convinced her that anybody who is against them can't be all bad. Mr. Gladstone sees the dangers of an Australian rising, as so do some of the English generals. But Queen Victoria pays more heed to her Scottish gillie than to her Prime Minister and her War Office. And Brown hates Gladstone as much as he hates the military.

"So, as far as London is concerned, the danger to the British Empire is in Canada, not here. But as far as Sydney is concerned there *is* danger here—but not yet from us. This huge, underpopulated land mass is now unprotected save for volunteer regiments and the decrepit gunboats owned by some of the States. Some, I say. New

South Wales has a navy but no ships. Victoria has only one war vessel of any consequence—am I not right, Mr. Grimes? —the turret steamer *Cerberus*. And in these waters—or in the waters not far to the north of Australia—there is the German Navy. There have been French and Russian warships prowling around your coast. Perhaps even the Japanese might cast covetous eyes upon this virtually defenseless island continent."

Kelly laughed loudly. "Now ye are goin' to absurd extremes, Kitty girl! The Japanese! Next ye'll be sayin' that the blackfellers'll be rising aainst us an' pushin' us all into the sea under a rain o' spears an' boomerangs!"

Red Kitty waited until the laughter around the table had subsided. Then she went on, talking calmly and convincingly.

"I have, as you should know by this time, my sources of information. A . . . friend in Sir Henry Parkes' office. Another friend who is a *Sydney Morning Herald* editor. And this, according to them, is the growing feeling in high places. A rising in Australia—preferably confined to Victoria—might well cause the Colonial Office in London to demand the withdrawal of warships from Canadian waters and their despatch to Australian ports. Killing, as the saying goes, two birds with one stone. Protecting these colonies from rapacious foreigners *and* crushing the Kelly Rebellion."

"An' for that," said Kelly thoughtfully, "they'll be needin' more than a few sailors servin' ashore as artillerymen. They'll be needin' soldiers, regiments o' redcoats. They'll be needin' troop transports to carry 'em . . . An' they'll still be havin' Riel an' Gabriel Dumont to worry about in Canada. An' what if there's a risin' in old Ireland herself?" He drummed the tabletop with heavy fingers. "An' 'tis a long way out here by sea, even by steamship through the Suez Canal. . . ."

I was both amused and impressed by his grasp of the situation. Oh, Red Kitty had taught him quite a lot but still he seemed to have an overall vision, of his very own, of the problems involved.

" 'Tis a pity," he went on, "that we've no ships of our own to intercept the troop transports. An' 'tis a pity that we don't yet have any o' those flyin' contraptions that Major Donnelly was tellin' us about. But we've time on our side. Sir Henry has yet to persuade London to send ships an' soldiers back here. An' we've the arms in Eden, waitin' to be used, an' more guns comin' in the next ship an' the ones after her.

"As we stand now, with our supporters all through Victoria ready to take an active part as soon as they have the guns, with the armored train that Reardon'll soon have ready for us, we can take Melbourne." He turned to me. "There're ships there, Johnny. Not only the Victorian Navy, such as it is, but merchant ships. Fast ships, some of 'em. Ships that we could mount Gatling cannon aboard."

"And crews?" I asked.

"What does that matter? We shall have men enough."

"But not seamen, Ned. You need seamen even aboard a steamer. You need trained, qualified officers. And, in a port like Melbourne especially, you'll need pilots to take them out through the Heads."

"We shall get our seamen, Mr. Grimes," said Red Kitty. "And our officers. And pilots. Most men, even professional gentlemen, will do anything, serve under any flag, as long as the pay is high enough. As for the ships themselves, any ships suitable to our requirements, we have only to declare ourselves the legally constituted government of Victoria and then invoke the Right of Angary."

"An' what's that when it's up an' dressed?" asked Kelly.

"The right of a government, in time of war, to seize neutral ships in its harbors and use them as auxiliary cruisers, transports or for any other purpose. It is quite legal. Compensation, of course, must be paid to the owners of such vessels."

"We shall still have the problem of finding willing, loyal—to us—crews," I said.

"We shall," she told me, "cross that bridge when we come to it. There is, of course, the possibility of using American Volunteers."

"Giving the Yankees," growled Kelly, "even more of a foothold in this country."

"We shall use them," she said, "and pay them for their

services, just as we are using and paying for the arms that they are sending us."

"With money," he said, "raised in America. I don't like it, Kitty girl. I don't like it."

"You will have to like it," she snapped, "or your rebellion will be of no greater consequence than the Eureka Stockade fiasco."

Kelly got to his feet, towering over the rest of us, who remained seated.

"I'm learnin'," he said, "that a leader often has to be doin' things that he doesn't like. But still he can remain true to himself. I give ye my word, all o' ye, that when the Union flag is hauled down, as it will be, the banner to replace it will not be the Stars an' Stripes but the brave standard o' the Golden Harp an' the Southern Cross. This country is rich enough—or will be rich enough—to pay for any and all help we receive from friends overseas. Aye, an' with interest.

"But our loyalties must ever be to our country an' to ourselves."

Joe Byrne caught my eye and whispered, "Our country? Is it Australia he's meanin', or is it Ireland?"

"Australia," I said.

CHAPTER 45

We left the next morning, shortly after sunrise.

Steve Hart was riding at the head of his ten horsemen, he alone in uniform, an outfit that he had seen—and requisitioned—in the window of the shop of one of the town's better tailors. It had been made for a wealthy squatter who was an officer in one of the Victorian volunteer cavalry regiments, who would never now be wearing this finery. Scarlet, gold-braided and-buttoned tunic, not too bad a fit . . . White riding breeches, only just a little baggy . . . A white-plumed helmet . . . The black riding boots were Steve's own. It was a pity, perhaps, that the tunic buttons bore the VR monogram but the curse was taken off them, Steve had said, by the emerald green silk sash that was a diagonal band of contrasting color across his chest.

His men, roughly clad in gray and black, with collarless flannel shirts open at the neck, with floppy, broad-brimmed hats on their heads, untidily bearded, were in almost ludicrous contrast to their sartorially elegant officer. But their carbines were clean, the lightly oiled barrels gleaming. Their horses were well-groomed and lively, although lacking the uniformity of size and appearance of what I was thinking of, rather snobbishly, as *real* cavalry. There was no attempt at riding in any sort of formation.

And what of me?

I was as roughly clad as any of the horsemen and already my hands were greasy after making a check of the Gatling cannon's machinery, and some of the black oil had gotten itself transferred to my face and clothing. I was standing in the turret of my clanking, hissing behemoth, peering out through the narrow vision slits. Flynn, my gunner, shared the cramped accommodation. He was sullen, smoking a blackened clay pipe, saying nothing.

We drove east, passing through Beechworth. There was some half-hearted cheering as we made our way through the town, Steve Hart, on his cavorting steed, lifting his plumed hat and waving it to his admirers. This ceased as my driver made his own salutation, a long-drawn-out tooting of the tractor's steam whistle. There were scowls as we passed through the small crowd on either side of the street. Somebody threw something—a stone?—that clanged loudly on the armor of the turret. It was fortunate that the traverse of the Gatling was limited; had it not been I am sure that Flynn would have opened fire on the spectators.

And then we were out into the countryside again, the road little better than a track, running between wooded hills, past the occasional patch of more or less level pastureland with grazing sheep or cattle, with lonely farmhouses that often were no better than the rude cottages of selectors but, now and again, the sprawling mansions of wealthy squatters.

One of these had been burned out recently. Others of them, I knew, would be abandoned; their owners, men who had done little to endear themselves to the small farmers—or to those whom Red Kitty referred as the toiling masses—having fled to the safety of Melbourne, or across the border into New South Wales.

We made a midday halt on the eastern bank of an easily fordable stream. A fire was lit and the billy boiled for tea. To eat there was bread and cold mutton and cheese. Then, grumbling, Hart's horsemen helped with the cutting of wood and the stowage of the split billets in the traction engine's tender. It was a great pity, I thought, that we did not have a good supply of coal. Eucalyptus burns all right—but it burns too well, too fast. Fortunately nowhere along our route would there be any shortage of fuel for the cutting and taking.

After our meal I walked with Hart out of earshot of the others.

He said, "I suppose Ned has given ye yer orders."

"Aye," I replied, "just as he's given you yours."

He didn't like that.

He went on, "Then you know we must cross the border on time to meet the supply wagons. I can't be stoppin' any place to allow your steam kettle on wheels to catch up."

I said, "There'll be no need for that, Steve. Don't forget that horses tire but a steam engine doesn't."

He snapped, "The horses aren't tired."

"Yet," I said.

He scowled at me.

"Things was much better before we had all these outsiders gettin' involved. Things was good when it was just Ned an' Dan an' Joe an' meself. But now there's Her Ladyship an' a limey sailorman an' all these bloody Yanks gettin' involved. All that's needed to fight a war's a good horse an' a gun. But now . . . Traction engines—may all the blessed Saints preserve us! Cannon that need an engineer to work 'em! An' this talk about flyin' contraptions . . ."

I said, "That's the way of it, Steve."

He said, "The name is Mr. Hart, Mr. Grimes."

I said, "If that's the way you want it."

And then, shortly thereafter, he was leading his men along the road to the southeast and I was trundling after. Despite the roughness of the track I had little trouble in keeping up. But when the evening halt was called the tender was almost empty of fuel.

We kept south of the border, making good time. There was a bitter wind on the second day, straight from the Antarctic it felt, bringing a thin, penetrating rain. We, aboard the tractor, were the lucky ones although, normally, both the gun turret and the driver's cab were comfortless. We made our stop for the night before sunset. Hart wanted to press on but his men persuaded him, not without some angry shouting on both sides, to take advantage of the shelter offered by an abandoned farmhouse. After a not too bad night's rest despite the icy drippings from the leaky roof, we made an early start, at first light. There were grumblings about the breakfast we ate before setting off. The bread, by now, was dry and stale, the cheese hard and the cold mutton stringy, its fat turning rancid.

There was a village on the shores of a small lake—Banambra. We stopped there. The few inhabitants turned out to stare at Hart, in his by now bedraggled finery, and at the big traction engine. I'd thought to conceal the multiple muzzles of the Gatling with some rags of canvas; it is possible that the villagers did not realize that the road locomotive was a war machine. Possible, but not probable. News, especially news of disaster, travels fast, even when telegraph lines have been cut.

The village store let us have fresh bread, and eggs and tinned meat and fish. Hart paid in gold coins—overpaid, I thought. But he must have had strict instructions from Kelly to avoid antagonizing the country people.

Then we were off again, pressing on through the drizzle which drifted in gray tattered veils along the hillsides, rent by the upthrusting gum trees. We overhauled a couple of bullock wagons, which pulled to the side of the rough, muddy road to let us pass. The driver of one of them yelled obscenities as we crunched and spattered by his stationary vehicle, as his patient team cringed away from the hissing, rattling mechanical monster.

"Who d'yer think ye are? Tearin' up the fuckin' patch with yer dirty great fuckin' iron wheels . . ."

The answering toot from our whistle drowned out anything further that he had to say.

So it went on.

That night we camped in the open, with the men huddling for shelter under the traction engine and the tender, with Hart himself condescending to sleep on the steel deck of the relatively warm and dry cab.

So it went on, although the weather improved, with the wind, still cold, coming from the west. Hart was becoming more and more bad tempered, complaining that we were behind time and claiming that it was because he was having to match his pace to that of the traction engine. I pointed out, reasonably enough, that my iron horse showed no signs of tiring, whereas his flesh and blood mounts did. I said that with the gunner as relief fireman and myself as relief driver we could keep going all night. Fortunately he did not take me up on that. The oil lamp mounted at the forward end of the tractor was far from bright and none of the crew possessed the local knowledge of the countryside that Hart did.

We were supposed to be crossing the border at Bendock—assuming that we got there first. Otherwise the convoy from Eden would be crossing at that point and we would meet them in Victorian territory. There was no Customs post in this small village but, so far as I knew, the local police officer would handle Customs matters. If he were still there, which was unlikely. I knew that the Victorian constabulary was being withdrawn from the smaller towns and villages, even those which had not been taken by the rebels, and concentrated in and around Melbourne.

And so, as had been anticipated, the traction engines, each towing a wagon laden with arms and ammunition, trundled into Victorian territory without let or hindrance. We saw them coming a long way off—or, to be exact, we saw their smoke, rising in the still, afternoon air, before they created the hill that we, headed in the opposite direction, were about to climb. Hart shouted something which, in the confines of the gun turret, I couldn't make out. I had a telescope with me and poked it through the narrow vision slit in the armor. The vibration and the jolting made it hard to hold steady, to focus. I saw the horsemen first, four of them, come up over the ridge to commence their descent. Soon, I thought, I should be seeing the first of the tall, smoke-belching funnels.

But something was happening there. The riders, who had already begun their downhill canter, reined in, turned. Very faintly there came the rattle of distant gunfire. There was a heavier explosion. Was somebody using artillery? But that dull-thudding detonation was repeated, after a short interval, only once.

I shouted down through the hatch into the cab, "Give her everything you've got!" and then, to Flynn, "Be ready to use the gun!"

"Loaded and ready, Mister!" he replied.

I heard the brief hiss as he bled steam and water from the cylinder of the little engine.

Our progress up the slope was painfully slow, it seemed. Yet we were overhauling Hart's horsemen; their mounts were, now, in no condition for an uphill charge. My driver tooted the whistle urgently. Some with reluctance, some with obvious relief, pulled off the road—it was little more than a track—to make way for us. Lurching and clanking we continued our painful ascent and, despite the mechanical noises, I could hear, faintly, the shooting and the shouting coming from over the brow of the hill.

We topped the crest, began to pick up speed.

And stopped.

A large gum tree had been felled—the first of the two explosions?—to block any passage, upwards or downwards, along the track. Beyond it were the traction engines and the wagons, their retreat blocked by another fallen tree. There were dead horses on and beside the road. There were two dead men. And there were bullets striking our armor, first single shots and then a sustained volley.

But what was happening? What had been happening?

There were men sheltering behind the wheels of the traction engines and of the wagons. They were firing rapidly—and apparently with little result—at those other men who, from the cover of the trees and brush, were firing back at them. And at us. I could see them, shadowy figures, crouched, scurrying from tree to tree, from rocky outcropping to rocky outcropping.

There were more of them on our right than on our left.

"Bring her round to starboard!" I yelled down the hatch. Then, "Bring her round to the right!"

Ponderously we turned as we backed, steam hissing, our big rear wheels scrabbling for a hold on the rutted surface of the road.

"Fire!"

Flynn pressed his trigger, opening the valve that admitted steam to the piston of the little stationary steam engine. The barrels turned about their common axis, faster and faster. Inside the turret the continuous detonation of the cartridges was deafening as the canister shot sprayed the trees and bushes beyond the roadside. It was as though, I thought, Death himself were wielding the scythe that was bringing down not grass but saplings and sturdy brush— and the men who had trusted in this arboraceous cover to protect them.

The gun fell silent.

I lifted the empty drum magazine from top of it, threw it to one side with a metallic clatter, picked up and dropped into its place a full drum. That thing was heavy. As it fell into position I felt a tearing sensation in my stomach muscles and fell weakly against the armored wall of the turret.

Flynn was firing again—but at what?

From below there came yells and screams and the sound of rifle and revolver fire. The ambushers had launched an attack from the left while I, who was supposed to be in overall charge, had devoted all my attention to the right hand side of the road.

I saw nothing of this fight.

I learned, afterward, that Coglin, the fireman, had struck down three men with his slice bar before being shot and that McTaggart, my driver, had used the Colt revolver that he carried to good advantage. By the time I scrambled down into the cab it was all over. Coglin, a gory mess where his face should have been, was bleeding all over the steel decking and McTaggart, fumbling badly, was trying, with trembling hands, to reload his pistol and, out on the road, Hart and his men were riding down the last of our attackers.

While I was supervising the attachment of ropes to the fallen tree, so that it could be dragged clear of the roadway, Hart came to me.

He said grudgingly, "Ye did well, Mr. Grimes."

"I did what I could," I replied shortly, stooping to make sure that the hitch about the trunk was secure.

"I suppose ye're wonderin' what all this was about."

"Frankly, yes. I know that it wasn't soldiers or police who were fighting us, but. . . ."

"There was a man," said Hart, "who wasn't killed outright but didn't get away with the others. He talked before he died, he did . . ."

"Yes?"

"It was Gilligan's mob behind the ambush. He wanted the guns an' the ammunition an' the steam engines . . ." He glared at me wildly as though it were all my fault. " 'Tis all wrong. Here's you, the outsider, the Englishman, fightin' on our side an' there's our own people fightin' against us. 'Tis 'gainst nature. Why are ye doin' it?"

"It's a long story," I said, "and I doubt if you'd believe it if I told you." I straightened up and waved to McTaggart, who was leaning out and looking back from his cab. "Take her away, Mac!"

Slowly, creaking in protest, with branches splintering, the felled tree was dragged clear of the road.

CHAPTER 46

Back in Wangaratta, shortly after our return to that town, I had occasion to recall this conversation with Steve Hart. It was when, after the evening meal that I had taken with Reardon in the dining room of the hotel that we had requisitioned, I went to seek out Joe Byrne. Somehow he had fallen into a job that could be described as Officer Responsible For The Allocation Of Personnel. It was my intention to persuade him that there should always be a loading number for the Gatling cannon carried in the traction engines. (Those drum magazines, charged with one-inch canister shells, were *heavy*.) I found his lodgings, in one of the other hotels, without any trouble.

Standing there in the poorly lit corridor, with its frayed and faded carpet, I rapped on his door.

I rapped again.

A sleepy voice called, "Who is it?"

"It's me. Grimes."

I heard what sounded like bare feet shuffling over the floor inside, then the sound of the bolt being withdrawn. When I opened the door Byrne—he must have moved fast—was back on his disordered bed. It was obvious what he had been doing. I had smelled that sickly sweet odour before, in ports on the China Coast. Too, there on the bedside table were the paraphernalia—the little oil lamp, the heat-dulled metal stylet, the tiny-bowled pipe.

"Ye'll excuse me, Johnny," said Byrnes, "if I finish me smoke. 'Tis a great pacifier this is—an better far than brandy or whiskey or rum. . . ."

The nineteenth century part of my mind was horrified but my twentieth-century self was not. Those words of Joe's had a familiar ring—although this was the first time that I had heard them applied to opium.

"Ah, 'tis out," mumbled Joe, "an' wi' no more'n one puff taken. . . ."

He held the inverted bowl of the pipe briefly over the smoke-blackened chimney of the lamp, then brought the stem to his mouth. He inhaled deeply, then again, and again, all the time regarding me out of eyes that seemed to have grown too big for his face. And was that fear I read in his expression?

Fear of what?

"Bring me the mirror, Johnny," he croaked. "That shavin' mirror hanging on the wall over the washstand. . . . Hold it up to me, there's a sweet man. . . ."

I did as he had requested.

He stared into the glass. Suddenly he smiled.

"So I'm still here. I'm still in the blessed land o' the livin'."

"What's all this about, Joe?"

He put down the pipe on the bedside table, stretched out a hand to touch me.

"An' ye're here, real enough. Yet there's somethin' odd about ye. Young Steve was talkin' about you to me. Ye . . . ye don't belong."

I said, "But I do. I was a fugitive from British justice—so called—when I joined up with you."

"Ye didn't get me meanin' straight. When I've taken a pipe or two I . . . I see things. I see things different, like. An' now, with you here, I'm seein' things I've not seen before. . . . Like young Steve an' young Dan, burned to cinders, bein' dragged out o' the smoulderin' ruins of Ma Jones' hotel. . . . Like meself, riddled wi' bullets an' dead as a doornail, bein' tied up against a brick wall an' havin' me photograph taken. . . . Like Ned hisself swingin' on the end of a rope in Melbourne Jail. . . . Oh, we're dead, all of us, but *you*. Dan is dead, I know, but the rest of us aren't. Or aren't we? An' Kate is dead but I have the feelin' that she's not, not yet, anyway. . . .

"But you. . . .

"Ye're not here wi' me. Ye're walking up an' down on the bridge o' some steamship, lookin' important . . ."

I said, "Rubbish, Joe. You're seeing things."

"Indeed I am, Johnny boy. I can see that ye don't belong. There're the things ye know an' the odd things ye say, sometimes. I've the feelin' that ye could, if ye so wished, change things back to the way they would ha' been if Curnow—may Old Nick be takin' his black soul! —had stopped that train before it got to Glenrowan . . ."

I said, believing it, "You need have no fears on that score. What you're saying is all a load of hogwash, anyhow."

"Smoke a pipe, Johnny, just one pipe, an' see what ye say then . . ."

He dipped the end of the stylet into something that looked like a cake of soft, dark brown pitch partly enclosed in some vegetable fibre wrapping. He twirled it expertly, then withdrew the tool with a sticky ball on the end of it. This he held over the flame of the lamp, where it bubbled and made almost inaudible hissing noises. He transferred the mess to the now empty pipe bowl. This, in its turn, he held over the flame. Then he handed the pipe to me.

"Draw in deep," he said, "deep down into yer lungs . . ."

It would be no worse than marijuana, I thought. I'd smoked that, in my other life, once or twice and with no ill effects.

The bore of the pipe seemed to be clogged.

I sucked. Hard.

The obstruction cleared itself and there was a rush of sweetly acrid smoke into my mouth. I drew it in, and down . . .

I was slumped in the chair, staring at the assemblage of rotating, precessing wheels. It was doing nothing to me or for me. It was no more than an ingenious mechanical toy. And I was hungry, and I was thirsty, and although my bladder was not exactly bursting I was in need of relief.

I got up and walked out of the laboratory, to the bathroom.

When I came out I ran into Major Duffin. He stared at me as though as at a ghost.

"Grimes!" he said at last, "you're not supposed to back yet."

"I am. What about rustling up some tea or coffee?"

"But the machine's still running. I can hear it. What happened? Did you get killed back in the Past?"

"If I had been," I said. "I should never have become my own ancestor."

"Go through to the kitchen," he said. "You should be able to make yourself a cup of tea. And I'll try to get hold of Graumann. He said he was havin' a night out with some American friends from the Consulate. Oh, it's lucky we are that Ned's not here. If we were he'd be after havin' all of our guts for garters."

"Where is Ned?"

"In Glenrowan. Where else? In a huddle wi' the Chiefs of Staff. Decidin' whether or not to use the Sunday punch in the Nam."

I said, "Things must have gotten worse quickly."

"And they're getting much worse even quicker. But have your tea an' a bite to eat, an' then get all ye've been seein' and doin' and hearin' down on tape while it's fresh in the memory."

"And the machine? The time twister?"

"Let it run. I'm not touchin' those controls—an' if you have any sense you'll keep your paws off 'em too."

CHAPTER 47

I made myself a mug of tea and carried it through into the sitting room. I glanced at the wall clock and saw that it was almost time for the Nine O'Clock News. I switched on the TV before settling down into an armchair.

As Duffin had told me, things were going from bad to worse in Vietnam. The Viet Cong were using a new tactic—or, to be more exact, had revived a very old one, ironically one that we had introduced into warfare during the Australian Revolution. They had manufactured, in jungle workshops, a fleet of primitive Andies, flimsy, motorless affairs of silk and bamboo, hydrogen filled and carrying incendiary bombs with plastic casings. They were silent and, as there was no metal at all in their construction, undetectable by radar. There were shots of a fire bomb raid on Saigon. The cameraman, more by luck than any special skill, had caught a picture of one of the little airships swooping down from the black sky, its underside ruddily illuminated by the glare from the burning buildings. I saw the bombs falling and the dirigible, positively buoyant again, soaring up and away into the smoky darkness, pursued by a stream of tracer fired by some panicky gunner who was missing well astern.

And then there was the coverage of anti-war demonstrations in Australian cities—water cannon and tear gas in Sydney, machine guns, used by both sides, in Melbourne.

Victoria again, I thought. That was where the first revolution—the one that I was reliving—had started. And who would be the new Kelly? Jim Cairns? No. Although he possessed charisma and the gift of the gab he was too old. Ned, at the time of Glenrowan, had been a young man, budding military genius as well as rabble rouser.

Talking of Ned—here was his descendant on the screen, bearded, handsome, looking as the original Kelly would have looked if dressed in late-twentieth-century clothing.

"I appeal to ye all," he was saying, "to present a united front to the world in this time of crisis. We, with our co-religionists in Vietnam, are in the forefront of the battle against Godless communism. Those of our own race, our own blood, who helped us to found this great republic of ours, have deserted us, are squandering their wealth in futile attempts to plant their once proud flag on worthless hunks of rock throughout the Solar System. They say that they cannot afford as much as one cent to support us in our struggle. Not one cent, not one gun, not one man. But I say this—not without sorrow—we do not need them. We are not a giant among nations—as they are. There are, as at last count, only fifty million of us. But we are true to our given word. We shall never desert—as others have done— those who are fighting the good fight beside us.

"Despite the machinations of traitors in our own ranks we shall stay in the Nam until victory is ours. There is weaponry that we have not yet deployed—but we shall do so should the need arise. We are not as timorous as our American cousins in such matters. In Korea they had the God-given opportunity to teach the godless Red Chinese a lesson that they would never forget. They did not have the courage to take it.

"We, with God's blessing, shall not be lacking in courage when the time comes."

"The man's mad," somebody was saying behind me. "He's dangerous. He should be put down."

"Watch what ye're sayin', Doctor," came Duffin's voice. " 'Tis treason ye're talkin'. 'Tis lucky for ye that only Mr. Grimes an' meself heard what ye were sayin'."

I turned in the chair as far as I was able, looked behind me.

Graumann, dragged from some party, was obviously the worse for wear, flushed in the face, his hair untidy, his necktie loosened, his collar open. I could smell the liquor on his breath.

He said indignantly, "Treason, Major Duffin? How can it be? I'm an American, not an Australian."

"Then ye're an undesirable alien. Ye can be deported."

"Deport me as soon as you like. I want out of this crazy country."

"Easy now, Doctor, easy. Ye've a job to finish, just as Mr. Grimes has. Himself wants that history written, up to an' includin' the inauguration o' the first president, the first Ned. An' so I'd like ye to be stoppin' that time twister o' yours before it does some harm to itself an' then you can get things sorted out wi' Grimes, how t'is that he's back in the here an' now while he should still be doin' his bit in the War of Independence. An' then, after he's said his piece on tape, ye can send him back again."

"First," I said, "I shall want a shower and a change of clothing. Then a meal. And then, when I'm ready, I'll get things down on tape."

"You," Duffin told me, "are an Australian citizen, unlike the good doctor here. Which means that you will do as you are told. Ned declared a State of Emergency a couple of days ago, while you were snoring your head off in the chair. The country is under Martial Law. Which means that you will be doin' as you're told."

"Unless I co-operate," I said, "this project goes no further. I've only to scrounge a pipe of Joe Bryne's opium or take some other mind-liberating drug—there must have been some around in the 1880's—to escape from the Past whenever I feel like it."

"So that's what it was . . ." muttered Graumann.

Duffin laughed nastily.

"An' if ye do escape, as ye put it, an' come back here before ye should ye'll be wishin' that ye stayed put. Just see to it that your ancestor confines himself to a Christian man's booze an' tobacco from now on."

I looked at Duffin and read in his face a hardness, a ruthlessness that I had not realized, until now, was there.

CHAPTER 48

It was a Major Kennealy, of the Australian Army Medical Corps, who gave me a check over. I gained the impression that he knew something about the project but did not believe what he had been told. He was regarding all three of us with extreme suspicion.

He said to Duffin, "You tell me, Major, that this man has been smoking opium. I can find nothing in his physical condition to support that statement. But he has been under strain of some kind."

"Is he fit, Doc, to carry on with the . . . with the experiment?" asked Duffin.

"If he's fit now, he won't be after he's been staring at that cock-eyed mess of wheels in the other room. Such a contraption, when in motion, would be enough to give anybody hallucinations." He glared at Graumann. "Oh, I know, *Doctor*, that you've sold the President on the idea that you've a sort of peep-hole into the Past. This is Nazi Germany all over again, so it is."

"Nazi Germany?" asked Graumann, bewildered.

"Yes. When all the quacks—the astrologers and the hollow earth people and the Lord alone knows who else— won the support of Hitler for their crack-brained theories."

"Careful, *Major*," warned Duffin. "You're in uniform. You hold the President's commission. If ye'll just do yer job an' get out of here I'll say nothing about yer treasonous talk."

Kennealy's ruddy face paled.

He said, "I thought. . . ."

"Ye're not paid to think. Ye're bein' paid either to certify Mr. Grimes fit in wind and limb or to tell us when he will be."

"There is nothing wrong with Mr. Grimes that a good night's sleep won't cure," said Kennealy at last.

"An' there'll be nothin' wrong with you as long as you keep your mouth buttoned. Just don't go around sayin' that Ned's like the late, unlamented Adolf. That sort of talk is dangerous. To you."

The medical major put his things back in his bag and, with only the curtest of goodnights, left.

"I think," said Duffin, "that he's about due for a tour o' duty in the Nam."

It was well after midnight when I slid between the cool sheets and tried to sleep. I was tired—but tense. I was not imagining the occasional faint rattle of distant machine gun fire or the less frequent, heavier explosion. And there were sirens—police? fire engines?—some of which seemed quite close. But the screaming of the sirens, their pitch deepening, faded into the distance and died away. And those machine gunners, whoever they were, must either have killed each other or knocked off for the night.

The silence persisted.

I dropped off . . .

And down . . .

And back.

We were standing in a large paddock on the outskirts of Wangaratta, looking at the first of the Aereons. The airship had already made three short test flights and had performed well. A few small leaks had developed in the varnished silk envelope but had been discovered in good time and then patched. Sent out with it from the U.S.A. had been a mobile hydrogen gas generator, that lead-lined, wooden tank on wheels invented by Professor Lowe when he was the Union Army's Chief Balloonist during the

War Between The States. This was working well and was capable of fully inflating the twin gas bags in a little over six hours.

Essentially this early Andrews Airship was little different from the Andies seen in our skies today, although its descendants are used only for recreational activities—or were so used until the Viet Cong launched their fire bomb raids on Saigon. But this was a big beast, its twin, cigar-shaped balloons over one hundred feet long and each almost twenty feet in diameter at the thickest. The slightly wrinkled yellow skin—it would be taut when pressure height was reached—gleamed greasily in the late morning sunlight. Slung below the balloons was the long, wicker-work car with, at its after end, a large rudder. The skids under the gondola rested firmly on the trampled grass and would do so until the first of the ballast was dumped.

Handy to the car was a row of what might have been five-gallon drums—but they were something much more deadly. These were the new dynamite bombs, manufactured by the versatile Dr. Gatling and shipped out to Eden as part of yet another shipment of "agricultural machinery." (On the ship's manifest they had appeared as fertilizer.) They were ingenious devices, set to explode on impact and quite safe (in theory) until primed and armed. We had yet to try one of the things.

There was Kelly, wearing the uniform that had been sent to him by his American Irish supporters, brave in green and gold and with an elaborate golden harp badge at the front of his broad-brimmed hat. There was Red Kitty, also in donated finery of green and gold. (She had shocked Ellen, Ned's mother, when she had had the long skirt shortened to knee length.) The rest of us were in uniform too, as befitted the staff officers of the Army of the Republic of the North East. We were wearing military tunics that were part of the spoils of war over trousers that, in most cases, were obviously of civilian origin. (My own jacket had once belonged to a Victorian Navy lieutenant. I had examined it carefully when it was given me and had been relieved to find neither bulletholes nor bloodstains.) Green silk sashes were the badges of our allegiance.

There was one of us, however, who outshone our Captain General in his sartorial finery. This was "Professor" Duval, our Chief Aeronaut, a carnival balloonist who had been recruited in New York, who had accompanied the Aereon on its voyage out to Australia and who had supervised the assemblage of the motorless dirigible. He was wearing what he had always worn during his exhibition ascents in free balloons—a heavily gold-braided shako, a befrogged Hussar jacket that made him look like a refugee from an Hungarian cavalry regiment, beautifully cut riding breeches and black boots polished to a mirror finish. He was beardless but sported a magnificent moustache waxed to two needle points. He was the very antithesis of Bill Brown, Ground Crew Chief, whose plain blue tunic was stained and in places eaten through by the sulphuric acid that, interacting with iron filings, produced the hydrogen with which the Aereon was inflated. His sparse, untidy beard looked as though it, too, had been splashed by the corrosive fluid. Before joining the forces of the revolution he had been a pharmacist's assistant in Melbourne. When Kelly had called for a volunteer to look after the mobile hydrogen gas generator he had stepped forward. (Such matters were beneath Duval's dignity. "Mr. Kelly," he had said, "I am an aeronaut, not a chemist.")

"She's ready to fly?" Kelly was demanding.

"She's filled to initial lift-off capacity," Brown told him.

"Good. Then get the ballast out, all save what's required for . . . for . . ."

"Maneuvering," I suggested.

"Ye've a word for everything, Johnny," he said. "Then get the ballast out an' the bombs in."

"The *bombs*?" whispered Duval, his flamboyant moustache suddenly very black against the pallor of his face.

"Ye heard me."

"But my understanding was that the *Aereon* was to be used only for observation purposes. To take it aloft with untried weapons that are liable to explode in midair is suicidal."

"There's no choice," growled Kelly. "We've got the word that Steve Hart an' Reardon, an' all the crew o' the armored train, are trapped 'atween Seymour an' Tallarook, ambushed, wi' the line blown up ahead an' behind 'em.

There's been no further word from Seymour. Some bastard must ha' cut the telegraph wires. . . ." His face darkened. "I told the bloody young fool," he said harshly, "not to run south o' Seymour. But it'd be just like him to attempt a raid on Melbourne itself!"

" 'Tis game as Ned Kelly that he is," murmured Joe Byrne.

Kelly turned on him furiously.

"An' that'll be enough from you, Joe. Yer wits are addled wi' what ye've been smokin'." He turned to Brown and Duval. "Get five o' the bombs into the car an' be ready for lift off."

"I'll have no part of this," cried Duval, brave in his cowardice.

"The bombs haven't been tested yet," protested Brown.

"Listen, both o' ye. That train, wi' our friends aboard, is over one hundred an' fifty miles from here. How long will it take us to ride to their help on horseback or in the panzerwagens? Correct me if I'm wrong, Professor, but it's my thinkin' that we can do it in three hours or less in the flyin' ship. But we'll not be doin' any good at all, at all, if we're doin' no more than observe the massacre."

Brown had called some of his men. They were passing bags of sand out of the car. The *Aereon* stirred as a sudden, light draught of air caught the big balloons. Two of the ground crew lifted, between them, one of the bombs.

"Arm the things," ordered Kelly. "Shove in the primer an' the pistol."

"But, Mr. Kelly, even a slight jar will be liable to set it off."

"I don't want to be fumblin' around at the last minute. Get into the car, Professor."

I thought at first that the balloonist was going to obey. But just as he was walking slowly past the row of bombs Joe Byrne brought his hands together with a loud clap. Duval actually squealed. And then he had turned about and was running, running for his precious life, pursued by derisive laughter and volleys of hand-clapping. He tripped over some obstruction, fell heavily on his face. Two men lifted him roughly to his feet, dragged him back to the airship.

"Take him away," ordered Kelly. "Lock him up. We'll manage without him."

I said, "You must have a pilot."

"An' I've got one," he told me. "You. Ye've been on one o' the test flights. Ye were tellin' me that handlin' one o' these things is like handlin' a sailin' ship. An' ye'll not be needin' a compass. All ye have to do is follow the railway line."

"But . . ." I realized that argument was useless, unless I were to suffer the same fate as Duval. So I said, "I shall need a bombardier."

"Ye've got one. Didn't I say that I was comin'?"

Red Kitty said, "I think that I should go."

"No, Kitty girl," he told her, "these bombs are heavy things to be liftin'."

She said, "As pilot."

"Again no. If it should be I'm not comin' back, who's to be runnin' things?"

"Not a woman," muttered Byrne.

Kelly did not hear but she did. I saw her slim hand hovering over the butt of the revolver that was bolstered at her belt.

"Get ye aboard, Johnny," roared Ned.

I clambered over the low rail into the car, took my place by the tiller. Kelly followed me, crouched over the little pile of sandbags that was forward of the single tier of bombs.

"Ye're the skipper," he said to me. "Start givin' orders."

"Throw out two bags," I told him. I felt the airship coming alive. "One more. Now come aft."

We were lifting from the paddock, at first rising almost vertically.

There was, at first, no time for sight-seeing. I had to get the feel of the ship. As I have said, she was rising. Then, with the shift of human ballast, she was coming under control, behaving like a glider—but one gliding upward rather than downward. I felt the wind on my face as our forward motion through the air gathered speed. I heard the ragged cheer from those left on the ground. By this time, I thought, control surfaces should be operative. I looked ahead at a distant clump of cumulus, snowy white against the pale blue sky. I pushed the tiller over to the right. Almost immediately the *Aereon* started to come round to port. I had steerage way.

I kept her coming around until we were almost over the southbound railroad track from Wangaratta. Then I checked the swing. Looking ahead and down I could see Glenrowan in the gap between the hills. We must already be quite high although, with no altimeter, it was impossible to gauge our rate of ascent. I looked up at the gasbags. They were still slightly wrinkled, their surface crawling as the air rushed through the division between them.

Kelly came farther aft to stand beside me, trimming the *Aereon* still more by the stern. The bombs shifted with a faint metallic clanking.

"Get those bloody things chocked off with sandbags!" I yelled.

"Sorry, Johnny. I wasn't thinkin'."

He did as I ordered and then joined me at the helm.

He said, "Apart from one other thing I always thought that ridin' a good horse was best of all. But now I'm not so sure . . ." He made an ineffectual grab as the wind took his gold-braided hat. He laughed. "Oh, well, 'tis a small price to be payin' for this ride!"

I looked up again. The envelope was taut now.

"Run for'ard!" I shouted.

He grumbled, "I was just beginnin' to enjoy it here. . . ."

But he obeyed and as he shambled to the front end of the car I tugged on the cord that would open the two simple valves in the underside of the balloons. I heard the hiss of escaping gas. For long seconds we seemed to be hanging motionless in the air and then, as our nose dipped, we began our downward swoop, picking up speed again until the wind was whistling through the rigging that secured car to envelope.

So it went, swoop after swoop, while the sun declined slowly from the meridian. We both of us wished that we had thought to put on overcoats before lifting off. We were shivering and the chill wind created by our passage was making our eyes water profusely. But we were making good progress to the southwest, keeping the shining ribbon of the railway line below us. It was easy to see, having been kept burnished by the regular sorties of our armored train as it imposed our suzerainty as far as Seymour, maintaining a constant threat to Melbourne. I made no attempt to bypass any of the towns and villages along the track. This would have wasted time and, in any case, it was unlikely that anybody would be looking up to mark us in our flight.

We saw the fighting before we were over Seymour. There was the dirty white smoke drifting between the gum trees; there were the faint muzzle flashes. We heard, diminished at first by distance, the rattle of automatic fire, the ragged rifle volleys, the occasional angry bark of field artillery. And then, beyond the smug town (looking, from the air, an unlikely site for violence—but so Glenrowan, where it all had started, must have looked) there was the armored train, a crippled steel caterpillar assailed by vicious ants. It was fighting back still. There was still ammunition for the heavy Gatlings, still steam to operate the guns.

A last downward swoop brought us directly over the battle.

Behind the train the lines had been blown up, blocking its retreat to the northeast. (Not that such retreat would have been possible, with both locomotives out of action.) The twisted rails were pointing skyward, like the branches of some strange, metallic tree. Then there was the rear coach with its revolving gun turret and the heavy Gatling spitting out round after round of canister. There was the armored ammunition carrier and then another turret coach. Its gun, too, was hammering away. There was the armor-plated car in which was a boiler taken from a stationary steam engine in the Beechworth mine workings. Its funnel was smoking heavily.

There was the horse wagon.

Somebody must have opened a side door, letting down the ramp, possibly with the intention of mounting a cavalry charge against the ambushers. At least one explosive shell had burst inside the coach. There was tattered flesh, red where it was not fire-blackened, and jagged splinters of white bone. There were great gouts of blood. There was the wreckage of men among the animal wreckage.

I heard Kelly curse.

I think that he was more affected by the fate of the horses than that of the human train crew.

But we were low, too low.

"Ballast!" I yelled. "Come aft!"

One of the little sandbags burst harmlessly by the funnel of the Number Two locomotive. It had been derailed but was still upright. Number One had not been so lucky. It was on its side and there were bodies sprawled on the ground just a few feet from it. They must have been thrown clear, and then mown down by e rifle fire of the attackers. Ahead of it was the wreckage of the turret coach, with its ammunition tender, which had been the leading vehicle of the train. The mine must have exploded directly beneath it. I had time for no more than a hasty glance as we swept over it with a clearance of only a few feet, rising rapidly as bullets whined harmlessly beneath us. (Those riflemen weren't used to firing at targets such as ourselves.)

I heard the barking of the field gun astern of us.

"We have to get those bastards!" growled Kelly. "They're bombardin' the train. Why don't ye turn, damn ye?"

I said, "We have to gain height first."

So we gained height, still following the railway track, and then I brought her around as tightly as possible. She handled well. We were now to the right of the railway lines and, farther still to the right, I could see the field gun, well sited in a clump of trees, further protected by earthworks. (The ambush had been well planned.) I could see the blue uniforms of the gunners, some of them around the cannon, others standing by the ammunition cart. Not far from them were other blue uniforms, sailors not artillerymen, and these were serving two Nordenfeldts on wheeled carriages. I could see the smoke and flame spitting from their laterally disposed barrels.

We were diving now, with the gun directly ahead. It fired as I watched. I saw the orange flame and dirty white smoke, mixed with a spray of upflung soil, as the shell burst just short of the train. A man was sponging out the barrel while others stood by with cartridge and shell. They didn't seem to have seen us. But the sailors had. They were struggling with one of the Nordenfeldts, trying to increase its elevation by jamming the trail of the carriage into a shallow gulley.

"Bomb ready!" I yelled.

Kelly lifted one of the drums, held it poised over the side of the car.

"Now!"

He dropped it, scrambled aft, and we began another upward swoop.

I had over-estimated our speed, or our altitude, or both. I heard the roar of the exploding dynamite but Kelly, who had joined me by the tiller and who was looking astern, muttered, "All o' twenty yards short. Let *me* be the judge next time, Johnny . . ."

I turned to starboard, away from the railway tracks. I thought that we should have a better chance of getting the gun if we came in from behind it as the rear of its position was unprotected by trees. Too, we should be out of the line of fire of the Nordenfeldt. I didn't like to think of what would happen if one of its bullets should strike a dynamite bomb.

We made our second dive with Ned at the forward end of the car, a bomb in his big hands, held over the side, ready to be dropped. There were the beginnings of panic among the scarlet-coated infantry on the ground although a few brave men did not run but stood in the open, blazing away at us with their rifles. We were a big enough target but we were fast, too fast for soldiers who had yet to learn the techniques of anti-aircraft fire. I saw one officer emptying his revolver in our general direction.

I saw, too, that at least fifty redcoats were running toward the armored train. Perhaps they thought that they would be safe there from our bombs. Too, the fire from the Gatlings seemed to have ceased. Ammunition must be running low.

"Now!" grunted Kelly.

He dropped the bomb and there was an immediate change of trim and transition from negative to positive buoyancy. We were swooping upward—impelled, it seemed, by the explosion astern of us as the field gun and ammunition supply were destroyed.

"Now!" grunted Kelly again.

Those running soldiers, bunched together, were a tempting target. (Their officer must have been a fool not to have commanded an open order attack on the train; he did not know, any more than we did, whether or not the Gatlings were completely out of ammunition.)

We were lifting at a steeper angle, still picking up speed.

"Now!" Kelly shouted.

The man was berserk.

I heard—and felt—the explosions astern of us. I thought, *This is how a fly must feel when being swatted at* . . . The last detonation sounded heavier than the others.

Somehow I managed to get the *Aereon* back under control. Something seemed to be wrong with the rudder. But I brought her around, ready to make another run across the railroad track. I was not prepared for what I saw and cried out in horror and disbelief. The train was now a total wreck, broken in two and with only a crater where the boiler car had been. Steam from its bursting still mingled with the smoke from exploding dynamite. There were bodies everywhere, some red-coated, some with the broad green sashes that identified them as members of the Army of the North East.

But the sailors manning the Nordenfeldts had escaped the general carnage. They opened fire as we drifted slowly toward their position. A projectile penetrated the flimsy wickerwork of the car as though it weren't there, struck the metal casing of the last bomb a glancing blow. The *clang* as it hit was deafening.

I thought, *This is it.* . . .

And awoke in a tangle of bedclothes, soaked in a cold sweat.

CHAPTER 49

I told Duffin and Graumann of my dream, if dream it was, over breakfast the next morning. The major was amused. He said, "It looks as though we don't really need your time twister any more, Doctor. Mr. Grimes relived the Battle of Seymour—although his version doesn't quite coincide with that in the history books."

"Mr. Grimes," said Graumann stiffly, "has now the ability to relive, in his dreams, the experiences of his ancestors. But it is not a selective process, as has become obvious. We have had glimpses of the Battle of Batoche, in Canada, and of events that occurred during the First World War. Mr. Grimes and I are being paid by your President to write a history of the Australian Revolution. It was purely chance that last night he dreamed of one of the battles."

"Not altogether chance," I said thoughtfully. "Before retiring I watched the news on TV. I saw shots of the fire-bomb raid being made by the Viet Cong on Saigon, using Andies. So, when I went to sleep, I had the Andrews Airship on my mind."

"It ties in," said Duffin. "But do you think that you'll be allowed to put your version of what happened outside Seymour in your history?"

"Why not?" I asked.

"Does the President," he countered, "want a warts and

247

all portrait of the first Ned? Ned Kelly, the military genius, who never put a foot wrong. And now you're tryin'
to tell us that he blew up his own people with a misaimed
bomb. About the only thing that tallies in your account
and the official one is your story about a bullet hitting that
drum o' dynamite an' not setting it off—an' that's the one
that I never quite believed, until now. The Almighty
Himself intervening so that the Sacred Ned was spared to
lead Australia to freedom."

"In any war," I said, "there are dud shells and dud
bombs."

"What is the official version of what happened at Seymour?" asked Graumann.

"According to the history books," I told him, "word
reached the Kelly headquarters at Wangaratta that the
armored train had been ambushed. Ned realized that the
only way to rescue his friends was by using the almost
untried *Aereon* to bomb the Victorian Government forces.
As in my dream, the Chief Aeronaut, Duval, refused to
risk his life on this expedition and so the airship was
piloted by my great-grandfather, with Ned as the bombardier. By the time they got to the train it was too late to
help anybody aboard it; it had been shelled into smouldering wreckage by the ambushers' artillery. So Ned avenged
his friends by dropping his bombs on the Government
troops. That fifth one, the one that did not explode when
the bullet hit it, went off all right when it struck the
ground."

"But why the lie in the history books?" persisted
Graumann.

"Why the lies in any and all history books? If the
Revolution had failed the official story of the Battle of
Seymour might be nearer to the truth—but there would
have been other lies about other battles. . . ."

As I talked I seemed to be slipping back again into the
Past. I was bringing the *Aereon* down to that paddock
outside Wangaratta. We had only just been able to make
the distance, jettisoning our boots and tunics and our
revolvers to maintain buoyancy. We . . . flopped down on
to the trampled grass and it seemed that the twin gas bags

were about to collapse over us. They did not, of course. There was still hydrogen in them.

Brown and Byrne were the first to run up to the car.

"Are they safe, Ned?" cried Byrne. "Did ye save them?"

"No," growled Ned.

He got out of the car. Brown hastily threw in bags of sand before the airship could lift sluggishly. I got out.

Red Kitty took one of Ned's hands in both of hers, began to lead him to the tent that had been set apart for his use. She frowned at Byrne as he began to follow, shook her head. Then, in a soft voice, she said to me, "Come with us, Mr. Grimes."

There were just the three of us in the tent, standing there in the semi-darkness. The dim light of evening could not penetrate the thick canvas.

She asked sharply, "What happened? You're back safely, but there was something . . . bad. What happened?"

"Ask Johnny," muttered Kelly. "He was captain of the flying ship."

So I told her to the best of my ability, leaving out nothing.

She said, "This story you must keep to yourselves. You have our image to consider, Edward. A military leader who blunders will soon lose his following, especially one who, by his blundering, slaughters his own men. This is the way you must tell it. Through no fault of your own you were too late. The train had been destroyed and its wreckage was being overrun by the enemy. All that you could do was to make them pay dearly for their victory. *Your image must not be tarnished*.

"Do you understand?"

"Yes," he muttered. "But young Steve . . . And Reardon . . . And . . ."

"They were probably already dead when you got there," she told him. "You could have done nothing to help them. For their sakes you must help yourself, and the Cause. Without you the revolution will never succeed."

He said, "But I'm not in the habit o' lyin'."

She said, "Today, Edward, wars are fought with words as well as with guns. The skilled user of words can build—and destroy—images."

"It always has been so, Kitty girl," he said thoughtfully. "There were the minstrels of old, a-singin' the praises o' their kings . . ."

"Yes, yes. But we are living in the age of the printing press and the submarine cable. What you do today will be talked about in New York tomorrow—and do not forget that without the support of the Americans our cause would be hopeless. We must have their money and their guns, and the volunteers who must soon now be coming. And who would volunteer to serve under a blunderer, no matter how brave he is?"

I thought, *All through history lions have been led to their deaths by asses. . . .*

"And, of course, Doctor," Duffin was saying, "you must realize what asses the top brass in Melbourne were at that time. . . ."

I blinked, looked across the breakfast table at my two companions.

"They just couldn't believe," the major went on, "that the Army of the North East had at its disposal a dirigible airship. They could have made preparations for countering such a weapon, adapting Nordenfeldts and other automatic weapons for high angle fire. Of course, it seems that the Victorian Navy's Nordenfeldt crew, the men who were quick-witted enough to convert their weapon into an anti-aircraft gun of sorts, were all killed by that last bomb, the one that should have exploded when it was hit by one of their bullets. And the story that got back to Melbourne was that an observation balloon had drifted over the battle, dropping bombs and had last been seen blowing away back to the northeast, losing altitude as it went, probably holed by rifle fire. That was the word that got back to London. But the English War Office probably wouldn't have believed a story about a dirigible airship even if it had been told to them."

"The workings of the military mind are fascinating," said Graumann rather nastily. "Another thing that I can't understand about that war is why the Aereons, once a fleet of the things had been built up, weren't used to batter Melbourne into submission.

"Ned Kelly was a gentleman," declared Duffin. "After

that first experience of his he must have realized that precision bombing was impossible. He refused to entertain the idea of raining high explosives on to civilian men, women and children."

"It's a pity that there are no gentlemen in your military high command today," said Graumann. It's no secret what your Air Force has been doing in Vietnam."

"You were there too!" snapped Duffin.

"But we aren't there now, Major. And neither should you be."

"We keep our word to our Christian allies—which is more than your President Kennedy did!" He took the last piece of toast from the rack, smeared it thickly with marmalade. "And what if we have bombed the hell out of a few Cong villages? They're only Godless, Commie Gooks!"

I wondered what Red Kitty would have thought of Duffin.

CHAPTER 50

And then I was sitting in the chair again, staring at the complexity of shimmering, gleaming rotors which, even while still motionless, exercised their hypnotic effect. Behind me and to my right Duffin and Graumann were continuing their conversation.

"Himself is gettin' impatient," said the major. "He's wantin' the job finished."

"And so am I, you can tell him," said Graumann. "From now on we shall be concentrating on key events. Mr. Grimes will decide what they are. After all, he's the historian."

"But one with a bias, Doctor. I doubt if we shall ever have a first hand account of one of the cavalry actions. Surface ships and airships are all that Mr. Grimes seems to care about."

I turned my head as far as I could and said, "My great grandfather was not a cavalryman. He was a seaman and an airshipman. I can remember only the actions in which he took part. They are the only memories to which I have direct access."

"And so," said Duffin, "you want to be sent back to Eden so that you can participate in an act of piracy that, you claim, was important to the course of the war."

I said, "It was not piracy."

"Opinions differ," Duffin told me. "Even the official historians have doubts about the legality of what was done."

"Angary was legal," I said. "It still is. And compensation in excess of £80,000—a lot of money in those days—was paid to the Union Steam Ship Company of New Zealand."

"All right, all right," growled Duffin. "Send him back, Doctor, so that he can seize his bloody ship, at the Australian taxpayer's expense!"

The gleaming rotors began to turn, to spin, to precess, tumbling down the dark dimensions, dragging me with them.

It was windy on Lookout Point, even though Twofold Bay was sheltered from the westerly gale that had been blowing for three days, lashing the Tasman Sea to fury, making the Bass Strait impossible. It was not conditions in the Strait that were worrying me; it was the weather to the east of Australia. The steamer *Sarah Maddox*, bound to Eden from San Francisco, was overdue. Her continuing non-arrival was a matter of some concern. She was supposed to have among her cargo three Aereons; the gas cells of the original one, Bill Brown had said disgustedly, had gotten to the stage where they couldn't hold small coal. There were crates of rifles and more of the steam-operated Gatlings, some of them of 2″ calibre. There was ammunition for these guns, both 1″ and 2″. The 1″ ammunition was badly needed. We had been obliged to save cartridge cases and to refill them. As a result our Gatling gunners had become expert in coping with misfires and jammings but our solid bullets were not as effective as the factory-made canister. If Melbourne ever learned of our deficiencies a determined attack might well be made on Wangaratta, a well-equipped and -armed drive to the North East.

The Victorian capital had proven to be a very hard nut to crack. Our supporters in that city had demonstrated their capacity for destructive rioting but not for real fighting. The best of them had escaped, to join the Army of the North East. Others were in jail. Some had been executed. The seaport was still functioning, almost as in normal days, with ships coming in from around Australia, from

Europe, from the Americas and from New Zealand. And all that we had was this one small port, which would be ours only for as long as the Government of the Colony of New South Wales continued to turn a blind eye to our presence.

Of course, I wasn't thinking all this as I stood there, staring out to sea. But it is hard to avoid the merging of my two personae, that of my great-grandfather and that of myself. I knew more than my ancestor did of the actual political situation at the time—but he was living through it all while I was no more than an occasional observer. (After what had happened at Glenrowan I had lost all desire actively to intervene.)

So I (great grandfather Grimes) was standing there, on Lookout Point, staring out over the empty, storm-tossed Tasman Sea and wondering when (if ever) the upperworks of *Sarah Maddox* would lift above the horizon. I had my telescope with me and, steadying the long, brass tube against the flagstaff, swept the horizon to the east. I adjusted the focus. The magnification was sufficient for me to see the line dividing sea and afternoon sky as a broken one, with serrations marking wave crests and the troughs between them. But there was never a mast to be seen, never a funnel, not so much as a puff of smoke from a coalburner's furnace.

Perhaps, I was thinking, the overdue ship had made a poor landfall, had raised the coast either well to the north or well to the south of the track laid down on her charts. I swung the telescope to the northeast, to Worang Point. There was nothing there. I swung it back in a southerly direction. And there, quite suddenly, was a ship coming up from the south'ard, just clearing Red Point. She was on a northerly course. Bound for Sydney? I wondered, Hugging the coast to take advantage of the lee of the land? I had known at once that she was not *Sarah Maddox*, which vessel was no stranger to the port of Eden. *Sarah Maddox* was an ugly little brute. This was a big ship, with clipper bow and very tall raked funnel, square rigged at the fore but with sails stowed. Her hull was green, with a yellow ribbon, her upperworks white, her funnel, its color dulled by dried salt spray, red with a black top and three narrow black bands.

She maintained her course until she was well past and clear of the Seahorse Shoals and then turned to port. By this time I had recognized her. She could only be the Union Steam Ship Company's crack trans-Tasman liner *Rotomahana*. But what was she doing here, putting into Eden? I saw her ensign being hoisted aft, the Red Duster, and her houseflag broken out at the mainmast head. It, too, was red, a square flag with the English union jack in its center and around this, in white, the letters U S S Co.

We had been keeping a permanent lookout on Lookout Point. The man on duty was Smith, one of our local recruits. I ordered him to fire the signal cannon. He demurred. (He was one of those people whose distrust of firearms increased in direct ratio to their calibre.)

"But ye've already seen the ship, sir."

"But the others haven't," I told him. "Fire the bloody thing."

He stopped, hooked a cautious finger around the trigger. He jerked it. The flint sparked at the first attempt and there was a satisfying orange flash and deep *boom* as the blank cartridge exploded. The gun rattled back on its carriage.

"Bloody near took me legs off," complained Smith.

"You were well clear. You know how to reload, don't you?"

"Yes, but . . ."

"Reload. With all these visitors you might have to sell your life dearly."

I took pity on him them and reloaded the cannon myself before making my way down the hill to the jetty.

Ned and Red Kitty were on the pier, with others, by the time that I got there. They were making a brief visit to Eden, leaving Joe Byrne in charge at Wangaratta, so that Ned could spend a few hours with his mother, who was in bad health. I stood with them and watched the liner coming in to her anchorage. There was the flurry of white water around and under her counter stern as the powerful, compound engines were reversed, killing her way through the water. There was a splash below her graceful bows as the anchor was dropped and then, sounding loud across the water, the rattle of chain cable running out.

"What ship is it?" Kelly was demanding. "What is it doing here? I was expectin' the American ship . . ."

I said, "She's *Rotomahana,* owned by the Union Steam Ship Company of New Zealand. My guess is that she was bound for Melbourne and found the weather in the Bass Strait too much for her, and put in here for shelter until it's blown itself out."

Red Kitty said, "It looks like a fast ship."

I said, "She is."

She said thoughtfully, "We could use a ship like that. . . ."

"Too right," I said.

She said, "We have talked, in the past, of exercising the Right of Angary. We have always assumed that we should be seizing ships berthed in the Port of Melbourne. But Melbourne is not yet ours . . ."

"So?" I asked, although I could guess what she would be saying next.

"New Zealand is a neutral nation," she said. "And now a New Zealand ship is in one of our ports."

"Eden," I told her, "is not within the territory of the Republic of North East Victoria."

"But it will be," she said. "And, in any case, we can say that it is when we seize that ship."

"The captains of trans-Tasman mail liners aren't altogether fools, you know," I said. "If we go marching aboard *Rotomahana* invoking the Right of Angary the Old Man'll just tell us to get lost. And if we use force Sir Henry, in Sydney, will be bound to hear about it. He's been tolerating quite a lot but he'll not tolerate piracy in a New South Wales port. And just imagine the screams from Pig Island!"

Kelly entered the conversation.

"Ye're the expert on ships, Johnny, an' the law as it applies to ships. There must be some way that we can get our paws on that beauty without treadin' on too many corns . . ."

But how? I wondered. *But how?*

I looked out at the graceful liner, riding quietly to her

anchor in the middle of the bay. She was a beautiful ship and, far more important, she was fast. She would have the legs of anything in the Royal Navy—and as for the ships of the Victorian Navy they would be to her as elderly tortoises to a young and sprightly hare. With her speed, and armed with the 2″ Gatlings—when we got them—and, perhaps, with the new-fangled locomotive torpedoes she would be the pride of anybody's fleet. She was an almost perfect auxiliary cruiser presented to us on a silver tray, and we couldn't touch her.

I looked at the ship. We looked at the ship. Save for the officer of the watch on the bridge and a few hands engaged on various tasks about the decks there were very few people looking at us.

"There must be some way . . ." repeated Kelly.

And I could see, quite suddenly, what that way would be.

Before I could put my ideas into words Dalziell, the new Customs Officer, came hurrying down to the jetty. He was a man at least as venal as Daniels, his predecessor, and even lazier. (Daniels, who could never refuse a free drink, had fallen overside from the boat on the way back from a ship at the anchorage, and had drowned.) Dalziell, obviously, had been awakened from his afternoon sleep. He had put on his rumpled uniform but a large brass collar stud made it plain that he had been unable to find his necktie.

He grumbled to me, "I suppose I'd better go out to her, Captain Grimes. But if she's only in here for shelter she'll not want clearing inward."

"Probably the purser will shout you a drink or two," I told him. "Would you mind if I came out with you?"

"I s'pose not. But you've no business, have you? All o' Stolzberg Brothers' cargoes have been coming in from the States, not from New Zealand."

"True. I thought I'd just like to set foot aboard a real ship again."

Dalziell shambled off to organize his boatmen.

Red Kitty said, "You have something in mind, don't you?"

"I have," I told her. Then, to Ned, "Can you round up a

dozen or so good men to be aboard *Rotomahana* when she weighs anchor? As many seamen as possible; it's a good thing that this weather has kept all the fishermen in port. Uniforms. Shooters."

He laughed incredulously.

"Are ye mad, Johnny? Thinkin' o' invadin' Melbourne with a dozen men?"

"I'm not that daft, Ned. Only one of us can be game as Ned Kelly—and it's not me. But this is the way of it. The border between New South Wales and Victoria—or the Republic of the North East as far as we're concerned—is just over two hours' steaming time from here. I shall tell the captain that here, in Eden, are a number of men whose families are in Melbourne. They are worried about them. The way that things are now it's impossible to make the journey by road and rail. But it is possible to make it by sea."

"And you will board the ship," said Red Kitty, "with your uniforms and your revolvers in your baggage . . . And when you are in *our* territorial waters you will get dressed as soldiers of the Republic and, quite legally, seize the ship."

"Correct," I said.

"But why so many o' ye," demanded Kelly, "when what ye'll be doin' will be legal?"

"The captain might think otherwise. After all, New Zealand has not yet recognized the Republic of the North East."

"Any more than any other bastard has," grumbled Ned.

"How do you know that there'll be accommodation for extra passengers?" asked Red Kitty.

"How many people, apart from the crew, did you see on deck when she came in to the achorage?" I said. "If she'd been a full ship the decks would have been crowded with gawking passengers. There'll not be many traveling from New Zealand to Victoria these days."

"I'd like to be goin' with ye," said Ned.

"You will stay ashore," his wife told him firmly. Then, with one of her rare exhibitions of humor, "You are a bushranger, not a pirate."

Then Dalziell was calling out that the boat was ready.

CHAPTER 51

I clambered down the ladder, at the head of the jetty, into the waiting boat, Dalziell was in the sternsheets, grasping the tiller. On their thwarts, oars tossed, were two of the local fishermen who made the occasional honest shilling by ferrying the Collector of Customs back and forth. I took my place forward, loosened the simple hitch that held the bows to an eyebolt, used the boathook to shove us off from the piling.

"Give way," Dalziell ordered. He liked playing the naval officer. (He had, in his younger days, been a junior paymaster in the Royal Navy.)

The oarsmen pulled with a will and Dalziell maintained a fairly straight course toward the anchored ship. I saw a gleam of reflected light from the port wing of her bridge. Somebody, probably the officer of the watch, had his telescope or binoculars trained on us. Faintly over the water came the sound of a mouth whistle.

I could see activity on the foredeck. A boat rope was being run out, from a forward lead to a position aft. Then there was a clatter as a pilot ladder was lowered over the bulwark until its bottom rung was just clear of the water.

"They might ha' put out the accommodation ladder . . ." grumbled Dalziell.

"They weren't expecting visitors," I said.

Dalziell grunted, concentrated on bringing his boat alongside the liner. He didn't make too bad a bungle of it, although he gave the order, "Oars!"—to cease rowing—a little too soon. But I was able to catch the boat rope with the boathook. I pulled us up to it, secured us to it with the painter. We were directly under the Jacob's ladder. The customs officer went up it first, puffing and complaining. I followed, after the short climb jumping down from the bulwark rail to the deck.

There were two men in blue jerseys with the letters USSCo, in red, on their chests. They looked at us with some distaste. After all, we had shattered the calm of a quiet anchor watch. There was a junior officer, smart in his brassbound, double breasted uniform. His cap band was plain and, apart from the badge, his Company's houseflag with its gold laurel leaf surround, the only golden accessory to his headgear was the chinstrap over the patent leather peak. From what I knew of shipping companies' uniforms I assumed (correctly) that this must be the liner's fourth officer.

The young gentleman regarded the collarless Dalziell disdainfully.

"What is your business, sir?" he asked.

"I am the Collector of Customs for this port," blustered Dalziell. "And this is Captain Grimes, Wharf Superintendent for Stolzberg Brothers."

"We are here for refuge only," said the officer. "There will be no need for Inward Clearance. And, in any case, we have no cargo for discharge in this port."

I looked at him severely. I knew the type. (I had passed through such a phase myself.) Probably he was studying for his next certificate of competency and his brain was full of half digested information on such matters as Shipmaster's Business. He was airing his knowledge.

I said, trying to use the sort of voice that would go with my courtesy title, the stevedore's captaincy, "Mr. Dalziell would like to see the purser. And then I shall be obliged if you will take me to the captain."

The two seamen, standing in the background, exchanged furtive grins. The young officer flushed angrily but swallowed an angry retort.

He said, addressing me, "If you will be so good as to follow me. Sir."

We followed him, through a weather door into the port alleyway of the upper deck accommodation. The purser's cabin, with adjoining office, was at the forward end of this. The purser, jacketless but with brass-buttoned waistcoat over his white shirt, with its stiff white collar and black necktie, was seated at his paper-strewn desk. He looked up as our guide rapped on the frame of the hooked-back door.

"Yes?" he demanded.

"The Collector of Customs is here to see you, Mr. Ling."

The purser threw down his steel-nibbed pen irritably.

"What for?" he demanded. "The captain said that as we were only here for shelter there'd be no formalities, Mr. Davies."

I said, "It may be necessary for the ship to be entered inward and cleared outward, Mr. Ling."

"What's all this about, Captain Grimes?" demanded Dalziell. "I didn't bring any of my documents and stamps with me."

"You can get the preliminaries sorted out," I told him. "It could be that there'll be some passengers from here to Melbourne."

"Nobody ever tells me anything." Dalziell complained.

"Or me," agreed the purser dolefully.

When we left them, on our way up to the bridge deck, the bottle and the glasses were already out.

The master's accommodation was a cabin situated, in solitary state, directly under the bridge, its windshielded entrance on the starboard side. I looked around me as we approached this. It was good, I was thinking, to be aboard a ship again, especially a ship such as this with her holystoned wooden decks, her gleaming white paintwork and glossy brightwork, the burnished brass of port rims and fittings. There were, inevitably, rust stains but these would not be in evidence for long, any more than the white dusting of salt, dried wind-driven sea spray, that dulled the brave red of the tall, raked funnel.

I (or my great-grandfather) was beginning to feel a little

scared. Would I be biting off more than I could chew? Oh, I had already been in command, of a small squadron of panzerwagens and of the *Aereon*—but this vessel was so . . . *big*.

Mr. Davis was knocking on the captain's door.

"Come in!" I heard an authoritative voice from inside the cabin.

The fourth officer opened the door and poked his head inside.

"Sir, there is a Captain Grimes here. . . ."

"I don't know any Captain Grimes. But send him in."

Davis stood aside to let me enter.

The shipmaster was sitting on the long settee upon which he had been stretched out. With slow deliberation he put on first his left boot and then the right, knotting the laces in neat bows. As the purser had been he was in his shirtsleeves but his collar was of the turn-down variety and his black necktie a bow, its end tucked under the collar points. He got up, opened the door of his wardrobe and took from it his double breasted jacket with the single gold band on each sleeve. After he had it on and buttoned up he turned to face me. He was a big man, stout rather than fat, his heavy face clean-shaven. He looked at me for a few seconds, his features creased in a frown, his pale eyes obviously weighing me up. Then he smiled and extended a big hand. I took it. His grip was warm and firm.

"Captain Grimes?" he asked rather than stated.

"Yes, Captain. . . ?"

"Carew." He gestured toward the settee, said, "Be seated."

He lowered his own frame into the swivel chair at his desk.

"And what can I do for you?" he asked.

I said, "I'm wharf superintendent for Stolzberg Brothers. You may have heard of them." (He hadn't.) "Exporters and importers."

"So you may have some cargo for me? To Melbourne, or to New Zealand?"

"Not cargo, Captain. Passengers. For Melbourne. From what I could see as you came in you have an almost empty ship."

"That is so, Captain. There are very few people wanting to travel to Melbourne these days. I can't say that I blame them, with the entire colony of Victoria in a state of turmoil. It seems hard to believe that the man Kelly was not firmly dealt with from the very first moment after the trouble started. But, of course, he's getting help from outside. Each time in Melbourne I hear tales of all sorts of fantastic American weaponry, even balloons." He looked at me keenly. "And would this company of yours, Stolzberg Brothers, be in the business of importing agricultural machinery?" He laughed. "But, by your accent you're English. You'd not be aiding and abetting an Irish rebel."

I let him go on thinking that, although I hated myself for doing it.

I said, "At the moment, Captain, I'm concerned with aiding some people in Eden who are worried about their relatives in Melbourne. As you must know, it is practically impossible to get from Eden to Melbourne by road and rail these days. The railway is nothing more than a private track for Ned Kelly's armoured train—the Shamrock Express they call it. The roads are infested by bands of irregular cavalry, little better than bushrangers." (That much was true) "And the Kelly forces have their huge, steam-driven traction engines with their Gatling cannon. . . ."

"The Americans must be behind him!" Carew told me. "Just as they're behind Riel and Dumont in Canada. And then there's the trouble in the Sudan *and* the rebellion in Ireland. It's not surprising that there's talk of a peace being made between the Canadian rebels and the Canadian government, with the formation of a Republic of the North West. The British Army and Navy can't be everywhere. Now, perhaps, they might be able to spare some ships and men to put down the Kelly rising."

I said, "From what I hear, Dumont has been putting up a good fight."

"And so he should, Captain Grimes, so he should. American arms and American volunteers. They say that it was the Yankee Gatling guns that won the Battle of Batoche for Dumont."

"I've heard the same, Captain," I said.

"They must be really dreadful weapons. Especially the big ones, worked by steam. I'm surprised that nobody has thought of mounting them aboard a ship yet."

"Perhaps somebody has," I said. I laughed. "They'd be ideal for a ship like this. Just the thing for a commerce raider."

"How did you guess?" he asked. "Each time in New Zealand I have all sorts of military people getting underfoot while they decide how many guns the old girl can mount. But they're more interested in the big weapons, six inch and such."

He opened a locker under his desk and brought out a rum bottle and glasses.

"You'll join me?" he asked. "I'll not be shifting out of here tonight or, the way things look, tomorrow. The bottom's fallen out of the glass . . ." I looked at the aneroid barometer on the bulkhead over his desk. The needle registered well below twenty-nine inches. "I don't drink at sea," he went on, "but this is a safe anchorage."

He splashed a generous dollop of the spirit into each of the two tumblers, made a token gesture with the water bottle. He handed me my drink and then raised his own in salutation.

"To your very good health, Captain."

"And to yours, Captain."

"Who were you with before you swallowed the anchor?" he asked.

"Nobody like your company," I said. "Just tramp windjammers, mostly, although I've done time in steam."

"You were in command, though, weren't you?"

"I never got that high. The 'captain' is only a courtesy title."

"Is that so? But there's something about the cut of your jib that makes you look as though you've been in command."

"Small craft, now and again," I admitted. "But nothing big. Nothing as big as this ship of yours."

There was a brief silence as we sipped our drinks.

Then, "I suppose that we'd better get around to business. About these passages . . . For how many would it be?"

"For thirteen, including myself."

He laughed. "An unlucky number! And do *you* have people in Melbourne?"

"The young lady who is to be my wife," I lied. "She was supposed to be joining me in Eden, to marry me here. Now I shall have to go to fetch her. Apart from anything else I want her out of Melbourne before the city falls to the rebels."

"Do you really think that Melbourne will fall, Captain Grimes? Fall to a rabble of bushrangers and peasant farmers?"

"I've been across the border into Victoria," I said. "I've seen something of the weapons that the rebels are using. I've even met their Captain General, as he calls himself."

"You have? What is he like, this Ned Kelly?"

"He's a *big* man, big in all ways. In another time he could have been a king. He is a man with great personal charm. When he speaks it is with a voice, as his men put it, that could charm the birds down from the trees. He is famous for his courage."

"He seems to have made a big impression on you, Captain Grimes. I'm rather surprised that you, an English ship's officer, should speak so highly of an Irish rebel."

"I think, Captain Carew, that he regards himself as an Australian."

"But still Irish Australian. And a rebel. And a rabble rouser. But he could never have won his victories against well-led, well-disciplined British troops. If the stories about peace in Canada are true England will be able to send men and ships to Australia, soldiers with battle experience."

Battles which they lost, I thought.

From somewhere below decks came the sound of a gong.

"You will dine with me?" asked the shipmaster.

"Thank you, Captain. But I came out with Mr. Dalziell, the Collector of Customs . . ."

"He's with the Purser, isn't he? I think that the Company will be able to afford a couple of extra meals this evening."

"And there are the boatmen . . ."

"You do worry, Captain Grimes, don't you? I'll tell the Chief Steward to see that they're fed."

We stopped off at the Purser's office on the way down to the First Class Saloon. Obviously Mr. Dalziell and Mr. Ling had already left for their meal. Captain Carew looked disapprovingly at the almost empty gin bottle on the desk, the two used glasses.

He said, "I suppose that alcohol is one of the best lubricants for the machinery of ship's business, and always will be. But I never cease to wonder at the capacity of port officials."

We made our way aft along the port alleyway and then down the companionway to the saloon.

I quite enjoyed the meal. It was good to be sitting down to table aboard a ship again, to be served by a white-jacketed steward, to handle good silver bearing the Company's houseflag, to eat from china similarly decorated. At the Captain's table there were Carew, Mr. Mason, his Chief Engineer, Mr. Taylor, his Chief Officer, and a Mr. and Mrs. Willard. They were the only First Class passengers on this voyage. Captain Carew introduced me to them.

"And how are things in Melbourne, Captain Grimes?" asked the fat, blonde Mrs. Willard. "There has been news published in Wellington, reports by electric telegraph. Even so, we were reluctant to return. If Percival, here, had any trust at all in his chief clerk we should have stayed in New Zealand until it'd all blown over. . . ."

Willard mumbled something about bloody bushrangers and incompetent policemen.

I told them that Melbourne was still holding out and that the Army of the North East controlled only a narrow strip to each side of the railway line.

"Sea power!" grunted Willard. "Sea power! The man Kelly has no ships and wouldn't know what to do with 'em if he had 'em. Ain't I right, Captain Carew?"

Carew agreed.

And while we were talking I enjoyed the pea soup, the poached smoked fish, the mutton pie and the suet pudding with its generous coating of treacle. As we were dealing with this last course the electric lights came on. I looked with some wonderment at the bulbs with their brightly glowing, coiled, carbon filaments. Aboard any ship in which I had served there had only been smelly oil lamps.

Carew saw my expression and laughed.

"Nothing but the best for the pride of the fleet," he said.

"And do ye know how much that dynamo costs in steaming coal, Captain?" asked Mason sourly. "I don't hold wi' wastin' good steam on luxuries."

"I suppose," I asked, "that this dynamo of yours could be used for a searchlight, Chief?"

"Aye, it could. But what would we be wanting a searchlight for?"

"If the Navy takes us over they'll be fitting one," said Carew.

"If the Navy takes us over," said Mason, "they'll be filling the bunkers. But as long as we're running for the Company I have to account for every lump o' coal."

I said, "You must be running a bit short now."

Carew told me, "By the time we get to Melbourne there'll not be much of our reserve left. At full speed we get through nearly sixty tons a day. That's why I'm not stirring from here until I'm sure of the weather. But as soon as I am sure I'll weigh and get going. That's why, Captain Grimes, I shall want you and the other passengers aboard by ten tomorrow morning. After dinner you can see the Purser and make arrangements for paying the fares."

"And then, Captain," I said, "I must get back ashore to tell the others and to make sure that they have the money."

CHAPTER 52

I took charge of the boat on the way back ashore from the anchored ship; Dalziell, obviously, was in no fit state to do so. He was snoring, huddled in the bows, long before we got to the jetty.

I left the two boatmen to look after him and made my way up the hill, stumbling, in the darkness, over the ruts, to the building that housed the office of Stolzberg Brothers and accommodated that company's management. In the large living room were Ned, his mother, and Red Kitty. Ellen Kelly was engaged in sewing. She had a navy blue frock coat and was replacing its plain, bone buttons with large brass ones. On the sofa beside her was a blue, peaked cap. To this she had already attached one of the golden harp badges which had been sent to us by the Harp In The South Committee. Ned and Kitty were studying papers spread on the table. She was writing something on one of the sheets with a steel-nibbed pen.

"So ye're back, Johnny," Kelly said. "How did it go?"

"It's all arranged," I told him. "As I said, there's plenty of passenger space. All I have to do is to pay the sixty-five pounds the captain is wanting."

"Sixty-five pounds! The man must be thinkin' we're made of money."

"If he were not embarking passengers here," I said, "he'd not be liable for any port dues. And, as he put it to me, the Union Steam Ship Company of New Zealand is not a charitable institution."

"And they call *me* a robber!" grumbled Ned.

"Making a profit is robbery," said Red Kitty. "Morally there is no difference between running a business, such as a shipping company, and robbery under arms."

I asked, "Have you the prize crew organized?"

"The prize crew?" she asked.

"The men who're going to seize the ship."

"Yes," Ned told me. He picked up one of the sheets of paper on the table, squinted at it in the light of the oil lamp. "There are four o' the fishermen who're with us— the Penruddock brothers, Dai Evans and Charlie Moore. Then it seemed to me that ye'd be needin' somebody who knows something about steam engines, so I'm lettin' ye have Mackintosh—he used to be a stoker in the English Navy—and Wallace. He was on the railways. The other six are just men like meself—small farmers, ruined by the banks and the squatters, an' now good soldiers."

"Uniforms? They must have uniforms to make everything legal."

"Don't ye worry. All o' them will be in the green o' the Army o' the North East when the time comes. Exceptin' you, o'course."

Ellen Kelly got up from the sofa, holding the blue frock coat.

"Try this on, Johnny," she said.

I took off my jacket and then was helped into the frock coat by Kelly. It seemed to fit well enough. I looked at what I could see of myself in the wall mirror, then took the cap that Ellen handed to me and put it on my head. Apart from the badge there was no gold on it but it would have to do. Come to that, there was no gold on my sleeves or shoulders—but, after all, Captain Carew, master of that fine, big ship out at the anchorage, was deemed by his employers to be worthy of only a single band on each sleeve while his officers had nothing but brass buttons at their cuffs.

In any case, I thought, a pirate's gaudy finery might be more suited for what I was going to do.

"And when do ye all have to be aboard?" Ned asked.

"Captain Carew wants us to embark no later than ten tomorrow morning," I told him.

"In that case," he said, "I'll send for your twelve good men and true an' you can give 'em their instructions in the warehouse." He raised his voice. "Mick!" Then, "Where is that lazy spalpeen?" Again, louder, "Mick!"

Mick Flannery, who seemed to have become Ned Kelly's doggy, sidled into the room.

"Yes, Ned?"

"See to it that there are lanterns in the warehouse. An'a bottle or two. An' mugs. Then round up the men—ye know who they are—who'll be takin' passage to Melbourne in the Pig Island ship."

"Where shall I tell 'em to meet, Ned?"

"Why d'ye think I'm wantin' lanterns an' bottles in the warehouse? Off with ye, now."

Ned had made a good choice, I thought, as I looked at the men assembled in the warehouse. The Penruddock brothers, black-bearded, blue-eyed Cornishmen, the always cheerful, little Dai Evans, his face, framed by his sidewhiskers, like that of an intelligent monkey, and big, heavily moustached Charlie Moore. And Mackintosh, another big man, his fleshy, ruddy face clean-shaven. And Wallace, in his oil-stained clothing but with an amazingly neatly trimmed beard, who had replaced Reardon as our master mechanic. And there were the others, whom I did not know as well, but who conveyed an impression of reliability under stress.

They looked at me with some curiosity; I was still wearing the uniform that Ellen Kelly had contrived for me.

Ned announced, "Captain Grimes'll be tellin' ye what ye're to do. I've already given ye some idea, but he'll be in command."

I said, "We're to board the ship at nine o'clock tomorrow morning. We shall be, as far as the ship's people are concerned, civilian passengers. Our uniforms, and our revolvers, will be in our baggage. When aboard the ship you are to comport yourself quietly and decently, as first class passengers should. . . ."

"I still can't see, Johnny," Kelly interrupted me, "why

ye should ha' gone to the expense o' booking first class passages, especially when it'll be only for a very short voyage."

"The cabins I've booked," I told him, "are on the upper deck, handy to the bridge. There'll be no need for us to make our way through miles of alleyways and up narrow companionways when the time comes. And in any case, if all goes well, we shall be getting our money back." I addressed the men again. "I can't say, of course, just when Captain Carew intends to weigh anchor. It all depends upon the weather. But once the ship is clear of Twofold Bay you will all go to your cabins and change into your uniforms. Don't come back on deck until I give the word. And then I shall go up to the bridge, and Jack and Peter will come with me . . ." The Penruddock brothers nodded. "Ian and Lew will go down to the engine room, to take charge there." Mackintosh grunted assent and Wallace grinned. "Dai and Charlie—it'll be your job to keep the off duty officers and engineers under control. The rest of you? Stand by, under arms. But remember—*no shooting*. This is a legal operation."

"What shooters do the captain and officers have?" asked Ned.

"That I can't say. Possibly the Old Man has a couple of revolvers in his safe—but he certainly won't be going around armed to the teeth during the course of a normal voyage. Too, shipmasters employed by major companies are supposed to co-operate with local authorities."

Then we partook of a few drinks and engaged in a general discussion and, finally, went to our various lodgings to do our packing in preparation for the following day.

CHAPTER **53**

The following morning, after a good breakfast, I left my lodgings and made my way down to the jetty. My baggage—a small trunk—had been picked up earlier and now, with the luggage of the other members of the prize crew, was waiting on the wharf to be loaded aboard our little steamboat-of-all-trades, *Wombat*. She was an ugly little brute, tug, tender and what ever other use we could find for her. I noted that the canvas cover that hid the Gatling gun mounted on the foredeck was in place. If anybody aboard *Rotomahana* noticed it he would assume that it was just a piece of deck machinery.

Kelly was there, and with him was Red Kitty. They turned to greet me.

"Ah, the admiral has condescended to show his face on deck," said Ned sarcastically. "All yer crew's here, Johnny boy, chafin' at the bit. . . ."

Nobody, I noticed, seemed to be in overmuch of a hurry. The men were sitting on trunks and chests, smoking, talking quietly among themselves. They did begin to bestir themselves as they saw me, using the little, hand-operated crane at the jetty head to lower the baggage down to the tender's foredeck. Then, one by one, they clambered down the ladder to board the steamer.

"And when do we expect to be seein' ye back?" asked Ned.

"That all depends on when Captain Carew decides to sail," I said. "But, at a guess, I'd say about five hours after he does so."

I looked out to the liner, saw that a gunport, beneath which an accommodation ladder had been rigged, was open, also that one of the mainmast derricks had been broken out in readiness to handle our gear.

"He's waitin' for ye," said Ned.

I saw a white burst of steam from just forward of the liner's funnel. Seconds later came the booming note of the whistle. The skipper of *Wombat* tooted in reply. So, I thought, the glass was rising. So Captain Carew wanted to be on his way. I shook hands with Ned. He said, "Look after yerself, Johnny." I was surprised when Red Kitty threw her arms about me and planted a kiss full on my mouth.

And then I scrambled down the ladder to the tender's deck, and then climbed the short flight of steps to the little wheelhouse, standing beside Terry Clancy, *Wombat*'s grizzled skipper.

His crew cast off fore and aft and we chugged our way out to the big ship. I noted that, on the forecastle head, hands were already standing by. I heard the rattle of chain cable as the anchor was being hove short.

The fourth officer, who was standing by at the accommodation ladder head, handed us over to a senior steward. He assured me that our baggage would be brought on board as soon as *Wombat* dropped astern to where that after derrick could plumb her foredeck. I walked aft, saw men at the steam winch controls and at the derrick guys, watched as the cargo net was lifted and then swung overside. The second officer, distinguishable by the two stripes of gold braid around the band of his cap, was in charge of operations. He said cheerfully, "Your gear'll be aboard in two shakes of a lamb's tail, Captain Grimes. And then we'll be on our way."

I went to the rail and looked down. Clancy's men were throwing the baggage into the net, none too carefully. I hoped that nobody had been fool enough to pack a revolver loaded and cocked. (This was unlikely but some of the accidents happening with firearms are the result of stupidity more than anything else.)

The steam winch rattled. The net was lifted clear of the tender, hoisted above the rail and then swung inboard. From his wheelhouse Clancy waved to me. I waved back. *Rotomahana*'s crew cast loose the tender's mooring lines. And then, with black smoke belching from her tall, thin, rusty funnel she was chugging back toward the jetty.

White-coated stewards were helping my men to sort out their possessions, were carrying most of the trunks and blanket rolls to the small block of accommodation on the poop, cabins F to J (omitting I) each of them two berth. My own trunk was taken to M, at the after end of the midships house.

The second officer said, "The captain would like you to join him on the bridge, sir."

I said, "If he doesn't mind I'll see my gear stowed first. There could be some swell outside."

"As you please, sir."

From forward I heard the rapid ringing of the fo'c's'le bell, indicating that the anchor was aweigh. I heard the jangle of the engineroom telegraph bells and felt the slightest of vibrations as the powerful compound engine began to turn. There was no need for Captain Carew to turn his ship; she was already heading to seaward.

It was noisier inside the accommodation than it had been on deck. The steering engine was situated at the forward end, directly under the bridge, and it rattled with every movement of the wheel, as did the rods and chains connected to the rudder.

I pulled out my watch. The time was ten-thirty. The midday meal would be at twelve. We should have to miss it. At that time we should be approaching Gabo Island, not far from the border between New South Wales and Victoria, almost in what I should say were our territorial waters. All of us would need to be in our uniforms.

I left my cabin and went forward to the purser's office, at the end of the alleyway. I had with me the £65 for our fares. Mr. Ling was busy at his desk. He looked up as I rapped on the door frame.

"Good morning," I said. "I've come to pay the fares, for all of us."

"I'll get the tickets ready," he said, but watched as I counted out the banknotes and gold coins from the leather pouch.

I said, "We should really be getting a reduction."

"Why?" he asked.

"Most of the men are already feeling seasick," I lied. "They'll be missing the meal at twelve o'clock. As I shall be myself."

"You, Captain Grimes?"

"I had a late breakfast. Too, I am trying to cut down on eating too much in the middle of the day." I patted my belly. "But I'll make up for it in the evening."

"The more you eat, the more you earn!" he laughed. "And when you're a passenger you should make sure of getting your money's worth. Oh, well. Suit yourselves. I'll pass word to the chief steward."

He gave me the tickets. I thanked him and then walked aft.

I made my way past the after hatch, to the poop passenger accommodation. All the men were at the starboard rail, looking out to the well-wooded shoreline sliding aft and astern. Red Point, marked by Boyd's Tower, was already abaft the beam. As we headed out into the Tasman, before making our turn to the south'ard, the ship was beginning to pitch gently to the swell. At least four of the landsmen in the party were beginning to look uneasy. It was a great pity, I thought suddenly, that I had not been able to assemble an entire prize crew of seamen—but it was too late now to do anything about it.

I addressed the Penruddock brothers.

I said, "You know Gabo Island, of course. . . ."

"Of course," they both said.

"I shall want you all in uniform before we have it abeam. That means that we shall have to miss the noon meal. I've already told the pursuer that none of us will be eating. I conveyed the impression that some of us aren't feeling too well."

"Some of us aren't!" groaned a man called Cowan. He

broke away from his companions, hung over the rail, retching. It was the weather side, of course.

I stepped hastily to one side.

"Stay out on deck, in the fresh air. But don't forget that I shall want you in uniform before we get to Gabo."

"We'll watch him, Cap'n," promised one of the Penruddocks.

"Good. I'll come for you as soon as I want you."

I went back to my cabin. I should have insisted, I realized, on having one on the starboard side so that I could watch the progress through the port. But this was, after all, no more than a minor inconvenience. I shut the door and, as a precaution, shot the bolt. I opened my trunk and took from it my uniform and the leather belt with its holstered Navy Colt revolver. I stripped to shirt and underdrawers, put on the dark blue trousers and resumed my black boots. I folded my civilian suit and put it into the trunk, on top of the green and gold ensign of the Republic of the North East. There would be time enough to get that out and hoisted at the gaff after I had seized the ship. The revolver and the uniform cap I put on the bunk, hiding them with the frock coat, folded so that the brass buttons were not in evidence. Then I let myself out and went back on deck.

The ship was rolling now to the swell that, even in the lee of the land, was evident. Quite possibly, I thought, most of my prize crew would not be feeling like a meal. I walked to the starboard rail, looking out to the land. We were making good time, I saw. Already we were past Green Cape, the long, low tongue of dark land thrusting out to seaward. Ahead was the hulking mass of Howe Hill and below it, to the left, Gabo Island, looking like a huge ship, almost hull down, with a single funnel, the lighthouse.

I looked aft.

Jack Penruddock was out on deck, ostensibly admiring the scenery. Like me, he was in his shirtsleeves, although he was wearing green trousers. They looked rather odd, but there was no law against it. He gave me a wave. I gave him one back.

Mrs. Willard joined.

"Aren't you *cold*, Captain Grimes?" she asked.

"No ma'am," I lied. "This is a pleasantly warm day."

(So it would have been, in the sun, but we were in the shade of the promenade deck above us.)

She laughed. "Oh, but of course you sailormen are used to really cold weather. Around Cape Horn, and all that . . ."

I wished that Captain Carew were hugging the land more closely; we were far enough out that the last of the westerly gale was making itself felt. It was one of those lazy winds; too tired to go around you so it just went through you.

"Why, Captain Grimes, you're *blue!*" said the annoying woman.

I said, "I'll be putting a coat on soon."

"You should look after yourself. You men are all the same. Like children. You have to be told to wrap up warmly."

"It is a bit chilly," I admitted. Then, "Excuse me, please. I'd just like a word with Mr. Penruddock."

"Mr. Penruddock?"

"One of the other passengers who joined in Eden. That's him by the rail, aft."

"Why is he wearing green trousers? Is that the latest fashion in New South Wales? Isn't it dreadful the way in which Melbourne has been cut off from Sydney by that dreadful Kelly person? We just don't know what people are wearing in Sydney these days. . . ."

I broke away from her without showing too much discourtesy and sauntered aft. Just abaft the block of cabins there was a sidehouse, with them WCs and a urinal. I ducked into this latter, out of the wind. Penruddock joined me there. We looked out through the port.

"Not long now, Cap'n," said Penruddock.

"Not long," I agreed. "Just before we have Gabo abeam we'll take over. How are the men? Are they ready?"

"Four of 'em have been spewing their guts up, but we have enough for the bridge and the engineroom."

"Good."

We heard the reverberations of the dinner gong.

"Isn't it strange," Penruddock said, "how things always seem to happen at mealtimes at sea. I could eat a horse. . . ."

"And I."

Through the forward partition we could hear the sound of somebody being violently sick in one of the WCs.

"It's all very well," remarked Penruddock gloomily, "for them that have no appetite for dinner. . . ."

Gabo Island was coming directly under Howe Hill now. It would not be long before we should be in what we should say were our territorial waters.

"All right, Jack," I said. "I'll get back to my cabin to get dressed up. And you'd better get your own tunic on, and see that the others are in uniform. Then come along to my cabin—you know which one it is—and we'll carry on from there."

I put on the frock coat, buckled the belt, with its holstered revolver, about my waist. I put on the cap. I sat on the settee to enjoy a quiet smoke while I was waiting. It was a very short one. Somebody hammered on the door as though he were trying to break in. I got up and opened it.

The Penruddocks were there, quite smartly attired as sergeants of the Army of the North East, with corporals Dai Evans and Charlie Moore. And there were two other sergeants, Mackintosh and Wallace. All of them were armed as I was. All of them, with the exception of Wallace, balanced themselves easily against the rolling of the ship.

"Where are the others?" I asked.

"We're better off without 'em, Cap'n," said Jack Penruddock. "They're curled up in their bunks groaning."

The engineroom door was just forward of my cabin, on the other side of the alleyway. When it was open we could hear the steady beat of the two pistons and were subjected to a gust of warm air smelling of oil and steam. This, obviously, did not worry Mackintosh but Wallace began to look green.

"All right," I said, "Dai can go down with Mack. It doesn't matter that he doesn't know about engines. And you, Lew, stay here in the officers' quarters. Jack and Peter, come with me."

A junior engineer, white-overalled, came out of the engineer's mess to stare at us.

"Who are you?" he asked. "What do you think you're doing?"

"Minding our own business," I said.

"Why are you going down into the engineroom?"

Mackintosh had his revolver out.

"I've always wanted to shoot an engineer," he said.

"Put that bloody thing away!" I told him. And, to the engineer, "Get to your cabin and stay there, if you know what's good for you."

He stared at us, his face suddenly pale. And from the open galley door two cooks and a steward were staring at us.

I drew my own revolver, deliberately fired a shot into the wooden deck. In the confined space of the alleyway the noise was deafening. Doors slammed and there was the sound of bolts being shot. Nobody hindered the Penruddocks and myself as we made our way up to the bridge.

Neither Captain Carew, his third officer or the quartermaster noticed us as we approached the open, port door of the wheelhouse. The master was bringing the ship around to her new course, with Gabo Island lighthouse already just abaft the starboard beam. "Steady so," he said at last. The ship's bows lifted and then slammed down and wind-driven spray rattled on the wheelhouse windows. But there was no heavy water. The run from here to Melbourne would be a fairly good one, with the weather abating all the time.

But *Rotomahana* wasn't going to Melbourne.

"Captain," I said, "I shall be greatly obliged if you will set course for Eden."

He straightened up from the binnacle, shifted his regard from the steering compass to me. He stared at me incredulously, and at the Penruddock brothers, both of whom had their revolvers drawn. The third officer stared at us. The quartermaster, to his credit, allowed himself no more than a fleeting glance before devoting his full attention to the steering.

"Captain Grimes," demanded Carew. "What is the meaning of this . . . this masquerade?"

"It is not a masquerade, Captain Carew. I am exercising

the Right of Angary. Your ship is now within the territorial waters of the Republic of the North East. As ordered by President Kelly I am seizing her for service in our naval forces."

He said, "You have to be joking."

I said, "I am not joking. Besides myself there are twelve armed men aboard your ship, all of whom have had battle experience. Your engineroom is under our control . . ."

"Mr. Crowley," he said.

"Sir?" almost whispered the third officer.

"Find out if he's telling the truth, will you?"

Crowley lifted the brass whistle out of the speaking tube, put his mouth to the now unplugged mouthpiece and blew. He blew again. And again.

And then we all heard the muffled voice in reply.

"What the hell is happening? There's two soldiers down here, in funny uniforms, waving revolvers around and saying that we have to do as they say . . ."

"This is piracy!" blustered Carew.

"Angary, Captain," I told him. "There's a difference."

"Try telling that to Head Office in Wellington."

"I shall, in due course. But I assure you that what I am doing is quite legal."

He changed his tack.

"Have you no shame, Grimes? You, a British officer, serving under a. . . . a bushranger and a rabble-rousing German trollop. Allow me to make prisoners of you and your men and I'll do my best for you in Melbourne."

"A good try, Captain, but not good enough."

Again I tried the firing-a-shot-into-the-deck technique. It worked.

"All right, Mr. Crowley," said Carew tiredly. "Bring her round to port. We'll leave it to the authorities in New South Wales to deal with these dangerous lunatics."

"Sir," said the young officer, "isn't it time that the second was up to take over the watch? Surely he should have finished his meal by now."

"Don't bother me about such things!" snapped Carew. "Ask Captain Grimes. He seems to have appointed himself master of this ship."

CHAPTER 54

Carew stayed on the bridge with me; after all, he was still responsible for his ship. I sent Jack Penruddock down to the officers' quarters to secure the release of the second so that he could come up to relieve the third. I told that sulky young man to arrange for sandwiches and a pot of tea to be sent up to the bridge.

"If you don't mind, Captain Grimes," said Carew, "I'll handle her until she's safe back at anchor in Twofold Bay." Then, suddenly, he laughed. "You know, I admire your cheek—although I doubt that there'll be much admiration for you in Head Office, in Wellington! I can just imagine the screams when they get my cable!"

"What is the feeling in New Zealand about the rebellion?" I asked.

"People call it the Bushrangers' Revolt. Oh, there is some sympathy for your cause among the younger people and among those of Irish origin—just as there must be sympathy for you among some members of my crew. But New Zealand, as a nation, will remain loyal to the British Crown."

"Even if—no, when—we win?"

"Very definitely. Your people have a far different attitude toward the Americans than ours do. We look across the Tasman and see American arms and American military advisers. . . ."

"All of whom," I said, "Ned tends to ignore."

"And there's talk of American volunteers. There'll be more, I suppose, now that they're no longer required in Canada."

I chewed reflectively on my thick ham sandwich.

"There has been word . . ." I admitted at last.

"You're selling your country to the Yankees, Grimes. Once they get foothold you'll become no more than an American colony."

"We shall not," I told him, "not so long as Ned's our leader. But suppose we did . . . Should we be any worse off than as a British colony?"

He said, "I never thought that I should ever hear a British officer say such a thing."

Oh, it sounds absurd, but I felt ashamed. I hadn't been brought up to say, My country, right or wrong. I'd been brought up to think that my country was never wrong. Had I not been caught up, against my will, in the Australian Revolution I should, no doubt, have been among those screaming that Great Britain should send a strong force to deal with the insolent rebels at the bottom of the world. And then the twentieth century, he laughed quietly. It is a fact of history that today's traitor is tomorrow's patriot.

"And what is so amusing, Grimes?" asked Carew coldly.

I said, "John Paul Jones, the British shipmaster who became the father of the American Navy, was called a traitor in his time. As was George Washington."

It was his turn to be amused.

"I might, I just might, see you as another John Paul Jones—but Ned Kelly as a second Washington! A man with no formal education, a criminal. . . ."

"And a man," I said, "who has the imagination to use weaponry that is considered too fantastic to be taken seriously by the generals and admirals."

"And how will he use this ship, then? Fit her with big guns so that she falls apart at the first salvo? Put armor plating around her so that the decks are awash with the weight of it?"

We have moved out from the chartroom to the wing of the bridge. Green Cape was abaft the beam again. The duty quartermaster was steering a good northward course, the officer of the watch was pacing up and down, his face expressionless. The Penruddock brothers were standing in the wheelhouse, their big hands resting on the butts of their holstered revolvers. I looked aft. Somebody had taken the ensign from my cabin; flying from the gaff was the big, green, silk flag with the golden harp at the hoist, the golden stars of the Southern Cross at the fly.

"Should not that be the Jolly Roger?" sneered Carew. "The black flag with the white skull and crossbones? I wonder if they'll take you home to England so that you can be hanged at Execution Dock"

But I knew what was going to happen, I thought smugly.

But did I?

If the course of history had been changed once it could be changed again.

CHAPTER 55

We steamed back into Twofold Bay with the afternoon sun a blinding dazzle in our faces. But it was not so dazzling that I could not see a ship alongside at the jetty; so *Sarah Maddox* had finally arrived and was discharging her cargo quite happily without the supervisory services of Stolzberg Brothers' wharf superintendent. Belatedly, just as *Rotomahana*'s main engines, obedient to Captain Carew's engineroom telegraph, went astern the saluting cannon on Lookout Point boomed to announce our return. Shortly thereafter there was the rattle of chain cable as the starboard anchor was dropped, the tolling of the fo'c's'le bell to give the count of the shackles out through the hawsepipe.

"Four shackles do you?" asked Carew.

"Make it four in the water," I said.

He gave a blast on his mouth whistle, then signaled to the chief officer on the fo'c's'le head, his arms raised and crossed, to secure the windlass.

"What now?" he demanded.

"Tell your people to pack their gear. I'll arrange for you all to land as soon as possible."

"Is there a telegraph office here?"

"No," I said. "The closest is in Bega. You'll be passing through there on your way to Sydney."

I looked out to the jetty, saw that *Wombat* was chuffing out to the anchorage. The canvas cover had been removed from her 1" Gatling and she was wearing the green and gold flag of the Republic at her ensign staff, and green uniformed figures were about her decks.

I said, "I'll be obliged if you put out the accommodation ladder."

He said, "The fourth officer's attending to it now."

From the wing of the bridge I watched *Wombat* coming alongside and the soldiers making their way up the gangway. I had been expecting that Kelly would be leading them, but he was not. It was Mick Flannery, in his lieutenant's uniform, who found his way up to the bridge and saluted me smartly enough.

"The Captain General's compliments, sor," he said. "Will ye please report to him as soon as is convenient?"

I looked at Jack Penruddock and told him, "I'm leaving you in charge. You'll be the senior seaman aboard when I've gone ashore. See that the ship remains at anchor." I turned to Carew. "Will you come with me, Captain? It is time that you met our leader."

Carew didn't like it. He knew that he would be a hostage rather than a guest. But he was in no position to refuse.

One thing that I had not been expecting was a tea party.

There was a starched white cloth on the table at which Ellen Kelly, very ladylike in her best black, with ivory lace at throat and wrists, presided. There was the big teapot and the milk and hot water jugs and the sugar bowl and the cups and saucers with their floral pattern. There was the dish of freshly baked scones, and the butter dish and the jars of honey and homemade jams.

Sitting at the table were Ned and Red Kitty, he in one of his gold-encrusted green uniforms, she in scarlet silk shirt and black trousers. And there was a stranger with them, another woman, in a long, black skirt and white blouse, still wearing a broad-brimmed black hat. But I could see her features—the prominent beak of a nose, the wide mouth, the firm chin. She looked at me curiously.

"Ye're just in time, Johnnie boy," said Ellen. "Pull up a chair an' take some tea. An' yer friend. . . ."

The look that Carew gave me made it plain that he did not consider himself such.

"Ned," I said, "this is Captain Carew. He has come ashore with me to arrange for the transport of himself and his people to Sydney." Kelly pushed his chair back, thrust out a big hand which Carew affected not to see. "And, Captain, this is our Captain General, Ned Kelly. And Mrs. Ellen Kelly . . ." Carew bowed stiffly. "And Mrs. Kitty Kelly. . . . And . . . And . . ."

"Mrs. Louisa Lawson," said the stranger. "From Sydney."

"Louisa," Red Kitty told us, "is a well known advocate of women's rights. Not only of women's rights, but the rights of the common people. She has been telling us of the newspaper she plans to start. It is to be called *The Republican*."

"I had to come here to see for myself," Mrs. Lawson said, "if your revolution should be supported by the republicans of New South Wales. Frankly, I had my doubts. But the baroness has dispelled them." She flashed a brief smile at Ned. "You, sir, have a wife who is your equal, a wife without whom you would never have risen to the heights that you have."

Kelly smirked with embarrassment.

His mother snapped, "And did not I, by bringing Ned up to be proud of the Kelly name, play my part?"

"Of course, Mrs. Kelly," said the Lawson woman. "But, with no disrespect intended to your good self, your views are narrow. Your upbringing is to blame. In your world the woman waits at home, eating her heart out, while her husband or her son goes out to fight the battles. In the world that is to come the woman will fight by her man's side."

"Somebody must be the homemaker," said Ellen Kelly stubbornly.

"A duty that will be shared," Louisa Lawson told her.

"An' while ye're talkin', these men are near to starvin'."

She poured tea for Carew and myself, indicated that we should help ourselves to the freshly baked scones. Rather to my surprise Carew did so, splitting one and making a generous application of butter and jam to its surfaces. I thought that I might as well do likewise.

"How soon will you be able to get your men off your ship, Captain?" asked Red Kitty.

"Let the poor man enjoy his tea," chided Ellen Kelly.

"Ye have Irishmen in yer crew, Captain?" asked Ned. "Perhaps I had better go on board to talk to them. They might be willing to join the Army of the North East."

"Or the Navy," I said. "If there's the promise of prize money . . ."

"Must you make everything so commercial, Captain Grimes?" demanded Louisa Lawson.

"Prize money," I told her, "has always been one of the prerequisites of naval service."

"With the lion's share," she sneered, "going to the officers."

"In *our* Navy," said Red Kitty, "it will be a case of from each according to his ability, to each according to his needs."

"You can't run a ship that way," said Captain Carew. "Or a navy."

Both the younger women glared at him.

Then Louisa looked at him earnestly across the table and said, "But you must realize, Captain, that you have been privileged to be present at the birth throes of a new world—a world in which the worker will be properly compensated for his labor, a world in which both men and women will enjoy the freedom that, now, is enjoyed only by the rich and the powerful. In my own humble way, when I am back in Sydney, I shall labor as one of the midwives. I shall speak, and I shall publish. When the time comes I shall take my place on the barricades, just as the baroness already has."

"These are excellent scones, Mrs. Kelly," said Carew to Ellen.

Louisa Lawson muttered something about brassbound pigs.

Ned said to me, "D'ye think, Johnnie, that I should go aboard the ship to talk to the men?"

"Yes," I told him. "The greater number of her own seamen—deckhands and black gang—who come across with her, the better. She's a *big* ship, Ned. She'll take some running. And until we're able to get some naval recruits locally. . . ."

"There're the fishermen, Johnnie."

"How many of them? And how many of them used to be deep-water men?"

"Ye're the expert on such matters. What d'ye say, Captain Carew?"

"I can hardly be expected to have an opinion to offer, Captain General Kelly," said Carew coldly.

CHAPTER 56

We talked until late in the evening—over drinks, over a meal of roast beef and boiled potatoes produced by Ellen Kelly, over more drinks. Ned was exerting all his charm and Carew was beginning to thaw, slowly at first and then quite rapidly.

" 'Tis a great pity, Captain," said Kelly, "that ye'll not be comin' to us along with yer fine, big ship. . . ."

Carew laughed. "Do you know, Captain General, for two pins I'd be doing just that. I do not advertise my feelings in such matters—in my position it would be improper for me to do so—but think that it is high time that our two nations, New Zealand and Australia, shook off the shackles of England."

"But what are *you* doing about it?" demanded Louisa Lawson. "What is anybody in New Zealand doing about it? We, in Australia, have made a start—with the rebellion in Victoria and a strong republican movement in New South Wales. And in another British colony, Canada, there is also rebellion."

The shipmaster stared at her. Kelly he had been talking to as an equal but he had not known how to treat the two "new women," Louisa Lawson and Red Kitty, one Australian, one German.

He said, rather lamely, "But I still do not think that it is right for ladies to concern themselves with such matters. Wars are for men."

"Would you have said that to Queen Boadicea or to Queen Zenobia, Captain?" demanded Red Kitty. "Both of them were warrior queens who led armies against the Romans who, at that time, were the major military power on this world."

"And both of them lost," said Carew. "At least, Boadicea did. I don't know about the other lady."

"They lost, Captain," she told him, "because the numbers were against them. They were petty imperialists pitting themselves against a great one. But if they had lived today they would have realized that they must gain support inside the enemy's camp—the support of the downtrodden, the slaves and the women. Had they done so they could have won."

"And do you really believe," asked Carew, "that women will play a big part in this rebellion of yours? In any rebellion?"

"There are women in Europe," she said, "who are already doing so. There was a girl I met in Poland, not yet twenty, already known as Rote Rosa. Red Rosa."

"As you are known as Red Kitty," said Carew.

"And Kitty," Kelly said, "does more, much more, than just talk. She is the most trusted of my officers."

"And will she ever be more," asked Louisa nastily, "than just one of your officers?"

" 'Tis content she should be," said old Mrs. Kelly, "to be Edward's wife. And 'tis at home she should be stayin', to wait for her man to come back after the day's hard fightin'. I had hoped to see grandchildren around me as a comfort for me old age—but shall I live that long? Dan in his grave, an' poor Kate, an' now there's you, your ladyship, tryin' to make yerself out to be more of a man than any man ever was."

Carew was unwise enough to mention Joan of Arc.

"An' she was burned by the English, was she not? She came to no good end!"

"Joan of Arc . . ." I murmured. "The Maid of Orleans. A mystic. She heard voices . . . But what voices do you hear, Mrs. Lawson?" Perhaps it was surfeit of rum speaking, my philosophical mood induced by too much alcohol. "But you have had a hard life, haven't you? You have seen social injustice from the viewpoint of those unjustly treated. You have . . . motivation. I think that I am near to understanding you, Louisa. But you, Red Kitty, are still a mystery to me. Titled parents, enough money—more than enough money—to pay for education and travel and a life of luxury. Yet you are not a typical, jet-set, rich bitch . . ." Oddly enough she seemed to be the only one to notice the anachronistic slip of the tongue. Then another twentieth-century expression slipped out. "What makes you tick? Oh, you love Ned, and you're his wife, but you were known as Red Kitty before you came to this country."

She stared at me across the table. She, too, had taken rather too much to drink.

"And what makes *you* tick, as you put it, Johnnie? I'll tell you. You were thrown by chance into the company of one of the most accomplished spellbinders of this age. You have hitched your wagon to his star. And you feel, don't you, that you will rise to heights which you could never have attained as a merchant seaman. But, essentially, you are a mercenary, taking your pay in reciprocated loyalty.

"But what of myself, you ask?

"I will tell you. My father made me what I am—although I think that the way that I turned out finally rather shocked him. He was a man very keenly interested in all the sciences. The *schloss* was always an asylum for philosophers of all kinds. I remember a man who was trying to build a perpetual motion machine, a strange assemblage of wheels and shifting weights. There was another, a chemist, who was endeavoring to produce the universal solvent. There was an explosion, which killed him and destroyed his workroom and damaged adjacent apartments." She laughed. "I was only a small girl at the time, but I remember that it was after this disaster that my father's guests were mainly philosophers who did all their work on paper or inside their own minds. I was allowed to sit up and listen to them talking, to hear their theories about how the world came to be the way it is and how it might be improved."

"It can't be improved by sittin' on yer backside talkin' about it," growled Kelly.

"I know. I know. But there must be talking before there is action. And now, back to my father. He always wanted a son to follow in his footsteps and to become a patron of the arts and sciences or, even, to become a famous scientist himself. But there was to be no son. After my mother's first child, myself, she was told that there could never be another. So my education was one more befitting a young gentleman of my class than a young lady. Philosophy, the sciences. My father could afford the best tutors and, being the man that he was, did not disapprove of the revolutionary ideas that were, at times, propounded. He sympathized with the anarchists and others of their ilk in Russia." She laughed indulgently. "Germany, of course, was different. Was not Bismarck doing his best to ameliorate the lot of the working man? He never realized, of course, that Bismarck was doing no more—or less—than to steal the thunder of the National Liberals by giving his blessing to reforms that were long overdue and that, if not initiated, might be forced at the cost of severe social upheaval.

"I became of age. I said that I wanted to go out into the world to earn my own living. My father humored me. One of his friends was the proprietor of the *Berlinische Zeitung*, one of our more influential newspapers. He persuaded Herr Emmell to create a post for me. It translates roughly to Editor for Ladies' Affairs. But I wanted to be a reporter, to go out in search of news, to find out all about people and to see my findings in print. I wanted to feel that I was helping to influence public opinion.

"I was able to persuade Fritz—Herr Emmell—to allow me to become a reporter. . . ."

(*And what methods of persuasion did you use?* I wondered, not without an absurd twinge of jealousy.)

"I cut my hair, dressed in male clothing. Always with me was one of the men, usually Wilhelm Forster, who usually specialized in political news. With him I attended meetings. I learned about Marx and Engels and their theories. Later I was privileged to meet Karl Marx himself. And, you know, Marx is right. His monumental work,

Das Kapital, will be to future generations what the so-called Holy Bible was to past ones. . . ."

"I'll not have such blasphemy in my house!" cried Ellen Kelly.

"*My* house, mother," corrected Ned sadly. "But go on, Kitty."

"It is all so obvious," Red Kitty continued. "Remember, all of you, that I received a scientific education. I sat at the feet of philosophers. I had read the works of Charles Darwin in the original English. The theory of evolution is, to me, more than a theory. It is a fact. And Marx has done what Darwin did. His dialectic is no more and no less than the application of the principles of evolution to the development of social and economic systems. And Marx tells us how we can control such evolution."

She was making sense to me, although perhaps not to the others. She had become a convert to Marxian socialism—but an intellectual convert, not an emotional one. She, although taking risks when it was necessary, would never be one to die on the barricades. She would trim her sails, as required, to the shifting winds of change. She would get to the top, or as near to the top as one of her sex could in this period. And somehow, along the way, the vision of an Australian Workers' Republic would get mislaid . . .

But Kelly was not thinking on the same lines as I was. Somehow her story—it might have been the first time that he had heard it in its entirety—had planted the seeds of suspicion in his mind, suspicion and jealousy.

"This Wilhelm Forster . . ." he growled menacingly. "An' before him that Fritz whatever his name was . . . You seem to have had them both eatin' out o' your hand . . ."

"They helped me, yes."

"An' they must ha' done more than just . . . help."

She said, "You are absurdly jealous, Edward. But what if there was anything between them and me? Look at it this way. If they had not helped to make me what I am I should never have come out to this country as a roving correspondent. I should never have met you."

" 'Tis *them* that I'm talkin' about."

"A woman's body," said Louisa Lawson with an odd mixture of primness and passion, "is her own, to do with what she will."

Captain Carew stared at her, then at Red Kitty.

"We are not all like these brazen hussies, Captain," Ellen Kelly told him. "An' 'tis ashamed I am to have a guest o' mine forced to listen to such talk at my table."

"Mrs. Kelly," said Red Kitty. "I have respected you for your age, and your strong character, and because you are the mother of my husband. But, as Mrs. Lawson has said, I am my own woman. If my company displeases you, I shall take my departure."

"Perhaps you will accompany me to my lodgings, Catherine," said Mrs. Lawson.

"I shall be pleased to, Louisa. We shall leave the men, and you, Mrs. Kelly, to their drinking."

She got up from the table. She stood there for a few seconds, looking down at me intently. Her eyes seemed to be probes, boring into my brain. It still seems to be fantastic that none of the others noticed but, perhaps, what was to me a searching gaze was only, to them, a mere passing glance. The human mind plays funny tricks with Time—as I should know. And then the Lawson woman was also on her feet, assisted up by Captain Carew. She glared at all of us and then, accompanied by Red Kitty, swept out of the room.

Carew chuckled. "I hope, for your sake, Captain General, that you exercise more control over your army than over your women."

Ellen Kelly rushed to her son's defense.

"O' course he does, Captain. They'd follow him to Hell, so they would. The great pity of it is that Red Kitty will be behind him, doin' the pushin'. I know you Ned, as well I should. Left to yerself ye'd niver amount to anything. Ye've the brains an' the ability, but d'ye have the drive?" This, I thought, was becoming far too much of a home truth session for comfort. She went on, "Why, oh why couldn't ye ha' found a better woman for yerself than that stuck-up German female with all her godless socialist ideas?"

"Her ideas are not yours, mother," said Ned.

"An' more's the pity. Ye've picked a hard row for yerself to hoe, son."

"It's my choice, mother," he told her. "I'll hear no more of it."

CHAPTER 57

Eventually I left them to it. It had become obvious that Ned would not be going out to *Rotomahana* this night to try to enlist her people into the naval forces of the Republic of the North East, or that Captain Carew would be returning to his ship. Fantastically the two men, so very different in birth, background and upbringing, were hitting it off. Ned was more than a good talker; he was also a good listener. This, to him, was a golden opportunity to get the viewpoint of an intelligent outsider, to find out how his rebellion was regarded by the citizens of a neutral country. And Carew, flattered by the Captain General's attention, was talking freely and, when not talking, was listening intently to what Ned had to say.

Old Mrs. Kelly stayed up, her hands busy as she knitted something. She was pleased, I could tell, by the respect with which her son was being treated by the big, smartly uniformed, New Zealand sea captain.

I was tired. I wanted to be able to cope with all the problems that the next day would surely bring. I wanted to have a clear head on my shoulders. So I said good night to everyone—I think that only Mrs. Kelly noticed—and left them to it.

I let myself into my lodgings. My landlady had long since retired but had left a candle holder on the table in the parlor. I lit the candle, turned out the dimly burning oil lamp, and made my way up the stairs to my bedroom. I wasted no time undressing. I got into the clean nightshirt that was laid out on top of my bed and then, almost as an afterthought, hung my uniform in the wardrobe. I put the candle on the bedside table, slid in between the cool sheets.

Lips pursed, I was about to blow out the candle when I heard a soft creaking noise. I looked at the door. It was opening slowly.

Isn't a man entitled to his sleep? I asked myself indignantly.

It was Red Kitty who stepped into the room.

She shut the door behind her and whispered, "I saw the light in your bedroom . . ."

I said, "You almost didn't."

She came to sit on the bed.

"After tonight's exhibition of male superiority I had to come to talk to you, Johnnie. You are . . . different. You don't see things the same way that Edward sees them, or that dreadful man Joe Byrne, or that big, fat New Zealand captain. The idea of treating a woman as an equal does not appal you as it seems to the others. And yet you are an Englishman, a subject of the good Queen Victoria."

I said, "Women of your kind are rare enough in any country, Red Kitty. And, in any country, are mistrusted by most men."

She said, "It will not always be so. But until things change a woman must be content to be the power behind the throne."

She was leaning against me. I was increasingly uncomfortable. She was Ned's woman. What would happen if he decided to find out where she had gotten to, came looking for her? And what would happen to the revolution, with both the second-in-command and the naval advisor shot down by an irate husband?

But nothing could have happened.

If anything had happened, I, my great-grandfather, that is, would never have become the ancestral Grimes whose descendant was, through him, observing the Past. It was all very complicated—or very simple. I was here, wasn't I? Both of me were here. So obviously, Red Kitty had just said her piece—would just say her piece—and then go out into the night and find her own bed.

But I was entitled to a good-night kiss.

Her mouth was hot under mine, her lips mobile, and her tongue from between them made contact with my own. Somehow her shirt had become unbuttoned. Under it she was wearing nothing. I could feel, through my own night garment, the erect nipples of her firms breasts pressing into my chest.

I still can't remember who it was who unbuckled her belt, loosened the waistband of her trousers. It was, I think, a joint effort. But it was her hands that pulled up my nightshirt, drew it over my head and clear off my body, letting it fall to the floor. Even so, my cooperation was necessary.

We looked at each other in the candlelight.

I had not been exactly sex-starved since the death of poor Kate but I had become used, too used, to female bodies that, deprived of the support of corsets, flopped and sagged, the skin of waists ribbed by stays long after their removal. Red Kitty needed no corsetry to keep her body in shape. Her pink-nippled breasts were small but firm. Her narrow waist flared out to surprisingly wide hips; she was one of those women who look far slimmer clothed than naked. Her thighs were full but not overly so. Perhaps this detailing of her parts gives an impression of disproportion but, to me, she was beautiful.

I made to snuff out the candle between finger and thumb but she put out her hand to stop me. And then she was riding me, astride me, her hands on my shoulders while I tried to restrain her—that bed was *noisy*—with mine on hers, pressing her down upon my body.

Her wide open eyes reflected the candlelight. Her teeth gleamed in her open mouth. I was afraid that she would cry out loudly when she reached orgasm—as we reached orgasm—but she did not. She collapsed upon me, her body still throbbing, her mouth on mine.

She . . .

CHAPTER 58

I opened my eyes, looked dazed^l t the complexity of rotors that was slowing to a stop. ⸗ ɪelt uncomfortable. It was obvious from the stickiness between my thighs that my twentieth-century body had experienced what that of my great-grandfather had done almost a hundred years ago.

"He's back," I heard Duffin say.

"Is the recorder ready?" asked Graumann.

"O' course. As I've been tellin' ye, Himself wants the job over an' done with."

I turned in the chair so that I could see them.

"First I want some coffee." I told them. "Then I have to go to the bathroom to . . . to . . ."

"To what?" demanded the major.

"If you must know," I told him, "to change my trousers."

He guffawed coarsely, "Did ye shit yerself, then?"

"Yes," I lied after a few moments' consideration. That episode with Red Kitty would have to be left out of my report. I did not think, somehow, that President Kelly would be amused to hear that my great-grandfather had cuckolded his.

So I went into the bathroom for a hurried shower, then to my bedroom for a change of clothing. When I rejoined Graumann and Duffin I saw that the tape recorder had been set up. I refused to do any talking, however, until I had been given a mug of hot, sweet coffee and an egg and bacon sandwich. While I was enjoying these the windows rattled to the thud of distant explosions.

"What's happening *now*?" I asked around a half-chewed mouthful.

"Panzers in the streets," said Duffin disgustedly. "North Eastern Australia talkin' about breakin' away from the Federation, led by that Bible-bashing bastard Ballocky Petersen. Riots in Brisbane, Sydney an' Melbourne. 'Tis one o' ours ye're hearin' now."

"Ballocky Petersen?" I asked.

"That's what his name sounds like. Some sort o' blown-away squarehead. We should ha' kept Australia Irish, for the Irish. But say yer piece, will ye? Not that it'll be o' any great historical importance."

"But it was," I said. "Apart from anything else, it gave us the nucleus of our fleet. *Maeve*, as the ship was re-named, enabled us to establish a coastal blockade of Victoria. We seized a couple of colliers southbound from Newcastle to Melbourne—and that gave us bunker coal for our operations. And then there were the political repercussions. With Eden being used as a base for commerce raiding operations Sir Henry Parkes could no longer pretend that we didn't exist. He persuaded the Governor—or told the Governor—to send New South Wales land forces to take Eden away from the Victorian rebels. By this time the Army of the North East had been swollen by an influx of volunteers, mainly of Irish origin, from the United States. And a heavy Armstrong coastal defense breech loading gun had been mounted on Lookout Point . . ."

"We can get all o' that from the history books," Duffin told me. "What we want is an eyewitness account of the war. From you. Now."

So I spoke into the microphone while the tape spools turned, while Duffin and Graumann listened. I finished my account with the return of *Rotomahana*, wearing the flag of the Golden Harp and Southern Cross, to Twofold Bay.

"And is that all ye have to tell us?" asked Duffin. "Ah, well, at least we've learned one thing. Your great grandfather wasn't quite the hero that the history books make him out to be. What about the gun fight between him and his people and Captain Carew and his officers? What about his goin' down to the stokehole, when the stokers put on a go-slow, him with a revolver in each hand, bellowing, 'Blood or steam!'?"

"My great-grandfather played no part in writing the official history," I said coldly. "He just acted it, doing as he saw best. He seized the ship for Ned, didn't he?"

"I should have made a study of your Australian history," said Graumann. "However, I did not. I still cannot see why the seizure, legal or otherwise, of a passenger liner should have been of great importance."

"As I've said," I told him, "it enabled us to interfere with the coastwise traffic between Sydney and Melbourne, to impose a blockade. New South Wales had no warships and could do nothing to protect shipping. With the consent of Sir Henry Parkes the Victorian Navy sent *Cerberus* wallowing through the Bass Strait and up the coast to Twofold Bay. She could outgun *Rotomahana*—or *Maeve*—of course, but *Rotomahana* could outrun her. And nobody had bothered to tell her captain about that Armstrong breechloader, with its experimental armor-piercing shells, on Lookout Point. And meanwhile Ned Kelly, with his cavalry and his panzerwagens, had full control of all the roads into Eden.

"Overseas there were repercussions. New Zealand, many of whose people had tended to favor the Victorian rebellion, now adopted a pose of rather hostile neutrality. England decided—at last!—that something would have to be done about Australia. The rising in Ireland had been put down and peace had been made with Riel in Canada. General Middleton's army was available to be sent across the Pacific, from Vancouver, as soon as the ships were available. Admiral Tryon's squadrons were no longer required to maintain a British naval presence off the west coast of Canada."

"And aren't you playing down the help from us," complained Graumann. "Oh, I'm no student of your history, I admit, but I have read about the New York Irish Volunteer Regiment, and about those two American ships, the *Mary McCormack* and the *Colleen McCormack*, fitted out as privateers and, with their crews, sailing under the flag of your Republic of the North East."

I said, "You've missed out Calhoun's Californians and the Baltimore Brigade. But Ned was still *the* general. His was the strategy throughout. Much has been made by the historians of the part played by Red Kitty—but she was never more than a loyal lieutenant in military matters. Politics and finance were her strong points."

"Even so," said Duffin," she must have been quite a woman. Manning Clarke, in his official history, has suggested that there was bad blood between her and Joe Byrne and even hinted that she was implicated, somehow, in Joe's mysterious disappearance. It would be interesting if your great-grandfather knew something about it . . ."

"It would," I said.

CHAPTER 59

This time there was no physician, either civilian or army, to pronounce me sound in wind and limb, fit to carry on with the project. Both Graumann and Duffin seemed to expect that after I'd gotten my most recent experiences down on tape I should once again sit in the chair and allow myself to be sent back into the Past. But I was stubborn. I wanted time to relax, to enjoy a meal and a few drinks. I wanted a proper night's sleep in a proper bed before another session of sharing my great grandfather's life and hard times.

The scientist and the major were not pleased by my attitude but there was little that they could do about it. They took their evening meal with me and, while we were eating, they told me of what had been happening during my absence from the Present. The war in Vietnam was going very badly, with Australian forces withdrawing from the provinces to Saigon. At home the anti-war demonstrators seemed almost at the point of starting a civil war of their own. President Kelly was huddled with his Chiefs of Staff in Glenrowan, like the captain of some storm-tossed, foundering ship in the wheelhouse with his senior officers, desperately fighting to keep his vessel afloat, hearing reports of still more compartments flooded, bulkheads collapsed.

And he was not, I thought, the master strategist that his

great-grandfather, the original Ned, had been. This Kelly had the charisma without the ability—and now the charisma was wearing thin.

There was no TV to watch that evening.

Regular transmissions, said Duffin, had been suspended. He did not tell me why. Possibly he did not know.

So, after a last drink, I turned in.

As before, there were the noises of distant automatic fire, the occasional wailing of sirens. But these sounds did not keep me from sleeping.

Her wide open eyes reflected the moonlight, her teeth gleamed in her open mouth. I was afraid—but why should I have been, out here in this clearing in the bush about which only we knew?—that she would cry out loudly when she reached orgasm, as we reached orgasm, but she did not. She collapsed upon me, her body still throbbing, her mouth on mine.

" 'Tis a pretty sight," murmured a voice, a male voice. "The Lord High Admiral an' the Captain General's lady. 'Twill make Ned's day when I'm tellin' him what's been goin' on behind his back."

Red Kitty rolled off me, leaving me sprawling supine. I looked up into the sleepy yet mocking eyes of Joe Byrne.

"Ye understand that I must dob ye in, Johnnie boy," went on Byrne. "But I bear ye no malice—which is more'n I can be sayin' about that shameless hussy ye're with. Ned'll shoot ye both, like as not, when I tell him about these carryin's on. An' 't'will be good riddance to yer high an' mighty ladyship wi' yer airs an' graces an' yer tryin' to make godless socialists of us all." He laughed dirtily. "That's right, ye bitch. Cover yer nakedness. Ye stripped to the skin for this Englishman here; now ye can hide yer shame from an honest Irishman!"

On her knees Red Kitty was fumbling in the pile of the clothing that we had discarded. Byrne was watching her, as well he might. Her naked body was luminous in the moonlight, her posture as she turned her back to him provocatively erotic. I could have taken advantage of the way in which he was being distracted, scrambled to my feet and jumped him. He was holding a revolver loosely in his right hand but he was not pointing the weapon in any particular direction. He had been smoking, I thought, before he followed either Kitty or myself to our rendezvous. The opium would have slowed his reactions.

And yet . . .

And yet it was the sense of guilt that held me immobile. I had sinned. Red Kitty had sinned. I had betrayed my friend, she her husband.

Kitty got slowly to her feet.

It seemed that she had been unable to find her own clothing in the untidy tangle on the long grass. She was holding my shirt before her, hiding her breasts, covering her body to just below the knees. She turned to face Byrne.

"Joe," she said softly, "look at me . . ."

"I am so lookin'."

"Joe, you have always wanted me. You may have me." Her voice hardened, but almost imperceptibly. "As the price for your silence."

" 'Twould be too much to be payin' for used goods."

She took a step toward him, and then another.

"Used goods or not, you want me. And do not forget that Ned listens to me. You claim that of late you have been ignored, that your true worth is not recognized . . ."

" 'Tis true." Then the barrel of the revolver jerked in my direction. "But what about *him*? What about the Limey outsider?"

"He is not worth worrying about," she said contemptuously.

She was against him now. Her arms went about him and, after long seconds of hesitation, his about her.

Now! I thought. But still the sense of guilt inhibited me. Besides, I had always liked Joe Byrne.

I heard him utter an odd sort of gurgling squeal. Kitty pushed him violently away from her. He staggered backwards. He seemed to be trying to pull the shirt that Kitty had used to cover herself away from his body. He tripped and fell heavily on to his back.

"Bitch!" he gasped. "Whore of the devil!"

His right hand, still clutching the revolver, came up—

and then flopped lifelessly back to the ground before he could pull the trigger.

By this time I was on my feet. I approached him cautiously, stood looking down at him. His eyes were still open, staring sightlessly, his mouth twisted in a snarl. Suddenly the breeze was very cold on my bare flesh. Before I did anything else, I thought, I would get dressed. I tried to take my shirt from him. I had to disengage the cloth from the dead fingers of Joe's left hand. The material was entangled with something else, some protuberance on his chest. I got it clear at last, looked at the haft of the hunting knife that I had last seen in its sheath on Red Kitty's belt.

I put my hand about it to pull it from the fatal wound.

"Leave it there," ordered Kitty. "Leave it until we have carried the body away from the clearing, otherwise he will bleed and leave a trail. It is unlikely that anybody will come looking for him here, but it is possible."

"Let us get dressed," I said.

"Not yet. We do not want to get blood on our clothing." She took the shirt from me, examined it. "You will have to get rid of this."

The dark stain was clearly visible in the moonlight.

So we lifted Joe, I taking his shoulders, Red Kitty his feet, and carried him to a narrow but deep ravine not far from where he had surprised us. Before we threw him into it Red Kitty pulled out her knife, drove its blade into the ground. Blood began almost at once to well from the hole in his chest but was absorbed by his clothing.

Between us we swung the body; luckily she was a strong woman.

We swung the body—one, two, three!—and released it. We heard it crashing through the undergrowth.

She pulled her blade from the ground. The soil had cleared the blood from it and it gleamed evily in the moonlight. She stood there, a naked woman with naked steel in her right hand.

She whispered, "Perhaps I should make a clean sweep . . ."

Knives have always frightened me and she had made it plain that she knew how to use one.

She laughed. "But you are too useful, Johnnie. Not like poor Joe."

But if she had not dropped the knife I should never had allowed her to approach me closely, to throw her long, bare arms about me. And yet I was slow to react. I know that violence and danger are supposed to be aphrodisiac—but guilt can kill desire.

But not for long.

Her hot, moist mouth with its questing tongue was on mine and she pulled me down with her, on top of her, and I was a willing, energetic prisoner in the cage of her strong limbs.

The climax, when it came, was explosive . . .

. . . and I awoke in a tangle of sweaty sheets, by myself, bewildered, utterly lost in Space and Time.

The wail of a siren, a distant rattle of automatic fire, bought me back to the Present.

CHAPTER 60

I joined Duffin and Graumann at the breakfast table.

The major looked up from the morning paper that he was reading and gave me a sour look. He demanded, "Did ye dream again last night? And what did ye dream about?"

I said, "That's my business."

He said, "Anything ye dream, either in the chair or in yer bed while ye're employed on the project is *our* business. The Australian nation's business."

I said, as I took my seat and reached for the coffee pot, "All right. So I dreamed. So what?"

Duffin sneered, "Accordin' to the orderly corporal who looks after yer room it must ha' been some dream. Maps of Ireland all over the sheets. Aren't ye goin' to share the details of yer great grandfather's amors with us?"

"No," I said firmly, then addressed myself to the plate of eggs and bacon that the mess waiter brought me.

"Anyhow," Duffin said, "yer dreamin' days'll soon be over. 'Tis time the project was wound up. The whole, blessed country is fallin' apart about our ears. As a soldier I should be out fightin', not playin' nursemaid to a dim-witted wordsmith an' a mad scientist."

"Thank you, Major," said Graumann coldly. "May I take it, then, that my services are no longer required? That I am free to return to my own country?"

"Not yet, Dr. Graumann. Grimes still has some work to

do. There has to be his version o' the Battle o' the Tasman Sea. His great grandfather was there, an' so was the first Ned. If that ancestor o' Grimes' had been capable o' writin' more than log entries, if Ned hadn't had more important things to do than puttin' pen to paper, there'd already be a decent account o' what happened.

"But there's not."

"And this will be last session?" pleaded Graumann.

"We'll see," grunted Duffin.

I looked out of the window, watched a destroyer making her way down the harbor, bound seawards. I wondered where she was bound, against whom her guns and missiles would be turned.

"Finish yer tucker, Grimes," ordered the major. " 'Tis time we were gettin' the show on the road again."

So I was sitting in the chair, watching the spinning complexity of gleaming wheels, the ever precessing rotors. The roaring of the Time Wind was loud in my ears. No, not a roaring. It had diminished to a sound that was as much whisper as whistle, the noise of a breeze of less than ten knots blowing through rigging of some kind. I looked around me. I was in the car of one of our small fleet of Aereons, my hand on the tiller. On the fragile deck ahead of me were five dynamite bombs, secure in the frame that had been devised for their safe carriage. Sitting on one of them was Colby, my bombardier. He had been one of *Rotomahana*'s quartermasters, one of her crew who had come across with her after Ned's impassioned recruiting speech. Somehow he had transferred to the aeronautical branch of our naval service.

He turned to look aft. A gleaming, white smile split his dark bearded face. "Smoke ahead, about one point to starboard, Commodore. Looks like the Limey fleet."

"I see it," I replied.

I looked out over the side of the car and down, remembering as I did so (for the benefit of my twentieth-century self) all that had gone before, the trials carried out in the Tasman Sea, out of sight of land, of release and picking up techniques, the dummy bombing runs, using sandbags, on the target towed by the faithful *Wombat*, the working out of a simple code of signals using the newfangled flare pistols that had been among the material sent to us by our American well-wishers. I remembered, too, how Ned had pushed the idea. When he first proposed it I—as had been many others—had been incredulous.

"Surface ships towing airships? It can't be done. The Aereons, for all their size, are flimsy things. They'd tear themselves to pieces."

"Would they, Johnnie? How d'ye know? After all, the surface ships will not be doin' more than about ten miles an hour—and the Aereons, on their downward swoops, do all o' fifty. An', in any case, it's already been done."

"*What?*"

"Ye heard me, Johnnie. Ever since we started playin' around wi' these dirigible balloons I've been doin' a power o' readin'. Observation balloons—just the ordinary round ones—were used by both sides durin' the Civil War in America. The Union Army used to tow them up an' down rivers; they were towed from barges which were towed by tugboats. If it worked for the Yankees it should work for us."

I said stubbornly, "I still can't see the point of it. When the Limeys come we lift off from our base here, in Eden, drop our bombs and return, to load more bombs if necessary."

"An' meanwhile, Johnnie, those ships that haven't been sunk will be gettin' in close an' will have us within range o' their big guns. Too, accordin' to Louisa—I still don't know where she gets all her information from—General Middleton's intention is to land his troops in Sydney, from where they will march south, releasing the escorting warships, under Admiral Tryon, to come an' batter us into submission from the sea. Oh, *Maeve* an' the McCormack girls'd have the time o' their lives if they got among the troop transports—but they've no armor an' only 2" Gatlings. Tryon's steam frigates'd blow 'em out o' the water before they got close enough to fire a shot o' their own."

"I still don't think that it would work," I said.

He told me, "There's only one way to find out."

And so while the invasion fleet, vessels of the Royal Navy and requisitioned passenger liners, made its way from Vancouver to Wellington, we played around with our flimsy gasbags. Our aeronauts were a mixed bunch. There was Ned himself, saying, over Red Kitty's protests, that he would never tell any man to do a job that he was afraid of doing himself. Red Kitty wanted to fly with him but, for once, he put his foot down firmly—and, for once, she submitted. (At the time I wondered why.) There was Jim Kelly, who had come wandering into his brother's headquarters to join him in his fight for freedom. There was Flannery, who usually was second mate of *Mary McCormack*, and Shawcross, a lieutenant in Calhoun's Californians. There was myself. I didn't like having to hand over command of the surface fleet to Captain Reilly of *Colleen McCormack*—he was the senior of the two American captains—but I couldn't be in two places at the same time. I had to be content with being second in command of our tiny squadron of five airships.

Crowley—who had been third officer of *Rotomahana* at the time of the takeover—had become my chief officer in that renamed ship. Apart from his tendency to sulk if meals were not on time he was an extremely capable young man, a good seaman and navigator. His appointment as acting master of *Maeve* gave me no cause for worry.

Anyhow, I was looking out and down from the car of my Aereon, which I had named *Kate*. Almost directly below, but a little ahead, was *Maeve*. She looked surprisingly small from the air. I could see on her decks the dull-gleaming shapes of the 2″ Gatlings and even the wisp of steam that leaked from the actuating machinery. The guns were cleared away and ready but, if all went well, they would never be used. To starboard of *Maeve* was *Mary McCormack*, like her with a green hull and funnel and white upperworks. She was a far less graceful ship but almost as fast. Then there was her sister, *Colleen McCormack*, and then the coastal steamer *Merino*, one of our prizes and now wearing the colors of the Navy of the Republic of the North East. Another prize was *City of Melbourne*, repainted but not renamed.

The wakes of all five ships were straight white lines drawn on the surface of the calm, blue sea. Conditions were almost ideal for an aerial attack, with no wind to add complication to the maneuvers of the Aereon pilots. Our first assault would be from the south, our second from the east, out of the sun. If anybody aboard the ships had the initiative to organize massed rifle fire after the first bombing the men would be dazzled, unable to take proper aim.

I looked aft.

Wombat was well astern, struggling to keep up with our flotilla, her rusty funnel belching thick, black smoke. But she was hampered far more than were the other ships. Instead of towing a relatively streamlined, airborne craft she was dragging an ungainly barge on the deck of which were a steam winch and one of Professor Lowe's mobile hydrogen gas generators. Below decks were dynamite bombs and supplies of another weapon that, Kelly and Red Kitty hoped, would be even more effective.

I looked ahead again. The invasion fleet was still hull down but I could see masts and funnels, the glimmer of white upperworks. Their course was practically at right angles to ours and the leading ships were already to port of our course. It was a pity, I thought, that we had not worked out some systems of signals whereby the Aereon commander could give steering orders to the surface ships. Nonetheless, I thought smugly, I had done my sums well. After I had received the news that the British had left Wellington I had worked out just where our interception would take place. I was only a few miles and just over half an hour out.

From starboard I heard a rather dull pistol report. I looked around in that direction. Ned, from the car of *Ellen Kelly*, had fired a white flare, the signal to stand by. I grabbed my own already loaded pistol and discharged it to acknowledge and repeat. From *Mary Two*, *Liberty Belle* and *Peggy Girl* the whitely incandescent signals were falling and on the poops of the steamers men were grouped around the special towing cleats that we had installed.

Ned fired again—this time a green light.

We all repeated.

I could feel *Kate* lifting under me as, with her trailing towline clear, she dropped astern of *Maeve*, rising almost vertically. One of the surface ships was blowing her whistle, three long blasts and again three long blasts. It was the Morse letter O, the signal for Man Overboard. I looked to starboard. *Liberty Belle* was lifting much more slowly than the rest of us. It was at once obvious why this should be so. When the towline had been cast off the cleats one of *Colleen McCormack*'s seamen had stepped into a bight of it which had become entangled about his foot, snatching him from the deck as the airship began to climb.

Shawcross and his bombardier, both at the forward end of the car, were trying to pull the unfortunate seaman up to the airship. Their efforts did little more than to cause the towline to oscillate and the human weight at the end of it to swing like a pendulum. Perhaps it was this motion, perhaps it was the man's own struggles, but that fortuitious and fatal hitch about his ankle was loosened. He fell, head down. I thought that I heard a thin, high scream but this may have been imagination. One thing alone was certain; he could never survive that two hundred foot plunge to the surface of the sea.

Colleen McCormack had stopped her engines, was falling astern of the rest of the squadron. She would be putting out a boat but it was only a corpse that would be recovered. And from *Ellen Kelly* shot the red flare, the signal to attack.

The five airships commenced their upward glide, bringing the invasion fleet right ahead.

CHAPTER 61

They were steaming in good formation, in two columns.

We already knew something of the make-up of the fleet; our friends in Sydney had passed on to us all the information that they had been able to obtain. The flagship was the modern steam frigate H.M.S. *Nelson*, square rigged on all three masts and with two funnels. Then there was H.M.S. *Shah*, a similar ship. Both vessels were heavily armed but lightly armored. There was *Wolverine*, another steam frigate, an old ship, little better than a man o' war from the days when sail reigned supreme with engines added as a sort of afterthought. There was H.M.S. *Glatton*, with her twin, 12″ turret guns. (When we had been told of the composition of the naval force I had expressed both surprise and doubt. First of all that not very seaworthy monitor type vessel would have had to make the long voyage out from England to the west coast of Canada, and then from Vancouver to Wellington. She must have been very lucky insofar as weather was concerned, just as she was lucky during this trans-Tasman voyage. And there she was, abeam of the old *Wolverine*, waddling along at the rear of the troop convoy.)

There were the requisitioned liners—troopships and storeships, still in their peacetime colors. There were red funnels and black ones and some a sort of salmon pink. Colby took it upon himself to identify the various ships.

"There's the Shaw Savill liner *Arawa*, Commodore. I came out to New Zealand in her and jumped ship. Her mate's a bastard—or he was then. And there's *Tarawera*. I've sailed her. And *Wairarapa*. And *Waihora* . . ."

Still we were climbing, maintaining a fairly good line abeam formation. *Liberty Belle*, despite her poor start, had regained her station. It was extremely unlikely that anybody would have sighted us from the surface ships. Their lookouts would be scanning the sea horizon—to port and to starboard, ahead and astern—and not the sky. Even if Admiral Tryon had believed the stories he must have heard about the Kelly army's dirigible balloons he would not be expecting to meet with any such out here, miles from the nearest land.

Our own disposal was as had been agreed upon before departure from Eden, had been attained after some rather complicated aerial maneuvers. It would vastly have simplified matters if our surface ships had been steaming in the correct formation. But this was the first use of air power at sea; we were having to make up the rules as we went along.

Ellen Kelly was to port. Ned had taken it upon himself to attack the flagship. Then there was *Liberty Belle*, and to starboard of her *Peggy Girl*, and to starboard of her *Mary Two*. These would bomb the transports. And I, in *Kate*, should have the privilege of dealing with *Wolverine* and *Glatton*. ("I'd been hoping to get a chance to lay an egg on that bloody *Arawa*," complained Colby.)

From *Ellen Kelly* came the dull report of Ned's flare pistol, repeated along the line. The incandescent white stars dropped slowly through the clear air, guttering out one by one. *Stand by*. Another report and a red light. In the cars the bombardiers scrambled forward, each taking with him one of the dynamite bombs while the pilots valved hydrogen. It was an intentionally steep dive. If Tryon got any warning of the attack it would be only at the very last moment. I had no time to see what the other Aereons were doing. My intention was fixed on old *Wolverine*, steaming sedately along, the yards of her lofty masts bare of canvas. Her funnel was belching thick, dirty smoke that streamed astern. Her black-painted gunports

on the broad, white strake were all closed, I noticed; but a
broadside from the heavy weapons would not worry me
unless I were coming in at sea level.

I could see two officers on her poop, pacing from side to
side, apparently engaged in conversation. I could see the
two men at the huge wheel, and other men, the lookouts,
in the tops.

And still nobody had seen me.

Suddenly, drowning out the thin whistle of the wind
through and around the rigging of the car, came the
thunder of heavy explosions from port. Kelly, the first to
go into a dive, had made his strike. I heard other explosions. Aboard *Wolverine* there were bugle calls and the
shrilling of whistles. Gunport doors crashed open and the
gaping muzzles of cannon were revealed.

And still nobody looked up.

It was the foretop lookout who finally saw me—and that
was after Colby had dropped my first bomb, at my orders,
and was already trimming the airship by scrambling aft. I
was rising steeply, although not steeply enough for my
liking. The bottom of the car must just have cleared the
fore trunk. As I looked down my expression must have
betrayed anxiety; as he looked up the seaman's face was
a mask of amazement combined with terror. And then he
was behind me and I was clear and lifting fast. I heard the
dull explosion of the impact-fused bomb and then, fantastically, a series of relatively minor booms, the sound of a
broadside. What were the fools firing at?

(According to the accounts of survivors *Wolverine's* captain had thought that the convoy was under attack by fast,
low-in-the water torpedo boats.)

I looked to port.

All four of the other Aereons were there, in ragged
formation, climbing, like me, into the sun. I looked aft.
Wolverine was stopped in the water, listing heavily to
port. The mainmast, trailing rigging over the decks and in
the sea, was down. It must have smashed the funnel in its
fall; where this had been was a ragged hole in the deck
from which mingled smoke and steam billowed. *Glatton*
was just coming alongside the crippled steam frigate to
render assistance.

There had been havoc among the transports. *Arawa* was down by the head and already putting out boats. Another ship—I could not see who she was because her funnel was gone—was on fire and being torn apart by a series of explosions. She must have been an ammunition carrier. *Tarawera*—according to Colby that was who she was—was on her beam ends, rolling over to port.

But *Shah* and *Nelson*, apparently undamaged, were standing on, followed by two passenger liners and four storeships. Callous it may have been, callous it most certainly was, but Admiral Tryon, no fool, must have decided that his duty was to bring what ships and men he could into Sydney, must have realized that anybody who stopped to render assistance to the stricken vessels would make of himself a sitting duck.

And in the air we regrouped, but only to the extent that *Ellen Kelly* was now at the starboard end of our line and *Kate* at port. Our major targets were as before, although, in my case, I should now have only *Glatton* to deal with. We reached our ceiling, shifted weight forward and dived. Aboard our potential victims there had been some quick thinking, some improvisation. Riflemen were lined up on the decks of all surviving ships, only small parties of them aboard the smaller ones but masses of them aboard the steam frigates and the troop transports. But they were firing into the sun, dazzled, and they opened fire too soon. We could hear the thin crackling, see the powder smoke, as they poured their ineffectual fire at us and then, when they might have got in some lucky shots, they had to reload.

I swooped down on *Glatton*. This time I did not have *Wolverine*'s high masts to worry about. One was down, as I have said, and the ship was now listing at such a steep angle that the fore and mizzen trucks were no longer very far above the water. (It occurred to me that she might loose off her starboard broadside but to serve the guns with the vessel listing so heavily would have been almost impossible and, too, would have done no good at all to *Glatton*, alongside her to starboard.)

My second bomb was dropped too late. *Glatton* was enveloped in a smokescreen of *Wolverine*'s making, by the steam and smoke pouring from the ragged hole in the frigate's deck. I peered through the evil-smelling fog with smarting eyes, trying to distinguish the turret ship's outline in the swirling obscurity. But the riflemen, or some of them, could see me. *Kate*, with the sun behind her, its radiance veiled, must have been visible in silhouette.

A bullet whistled through the floor of the car, then another, then another. Luckily they missed both Colby and myself, and even more luckily they missed the dynamite bombs with their touchy fuses. And there was *Glatton*. I ordered Colby to drop the bomb that he was holding. It burst, as nearly as I could determine, just off *Wolverine's* port side. It finished her off, I think, but she was finished in any case.

And then as we rose I was able to look astern.

There was trouble at the head of the convoy. *Shah*, white water foaming about her stern as her engines were running at full reverse, was backing away from *Nelson*. *Nelson* was heeling over to port. Even from a distance I could see the gaping hole in her side. Later, when we were back aboard *Maeve*, proceeding to Sydney, Ned told me what had happened, or what he thought had happened. He was no seaman but his grasp of all military affairs was sound.

"The admiral," he told me, "was tryin' to take what ye'd call evasive action, an' all this while his riflemen were pourin' a hail o' lead at me. Lucky 'twas that there was niver a good shot among the bunch of 'em. An' I saw a string o' pretty signal flags goin' up to a yardarm; don't ask me what they were or even what they meant, although I can guess the latter. I could see him out on the open bridge, a big, bearded bastard in his blue an' gold, starin' at me through a telescope. An' then, just as me bombardier let go o' the bomb, I saw him wave to somebody an' the flags came flutterin' down an' the ship made a sharp turn to the left, or to port as ye'd be sayin'. But the captain of the other ship, the *Shah*, wasn't quick on the uptake. Me bomb fell short—but, as it happened, 'twasn't needed. There was a most unholy blowin' o' steam whistles an' a crash like a herd o' bulls in a china shop an' when I looked down an' back there was the pair of 'em locked

together, wi' the *Shah* stuck into the *Nelson*'s side just by
the funnels, an' there was smoke, an' steam, an' more
steam as the boilers blew up.

" 'Twas a pretty sight, to be sure."

I told him that I didn't think that it was very pretty.

"But ye're a sailorman, Johnnie. Ye don't think the
same as we poor, ignorant landsmen. But what about you?
Didn't ye keep on after that poor little ship, the *Glatton*,
not happy until he'd put a bomb right down her funnel?
Couldn't ye have let her go limpin' back to Pig Island?"

"A ship with twelve-inch guns?" I demanded. "Have
you any idea what she could have done to Eden?"

"If we'd let her," he laughed.

But I'm getting ahead of myself.

We turned, avoiding the convoy (what was left of it) so
that we could make our third attack out of the sun again.
Nelson was gone (and, with her, Admiral Tryon) and *Shah*
was in no condition to put up much of a fight. *Glatton*'s
luck finally ran out when *Wolverine* went down and the
smoke and steam of her prolonged dying dissipated, giving
me a clear view of my target. The explosion of my last
bomb must have set off the turret ship's magazine; it was
as though some giant, open hand had slammed into us
from behind, swatting us upward (fortunately) and away
from the scene of our . . . crime.

Yes, crime. That was the way that I was thinking of it as
I brought *Kate* around and then drifted slowly over that
wreckage-strewn patch of sea. There were men in the
water, dead men mostly, although a few, a pitiful few,
were clinging to gratings, wooden spars and other floating
wreckage. I saw bodies with arms missing, and legs. There
was blood in the water, mixed with ashes to form an
obscene scum. Air bubbles, from the sunken ships, were
still rising from the ocean depths.

I hung over the side of the car and vomited.

"Commodore!" Colby was insistent. "Commodore! General Kelly has fired a green light!"

I wiped my mouth with my sleeve, then found and
loaded my own flare pistol, fired it to acknowledge and
repeat Kelly's signal. Although all the bombs were gone
there were still bags of sand ballast. I told Colby to dump

one of these and then come aft to trim the ship. We slanted up into the sky—cloudless apart from the drifting fumes of battle, the smoke from the funnels of the surviving storeships—climbing reluctantly. I looked aloft to the wrinkled skin of the gas cells. Perhaps, I thought, during my series of attacks on *Glatton* I had valved hydrogen too recklessly before each steep dive. And then I saw the bullet-holes. I hoped that our buoyancy would hold until I could reach *Wombat*.

Ahead of me, at various altitudes, were *Ellen Kelly*, *Mary Two*, *Peggy Girl* and *Liberty Belle*. There was now no attempt at maintaining any kind of formation. And on the sea horizon were the masts, funnels and upperworks of our own surface fleet. I could make out *Maeve*. But I should not be passing over her with weighted towline trailing to be caught by seamen and thrown around the towing cleats. I was one of the lucky ones. *Kate* was to be winched down to the broad deck of *Wombat*'s barge, there to take on a new bomb load and to have her gas cells replenished and her envelope patched. (I looked up again. Major Brown and his sailmaker would be busy, I thought.) Colby and I would be able to escape for a while the cramped, comfortless confines of the *Aereon*'s car which, apart from anything else, had no toilet facilities except for a battered bucket. Most of the other pilots and bombardiers would be obliged to bob astern of their parent ships, depending upon an all-too-liable-to-jam heaving line and traveler arrangement for supplies of sandwiches and bottles of lukewarm tea, enduring these conditions until it would be possible for them to fly off to the airfield just outside Eden.

Meanwhile, I saw, *Liberty Belle* was having her troubles. She was struggling to maintain altitude. I was close astern of her now, and above her. I could see that all manner of things were being dumped from her car—the boat compass (I thought it was), the sanitary bucket, bottles, some clothing. And then . . .

I stared in horror.

A man was falling, tumbling end over end as he dropped. "The bastard!" Colby was swearing. "The bastard!" And then, with a flash of gallows humor, "And would you do that to me, Commodore, to lighten ship?"

I said, "Whoever it was who got jettisoned, he was already dead. It's obvious that *Liberty Belle* got shot up more badly than we did . . ."

Yes, it was obvious.

As we passed over her I could see the rents in the envelope fabric, watched the two once-fat cigars of the twin balloons crumpling in upon themselves. *Liberty Belle* would never make it back to her mother ship, or to *Wombat*. But she—or the wreckage of her—would stay afloat and, unless he were very unlucky, Shawcross or his bombardier (I still didn't know whose the body had been) would be rescued.

And our ships were close now.

I watched *Mary Two* drifting over *Mary McCormack*. As far as I could see the often-rehearsed pick-up technique had worked successfully. Jim Kelly's *Peggy Girl* had to make a second pass over *Merino* and then was brought under tow. And I could hear the rattle of the steam winch aboard *Wombat*'s barge as Ned's *Ellen Kelly* was pulled down to the deck. I should have to wait my turn. As long as I didn't lose too much gas there were no worries.

At last there came a prolonged blast from *Wombat*'s steam whistle.

I glided slowly over the barge, weighted lines dangling from each end of the car. I valved gas cautiously. Men caught the forward line, took it to the winch drum. We were drawn down to that broad, dirty, blessed wooden deck and, after only minimal confusion, tethered alongside *Ellen Kelly*.

"Glory be to Jaysus!" Ned Kelly shouted to me, "An' didn't we clobber the bastards!"

"We did," I said glumly.

CHAPTER 62

Crowley sent a boat from *Maeve* to pick up Ned and myself.

We went at once up to the bridge. Crowley suggested that my commodore's broad pennant, emerald green with the stars of the Southern Cross in gold, be broken out at the fore to signify that I was once again in command of the surface fleet but I told him that this would only complicate matters. Captain Reilly, in command of *Colleen McCormack*, had seen long service in the United States Navy and surely was capable of handling the final stages of the battle, the rounding up of the surviving merchantmen and shepherding them into Twofold Bay. He had been appointed Acting Commodore before our departure from Eden; he could continue in this temporary rank.

So I was little more than a passenger.

I watched the hoists of signal flags going up and, between times, swept the sea horizon ahead with my telescope. When, finally, I saw the smoke from the funnels of what ships had survived our attack this was well on the starboard bow. The enemy vessels must be making back toward New Zealand.

Our own squadron altered course accordingly, all ships proceeding at full speed. *Maeve* took the lead while the two *McCormacks* dropped slowly astern. *Merino* and *City of Melbourne* were straggling badly and *Wombat* was already hull down to the west'ard. A stern chase is, as the saying goes, a long chase but our quarry, already slow, was slower still because of the overloading. The relatively small storeships were crowded with men rescued from the sea, their decks almost awash with the weight of these survivors. It was fantastic, I thought, that there should have been so many—but, unlike the warships, with their magazines exploding, the troopers had gone down slowly enough to allow almost leisurely abandon ship procedure.

We came up, at last, with the rearmost ship, passing close alongside her. She was the Union Steam Ship Company's *Wairarapa*. Her decks were crowded with men who had no room to sit, whose exhausted (and, in some cases, wounded and dying) bodies were held upright only by the pressure of those about them. I swung my telescope on to her bridge. A portly, blue-uniformed figure was on the starboard wing, his own telescope trained on me. I recognized him. It was Captain Carew. He recognized me. He lowered his glass so that his right hand was free. He shook his fist violently. He shouted something which I could not hear but knew was surely uncomplimentary.

We passed through what was no better than a rabble of unarmed ships, with *Mary McCormack* and *Colleen McCormack* close astern. About half a mile ahead of the leading vessel we turned, so that we were beam on to the line of advance. Our heavy Gatlings opened fire, the 2" shells kicking up a long line of spray that could almost have been the indication of some just-under-the-surface reef. Reef it was not, but it was even more deadly. Should any of the merchant captains attempt to cross that line his decks would be swept clear of life by our automatic fire. There was a blowing of steam whistles, a going astern of engines, as way was gotten off the storeships. On the other side of this pitiful apology for a convoy *Merino* and *City of Melbourne* had come up, were noisily firing their guns.

And from gaffs and ensign staffs, with haste or with slow deliberation, the British Red Ensign was fluttering down.

* * *

After the surrender Ned took charge.

All the ships but one were to be sent, under escort, to Twofold Bay. The exception was Captain Carew's *Wairarapa*. She, also under escort, was to proceed to Sydney. Her people would be able to tell the authorities—and the press—about the battle. The propaganda value of this would outweigh the danger of presenting a few hundred badly demoralized soldiers to the New South Wales military forces.

I was responsible for the choice of Carew's vessel. I felt that I owed him something. He would not be subjected to the rigors of the prison camp that we should have to set up, the poor food and the inadequate medical facilities. Ned suggested that I go myself in the boat to tell him of his fate. I declined and, in my turn, suggested that Mr. Crowley, who had been Carew's third officer, be the messenger. That young gentleman made mutinous noises.

And so it was that *Mary McCormack*, *City of Melbourne* and *Merino* set course for Eden, the prizes, with their huddled, miserable prisoners menaced by their guns, while *Maeve*, *Colleen McCormack*, *Wombat* and *Wairarapa* stood on for Sydney.

CHAPTER 63

It was just before noon when we hove to off the Heads, well to seaward, out of range of the coast defense guns of the South Head battery. A flutter of signal flags at our fore yard told Captain Carew that he was now on his own, was free to enter port. He acknowledged with a short, almost derisory toot on his steam whistle. (His decks were so crowded that it would have been hard for anybody to get near a set of signal halyards.) He stood in to the Harbor entrance. Watching through my powerful telescope I could see a flotilla of small craft, steam launches and pinnaces, coming out to meet her. Already, I knew, the bad news would be starting to spread through Sydney. A big troop convoy with a powerful Royal Navy escort had been expected—and now here was a solitary, trans-Tasman cargo liner, bringing with her the survivors of some major disaster, while out at sea were green-hulled, green-funnelled ships that could only be vessels under the rebel flag.

Ned and I went down to *Maeve*'s foredeck, where we were joined by our bombardiers. We clambered down the pilot ladder, into the boat that had been lowered for our use. The seamen, in their uniforms of blue jerseys with bright green neckerchieves, bent to their oars with a will. The third officer—like myself he was a deserter from a British merchant ship, although he had been an apprentice, not yet a qualified officer—brought us smartly alongside *Wombat*'s barge. The ungainly thing was so low in the water that there was no need, there, for a ladder.

Major Brown, his acid-stained uniform as scruffy as always, greeted us.

"Your ships are ready, sirs," he said. "Ready and loaded, and the new patches on the envelopes are holding well."

We thanked him.

Kelly and Peterson walked across the gently heaving planking to *Ellen Kelly*, climbed into the car. Men stood by the four lines, made fast to cleats in the deck, that held her down.

"Ready, boys?" asked Ned.

"Ready, General!" came the reply.

"Let go!"

The Aereon lifted almost vertically. There was a very light breeze but it blew her clear of the tall, stovepipe funnel that supplied the draught for the barge's donkey engine furnace, which was below decks. Then it was my turn. As *Kate* gained altitude I was almost looking down into the mouth of the smoke-stack. I noticed—oddly enough I hadn't known about it until now—the copper gauze spark arrestor that covered the aperture. He was a good man, Brown, I thought. He took no chances, especially when playing around with hydrogen. Game as Ned Kelly he might not be, would never be, but he did not take foolish risks.

And Ned was now making his upward glide, his course set for the South Head. I followed him. *Kate* was handling well, responsive to the lightest touch on the tiller. We lifted, *Ellen Kelly* and *Kate*, and, paradoxically, the South Head cliffs seemed both to advance and to recede, the first on the horizontal scale and the second as measured vertically. Ned fired his flare pistol and the red light fell slowly, leaving behind it a long streamer of white smoke. He put the nose of *Ellen Kelly* down, started his attack swoop. I was in no hurry to follow. I had no desire to fly into the burst of his first bomb, especially if this should set off a supply of ready use ammunition. I reached my ceiling and hung there, watching the twin cigar shape dwindle as the Aereon whistled down to the target. I saw the explosion as the bomb hit, thought that I saw human forms

among the wreckage thrown up by the blast. I followed
then. One of the big guns was, possibly, still serviceable.
One had been blown right off its mounting.

At the forward end of the car Colby had the bomb
ready. I gauged distance and trajectory, gave the order to
drop. The bang, which I heard as we were already well
into our upward glide, was a very satisfactory one. We
were over the Harbor now. I could see the red-funnelled
Wairarapa, limping slowly toward her Circular Quay berth,
steam launches trailing her. I could see the next target,
Fort Dennison, once the notorious Pinchgut Island. It was
an absurd harbour defence; its short range cannon could
be used only when any seaborne invader had actually
entered port, was already landing troops on the harbourside
beaches. Against an aerial raider it was utterly useless.
When we had done with it the fortifications were a heap of
rubble.

And now it was time for our last bomb run.

We—*Ellen Kelly* and *Kate*—lifted, flew out over Milsons
Point on the north side of the harbor. We turned and
came down in a shallow glide, steering for the Circular
Quay and for the broad, dusty ribbon of George Street
that ran inland from the wharves. There was panic in the
streets but nobody was running for cover. There was a sea
of pale faces, staring upward. As my bombardier, at the
forward end of the car, did his work I was obliged to valve
gas, little by little, to compensate for the loss of weight.
We wanted the good citizens of Sydney to have a good
look at us.

We flew the length of George Street and then turned,
following Pitt Street back to the harbor. I don't know
about Ned's bombardier but Colby was sweating like a pig
by the time that we were rising, looking down at the
smoke still rising from Fort Dennison, at the far bigger
column of smoke that marked where the South Head
battery had been.

He drew the sleeve of his jersey across his forehead.

"Am I glad to be rid of that lot!" he said. "Ye'd never
think that paper'd weigh so much!"

One of the leaflets had blown back into the car, was at
my feet. I knew what was on it; with Red Kitty I had

helped Ned to compose the message, had restrained him from producing one that would have required a book for its promulgation, not a single sheet of paper. But the original idea had been his alone.

TO THE PEOPLE OF NEW SOUTH WALES it started.

SURRENDER, BEFORE YOUR CITIES ARE DE-STROYED, AS THE ENGLISH INVASION FLEET WAS DESTROYED IN THE TASMAN SEA.

("The fleet *will* be destroyed," Ned had said confidently. "An' if 'tis not, then we'll just be out the cost o' the paper an' the printer's bill.")

("We can always use the paper even though it's been printed on," I said.

(He laughed and said, while Red Kitty tried to look disgusted, "Then surely 't'will be the world's most expensive arse fodder!")

THROW OFF THE CHAINS OF THE FALSE MOTH-ER ENGLAND.

EVERY MAN WHO CAN HOLD A GUN WILL BE WELCOME IN OUR ARMY AND WILL BE REWARDED ACCORDING TO HIS DEEDS.

THOSE WHO PERSIST IN OPPOSING US WILL SURELY PAY THE PRICE.

And the effusion was signed by Edward Kelly, President of the Republic of Australia.

CHAPTER 64

From aeronaut back to wharf superintendent was just one step.

Back in Eden I was kept busy, overseeing the discharge to the stores from our prizes. There was ammunition a-plenty and rifles—not as modern as those that we had been getting from America but still usable—and casks of salt beef and salt pork, sacks of flour and rice and sugar and, best of all perhaps, tents enough for the housing of a small army in field conditions. We needed those tents for the prisoners, and for their guards. It was the Americans, Calhoun's Californians, who undertook this duty. Perhaps Ned made a mistake in accepting Colonel Calhoun's offer. Calhoun hated the English more than Kelly did and his guards had orders to shoot at the slightest provocation. There were attempts to escape, of course, and some of them were successful. Ironically some of the absconders were shot when trying to break back into the stockade; the fine, sunny autumn had degenerated quite suddenly into wet, cold winter and it was no weather for Englishmen to be out in the bush.

There was the successful Aereon raid on Williamstown, Melbourne's naval base. I did not take part in this; I was too busy running the port of Eden, arranging for the reception of the occasional prize brought in by *Maeve* or *Mary McCormack* or *Colleen McCormack*, which three ships were maintaining an effective coastal blockade from Newcastle to Port Phillip.

There was the news of street fighting in Sydney, in which city the Sons and Daughters of Freedom—to whom a quantity of the captured arms had gone—seemed on the point of wresting complete control from the authorities. There was the spectacular dash of the Shamrock Express all the way into Spencer Street Station and the Kelly cavalry and the panzerwagens, carried to the scene of battle on special flat cars, ranging at will through the streets of the demoralized city.

I can give no first-hand account of any of these actions; I was no more than the harbormaster of a small port the resources of which were being taxed to the uttermost. I was busy, very busy.

And all the time I was the prey to a gnawing anxiety.

Why was I marooned here in the Past, sharing the mind and body of my ancestor while, almost a hundred years in the future, my own body in the chair of Graumann's time-twister slowly deteriorated, deprived of proper nourishment? What had happened? Had the scientist packed his bags and flown back to the U.S.A.? Had Duffin rejoined his regiment? Was there nobody in that harborside apartment who could bring me back to where I belonged?

I was increasingly lonely.

I saw little of Red Kitty and when I did meet her she was brusque and unwilling to talk. Ellen—old Mrs. Kelly—for some reason had taken a dislike to me. Ned was most of the time at his headquarters in Wangaratta. I had little in common with Colonel Calhoun and his officers and the colonel had made it quite plain that he did not approve of my visits to the camp to see if I could do anything to make conditions more comfortable for the captains and crews of the merchant ships that we had seized.

"You run your port, Commodore," he drawled around the cigar that was almost part of his uniform, "and I'll run my prison."

And so it was, one stormy evening, that I was sitting alone in the parlor of my lodgings, reading, by the yellow light of the oil lamp, a listing of the goods discharged that day from the coastal steamer *Black Swan*, which vessel had been bound from Fremantle, in the west, to Melbourne.

There was a tap at the door.

"Come in!" I called.

Red Kitty entered, bringing with her a flurry of wind and rain, wearing a man's oilskin coat over her long-skirted dress.

She stood there looking down at me. I could not read her expression.

"Johnnie . . ." she said it at last.

"Yes?"

"There is something you should know. . . ."

The door, insecurely latched, blew open. Icy, wind-driven raindrops spattered on to the lamp chimney, which shattered. The flame blew out.

And I was falling through the darkness, with the roaring of the Time Wind in my ears.

Graumann's face was peering into mine.

"Wake up!" he was muttering urgently. "Wake up!"

I was awake, after a fashion. I was weak and my throat was dry. About my body was the stink of stale perspiration—and worse.

"Wake up! Perhaps together we can . . . get away. I couldn't by myself. They stopped me. The soldiers stopped me, at the airport. But you're the president's man . . ."

"Where . . . Where's Duffin?"

"How should I know? All that I know is that the shit's hit the fan and it's going on hitting it. Why did I ever come to this goddamn crazy country?"

"Get . . . get me a drink," I said.

He had one ready, a tumbler full of some dark fluid that was—I think—part alcohol and that contained other drugs or stimulants. I could focus my eyes properly again and it seemed as though cottonwool had been removed from my ears. I could hear the frightening sound coming from outside, the shouting and the screaming, the wailing of sirens and the rattle of automatic fire.

"What's happening?" I asked.

"The people . . . They're trying to get out and the army is stopping them. The roads are choked with anything and everything on wheels and with men, women and children on foot. There's been a multi-car pile-up in the middle of the bridge . . ."

"But why. . . ?"

"Where have you been, Grimes?" he exploded.

It was my turn to explode. "You know damn' well where and when I've been, Graumann. Start at the beginning. Put me in the picture."

He got some control over himself.

"It's that goddamn crazy president of yours," he said. "Saigon fell. It was bound to fall. There was—or so they say—a massacre. Some crack regiment calling itself Ned Kelly's Own, wiped out to the last man. *And* the Australian nurses in the military hospital, raped and bayoneted. President Kelly was like a madman when he got the news. The story is that he pushed the button with his own finger . . ."

"The button?" I repeated stupidly.

"Yes. The button. *The* button. Where Hanoi used to be is a radioactive crater. Kennedy should never have given a lunatic such dangerous toys to play with."

I said, "We were on the same side when the American ICBMs were installed. You people should have stayed in the Nam."

"Well, we didn't. And I haven't finished yet. Those ICBMs must have had return postage attached to them. Rocket post—ha, ha. The fall-out over Hanoi had hardly had time to settle when Glenrowan was vaporized. . . ."

"Glenrowan?"

"Yes, Glenrowan, Your sacred shrine. But it's the end of crazy Kelly."

I asked, "And who fired those rockets?"

"I'm not a military man. How should I know? But I do know that the admirals and generals who weren't at Glenrowan with Kelly are getting ready for an invasion."

"From which country?"

"I don't know, Grimes. I swear I don't know. All that I do know is that Americans are suddenly as popular as pork chops in a synagogue. I thought that the soldiers who dragged me back here were going to shoot me."

It came to me with sudden clarity. The U.S.A., despite

its support of the Australian Revolution, had not gained the foothold in the Southern Hemisphere hoped for by industrialists and the military establishment. Now, almost a century later, was the golden opportunity for a take-over disguised as a virtuous attempt at peace-keeping in the South Pacific.

I didn't like it.

Over the decades, on that other time track, we had slowly shaken off the British yoke and, with it, our cultural cringe. We had fought in a war in which England had not been involved. (As we had on this time track.) And, at the beginning of 1979, our national capital had not been obliterated by rockets bearing nuclear warheads; we were not in a state of civil war and not threatened with invasion.

And, as I knew all too well, the course of history could be changed. It had been changed once, by myself. It could be changed back to the way that it had been.

"Dr. Graumann," I said, "do you want to get out of this country alive, back to your home and your career in the U.S.A.?"

"That, Mr. Grimes, is a singularly stupid question."

"Then I'll ask another, one that you might think is even more stupid. Do you believe that the course of history can be changed?"

"It's being changed all the time, isn't it? If your crazy president hadn't stayed in Vietnam after Kennedy pulled our people out . . . If that madman hadn't launched his ICBMs against Hanoi . . . If . . . If . . . If . . ."

"You didn't quite get my meaning, Doctor. What if the course of history was changed way back in 1880? What if that special train had not been derailed outside Glenrowan? What if the police party had cleaned up the Kelly Gang as they were then called?"

"You're talking absurdities," he snapped. "Oh, I know that you were there at the beginning of things. I sent you there. But you were an observer only, with no influence over your great grandfather's actions." He laughed. "And just suppose that you could do as you're hinting. Then *you* wouldn't be here now, and neither should I, probably, and neither would Major Duffin and neither would be countless other people."

"But history *was* changed," I insisted. "In the other world, on the other time line, I was a science fiction writer, not an historical novelist. You were in the same line of business as you are now, but you were doing your own research, trying to find evidence of visits to this world by people from the stars thousands of years ago. Duffin was a newspaper editor who hired the pair of us for a project of his own—an eyewitness account of the Siege of Glenrowan, to be published on November 11, 1980, one hundred years after the bushranger—he was never more—Ned Kelly was hanged in Melbourne Jail for murder. Oh, your time-twister was different. It was a sort of mobile Mobius strip rather than an assemblage of precessing gyroscopes. But it worked."

He said, "I don't believe you. But just suppose that I allow myself, for a few seconds only, a certain supension of disbelief. What happened at Glenrowan in this fantasy world of yours?"

"The village schoolmaster, Thomas Curnow, got away from the party in Mrs. Jones' hotel. He flagged down the special train while it was still south of the village. The police besieged the hotel. Dan Kelly, Steve Hart and Joe Byrne were killed. Ned was badly wounded, despite the protection of his armor. Eventually he was brought to trial, in Melbourne, and hanged."

"And what other differences were there, are there?"

"The Riel Rebellion in Canada was little more than an irritation to the English. The United States gave no support at all to the rebels. The Andrews Airship was never used in warfare—in fact there was no military aviation to speak of until the First World War. And it was during the First World War that the panzerwagens—but they were called tanks—were first introduced. The Bolshevik Revolution happened on time in Russia. And the rise of Hitler in Germany. World War II followed just about the same course on both time tracks although, on that one, the atom bomb was not dropped on any German cities and the Germans did not strike New York with their long range rockets.

"But the main flow of history was just about the same, although with . . . aberrations. It was John Kennedy who received the assassin's bullets that day in Dallas, not Jackie. And the U.S.A. stayed in Vietnam while your Australian allies pulled out. Eventually, of course, you lost that war and the world witnessed the spectacle of a humiliating withdrawal, by air, from Saigon . . ."

"And did," demanded Graumann, "whoever was our president at the time order the atom bombing of Hanoi?"

He did not—although there were many who said that such a thing should have been done."

He said, "Almost you convince me. But tell me, how was history changed? How did you, of all people, change history, as you are hinting that you did?"

I told him, "I stopped Thomas Curnow from flagging down the train. Send me back again to the right time and place and I'll make bloody sure that I don't go shoving my oar in again."

He laughed, a mirthless sound. "All right. I'll humor you. What have I to lose?"

"Your precious life, for a start."

We had not heard Duffin come into the room. He stood there, glaring at us, his once smart uniform muddied and torn, his heavy automatic pistol in his big fist. And with him was another man, also in a bedraggled green uniform from which one of the ornate gold epaulets was missing.

It was President Kelly.

"But . . ." stammered Graumann, "you were in Glenrowan . . ."

"I was not. When the rockets came I was in Williamstown, tryin' to talk the crews o' two o' our destroyers out o' stagin' a mutiny. But never mind that. I heard most o' what the pair o' you was talkin' about. The history that would ha' been if the first Ned had been put down at Glenrowan. An' d'ye really think, Johnnie Grimes, that Australia would be a better country if the Kelly dynasty had never been founded?"

"At least," I said, "we should not, at this point of time, be witnessing the start of a civil war with the Japs and the Yanks ready to move in to protect their interests. Our cities would not be living in dread of atom bombing."

Kelly laughed—and from him it came with genuine humor.

"Don't people say, Game as Ned Kelly? I'm game, just as my revered ancestor was. I'm willin' to take a gamble. *My* world against the world that you have the good doctor at least half believin' in. Let him set up another chair, alongside yours, an' the pair of us will go back in time to Glenrowan, to Ma Jones' pub. You do yer damnedest, Johnnie boy, to make sure that Curnow does flag the train down. An I'll do my damnedest to make sure that things went the way they did on that night."

"An' I promise ye that when we're both of us back here, in this proud republic that's fightin' for its very existence, ye'll be shot out o' hand for treason.

"Are ye game, Johnnie boy? Or is Ned Kelly the only one who's game?"

Somebody said, "I'm game."

I realized, with a shock, that the voice had been mine.

"And what about me?" bleated Graumann.

Kelly looked at him with contempt.

"Don't worry yerself," he said. "Just do as ye're told an' no harm'll come to ye. After this last . . . experiment ye'll be free to go, back to yer own country."

"But how?" muttered the scientist. "How? The American airlines aren't coming here any more. Our consul's office is closed, all the staff gone. There are no American ships in the harbor . . ."

"Ye seem to have been makin' inquiries. But ye'll be free to go. How ye go is a matter for yourself to arrange."

Graumann had to be content with that.

He fussed about arranging the second chair and then setting the controls of his time-twister. An army corporal brought coffee for Kelly, Duffin and myself. The president demanded something stronger and a bottle of Irish whiskey was produced.

Ned addressed me over his glass.

"Ye're thinkin' that the situation is hopeless, Johnnie boy. I can tell that, otherwise ye'd not ha' come up with this harebrained scheme o' yours. But 'tis not hopeless. The Kelly blood runs in my veins an' there is magic, strong magic, in the Kelly name. Ye should ha' heard the sailors cheerin' me when I left Williamstown, cheerin' me an' cursin' the leaders of the mutineers even though by this time they were dead, all o' them, their bodies danglin' from the signal yards o' the ships. Ye should ha' heard the crowds in the streets o' Melbourne cheerin' an' singin'. . . ."

"And that was before the rockets fell on Glenrowan," I stated rather than asked.

"What of it? Let's face it, Johnnie. Glenrowan was nothin' but a nest o' bludgin' bureaucrats an' deskbound generals an' admirals. 'T'was not much loss. O' course, when this mess is over that crater will become a national memorial."

"When this mess is over?" I asked. "How many of us in Australia will still be alive when it is? We're alone in a world full of enemies, Ned. Those who used to be our allies have disowned us . . ."

He laughed and said, "And those who used to be our enemies are now prepared to become friends. The U.S.A. and Japan aren't the only Pacific powers, you know. Before I left Glenrowan I had some very constructive talks with a couple of ambassadors. . . ."

"And those ambassadors," I said, "have made their contribution to the fall out, together with the bureaucrats and all the rest of them."

"There are still the consuls general in the other cities," he said airily. "After I come back from my excursion into the Past I'll be talkin' to 'em."

"Giving away naval bases and mineral rights," I said bitterly, "in exchange for token support and a few shiploads of weaponry."

Again he laughed. "An' didn't the Americans think that they were goin' to gain absolute control o' this country in exchange for their arms an' volunteers? But they did not, did they? The first Ned an' his lady wife, Red Kitty, were too smart for the bastards."

Then Graumann said that everything was ready and Ned and I took our places in the chairs.

"See you in Glenrowan," said Kelly to me as the assemblage of spinning, precessing gyroscopes stirred into motion.

CHAPTER 65

I was looking out through my great-grandfather's eyes, listening through his ears. But I knew what was going to happen, he did not. He was asking himself, *What have I gotten myself into?* He knew, of course, that the special train was expected from the south and that the track had been torn up north of the station—he had been among those persuaded, at revolver point, to take part in this work. He knew, too, that it was not Ned Kelly's intention actually to derail the train but to trap it at Glenrowan by blowing up the lines, south of the station, after it had passed.

And I knew, as he did not, that soon Thomas Curnow would persuade Ned to let him leave the party, to be with his sick wife, and that the schoolmaster, with a candle and a red scarf, would attempt to flag down the leading locomotive.

This time that attempt must succeed.

I looked around me. This would be my last time here, where it all had started, *where it must not start.* I stared at old Martin Cherry, who was playing his squeaky fiddle when he was not sipping from his mug, and at Mrs. Jones' young son, who was singing "The Minstrel Boy" in his high, clear voice. I was condemning them to death. They would die, both of them, victims of the inexcusably reckless police fire when Superintendent Hare's men laid siege to the hotel. (But, I remembered, they were to die in any case.)

I looked at the outlaws. Steve Hart would die in the siege, as would Dan Kelly and Joe Byrne. Hart and Byrne I should be robbing of a few years of life. (But how many lives, over the next century, should I be saving? The War of Independence had been—would be—a bloody business, and there would be the war in Viet Nam, well in the future, with the final massacre at Saigon and the obliteration of Hanoi by Kelly's ICBMs, and the retaliatory—or cautionary?—strike at Glenrowan and all the troubles, civil war and invasion, that were yet to befall Australia.)

I looked at the little, club-footed Curnow. He, the village schoolmaster, in his respectable black suit, with high white collar and black silk cravat, obviously considered himself several cuts above his rough fellow guests in the Glenrowan Hotel. He sat by the blazing fire, sipping his drink sullenly, talking only when he was talked to. During my stay—my great-grandfather's stay—in the village I had met him more than once and had been looking forward to a conversation with an educated man. But, as far as he was concerned, I was just another laborer with brains to match. He had no time to waste on such as I. And now he was being forced to waste hours in the company of his intellectual and social inferiors.

But he'll get his revenge, I thought. *I'll make sure of that, even if I have to flag the train down myself.*

And where was Kelly, whose descendant had sworn to frustrate me in my attempt to change the course of history yet again, to change it back to what it had been. I could guess where he was. I should soon have to follow his example but I was reluctant to leave this overheated room— the blazing fire, the oil lamps, the people—for the bitterly cold night outside. I'd go when I had to go, but not before. Ned Kelly, I hoped, would not prevent any of his unwilling—although most of them seemed to be enjoying themselves—guests from answering the call of nature.

Kelly came back in, followed by a blast of freezing air.

Once again I was surprised by his youth. Not even the full, black beard could make him look older than his actual years. He was young, and he was a giant, and he moved with assured arrogance. His eyes were pale blue flames in his ruddy (what could be seen of it) face. Yet when he spoke his voice had a soft, Irish lilt to it. Should he be so minded he could charm the birds down out of the trees.

"I've been listenin'," he announced, "an' still there's not a sound o' the train a-comin'. But come it must, an' when it does . . ." He addressed himself to his brother, to Hart and to Byrne. "There'll be no bloodshed. I want them alive—Hare an' all his puppies an' O'Connor an' his black devils. Ye can't drive a hard bargain when ye've only dead men to exchange for what ye're wantin'. An' it's justice we're wantin'—justice for me an' for all the selectors of the north east . . ."

He went on. It was a rambling speech but, obviously, it came from the heart. The man had the makings of an orator, a rabble rouser. And while he ranted on I watched him carefully. To him I was no more than a member of his captive audience. Or so it seemed. Had Graumann's technique failed with his descendant, the last Kelly? Or was President Kelly, ensconced in his ancestor's mind, laughing at me, waiting for me to make my move before taking counter measures? He would be careful, I thought, not to kill the ancestral Grimes. My great grandfather had played too big a part—would play too big a part—in the war of Independence.

But President Kelly, with his republic crumbling about his ears, was no longer a rational man.

I returned my attention to Curnow.

Soon, I thought, very soon he would be making his move. He would be appealing to Kelly, taking advantage of the big man's generosity and decency, telling him that his sick wife would be worried about him and asking to be allowed to leave the party to go home. He was sipping from a small glass of rum. This time I would not buy him a drink. I would see to it that he was more sober than otherwise when he stumbled along beside the railway track with his candle and red silk scarf.

Curnow finished his rum and got to his feet. With his lurching gait he was making his way to the leader of the outlaws.

"Mr. Kelly . . ." he said, with oily politeness.

"Yes, Mr. Curnow?"

"It's my wife. She is not well, as you know. She will be worrying about me. I am not usually out so late."

Kelly looked down at the little schoolmaster.

"Off ye go, then. Never let it be said that I caused any member of the fair sex needless worry."

Curnow wormed his way through the gathering to the door. Steve Hart stopped him. Curnow started to expostulate, then Kelly called, "It's all right, Steve. He has to go home to look after his good lady."

And still Kelly, the last Kelly, had made no move.

But I had to go outside myself. (And while I was outside I would make sure that Curnow played his part properly.) I walked unsteadily toward the door. Steve Hart barred my way.

"Where d'ye think ye're off to, Limey?"

I said, not untruthfully, "I'm bustin for a Jimmy Riddle."

"Let him through, Steve!" roared Kelly. "He can't hold his liquor!"

There was an outburst of laughter, directed at me.

Hart unlocked the door again. I brushed past him with unfeigned urgency. The cold air was like an electric shock to the exposed skin of my hands and face, and, in seconds, permeated my clothing. Shivering, I walked hastily to the nearest tree, unbuttoned and fumbled, managed to get cleared for action before I wetted my trousers. It seemed as though that steaming stream would never stop.

At last I was finished.

I looked along the road that Curnow would be taking to his house. The moon, just past its full, was high. I had no trouble in seeing him, although he now had a fair start on me. There was no mistaking that little, black figure hobbling along the rough tracks.

I started to walk after him.

He must have heard me. He quickened his pace.

I walked faster.

He started to run.

I ran.

It wasn't much of a race. At the finish he panicked and scuttled into the brush at the side of the road, attempting to hide. He tripped and fell heavily, squealing like a trapped rabbit.

I found a heavy stone, stooped and pulled it free from the earth, lifted it and brought it smashing down, and again, and again.

The squealing stopped, although a faint whimpering persisted for long seconds.

And there was the voice in my mind, Kelly's voice, and his obscene, half-mad chuckling.

Ye weren't expectin' this, Johnnie boy, were ye, now? An' neither was I. But 'tis a wise child as knows its own father—or great grandfather . . .

And I—we—heard the noise coming from the south, faint at first, then becoming louder and louder. The distant rattling, the chuffing . . . The pilot engine came first, its headlight very dim, almost out. That of the following locomotive was bright enough. And there were the lighted carriages and, in plain sight through the windows, men in uniforms and civilian clothes. And two women—O'Connor's wife and her sister.

The leading engine seemed to be slowing. There was the shriek of escaping steam. So, despite the presence of the last Kelly in the mind of our common ancestor history might yet be switched back to its original track. The pilot engine would stop at Glenrowan station so that something could be done about the oil-burning headlight.

But the special train itself did not slow down. Its driver whistled impatiently. I left the road for the railway track to try to see what was happening. The pilot engine was picking up speed again, although by this time the two locomotives must almost have been in contact.

The train vanished around the bend beyond the station.

And then I heard the crash.

Inside our shared mind Kelly laughed.

I remembered another Kelly who had been a cartoonist, a comic strip artist in the world that was now hopelessly lost to me.

One of his characters had said, "We have met the enemy and he is us."

CHAPTER 66

I opened my eyes slowly.

I was still sitting in my chair. Kelly was out of his, standing there and glaring down at me. A heavy revolver was in his right hand. Behind him was Duffin, also with a ready weapon. And there was the terrified Graumann off to one side, literally gibbering with fear. He must have hoped that the attempt to change the course of history would be successful, must have convinced himself that he would magically be transferred to some happier, less perilous time track. The disappointment must have been mind-shattering.

"You bastard!" growled Kelly.

If he was going to shoot me, I thought, I might as well show some defiance.

I said, "As we've both of us found out, it was your grandfather who was the bastard."

Amazingly, he laughed.

"Trust a writer to play around with words! And now, cousin, what am I to do with ye? There's still the history to be written—an' the history o' what's to come to be lived through. If I am put down—but I shall not be!—'t'will be punishment for you to see one o' *your* blood sufferin' defeat. But I shall niver be defeated." He lifted his head and roared, "I am Kelly! I bear the name—an' the name is

343

more than the blood. 'T'will always be the biggest name, the only name, in this country of ours!

"I am Kelly!"

Duffin said, "Even so, ye'd better kill him, Ned. What if he should make another attempt at changin' things at Glenrowan?"

"Perhaps ye're right," Kelly said. He lifted that huge revolver and pointed it at me. It was like looking into the end of a drainpipe. His teeth gleamed whitely in his beard (and what did his face look like under all that hair? I wondered) as he grinned viciously. And then he turned and fired. The reports, within doors, were thunderous. Graumann screamed.

And with an odd, tinkling crash the assemblage of gleaming rotors disintegrated as wheels and spindles were struck by the heavy bullets. There must have been some sort of residual field about the machine. Outlines wavered, colors sagged down the spectrum, perspective became impossibly distorted. Kelly was gone, and Duffin was no longer in army uniform but was the editor whom I had known, who had commissioned me to write the eyewitness account of the Siege of Glenrowan.

But it didn't last.

Kelly, President Kelly, the last Kelly holstered his smoking revolver and, followed by Duffin, left Graumann and myself among the wreckage.

CHAPTER 67

I have stayed on in Sydney, despite the panic evacuation of the bulk of the population. I didn't much care if the city was to be bombed or not but, so far, the only use of nuclear weapons has been at Glenrowan. Graumann vanished shortly after the destruction of his machine. I don't know what happened to him and I don't much care. He left the tapes and records and, working from these and from memory, I have tried to write my personal record of the War of Independence. Meanwhile the American occupation forces have been behaving correctly, decently even. There has been no real shortage of food or of luxuries such as cigarettes and hard liquor. And we are much luckier than the people of, say, Brisbane. *Our* new masters do, at least, speak English. The really unlucky ones have been those in the north and west, whose territory is being devasted by the nasty little war that the Russians and Japanese are fighting in somebody else's country.

Services have been restored, among them radio and TV broadcasts. On these news has been hard to come by; there has been far greater coverage of the American expedition to the moons of Jupiter than of any events in our unhappy country. For a while the last stand of the Kelly loyalists in the south was almost ignored—I suspect that this was because things were not going at all well for the Americans and their puppets. (The government of the

U.S.A. had learned its lesson during American involvement in Viet Nam; TV coverage of an unpopular, incompetently executed war does little more than to engender alarm and despondency.)

But at last the Free Australian Army, with its American arms and advisors, took Melbourne while other Free (so-called) Australian forces drove south- from Wangaratta. And Kelly, badly wounded in the legs, was captured after the Battle of Seymour. His trial, as a war criminal, was inevitable.

(Here I stopped writing to listen to a News Flash.)

On November 11, 1980, Ned Kelly was hanged in Melbourne Jail.

It was just one hundred years too late—and, besides, it was the wrong man.

But was it?

He had said himself that the name was more important than the blood—and that name will live, no matter what happens, as long as there are those to say of somebody whose courage they admire that he is as game as Ned Kelly.

AFTERWORD TO U.S. EDITION
A. Bertram Chandler

In addition to Ned Kelly himself there were other real life characters used in this novel.

Ned's sister Kate is one. On our Time Track she, after her famous brother's execution, attempted to cash in on the publicity and embarked upon a not very successful career in show business. Eventually she married and settled down in the town of Forbes, in New South Wales. A traveling theatrical company came to this town with a play based upon the exploits of the Kelly Gang. Kate, who was known to the manager of this company, got a free seat in the front row. When the show was over the manager came on stage and said, "Ladies and gentlemen, you will never have guessed that the real life heroine of the play that you have just witnessed is sitting among you! Allow me to introduce Miss Kate Kelly!"

Poor Kate . . . It seems that, up to this time, her life had not been a very happy one. This unexpected exposure must have been the last straw. On her way home she either jumped or fell into the river, and was drowned.

Another character who met his end by drowning, both in my novel and in real life, was Admiral Tryon. For a while, at the time when my imaginary War of Independence could have been getting under way, he was Flag Officer of the Royal Navy's Australia Station. Some years later he commanded the Royal Navy's Mediterranean Fleet.

During fleet maneuvers there was a collision between his flagship, HMS *Victoria*, and another battleship, HMS *Camperdown*. *Victoria* went down with considerable loss of life, including that of Admiral Tryon.

As was the case in the fictional collision, in the novel, between HMS *Shah* and HMS *Nelson* there was some confusion regarding flag signals.

Throughout the novel I took no liberties with Australian geography or with the rail, road, sea and telegraphic communications of the period. All the vessels of Admiral Tryon's invasion fleet, Royal Navy and Merchant Service, were actual ships of the time. So was *Rotomahana*. During her heyday she was one of the fastest and most beautiful vessels on the world's seas.

And what of Gabriel Dumont, the military leader of the Riel Rebellion? On our Time Track those Gatling guns were used against the rebels at the Battle of Batoche, not by them. Dumont lost the battle and the rebellion collapsed. The political leader, Louis Riel, was captured, tried and hanged for treason. Dumont escaped over the border into the U.S.A. For a while he was a member of Buffalo Bill's Wild West Show, in which he performed as a sharpshooter. Some time later, after he had been pardoned, he returned to Canada, where he died of old age.

Some Australian reviewers, checking up on the thoroughness of my research, have tried in vain to find a real life "Red Kitty." She was straight fiction—but not an impossible character. Even so, during the writing of the novel complaints were made about her: "There weren't any women like that in those days!" "Weren't there?" I replied. "Weren't there?" So I brought in the real life Louisa Lawson, mother of the Australian poet Henry Lawson, just to show that during the 1880s, even in Australia, there were women who were outspoken feminists, socialists and republicans.

I make bold to say—after all, this afterword is for American, not Australian, consumption—that Louisa was a far more interesting character than her much more famous son.

DAW

DAW

DAW BRINGS YOU THESE BESTSELLERS BY MARION ZIMMER BRADLEY

- ☐ CITY OF SORCERY   UE1962—$3.50
- ☐ DARKOVER LANDFALL   UE1906—$2.50
- ☐ THE SPELL SWORD   UE1891—$2.25
- ☐ THE HERITAGE OF HASTUR   UE1967—$3.50
- ☐ THE SHATTERED CHAIN   UE1961—$3.50
- ☐ THE FORBIDDEN TOWER   UE2029—$3.95
- ☐ STORMQUEEN!   UE1951—$3.50
- ☐ TWO TO CONQUER   UE1876—$2.95
- ☐ SHARRA'S EXILE   UE1988—$3.95
- ☐ HAWKMISTRESS!   UE1958—$3.50
- ☐ THENDARA HOUSE   UE1857—$3.50
- ☐ HUNTERS OF THE RED MOON   UE1968—$2.50
- ☐ THE SURVIVORS   UE1861—$2.95

Anthologies

- ☐ THE KEEPER'S PRICE   UE1931—$2.50
- ☐ SWORD OF CHAOS   UE1722—$2.95
- ☐ SWORD AND SORCERESS   UE1928—$2.95

NEW AMERICAN LIBRARY
P.O. Box 999, Bergenfield, New Jersey 07621

Please send me the DAW Books I have checked above. I am enclosing
$_____ (check or money order—no currency or C.O.D.'s).
Please include the list price plus $1.00 per order to cover handling
costs.

Name _____

Address _____

City _____ State _____ Zip Code _____
Allow 4-6 weeks for delivery

DAW

The really great fantasy books are
published by DAW:

Andre Norton

☐ LORE OF THE WITCH WORLD   UE2012—$3.50
☐ HORN CROWN   UE1635—$2.95
☐ PERILOUS DREAMS   UE1749—$2.50

C.J. Cherryh

☐ THE DREAMSTONE   UE2013—$3.50
☐ THE TREE OF SWORDS AND JEWELS   UE1850—$2.95

Lin Carter

☐ DOWN TO A SUNLESS SEA   UE1937—$2.50
☐ DRAGONROUGE   UE1982—$2.50

M.A.R. Barker

☐ THE MAN OF GOLD   UE1940—$3.95

Michael Shea

☐ NIFFT THE LEAN   UE1783—$2.95
☐ THE COLOR OUT OF TIME   UE1954—$2.50

B.W. Clough

☐ THE CRYSTAL CROWN   UE1922—$2.75

NEW AMERICAN LIBRARY
P.O. Box 999, Bergenfield, New Jersey 07621

Please send me the DAW Books I have checked above. I am enclosing
$_____ (check or money order—no currency or C.O.D.'s).
Please include the list price plus $1.00 per order to cover handling
costs.

Name _____

Address _____

City _____ State _____ Zip Code _____
Please allow at least 4 weeks for delivery